Praise for the joyous novels of Emma Hannigan

'Warm, wise and full of joy. Uplifting and magical,
like Emma herself'
Cathy Kelly

'Warm, intelligent and brilliant'
Marian Keyes

'A beautiful book by an exceptional author. Lose
yourself in her wonderful writing'
Sinéad Moriarty

'The characters shine off the page. A tale packed
with warmth, empathy and a deep understanding
of the quirks and imperfections of family life.
A wonderful storyteller'
S Magazine

'Emma Hannigan pulls at the heartstrings . . . A
beautifully written, inspiring story of hope
and family bonds'
Express

'Hannigan's novel, much like the vivacious author
herself, is brimming with hope, joy and inspiration'
Sunday Independent

'A moving tale celebrating the bonds between women,
Emma Hannigan beautifully captures the difficult and
wondrous thing that is loving and learning to let go . . .
just a little. An excellent read'
Irish Tatler

Emma Hannigan was the beloved and bestselling author of thirteen novels, including the No. 1 bestseller *Letters to my Daughters*. Her bestselling memoir, *Talk to the Headscarf*, was updated and revised as *All To Live For: Fighting Cancer. Finding Hope.*

In 2007, Emma was diagnosed with breast cancer and her eleven-year battle with cancer began. As an ambassador for Breast Cancer Ireland Emma worked to dispel the fears around cancer and spread hope about new treatments. In February 2018, Emma shared that her team of dedicated doctors had exhausted all avenues in terms of her treatment. She launched a social media campaign #HelpEmmaHelpOthers to raise €100,000 for Breast Cancer Ireland. Two weeks later, shortly before her death, Emma's target had been reached.

In the final months of her life, Emma completed her thirteenth novel, *The Gift of Friends*, sending her acknowledgements to her editor just days before she passed away in March.

If you would like to donate to Breast Cancer Ireland in memory of Emma, please visit www.breastcancerireland.com

By Emma Hannigan

Designer Genes
Miss Conceived
The Pink Ladies Club
Keeping Mum
Perfect Wives
Driving Home for Christmas
The Summer Guest
The Heart of Winter
The Secrets We Share
The Perfect Gift
The Wedding Promise
Letters to my Daughters
The Gift of Friends

The Wedding Weekend (e-short)

All To Live For

Emma Hannigan

the Gift of Friends

HACHETTE
BOOKS
IRELAND

First published in Ireland in 2019
by Hachette Books Ireland

First published in paperback in Ireland in 2019
by Hachette Books Ireland

4

Cataloguing in Publication Data is available from the British Library

ISBN 978 1 4736 6007 6

Typeset in Palatino by Palimpsest Book Production Ltd, Falkirk, Stirlingshire

Printed and bound in Great Britain by
Clays Ltd, Elcograf S.p.A.

Hachette Books Ireland
8 Castlecourt Centre
Castleknock, Dublin 15
An Hachette UK Company
Carmelite House
50 Victoria Embankment
London EC4Y 0DZ

www.hachettebooksireland.ie

This book is for my family. They are the ones
I spent most of my time with and they're the ones
I'll miss every minute of every day.

For Cian, Sacha, Kim, Mum, Dad, Timmy,
Hilary, Robyn & Steffy, with all my love.

SHE WAS LOOKING FORWARD TO GETTING HOME. The day had started out beautifully, but now it had clouded over and the first drops of rain weren't far away. As she turned into Kingfisher Road and walked under the granite archway, she was thinking of fresh coffee and the Victoria sponge she had bought in the bakery. Bliss!

There was a car and a van in the driveway of number ten. The back doors of the van were standing open and as she approached, a burly man pulled a large For Sale sign out of the back and strode over to the garden wall. He dropped the sign on the ground, then went back to the van for a large hammer. So, it was up for sale, she thought. That was interesting. Who would the new neighbours be, she wondered. It wouldn't be on the market for long, that was for sure. These houses didn't come up for sale often, so when they did there was always a scrum of buyers elbowing each other out of the way to nab one.

A man in a sharp suit stepped out of the house and smiled when he saw her.

'Good morning,' he called out very loudly. 'Are you a resident?'

She nodded. 'Yes, I live just across there.' She pointed at the houses opposite.

'I was just about to deliver these to the other houses,' he said, waving a sheaf of papers in the air, 'so you've saved me one journey.'

She waited at the wall until he walked down to her.

'Here you go,' he said, peeling off one of the brochures and handing it to her. 'I'm Mark Scott, by the way. I'm with Berwick Estate Agents and Valuers and we would like to do business on Kingfisher Road.'

'I see,' she said. 'Well, I'll certainly take a look at this. Thank you.'

She crossed the road, walking slowly to her own house, looking at the brochure in her hand. It was a glossy full-colour production to sell number ten, and a page had been stapled to the front that said: *Similar Required. Please talk to us if you are considering selling. We are very eager to acquire properties on Kingfisher Road, Drake Avenue, Heron Way and Mallard Park. Contact us in confidence for a valuation.*

Well, she wasn't thinking of selling. She hoped to live and die in her beautiful home. It was perfect for her needs.

Once inside the house, she made a coffee, cut a slice of cake and went up to the small sitting room upstairs to enjoy them. The room had a wide bay window that jutted out over the front garden, giving her views up and down the road. She loved to sit here and read, or just watch the comings and goings on Kingfisher Road.

She brought the brochure with her and read it as she sipped her coffee.

Kingfisher Road is the most sought-after address in Vayhill. This stunning property is the first house on the left upon entering via the stone archway that announces the enclave. Kingfisher Road is situated a mere ten minutes' walk from the town centre, making it an easy commute to a vast array of shops, restaurants and bars . . .

Number ten is set behind wrought-iron electric gates, with imposing granite pillars. The grounds are landscaped and immaculately kept, with space to park six cars. The main house is finished in coarse granite and rendered plaster panels. Two brick chimneystacks stand majestically above the original clay tiled roof . . .

The interior of the property is wonderfully proportioned, with large rooms and high ceilings, with many original features still in place, such as ornate marble fireplaces and leaded windows . . .

There are lawns to the side and rear, surrounded by mature trees offering privacy to the sizeable paved patio. The entire glazed rear of this building can be folded back on warmer days . . .

This is a very special and enviable property. Houses on this prestigious street rarely come on the market, so this is a wonderful opportunity to join this exclusive community. Number ten is in impeccable condition and ready to move into for the lucky purchaser.

Well, they certainly made it sound desirable. It was a fantastic property, one of the best on the road. She couldn't wait to see who would snap it up. She turned to the last page.

Kingfisher Road is the home of your dreams: beautiful, secluded, quiet and meticulously maintained by all residents. It is a prestigious address where we promise you will live happily ever after. Make your dreams come true: Live Happy!

She rolled her eyes. What nonsense. These estate agents had really lost the run of themselves – *happily ever after?*

How could anyone promise that? Talk about false advertising.

She put down the brochure and sighed. Didn't people understand that having the home of your dreams didn't mean you'd have the life of your dreams? But then, she'd been naive enough to believe that once. She had thought she was going to have a wonderful life, she had honestly believed it would all go according to her grand plan. Instead, all her dreams had fallen apart, lying in pieces around her feet. This wasn't how it was supposed to be.

She looked out at Kingfisher Road, the other 'houses of your dreams'. Her best friends lived in those houses, wonderful women, but they didn't really know her. She'd never had the guts to tell them the truth, and she reckoned she never would. She wondered if they were as happy as they seemed or were their houses like hers – perfect façades to hide the pain and heartache that lived behind them. Was it all a lie, just keeping up appearances? That was her life anyway, but she couldn't admit that to anyone.

She impatiently rubbed away the tear that slid down her cheek. Self-pity wouldn't help her. She was ashamed, that was the real truth of it. The secret she hid from everyone made her feel pathetic and defeated. If her friends knew, they would shun her. So yes, she lived in a perfect home on the perfect street, where everything was beautiful and to outsiders it looked gorgeously glamorous, but behind her closed door it was a very different story. It was horribly far from perfect.

Chapter 1

BETSY COX WAS USUALLY THE FIRST TO KNOW about anything concerning Kingfisher Road. Proud to be the longest-standing resident on the salubrious and beautiful stretch of road she called home, she made it her business to know what was going on and to ensure her neighbours were well informed too. As head of the Residents' Association, she took her role very seriously. Kingfisher Road was special, and Betsy wouldn't let anything threaten its happy and civilised existence.

This was why the sight of the For Sale sign being removed at number ten made her stop in her tracks. She had only walked the fifteen minutes to the town centre to get the newspaper for Noel. When she'd left, everything had been quiet and the For Sale sign was standing erect in the spacious garden at number ten, but now, on her way back again, a man with a lump hammer was busy taking it down. A van was parked outside, its doors standing open and a jumble of signs inside. She walked determinedly over to him.

'Good morning. It's sold, I see. Can you tell me who bought it?'

The man looked up in surprise. 'Me? No, sorry, love, I haven't a clue about that.' He gave her an apologetic smile. 'They don't tell the likes of me that sort of thing.'

Betsy felt a shot of frustration dart through her.

'Right so. Well, thanks for doing such a neat job. Goodbye.'

Really, the estate agents should have to inform the Association in advance of anyone moving in, to give them an idea of their new neighbours. It was such a tightknit community here – the complex had just ten houses, which meant that every resident had a big impact on the whole look and feel of the place. It was essential to get people who were the right fit.

In fact, she'd had that thought after the last owners of number ten had moved in and out in jig time. They were a young couple and insisted on keeping to themselves, which was very annoying. A sense of community was very much part of the experience of living on Kingfisher Road, but those two had failed to realise that. Betsy had sent over invitations to various get-togethers, but she'd barely received an answer, let alone an acceptance. It didn't augur well to Betsy, and she'd been proved right. After a honeymoon period when they gazed adoringly at each other, no matter who was trying to talk to them, the pair of them started to look miserable.

The odd thing was, strange things started to go wrong with the house – there was a burst pipe that flooded the kitchen, an unheard-of occurrence for these houses. They had been built to the highest specification and with the very best materials, so problems were rare. But number ten suddenly went rogue, with the flood, and then part of a window-sill just fell off one day, one of the gates unaccountably came off its hinge and Betsy had heard that one of them had put a foot through a stair on the steps down to the basement, like something from a Laurel and Hardy movie. As far as Betsy was concerned, the whole fiasco was the house letting them know they didn't belong here – or with each other, for that matter. They finally got the message and went their separate ways and the For Sale went up. The houses on Kingfisher Road knew what was right, Betsy thought, unlike the estate agents obviously. As she made her way up to her own gate, she resolved to put that question on the agenda of the next Association meeting: should we petition Berwick Estate Agents and Valuers to supply information in advance of a house sale/ arrival of new owner?

As she walked up the driveway to her own house, Betsy smiled. She adored her home. Even the sound of the name made her feel happy. Mount Liah, with its fine red-brick finish, Edwardian proportions and sweeping flower gardens was the envy of most of the population of Vayhill. Betsy and her husband of thirty-five years, Noel, lived in the first house on the right-hand side of the road, number one. Each house was different and some were bigger than others, but all were set behind granite walls and wrought-iron gates. Nowadays, of course, they all had electric gates fitted. Mount Liah had been the first to get them installed. It was for security, Noel insisted, and besides, they couldn't let the standards of the road slip. It was important to Betsy, and to Noel, that they lived in such a beautiful, well-maintained and quiet area.

Before she married Noel, Betsy used to walk her dog down Kingfisher Road and wonder what the people in each of the houses were like. She was born and raised in Vayhill town, in a small ex-corporation house where every penny was counted and accounted for. Betsy came from a family of eleven children, and there had been no time or money for fawning over anyone. From the time she became a teenager, she had felt her life was narrow and claustrophobic. She had to mind the younger ones and do the lion's share of cooking and cleaning, so free time was a precious commodity. When she did manage to slip out with the dog, she came here, to walk through a dream. These houses and the lives of the people who lived in them seemed impossibly glamorous and free to Betsy, the opposite of everything she'd ever known.

She never dared think she could end up actually living on the road she admired so much, but fate stepped in when Betsy took a chance on Noel, a simple and quiet man her mother declared 'boring'. But after a run of selfish and rude men who were only after one thing, Betsy found Noel's gentlemanly ways to be a breath of fresh air. He did anything and everything she wanted and nothing was ever too much trouble. He may not have been the funniest or the most dapper, but he was always polite, and she could just tell he'd make a devoted husband and would always put her first.

Theirs was a swift and joyful courtship. They were married within eighteen months of meeting. That first meeting happened on Kingfisher Road, where Noel lived with his parents. Betsy had been walking the dog, staring longingly at the houses as usual, when a young man sitting on a wall had asked about Leila, her labrador. They got talking, and an hour had gone by before she knew it. Betsy had to run home, dragging the poor dog along behind her. She hadn't thought she'd see Noel again, but the following week he was again sitting on the wall and he smiled and stood up when he saw her coming along. And that was that. Her mother rolled her eyes when she announced her engagement, but Betsy was sure in her heart that Noel was for her. If she was honest, the fact that he lived on her dream road made him even more special, but it was the man himself she fell in love with – and had kept on falling more in love with over their decades together.

In those early days, Noel had talked fondly about the neighbours and how kind they'd been to him and his father when his mother passed away. She'd died when Noel was a teenager and his descriptions of the community on Kingfisher Road sounded like something from another world to Betsy. Her neighbours were a grabby, selfish lot who looked after themselves and nobody else. Her mother fell out with everyone and wasn't well liked. So Betsy had never experienced the sort of community living that Noel talked about, and she longed to be a part of it.

They were waiting for a house to come up in a new estate ten miles from Vayhill town when Brian, Noel's father, asked them to come and live with him. 'Don't spend good money on rent when I'm rattling around this great big house on my own. I'd be thrilled to have your company.'

It was a good idea, but Betsy wasn't sure how it would work out in reality. She needn't have worried. They got on so well that he begged them to cancel the estate house and stay at Mount Liah. 'I'll happily do you a deal,' Brian had said. 'If you stay and allow me to live out my days here in my beloved home, it'll be yours when I go.'

Betsy agreed wholeheartedly and proceeded to throw herself into being the life and soul of Kingfisher Road. She organised tea parties, set up a book club and maintained a list of trusted tradespeople that she gave to newcomers as part of a welcome hamper. Before long, she was a key member of the community. Brian lasted two years after their marriage, but then a heart attack took him from them. Betsy had grown so fond of Brian that she was more upset about his death than she was when her own parents passed away.

They didn't have a big wedding purely because Betsy didn't want her whole family turning up. None of them was happy for her, and they weren't shy about saying it. Instead, they were seething with jealousy and wanted to scratch her eyes out. Her older sister, Maggie, had actually told her that she wasn't worthy of Noel and that he'd see through her before long. 'I give that marriage a year,' Maggie had said to her sourly, and mentally Betsy had severed her connection to her sister.

Betsy's feeling was that she could either sit and cry and allow them to ruin her wedding, and possibly even her future, or she could give them two fingers by showing them how wrong they were. So she had a small wedding, invited only her parents and didn't care what her clutch of siblings thought about it.

As an only child, Noel was used to being treated like a precious jewel. All he knew was love and affection and the fact that he was cherished. He passed those sentiments on to Betsy, and she thrived in the warmth of his love. At first she made some effort to keep up with her own family, but after her first wedding anniversary they stopped talking to her. To her surprise, Betsy found it a blessed relief.

'I feel as if I've been freed from some sort of negativity prison,' she told Noel. It freed her so she could concentrate on being Betsy Cox, wife of Noel Cox, residents of Kingfisher Road.

They longed for children and eventually, when Betsy was almost forty and had long since given up hope of hearing the pitter-patter of tiny feet, Graham came along. Everyone was thrilled for them when Betsy announced her pregnancy and the other women on the road were there to advise and help her. Betsy thought her family might have a change of heart now that there was a grandson, but they stayed away and showed no interest in Graham. She went so far as to invite them to the christening, but not one of them showed up. She hadn't cared a jot before, but now she was upset by the thought that Graham had twenty-eight cousins he might never meet.

She made one final effort and dropped in to visit Mona, the sister closest in age to her. They'd shared bunk beds when they were kids and she felt she could trust Mona more than any of her other sisters. If there was a way back in, Mona would be the one to help her find it.

She couldn't have been more wrong. All she got from Mona was the unedited version of what they all thought of her.

'You're a turncoat, Betsy. You always thought you were better than us. Look at you living on that road, acting all high and mighty with your dinner parties and your fancy clothes.'

'Who told you I have dinner parties?' she'd asked in disbelief. 'Not that it makes a blind bit of difference if I have my neighbours over.'

'Barney, your postman?' Mona spat. 'He's still one of us, but he says the shite you come out with about the evenings you do have . . . You'd swear you were royalty. You're from Heather Greens and the day you walked out of here thinking you were better than us was the day you lost your place in this family. Don't come around here again, do you hear me? And don't bother sending any more of them swanky cards with printed photos of that pug ugly child in them. We don't want to know.'

Betsy held her tears at bay until she was well away from the twitching curtains of Heather Greens. She wouldn't let them see how they'd upset her. But once home, she collapsed on the sofa in floods of tears. As always, Noel was there to soothe her and tell her that he loved her. He didn't put her family down, he simply reminded her that they had their own family now.

'You, me and baby Graham. That's more than enough for me,' said Noel. 'You stood by me when my dad was dying and you nursed him as if he were your own. You've never been anything but wonderful to me. I'll look after you for as long as you'll let me.'

So that was that, Betsy was now alone in the world except for Noel and Graham, and she poured herself into caring for them. Graham was a cranky baby who never slept for more than five hours a night until he went to playschool. He was in trouble from the start. They were called in to see almost every teacher that came across him. Their remarks were all the same. 'He's rude and disruptive and picks on the weaker ones in the class.'

They were mortified by his behaviour and begged him to try and think before he acted, but sadly he went from bad to worse. As he matured and hit the teenage years, things escalated. He was brought home in a squad car on more than one occasion, and poor Betsy felt it was her duty to apologise to the neighbours for bringing such embarrassment to the road.

She'd host coffee mornings when she'd offer a wide selection of home-baked treats that she'd almost killed herself preparing.

'If I could have a bit of hush,' she'd say, delicately tapping the side of her teacup with her spoon. 'I wish to apologise profusely on behalf of myself and Noel for the disruption caused by Graham two nights ago.'

The women fell over themselves telling her it wasn't her fault, that she'd done everything right in raising Graham, that he was simply going through a bad phase and he'd be past it soon. Betsy nodded and nodded, but she worried that the truth was that he'd inherited her family's gene pool. As the years rolled by, Graham resented his parents ever more and told them they stifled him.

'I don't want you both putting me on a pedestal and treating me as if I'm a prize cow at a mart.'

'We don't want to make you uncomfortable, son,' Noel said patiently again and again. 'We love you and we want what's best for you. That's all.'

As soon as he'd finished his last exams in school Graham was gone, off to Australia with a mate for a gap year of travelling. The mate came back at the end of the year, but Graham stayed.

While Noel and Betsy were heartbroken at his decision, there was a collective sigh of relief on Kingfisher Road when news got out that Graham wouldn't be back. Through no fault of their own, Noel and Betsy had created a bad egg in Graham, and the general consensus was that Australia was welcome to him.

In time, he'd married a dreadful woman called Tasha, who made it very clear they were not welcome to visit after the wedding.

'She's literally stolen our son,' Betsy had sobbed into Noel's chest. 'How will we cope without him?'

'I don't know,' said Noel. 'For the first time since I met you, I feel I've failed you.'

'Darling, you've never failed me.'

'But Graham is gone and I can't fix it.'

Noel's sense of failure proved to be a wake-up call. Betsy realised that Graham was gone, that it was his own choice and that she and Noel couldn't take the blame any longer. He was twenty-five years of age now and they'd done right by him, so she decided that from now on, she was going to loosen her grip and just accept this was who he was. Graham had been gone almost six years, living his life as he wanted to live it. But she still had Noel, and that was what mattered. So just like when they were first married, she threw herself into caring for Noel and cherishing him, and enjoying his love in return.

Betsy shook her head as she let herself into the house and went through to the kitchen to put down her shopping. What was she like, roving back over her years? Sometimes the memories just picked her up and carried her off and it was like she wasn't here at all. Maybe that's how she missed the sale of number ten – she wasn't paying enough attention. She set about boiling the kettle to scald the pot and put the tasty cake on a serving platter, resolving in her head to let the past be the past and to focus on the here and now. She smiled to herself, thinking that she sounded like Nancy now, full of determined optimism!

'Is that you, my love?' Noel's voice called from the study next door.

'Yes, Noel. I'm back again. I'll have some tea and cake for you in a few minutes.'

'Perfect timing!' he called back.

Betsy believed in doing things right, so she always set the table properly, with napkins and the correct cutlery. She moved the vase of flowers she'd cut from the garden earlier to the centre of the table, enjoying the pretty red dash of the dahlias. She used Noel's mother's wedding Delft, a gorgeous blue-and-white patterned set that made food look even more tempting. She set out her bone china teapot and matching cups and saucers and stood back to assess the scene. Yes, it was just right.

She heard a beeping sound coming from behind her and was confused for a moment, then laughed at herself. At sixty-three years of age, keeping up with technology wasn't her forte, and her phone was still a bit of a novelty. Noel teased her for being half scared of it. He was probably right – she had a fear of pressing a button and breaking it somehow. She fished it out of her bag and saw that it was a text from Graham. Her stomach dropped – bad news? He so rarely got in touch, it always made her as anxious as she was delighted.

Hi mum – u free to tlk? I call in 10 mins?

Betsy stared at the phone in shock. He never, ever called. A few texts a year was the most she could hope for, and now this. She gripped the phone tightly, sure that something awful had happened. *Ring asap*, she texted back.

Noel walked into the kitchen. 'This looks wonderful, darling, I was just—' He stopped when he saw Betsy's face. 'What is it? Has something happened?' he said, his face full of concern.

Betsy shook her head. 'I don't know. Graham just texted to ask if he could ring me, to talk.'

Noel's eyebrows shot up. 'Right. That's unusual. What do you think?'

Betsy shrugged. 'I've no idea.'

The phone started to buzz in her hand and she looked at Noel.

'I suggest we sit down for this,' he said, pulling out a chair at the table for her. They both sat down and Betsy slid her thumb across the screen.

'Hello?'

'Hi Mum, how's tricks?'

'Graham, we're so thrilled to hear from you. Is everything okay?'

'Of course. Yeah, fine. No worries.'

'Oh good,' Betsy said, smiling at Noel, 'so no problems or anything, then?'

'I just said everything was fine,' Graham said, the irritation in his voice making her blush. 'I thought you might have grown out of that doomsayer's habit.'

'Oh no,' Betsy said quickly, 'I didn't mean . . . it's just we don't really hear from you, so I did just hope . . .'

Across the table, Noel was frowning. Betsy thought he couldn't hear Graham's end of the conversation, but he was obviously picking up on the tenor of it from her reaction.

'Sorry, darling,' she said, forcing herself to be composed. 'Just me being a silly worrier. So all's well, that's fantastic. How are you keeping?'

'Grand. No complaints. I just rang to ask you something. But don't freak out, okay?'

'What do you want to ask?' Betsy said, looking steadily at Noel.

'Well, I was thinking of coming back. To Ireland. And I

just wanted to know if I'd be welcome to visit with you guys. To stay in the house, I mean, while I'm there.'

Betsy felt like her heart was going to explode.

'Oh yes, of course,' she said. 'We would absolutely love to see you. We miss you, Graham. If you're coming back, your father and I will be so happy to have you here. I'm so delighted. So is your dad.' She looked over at Noel, who was not so much delighted as processing, but she was sure he'd get there in the end.

'So how long will you stay?' she asked tentatively. In the past when she'd questioned him, he flew off the handle and told her she was meddling again.

'Well, it'll be just for a visit. So I'm guessing two weeks, maybe three.' It suddenly struck Betsy that he sounded utterly exhausted. Maybe life in Australia wasn't all fun and games anymore, or maybe, please God, he was going through a break-up?

'Stay as long as you want. The longer, the better. And are you coming alone?' She held up her hand, with fingers crossed, and Noel put his hand over his mouth to stop the snort of laughter.

'No, I'll have Tasha with me,' he said. 'Is that okay?'

Betsy uncrossed her fingers and made a face at Noel. 'Yes, she's very welcome too, of course. I'll make up a nice room for you.'

Her heart dropped like a stone at the thought of sharing space with Tasha, but she'd welcome the devil himself if it meant she got to see her son.

'Actually, I've another surprise for you,' he said.

'A surprise?' Betsy said. 'What else?'

'The thing is, em, we've got a son. He's called Arnie and we'll be bringing him too.'

Betsy felt like her face had gone numb. It wouldn't work itself into an expression of any sort. Noel was staring at her anxiously.

'Pardon?' she said. 'You've got . . .' she looked at Noel, ' . . . a son?'

She thought Noel was going to fall out of his chair. His eyes widened and his mouth dropped open. If she hadn't been so much in shock herself, it would have made her giggle.

'Yeah, I kept meaning to tell you, Mum,' Graham was saying into her ear, 'but you know how time passes and all that, yeah?'

Betsy was too stunned to answer him. A grandson. A whole entire new person and he hadn't thought to tell her? The rush of love she felt was accompanied by a rush of unbridled anger. How could he not tell them this? She suddenly realised that she had missed what Graham had been saying.

'Mum? So can you help?' he said, sounding irritated. 'I'm a bit pressed for time. I've got to get to work. So what do you think?'

'Hold on a minute,' said Betsy, her voice shaking with the anger she was trying hard to control. 'We've barely heard from you for the past six years. When we saw you last you were so unwelcoming and rude that you made us feel ashamed that we'd done such a poor job of raising you. Now you're dropping a bomb and acting as if we're the ones being odd! Now just cop on here, Graham, really.'

There was a pause as he obviously registered just how strong her emotions were.

'Okay. I'm sorry,' he said, sounding anything but. 'I was

saying there's an issue with my ticket home. We can't really afford it.'

'You can't afford your ticket?'

'Well, I can't afford any of them – mine or Tasha's. I suppose Arnie might go free. But if you want to see us, you'll have to help me out, okay?'

'You need the money for two return tickets?' Betsy asked.

Noel flung up his hands and looked disgusted. She could tell he was about to shout 'No!' at the phone, but she looked at him pleadingly. She put her hand over the phone and whispered, 'Please, love. I want to meet our grandson.'

'How old is the baby?' Betsy asked.

'Four months,' said Graham.

Betsy blinked back tears as she tried to digest the information. How could their own son have kept this from them?

Noel was nodding at her.

'That's no problem at all, darling. You just tell us how much you need and give me the bank details and Dad will send the money.' She smiled gratefully at her husband. Graham had some cheek, but family mattered far more than money.

'Okay, great, thanks Mum. I'll book tickets for travel in the next couple of weeks. I'll let you know the dates. We're really looking forward to seeing you guys,' he said, sounding more Aussie than Irish. Betsy hated the fact he didn't even sound Irish anymore. Nobody would guess he was from Vayhill, that was for certain.

'We're so happy, Graham. Keep us updated,' she said, then he ended the call.

Betsy put down the phone and she and Noel looked at each other in silence.

'Well,' Noel said finally. 'It's going to take me a while to get my head around all this.'

'I know,' Betsy said, feeling a little dazed. 'My God, Arnie Cox. I can't believe it.'

Noel smiled and shook his head. 'A grandson.'

'It'll take me a while to forgive him,' Betsy said.

'For not telling us?'

'Yes. I mean, really, Noel, nine months of a pregnancy and the child is four months old and he never said one word in that whole time. What kind of a son does that?'

Noel reached across the table and took her hand. 'Don't upset yourself, darling. I feel the same way, but this is where we're at, and if we want to be in Arnie's life, we'll have to bottle up the anger. The important thing now is that they're coming over, and we'll get to meet him. That will be magic.'

Betsy sighed and nodded. 'You're right. I'll have to let it go. I'll work on it between now and when their plane touches down, I promise.' She grinned at Noel. 'Wait till I tell Nancy and Maia and Pearl,' she said. 'They'll be so shocked.'

'That they will,' Noel said drily.

Deep down, Betsy prayed that her son had matured somewhat. She also hoped that dreadful Tasha had mellowed since becoming a mum. Surely they would both be less brash and aggressive than before?

She'd tell the other women as soon as she saw them. They'd be delighted for her. Although whether it was in fact good news or bad news, only time would tell.

Chapter 2

'MUM, YOU HAVE *GOT* TO STOP LOOKING AT ME like that.'

'Like what?' Maia demanded. 'Can't I look at my beautiful daughter?'

'Not all . . . soppy-eyed.' Zara pouted. 'I can't look at that expression for the next two months.'

'Give me a break,' Maia said, raking her long blonde hair with her freshly manicured nails. She'd managed to get an early appointment with her favourite nail artist, Mila, and she kept holding out her hands to admire her expertly applied soft pink falsies. Mila was worth her weight in gold.

'You give *me* a break,' Zara said. 'You've still got me for another while, so no need to keep gazing at me like I'm a cute puppy.'

Maia laughed. 'I really can't wait for you to have children and finally understand all you put me through.'

Zara rolled her eyes. 'Okay, I'll leave you to your pity party.' She left the kitchen, wafting the scent of Coco Mademoiselle behind her. Maia watched her go, aching when she thought of what she was about to lose.

'You do keep looking at her like you're heartsick,' Nancy said. She was perched on a stool at the breakfast bar, nursing a black coffee.

Maia sighed heavily. 'That's because I am,' she said, taking the stool next to Nancy's. 'You know more than anyone what that girl means to me. The idea of her leaving home, I just . . .' She trailed off.

Nancy reached over and patted her hand. 'I know, Maia,' she said. 'I've watched that girl grow from a baby, and you grow into a woman and a devoted mother. I haven't gone through it myself, but I can imagine how torn you must be feeling. I'm sure you're proud of what she's achieved but wish you could turn back the clock at the same time.'

'Exactly,' Maia said. 'I'm so happy to see her do well and follow her dreams, but it makes me feel, I don't know, left out. I don't feel like I have any dreams. I've just poured myself into Zara and Zach for the past seventeen years, so who the hell will I be without them?' She bit her lip to stop the tears that were threatening. She was daft to be sitting here crying because her kids were high-achievers. What kind of nutter did that?

Nancy smiled at her. 'Always hard on yourself, Maia. Ever since I first met you. I remember you when you moved here, a skinny streak of defiance, weren't you?'

Maia grinned at her. 'Such a way with words, Nancy. Just lovely.'

Nancy threw back her head and laughed. 'It's true. You thought we were all going to look down on you, or make a fool of you, that you didn't measure up somehow. You were wrong then and do you know what? You're wrong now. You do have dreams, you've just ignored your own inner voice for so long, you can't hear it. But it's still there. I see it with you mothers all the time. Your worlds are so noisy for so many years, you go deaf to yourselves. Common complaint.'

'Thank you, Doctor Smyth, for your wise insights,' Maia said, pouring herself a cup of coffee from the cafetière. 'Maybe you're right,' she said. 'But right now, all I can think about is that Zara is going travelling for a year and then going to university in Belfast, and Zach . . .' Maia groaned and put her head in her hands.

'Ah now,' said Nancy, 'it's not that bad.'

Maia could feel the tears welling again. 'Yes, it is,' she wailed. 'At least Belfast is up the road and I can drive there in two hours, but *America*! Zach is going to be so far away. I mean, my little baby. How can he head off halfway across the world?'

'Little baby? He's six foot two and built like a brick shithouse,' Nancy said, making Maia laugh through her tears. 'He's won a scholarship to study and play the sport he loves, and he's going to do it in a fantastic college that will open up so many opportunities for him. Maia, my love, this is what you've worked so hard for, to give him a life he can live with passion. America will be the making of him.'

'I know it in one part of my brain,' Maia said, 'but that's not enough to cancel out the bit of my brain that's screaming with sadness. The idea of them not in the house. How will Frankie and me manage, just the two of us?'

'Sex from the chandeliers would be my suggestion,' Nancy said, and the two of them burst out laughing.

'You're such a tonic, Nancy,' Maia said. She smiled warmly at her friend. 'You've been an absolute rock to me all these years. I hope you know how much I appreciate it, and how much I love you.'

'We'll be weeping into these coffees if you keep that up,' Nancy said. 'Remember, I'm nearly thirty years older than you, which means I know that time truly is a healer. It'll be horrible when they go. I'll miss them terribly myself. But then things will move on and flow and change and you'll find yourself with a different perspective. That's always how it goes. You'll just have to hang in there.'

Maia nodded. 'By my fingernails,' she said.

'By your incredibly expensive talons, you mean,' Nancy said.

Maia regarded her nails and tried to believe in Nancy's words. The truth was, she felt a rising sense of panic every time she looked into the future. It was October now, and by January the twins would be gone, and their little family would be broken up. She hadn't even really thought that Zach would get a place on the scholarship programme. She'd encouraged him and told him he could, but privately she'd been relying on his results not being good enough to get him over the line. But he'd knuckled down this year and studied like a demon and surprised everyone – not least his long-suffering teachers – by scoring two points more than he needed. His soccer skills did the rest, and now her boy would move to the US in January for three years. She felt sick at the idea of it. It wasn't just losing them, it was that sickening feeling that she was going to lose herself right along with them. Who was she if she wasn't Zara and Zach's mum? She honestly hadn't a clue.

'You should plan something nice,' Nancy said. 'Something to look forward to, like a holiday.'

Before Maia could answer, there was a rapping on the kitchen window. The two women looked over. Pearl was outside, hair and makeup beautifully done and wearing a white shirt and jeans, gesticulating wildly at them.

Maia raced over and unlocked the sliding door and

pulled it open. 'Wow, you look gorgeous,' she said. 'Did you go to Mila's place like I suggested?'

Pearl nodded. 'They were so good. They sent two girls up to do our hair and makeup. The bridal party are being done now. I don't really ever get an up-do, but I decided to go for it. Is it alright?'

'It's perfect,' Maia said, appraising her with an expert eye. 'And I adore the fresh flower. Is that a gardenia?'

'Yes. Thank you,' Pearl said gratefully. 'Seth hasn't mentioned my hair, so I was starting to think I got it wrong.'

'No way!' Maia said. 'That's just him being a man. You look stunning.'

'I'll take my compliments wherever I can get them,' Pearl said, blushing. 'But I'm so glad you're both here. The caterer just delivered the tables and chairs, but they've left me eight chairs short. The guy said he couldn't get across town and back again in time. Would either of you have spares I could use?'

'You've come to the right house,' Maia said. 'I'm the queen of party planning, as you know.'

'That's exactly why I ran straight here,' Pearl said, laughing.

'I have stacking chairs in the garage that will be perfect. You run on back, okay? I am not letting you ruin your perfect look by lugging chairs. I'll bring them across.'

'I'll help,' Nancy said, hopping down lightly from the stool. 'I may be nearly seventy, but I'm a good old work-horse all the same.'

'Oh no, I'll send Seth over,' Pearl said.

'Not at all,' Maia said, waving her hand. 'He's probably in his suit by now. We can manage. You run back and we'll see you in five.'

'Lifesavers,' Pearl said. 'Thank you so much.' She jogged off down the driveway and next door to her own house.

'Fair play to her hosting that wedding,' Nancy said. 'I'd be a basket-case if I had that level of hostessing to do.'

'I'd love it,' Maia said with a grin. 'I'm thrilled we're getting a preview. Let's go.'

She led the way outside and to the two-car garage that stood separate from the house. She tapped the keypad on the wall and the doors raised up, revealing her BMW, Freddie's Range Rover and walls of shelving all neatly arranged with tools, boxes, hanging bicycles – and chairs.

'Dear God, Maia, it's like an OCD paradise in here,' Nancy said, looking around in awe.

'You know me,' Maia said, making straight for the chair section. 'Have to have everything in its place.'

'This is actually kind of creepy,' Nancy said as she followed her.

Maia made four stacks of two chairs each. 'That's enough to carry in one go,' she said.

They both picked up a stack and walked around to Pearl's house.

'Are you sure you can manage?' Maia asked.

'I'm grand,' Nancy said. 'Pilates keeps me fit as a fiddle.'

'I want to be just like you when I'm your age,' Maia said. 'Fit and naughty.'

Nancy laughed. 'Just keep doing what you're doing, that'll get you there.'

'Nancy! Maia! Hey!'

'Good morning, Drew. Isn't this an exciting day?'

Pearl's son came bounding towards them, his eyes lit

up with pleasure. He grabbed Maia in a hug, nearly sending her and the chairs flying.

'Hang on,' she laughed. 'Let me get these out of my hands then I can give you a proper bear hug.'

'Get away from her this instant, Drew,' Seth barked as he came towards them. 'Nancy. Maia. Very kind of you. I'll take those.' He took the chairs from Nancy's hands and glared at Drew. 'Are you capable of helping?'

Nancy winced at his angry tone. 'That's grand, Seth,' she said calmly. 'They're no weight, and Maia is dying to get a look around at the grand preparations.'

'This way,' Seth said curtly. 'Don't get in the way, Drew.'

Maia and Nancy exchanged a look and Nancy took Drew's hand and squeezed it. The boy shrank into himself whenever his father was around and it pained Nancy to see it. She knew Seth had wanted a son just like himself, but Drew was sixteen years old now and she couldn't understand why Seth hadn't moved on to acceptance. When Drew was born and they'd discovered he was never going to progress beyond the mental age of a child, Pearl had been devastated at first, but then she had quickly accepted Drew for who he was and loved him fiercely. Pearl was devoted to Drew, and it was down to her hard work that he had come along so well over the years, but as far as Nancy could see, she got precious little help from her husband. His focus was the army, and always had been.

'I don't know how she puts up with him,' Maia said quietly as Seth marched up the path ahead of them.

Nancy shook her head. 'Certainly wouldn't be my cup of tea.'

'Cup of tea?' Drew said, looking eager to help.

'No, no, you're grand, Drew,' Nancy said, smiling at

him. 'We just had one. Now, will you show us this fantastic wedding set-up.'

'Come on,' Drew said, dragging Nancy by the hand so that she had to canter to keep up.

They went around to the back garden and stopped in astonishment. The long garden was festooned in the colour theme of the wedding: cream and silvery-grey. The chairs were cream, with grey silk bows. There was a podium at the end of the garden, with a long wooden table set up with candles and a sweeping bouquet of gardenias. A flower-adorned archway stood nearby, for Lily-Rose to walk through on her way down the 'aisle'. Old Kilner jars hung from the trees by ribbons, each holding a nightlight candle. A 'red carpet' in the same silvery-cream was waiting for the bride's Louboutin-clad feet to sashay across it. Strings of tiny white Chinese lanterns were hung across the whole width of the garden. The whole scene looked like an extravagantly beautiful movie set.

'My God,' Maia breathed, 'Pearl has played an absolute blinder. I couldn't actually have done any better myself, and that's saying something. This is amazing.'

'Wow!' Nancy said. 'Drew, this is spectacular.'

Drew grinned at them. 'I know. I know,' he said, nodding enthusiastically.

Seth walked over to join them. 'Are there any more?' he asked, gesturing at the chairs.

'Yeah, another four,' Maia said. 'I'll just . . .'

'I'll get them,' Seth said and turned on his heel and walked briskly away.

'Don't mind him,' Pearl said, her voice at a nervous pitch. 'He hates all this girlie stuff. But I'd say he's enjoying it really.'

'The important thing is to ignore him completely if he's annoying you,' Maia said. 'You look gorgeous, the place looks gorgeous and it's going to be a fabulous day, so don't let Sergeant Grumpy-arse ruin it for you.'

Drew started laughing hysterically. 'Sergeant Grumpy-arse,' he gasped.

'Oh God,' Pearl said, going pale. 'Drew, you can't say that,' she begged. 'Daddy will be angry. Please don't say that. It's just our secret, okay? You, me, Maia and Nancy. Our secret. We don't tell Daddy, okay?'

Drew grinned wickedly, but he seemed to catch the note of terror in his mother's voice.

'Sergeant Grumpy-arse,' he whispered, giggling to himself. 'I'm going to tell Tommy.'

He walked off and Pearl took a deep breath. 'Maia, please don't say stuff like that in front of him. Seth will blow a gasket if he hears that.'

Maia looked stricken. 'Jesus, I'm so sorry, Pearl. I wasn't thinking that Drew was there. Will I go after him and tell him he's never to say it again?'

Pearl shook her head. 'It's okay. Tommy is brilliant with him. He'll understand and make sure Drew knows not to say it out loud in front of Seth.' Pearl smiled tightly. 'Don't mind me, I'm just nervous about today. The bride is nearly ready inside and guests will be here in less than two hours and my nerves are shot.'

'You need a nip of brandy in your coffee,' Nancy said.

'God, no,' Pearl said. 'I'd fall over in a heap if I touched alcohol. I'm so tired from all the toing and froing this week. It's been crazy to get it all done.'

Maia looked around the garden. 'But my God, Pearl, you've done yourself proud. This place looks absolutely incredible. If I ever dump Freddie and find a hot young thing to marry, you're definitely my event organiser.'

Pearl laughed. 'I'm never doing this again, not for any amount of money.'

'Is there anything else we can do to help?' Nancy said, as Seth arrived back carrying all four chairs.

'No, thank you,' Pearl said. 'The caterers are brilliant, they have it all under control. And now I have the right amount of chairs, I can breathe again. I just have to get changed myself and then hopefully it'll all go smoothly.'

'You'd think you were organising a military campaign that involved life and death,' Seth said scornfully. 'It's just a party, Pearl. Keep it in perspective.'

Maia turned on him. 'Excuse me, Seth, but being responsible for your niece's wedding is a huge stress, and it's all on Pearl. You should be thanking her for putting such a huge amount of care and effort into it. It might look easy to you, but these things are a nightmare to plan and get right. Pearl deserves a medal.'

'A medal,' Seth snorted. 'You women. Talk about exaggerating.'

Maia looked like she was going to explode with anger, so Nancy put a hand on her arm and said quickly, 'We should go get ready, too, Maia.'

'Yes, I'll see you later then,' Seth said and walked off towards the house.

'Jesus Christ,' Maia muttered.

'I'm sorry,' Pearl said. 'He's just useless at this sort of thing. He's not mad on socialising and people around the house, so this kind of a day brings out the worst in him. Sorry about him speaking like that.'

'You've nothing to apologise for,' Maia said. 'I just don't

know how you don't whack him with one of those damn chairs. He'd have had a frying pan in the face long before now if he was my husband.'

Pearl smiled. 'That beautiful image is going to sustain me today, Maia.'

'Then my work here is done,' Maia said, laughing. 'Right, we'll leave you to it. But text me if you need anything else at all.'

'Just turn up and keep me sane,' Pearl said.

Maia and Nancy walked back to Maia's gate and stood looking at each other for a few moments.

'When I see men like that,' Nancy said, 'I'm so glad I have no husband or kids. He's so stifling. It's like you can't even breathe properly when he's around.'

'Pearl is such a sweetie,' Maia said. 'It breaks my heart to see that. I mean, Freddie's not exactly going to lay his coat over a puddle for me, but my God, he's decent and talks to me like I'm a human being, with feelings. Well, most of the time at any rate.'

'Anyway,' Nancy said, 'as Pearl said, we can go along and help her enjoy it. Hopefully Seth will find some boring old fart to talk army stuff with and she can forget about him. I'll go over and get ready. I'll see you there in a while.'

'Okay, see you later,' Maia said. She stood at the gate watching Nancy walk in her sprightly way back towards her house. She was so lucky to have friends like these women. Even Betsy, she thought with a smile. She loved to shock Betsy with a choice comment every now and then, but she also knew Betsy had the biggest and warmest heart and would do anything to help a friend.

She turned and started to walk slowly up her curving driveway, admiring the new lavender border the gardener had added. It worked beautifully. Imagine her with a lavender border! It was far from that she was raised. When they'd first moved here, she'd found the whole friendly neighbour scene a bit much. She'd also felt very insecure because she was from a different side of town. But she soon learned that everyone was from different backgrounds and, more to the point, they weren't concerned about where she'd come from. They were so welcoming and genuinely seemed to want her to join in with them, that she'd caved and 'become one of them', as Freddie liked to tease her. He was a rough diamond, but she felt he liked the fact that she'd learned how to hob-nob with the best of them over the years. She'd learned so much from Betsy, Nancy and Pearl, and now she could host a book club evening as if she was born to it.

The first time she'd mentioned going to the book club, Freddie had nearly coughed up his dinner. '*You're* going to a bleedin' book club!' he'd teased her. 'Does that mean you have to read something that's not a glossy magazine?'

Freddie was a good sort, though. Nothing like that Seth fella, who had a poker up his arse and couldn't crack a smile for love nor money. Although Maia had been getting worried about her husband lately. He seemed distracted, and it was harder to make him laugh. There was something a bit distant about him, like he wasn't really there even when he was beside her. It was bothering her, truth be told, but she didn't know what to do about it. She looked across at Pearl's house, thinking about the beautiful wedding day that was unfolding, when she had a lightbulb moment. What had Nancy said – arrange something to look forward to? She knew exactly what to do.

Maia went into the kitchen and found that Freddie had emptied the remaining contents of the cafetière into a big mug and was slurping it contentedly.

'How's my loving husband?' Maia asked, kissing his forehead.

'In danger of being late,' Freddie said. 'I'll just finish this and go.'

'You're working a hell of a lot of hours lately,' Maia said. 'We must try to have a date night, get some time to talk.'

'Talk about what?' Freddie demanded, looking at her sharply.

'Jesus,' said Maia, 'you'd swear I was from the Revenue. It's me, Freddie, your wife, remember?'

He smiled. 'Sorry, love. It's just whenever someone says they want to talk to me, it usually ends up costing me money.'

'Funny you should say that,' Maia said, 'because I've just had a fantastic idea.'

Freddie groaned. 'How much?'

'It's a really good idea,' Maia said. 'I'm kind of dying inside with the kids getting ready to leave, and you won't admit it but I know you are too.'

He shrugged. 'They have to grow up and live their lives.'

'I know,' Maia said, 'but that doesn't mean I'm not sad about it. But while we still have them, how about we celebrate our family? You and me are twenty years' married this year, so I'm thinking a party, big celebration, get everyone around and toast you and me and what we've achieved in raising Zara and Zach. What do you think?'

He shrugged again, and she felt a flash of irritation. What was it with men and shrugging? It was like they thought it constituted actual communication.

'Well?' she demanded. 'Have you fallen so far out of love with me that you don't care anymore?'

Freddie looked at her in surprise. 'Where's that coming from? Look, I'm no good at the organising, so you go ahead and arrange whatever you like, okay? It's a great idea. And the kids will love it. We could all do with a lift, and it'll be a night to remember if you're the brains behind it.'

'That's more like it,' Maia said, reaching over to take his hand. 'Bit of enthusiasm.'

Freddie looked at his watch. 'Have to get going, okay? I'll see you later.'

'So you definitely can't come to the wedding next door?'

He shook his head. 'Told you, just can't fit it in. But I hope you have a great day.'

The front door slammed shut behind him, and Maia was left standing in her spotless kitchen, in the silence. She looked around her and couldn't help thinking that she was standing in her own dismal future: quiet, empty, on her own. It made her heart sink. If her mother could see her now, she'd laugh in her face.

From the time she could walk, Roisin White had made her daughter model. Maia hadn't minded until she'd hit her teens. By that point she found it excruciatingly embarrassing and wanted nothing more than to curl into a ball when Roisin marched her into constant auditions. Her mother despaired when she wasn't chosen, while Maia secretly rejoiced.

'You've been chosen to do a yoghurt commercial, Maia!' Roisin said one day when she came in from school. 'It's going to pay out thousands. We'll be able to go on a foreign holiday for the first time!' Maia knew she couldn't refuse and even though everyone at school would slag her to death, it had to be done.

Maia never saw a penny of the money. They didn't go on a holiday either. Her mother bought her some hair clips and a t-shirt and told her to be glad of it. In retrospect, Maia now knew that the extra cash had been a lifesaver for her parents. They had so many to look after and she hadn't understood then the pressure they must've been under, especially coming up to back to school time or Christmas.

One good thing came out of it, though. She'd met Freddie at that yoghurt commercial shoot. He was there with his equally pushy mother, Bridgie. Mercifully, Freddie understood how much she hated being paraded and made to perform like a seal. But like Maia, his ma was struggling to make ends meet and he was the golden boy with the good looks, and so it was his duty to bring home the bacon too.

'He's my star,' Bridgie said to Roisin. 'I've four others and they got the worst of me and the old man put together. This one is our looker!'

'Our Maia is the same,' Roisin agreed. 'We might as well make hay while the sun shines and sure, they love every second of it.'

In the commercial Maia and Freddie were playing childhood sweethearts and had to kiss at the end. There was lots of hand holding too, which made them both blush like crazy at first.

'This is kind of awkward, isn't it?' he said after the first couple of run-throughs.

'Yeah,' she said, blushing wildly and wanting the ground to swallow her up.

'I'm finding it much worse because I kind of like you,' he said. 'I've seen you before at other auditions and always fancied you.'

'You have?' she asked in astonishment. Maia had very little experience with boys and didn't really know how to react. So she went along with Freddie, who decided by the end of the commercial that they were an item. He put his arm around her when they weren't shooting and told her she was his girl. She didn't object, and neither did Roisin – the two mothers were delighted, in fact, and on board with the whole thing.

They married young, partly to get away from their mothers and partly because they wanted to. They got a small flat above a betting office where Freddie got a job. There he met some dodgy fellas who got him into 'business'. Soon they were living in a townhouse, then a semi-detached house where Maia thought she'd died and gone to heaven. She longed for a baby but none came. Month after month her hopes were raised and swiftly dashed again.

The day Freddie came home and threw a set of keys on the table and looked at her with an expression of pure glee on his face she was confused.

'We're going up in the world, baby! I've just bought a house on Kingfisher Road.'

'Whaaat?' she screamed. 'But how? I don't understand . . .'

'Ask no questions and hear no lies,' he warned. 'We're moving and that's all you need to know, my precious. Pack the house up, we're moving tomorrow. This place is sold and we're on the pig's back.'

Her ma was delighted and started to get pushy again.

'Tell me as soon as you're pregnant. That's a massive industry. They'll all want you with a bump, especially if you live in one of them posh houses. They can come to your place and do them classy shots for the lifestyle magazines.'

Maia shuddered as she thought of that dreadful time in her life. Once the twins were born, Roisin went into overdrive, going on and on about putting her babies into adverts. Maia just kept saying no, hoping one day her ma would hear her. Eventually, it all came to a head one horrible day. Roisin had been arguing her case for over an hour, insisting they bring the twins to an audition that day. Maia was on her last nerve.

'Twins! And one of each. You're mad, Maia. Have I taught you nothing?'

'Yes,' Maia spat, anger taking over. 'You've taught me that I don't want to exploit my children and push them into doing stuff they hate!'

The fall-out between her and Roisin was massive. Her ma took serious offence at being accused of ruining her childhood and Maia simply couldn't back down and tell her it was okay, because it wasn't. They drifted apart and before they knew it, years had passed. Roisin hated calling to Kingfisher Road, saying it was snobby and made her feel inadequate. Maia took that as a personal slight and couldn't understand why her ma couldn't be happy for her.

Freddie listened to Maia's grief about the situation for as long as he could, but eventually he snapped too.

'You're not here to act as a bleedin' counsellor to your ma,' he roared after yet another tearful rant by Maia about Roisin. 'If I come home and find you crying over her once more, I swear I'll drive over to that hell-hole you called home and tell her once and for all to keep to herself. She's a selfish cow, just like my ma. They used us when they could and now they can both sod off. Enough is enough, and we're old enough to make our own decisions now.'

Maia was a bit shocked at first, but then she realised Freddie was absolutely right. Zara would say it was a toxic situation, and that's exactly how it had been; Roisin's greed was like a poison, seeping into everything. But with Freddie's strength, Maia was finally able to make a break.

Of course, now that she needed him most, her husband seemed to be pulling away and disappearing. Maia felt like her whole world was turning to sand and running through her fingers. First her darling twins, and now Freddie. One way or another, everyone seemed to be leaving. No doubt about it, her mother would find her life a right old hoot if she knew how things were unfolding now.

Maia felt like lying down on the floor and crying, but she straightened up her back and ordered herself to cop on.

'Chin up, Maia,' she whispered to herself. 'Time to put the glad rags on and pin a smile to your face.'

Chapter 3

LILY-ROSE WAS A PICTURE-PERFECT BRIDE. HER makeup was dewy soft, her long, thick chestnut-brown hair styled in a chignon with a sprig of gardenia – simple but chic. It had taken them six visits to town to finally find the dress, and Pearl had enjoyed every moment of that precious time. Her niece was an absolute darling, and tripping about from bridal shop to bridal shop, sipping Prosecco in each one, had been some of the happiest times of Pearl's life. And it had been so worth it, looking at the beautiful young woman standing before her now.

'You are so beautiful,' Pearl said, taking her hand. 'Leo is going to melt when he sees you.'

'Thanks, Auntie Pearl,' Lily-Rose said, blushing. 'It's a bit weird, but God I love this dress. I don't know how to thank you for . . .'

'Forget it,' Pearl said. 'You know you mean the world to me. I'm so happy you let us host your big day.'

'What's the delay?' Seth's voice called from the corridor. 'Everyone is assembled and waiting.'

Lily-Rose grinned at Pearl. 'He's so nervous about all this, isn't he? He's covering it up by being all army efficient.'

No, he's not, Pearl thought. That's just him.

'He's so pleased that he gets to walk you down the aisle,' she said. 'You've made his day.'

In fact, the suggestion of hosting the event had been Seth's idea in the beginning. He might be gruff and harsh with everyone else, but Lily-Rose had had a special place in his heart from the day she was born. She was Pearl's sister Barbara's child, but you'd swear she was Seth's own flesh and blood the way he took to her. Most adults were wary of Seth, and children certainly didn't flock to his side. But Lily-Rose never seemed to notice that and would climb onto his lap with a book under her little arm and insist he read to her.

'No unka Seth,' she'd say. 'Do the voices. Little Red Riding Hood has a different voice to the wolf, silly!'

So he'd end up booming one minute then trying to be ladylike the next. Their special relationship warmed Pearl's heart and gave her faith in her husband over the years. He was such a difficult man to live with and was so incredibly staunch about rules and regulations that she often felt he still thought he was out in Cyprus ordering his troops about rather than here in Vayhill, where he was supposed to be a husband and father.

'Is the bride ready?' Barbara asked, bustling into the room. 'Full house down there.' She smiled at the sight of Lily-Rose. 'My own daughter, nearly a married woman. Your father may have dumped us but it's all turned out well, hasn't it?'

Pearl bit the inside of her cheek. Barbara could be trying at the best of times, but today she was playing 'heroic single mother' and it was doing Pearl's head in. Pearl had been like a surrogate mother to Lily-Rose, always there when it suited Barbara not to be. This sudden display of maternal pride was hard to take.

'I'm ready,' Lily-Rose said.

Pearl went behind, making sure the detachable train didn't snag on anything. Seth beamed when Lily-Rose emerged from the room.

'My goodness, you look perfectly beautiful,' he said, holding out his arm.

Lily-Rose took his arm and nodded at him. 'Let's do this,' she said.

'Your wish is my command,' Seth said, and the two of them laughed.

Pearl followed them down, then slipped into her seat, with Barbara beside her. The string quartet began to play *Clair de Lune*, and it was finally happening. All those long months of preparation had been for this moment. Pearl felt her shoulders relax a smidgen, knowing she could do no more. She watched Seth walk proudly next to Lily-Rose and she felt a stab of jealousy that he got to give her away. She'd felt all along that Lily-Rose really could have asked her, although she understood it would probably have caused trouble with Barbara. But still, she had been the rock Lily-Rose had built her whole life on, and she would have loved to accompany her down the aisle to her waiting Leo.

Seth looked the part, and it made Pearl remember their own wedding day. She didn't want to, she tried to stay away from those memories because all the promises of that day had fallen asunder over time. Seth had loved her then, in his way, and she'd really believed they were going to share a happy life together. She watched Leo smile at Lily-Rose and sent up a fervent prayer that they would make each other happy. It was such a deeply lonely sense of failure when a marriage didn't work out. She'd never been able to tell anyone about it.

They had married when she was almost thirty, and now she was forty-seven and could barely recognise her own life. Then, she had a good marriage, lived in a pleasant semi-detached house near the town centre and worked as a receptionist for a GP. She thought it would always be like that. But then she got pregnant. Seth was thrilled and kept talking about how he wanted a son, a 'chip off the old block'. Whenever he said it, Pearl felt uneasy, but she went along with it because he was happy. Going along with things was her speciality, she thought bitterly.

The reason she had acquired enough money to live on Kingfisher Road was down to Drew. He'd been awarded the largest amount of money ever recorded against the maternity hospital. They'd messed up during his birth and as a result he'd suffered a lack of oxygen to his brain. The effect was devastating and had left him with the mind of a six-year-old, along with behavioural disorders that meant he could only function within a strict routine. Pearl had lamented and grieved for the life she'd hoped her son would have, but as time passed she loved him more and more and simply accepted his shortcomings. They were part of him and although he required full-time care, Pearl mostly managed very well.

The money they got for Drew was in her name officially, so that was probably why Seth never grumbled about how she spent it. Seth kept his salary in his own account and that never bothered her either. To be fair, he had never protested about the money she lavished on Lily-Rose and her brothers and, by extension, on Barbara. He had been pleased that Pearl was paying for the whole wedding and thereby ensuring it was a truly memorable occasion. It suited his image of himself as the kind benefactor to

Lily-Rose. For his part, he never paid for so much as a cup of coffee when they were out. If they had a meal or drinks, he'd sit back and let her pay out of Drew's money. Seth wasn't in Drew's life in any meaningful way, but he didn't interfere with the childcare arrangements and as long as they stayed out of his way and didn't annoy him, he was fine.

She knew some people saw the award as a Godsend and envied her, but the money could never undo the damage or give back what had been robbed from Drew. When she'd first moved here, she'd been wary of everyone because she felt they would judge her for using the money to buy a beautiful house, but then she slowly realised that Betsy, Nancy and Maia weren't the judgey types. They all had colourful pasts of their own, and they accepted her without reserve. Their friendship had been her anchor for the past sixteen years. She would have crumbled without them. They never demanded to know what was going on behind closed doors, but she knew they were there if she ever did want to talk.

Since the day Drew came into the world, Seth had been moving further and further away from her. She honestly believed he would dump Drew in a care home without a backwards glance. When he looked at his son, he just saw an embarrassment, a shameful failure that branded him less than a man. Drew challenged his whole sense of self, which was built on him being army, being tough. There was no way Pearl could love anyone who didn't love Drew, so it was an impossible situation. The only saving grace was that Seth spent large stretches of time on duty, otherwise Pearl would have really lost her mind by now.

The house had been her idea, and Seth had been very

happy to go along with it. She knew that she and Drew would be spending much of their time at home, so she wanted him to have space to roam and lovely surroundings and a quieter environment than the town and its traffic. The estate agent had shown her lots of places, but the day he walked her down Kingfisher Road was the first time she'd felt she found home. She'd looked at number two and couldn't believe someone was willing to leave it. It was perfect. The long, beautifully landscaped garden, the large, spacious rooms and the calm, tranquil surroundings. She would have paid any price to get it for Drew. And she was right, because he loved it here.

She forced herself to refocus on the ceremony. It only brought her down to think over her life like this. A movement caught her eye and she glanced down at the mews. Two faces were in the window, framed by the wooden sash. Tommy and Drew. She smiled and winked at them. Tommy would keep Drew safe and happy until the party started. He was the other rock in her life, along with her friends.

'You may kiss your beautiful wife.'

The place erupted in clapping as Leo bent to kiss Lily-Rose lovingly. Pearl felt an ache in her throat and swallowed it down. It would all be okay. Lily-Rose would have a good life. Leo was a truly lovely man and they'd make it through, Pearl was sure of it.

The guests began to leave their seats and mingle, so Pearl took the opportunity to nip down the mews building to check on Drew. When she opened the door and stepped inside, he charged at her and enveloped her in a hug. She laughed and kissed him.

'Did you enjoy that?' she asked.

'I love Lily-Rose,' he said.

Tommy smiled at her. 'He was so good. I told Drew we had to be quiet like mice and he didn't say a word during the whole ceremony. He just watched quietly. I'm so proud of him,' Tommy said, ruffling his hair. 'He has earned his piece of wedding cake for sure.'

'Cake!' Drew roared. Alongside Ben 10, it was his favourite thing in the world.

'Don't worry about him at all,' Tommy said quietly to Pearl. 'He really is on his best behaviour today, and I won't leave him for a second. You just concentrate on enjoying it.'

'Thank you so much,' Pearl said. She glanced outside. 'I suppose I better get back to it. I'll sit with you two at the meal, though.'

'Sure,' said Tommy. 'I'll see how he's doing by then. If I feel he's getting tired or a bit overloaded, I'll take our plates back here and let him eat in peace.'

'Okay,' Pearl said. 'We need to be careful. Seth's a bit on edge about everything being perfect.'

Tommy shot her a look. 'Drew is always perfect.'

Pearl smiled at him. 'See you in a bit,' she said.

Tommy had been assigned to them when Drew was five. By then, Drew was ready to start school and they were advised that he would need constant help to attain any level of decent education in a mainstream school.

'But it's best to keep him there for as long as possible. It's better for his development if he interacts with other children,' his team at the children's hospital had agreed. 'We have found an SNA for you as requested. You said you wanted a special needs assistant who would also live in, that's correct, right?'

'Yes,' she said, feeling sick to her stomach. But she'd been told it was the best route to follow because Drew would become more and more difficult to handle and she'd need a man to help. With Seth being away so often, they decided it was the best plan.

'Tommy has extensive training and fifteen years' experience with special needs children and he will be your home help. But if he and Drew don't click or if he doesn't fit in with your family, that's no problem. Let us know and we'll find a replacement.'

Mercifully, Drew took to Tommy instantly. He wasn't a tactile child. The only other person he'd hugged without being asked to was Pearl. Otherwise he shook hands. Pearl was a stickler for manners and despite her son's limitations she insisted he maintain some sort of politeness. So he automatically shook hands with everyone. The moment he was introduced to Tommy, however, he spontaneously hugged him.

'Don't be scared, Tommy. I'll be your friend,' Drew said.

Tommy was a Cork man, one of those fit yet strong looking types who looked like he belonged in the countryside rather than on Kingfisher Road. With brown wiry hair and bright blue eyes, he had a ruddy complexion with a warm smile. It became apparent after a few days that he had an engaging personality and that Drew adored him.

There were two spare rooms in the main house, but Seth ordered the conversion of the mews to the rear of the house. 'I won't have another man in my house,' he'd insisted.

The mews was made of sandstone and was actually a beautiful building. Pearl went to town on doing it up. She asked Tommy's opinion before ordering things and together they created a welcoming and comfortable home. With a fully fitted kitchen-cum-living room complete with a washing machine and dryer, large bathroom and two double bedrooms, it was spacious and modern and Tommy loved it. The little yard to the rear was secluded from the main house so they decked it and put in a table and chairs and a sofa, where Tommy loved to read. It was a sun trap, so Tommy was able to take advantage of any of the rare Irish sunrays.

The three of them had fallen into a routine and once Drew was settled at school, Pearl felt she had a piece of her life back once more. Ever since he was born, she'd had Drew clinging to her like a koala. Now, though, having a second person to share the minding and to talk things over about Drew's development was absolutely incredible. Pearl couldn't believe the difference it made, to have another adult there who cared as much as she did. Between them, they ensured that Drew was well supported and loved beyond measure. Pearl gave up thanks every day that they had been sent Tommy. She knew Drew wouldn't have come so far without Tommy's input.

Pearl rejoined the guests, greeting and shaking hands and thanking people for coming. But all the while she was just trying to get to the little huddle seated together near the archway.

'Here's the hostess with the mostess,' Nancy said as Pearl finally flopped into a chair beside them. 'What a day, Pearl. It's just so beautiful.'

'I nearly cried when I walked in,' Betsy said. 'It made me think of our wedding day, and I wished I could do it all over again.'

'I'd marry you again in a heartbeat,' Noel said, gazing at her adoringly.

'You two,' Maia said, swatting at them with her hand. 'Sent here to make the rest of us feel like we have crap marriages!'

Pearl felt her face blush and laughed to cover it. She'd often envied Betsy and Noel. She had no idea how they still loved each other so much.

'Oh Maia,' Betsy said, in the voice she reserved for whenever Maia said something wicked, which was a regular occurrence. 'You've all got wonderful men, too. But now, I've got some really exciting news to share with you.'

'Is it the identity of the new neighbour?' Nancy said eagerly. 'I noticed the For Sale sign had been taken down.'

'Oh no, not that,' Betsy said. 'I'm afraid I've no information on that just yet. It has been sold, but the only thing I could find out was that it was meant to go to auction but an offer was made two days before the auction that, apparently, could hardly be understood, let alone resisted. So the buyers got in and swooped it off the market for God knows what price.'

'Wow,' Maia said, 'they must have offered a king's ransom. These places aren't cheap even at the going rate. And number ten is one of the best houses on the street.'

'Can't wait to clap eyes on them,' Nancy said. 'We could have royalty moving in for all we know.'

'Probably some horrible vulture fund accountant,' Noel said. 'He'll wear pinstripe shirts with white cuffs and collars and we'll all hate him.'

Maia burst out laughing. 'Yeah, bet you're right, Noel. Whoever it is will be wealthy enough to be a right pain.'

'So what was your other news?' Pearl asked, curious about Betsy's announcement.

'Oh yes,' Betsy said, her eyes glowing. 'We are having

some visitors to stay for a couple of weeks. Graham is coming home!'

There was a discernible lack of enthusiastic response, so Pearl jumped in and said, 'That's so wonderful for you two. How long has it been since you've seen him?'

'Almost three years, since the wedding,' Betsy said, feeling emotional now at the idea of it. 'I know he was a handful, but I'm hoping the years away have matured him. We do miss him.' She took Noel's hand and he nodded. 'And there's something else,' Betsy said. 'He's bringing our grandson.'

The women looked at her in shock.

'What grandson?' Maia said. 'You've never mentioned this before.'

'We didn't know,' Betsy said. 'He rang to ask about visiting and then dropped the bombshell that we have a grandson called Arnie who's four months old.'

'My God,' Maia said and her mouth dropped open. 'The little bugger didn't tell you his wife was pregnant and had *given birth*!'

'Now, Maia,' Noel said gently, 'you'll give poor Betsy a turn if you call him names. I know it's a bit unorthodox, but we've come to terms with it now and we can't wait to meet him.'

'Congratulations,' Pearl said.

'Yes, congratulations,' Nancy said, reaching over to squeeze Betsy's arm. 'That's a blessing. I'm delighted for the two of you.'

'I'm in shock, I can't lie,' Maia said, 'but I'm also thrilled. You two will be the best grandparents who ever lived. You were made for this. Arnie is one lucky baby.'

'Thank you,' Betsy said graciously. 'It is a bit mad, but

then, life with Graham was never dull. Hopefully being a father has mellowed him out.'

'Well, I've a little bit of news too,' Maia said. 'Save-the-date kind of news.'

'Oh, what's happening?' Pearl asked. 'Has today made you want to renew your vows?' she teased.

'Not quite,' Maia said, 'but you're on the right track. Myself and Freddie are going to be twenty years' married this anniversary, so I've decided to mark it and the kids' great results by throwing a party. So keep the first of December free in your diaries. And Pearl, please make yourself available for event consultation.'

Pearl laughed. 'I told you. Never again!'

'Well I want all your suppliers' details,' Maia said. 'I don't think we'll get the right weather in December, but I'll definitely get a marquee and I want it to look this good.'

'We'll all pitch in,' Nancy said.

'Of course,' Betsy said. 'It's a lovely idea to mark the new phase in the twins' lives. Good on you.'

Maia struggled to keep her smile in place, and she felt Betsy could see that. Time was flying by too quickly now. The twins would be gone before she knew it.

'Right,' Maia said, jumping up. 'Champers all round, I think. I'll mug someone with a tray.'

'Did you enjoy the day?' Pearl asked as she took off her makeup at her dressing table that night. There were still a few guests partying outside, but Pearl was too exhausted to stay up another minute. All she wanted was to be curled up and asleep. She was utterly exhausted.

'Yes,' Seth said. 'I particularly enjoyed escorting young Lily-Rose to her fiancé. It was a wonderful honour to walk her down the aisle. She's a fine young lady and I have to take my hat off to your sister when I say she's done a superb job of raising her.'

'That she has,' said Pearl, swallowing the moment of madness where she wanted to blurt out that it was *mostly* down to *her* that Lily-Rose and her brothers had turned out the way they had. Much as her sister Barbara had earned money to support her kids, she was never actually there.

Pearl had stopped wasting her breath by saying she had money there and would gladly give it to Barb so she could cut her hours and spend more time with her daughter and two sons. But no! She chose that blasted shop over her own kids. Just as she'd done so many times before, Pearl managed to work herself into a state of boiling anger when she thought of Barbara. She was her only sister and although she was only three years younger than Pearl, she acted about twenty at times.

She'd done nothing to help prepare for today and as usual she'd drunk too much and had to be put to bed by her sons. It made Pearl so cross that she couldn't put her kids first and attempt to behave in a more responsible manner.

'The boys were well turned out,' Seth continued, clearly oblivious to Pearl's emotions. 'I'm glad I polished their shoes. You wouldn't know about doing that properly,' he said in a sneering tone. 'But suffice to say that the shoddy attempt you'd made would've annoyed me all day.'

'Well, isn't it great that you sorted it then,' said Pearl through gritted teeth.

She walked to the en-suite and closed the door. She wanted to thump the wall. She'd organised every single thing for the wedding with Lily-Rose. She was the one who'd tested menus, researched florists, makeup people, the hairdresser, you name it and she'd done it. But all Seth could do was pick on the fact that she hadn't polished two lazy grown-up men's shoes. She should know better than to expect anything nice or kind from Seth. All he did was put her down and why should today be any different? He was the only person who hadn't commented on how she looked. Her outfit had worked out so well, and she'd felt gorgeous in it. It was a green satin calf-length dress in fifties style, cinched in at her waist and then falling gently around her. She'd teamed it with high-heeled court shoes in a beautiful shade of yellow. It was a bit of a statement, but it had worked. Everyone had told her she looked fantastic. Seth hadn't said a single word.

She took a deep breath to calm herself. There was absolutely no point obsessing over this stuff. She redirected her thoughts to Drew, thinking about how well he had managed the whole day as she carefully hung up her dress in its garment cover. Pearl was immensely proud of him. Oftentimes, he struggled dreadfully with people he didn't know. But perhaps it was the fact that it was Lily-Rose's wedding, and she was the closest thing to a sister he had, and also that it was in his own garden, a space where he was very comfortable. Whatever it was, he had done them proud.

'Didn't Drew do well today?' she called out to Seth, who was flicking through the Sky channels, looking for some war documentary no doubt.

'Uh-huh.'

'Did you see the lovely framed photo Lily-Rose presented me with?' He had found a documentary on gun cleaning.

She stood there for a moment, to see if he'd answer. After a pause he did.

'Nope,' he said sighing loudly, making it clear he had no interest either.

'What did you get? Did you open your gift? It was nice of Lily-Rose to present them to us during her speech, wasn't it? I certainly wasn't expecting it, were you?'

'No, it was very good of her for sure. She gave me an antique medal holder. I can put one of my own ones in at some point. She's a great girl the way she thinks of things that I'll like.'

Pearl looked at her husband and told herself that no matter how horrible he was to her, he couldn't take away the happiness she'd felt seeing her niece marry the man she loved. She would take that away as her memory of the day and leave the rest behind, with all the other things she hated to remember.

She climbed into bed and lay down with her back to Seth, assuming he was going to watch the rest of the documentary. Good, she thought as relief flooded her. She just wanted to drift away into her dreams. But her relief didn't last long as he spoke a few moments later.

'Are you asleep?'

Pearl stared at the wall, blinking into the darkness. He didn't whisper nor was his voice loving.

'Pearl,' he said loudly. 'I'm speaking to you. I said, are you asleep?'

She shuddered. If she had been asleep, she certainly wouldn't be still.

'No, I'm not asleep. But I'm exhausted.'

He put his hand on her back. That was his indication that he wanted her. She'd never enjoyed sex with Seth.

Just like everything else, it was on his terms. He had no consideration for her and he was about as tender as a sledgehammer.

She turned over and obliged him. As usual, there was no joy in it for her. She simply hoped it would be quick and wouldn't hurt.

He finished and rolled over and passed out on his back, so she knew she was in for a night of listening to his snores. She left the room. She'd long since given up creeping about. He was out for the count and even if she'd put on Irish dancing shoes and River Danced across his chest and into the spare room, he wouldn't have stirred.

The good thing about her duty being done for a while was that he'd be in slightly better form for a couple of days. So while she didn't gain any personal enjoyment from their deed, it would serve a positive purpose for everyone else around him. Sex put him in better form, and that was good for her and for Drew.

She'd never have really known the difference if it wasn't for Tommy.

Chapter 4

NANCY WOKE TO THE SOUND OF THE KINGFISHERS' calls. She turned her head on the pillow to listen. One called, and after a short pause the other would answer. A perfect pair, she thought with a smile. Last year, when she'd finally realised what type of bird was making that particular call, she'd phoned in to a wildlife radio programme she sometimes listened to and asked about them. The expert had been quite excited, telling her that the bird was amber-listed, which meant its population was somewhat depleted, and that she was extremely lucky to have a nesting pair that she could observe up-close.

Nancy was thrilled to have something so special in her garden. She collected tadpoles in the spring to feed them and any spiders or creepy-crawlies that ended up in her house were left on a little perch for them to snack on. She'd named them Bonny and Clyde because they were so tame and cheeky. They'd come right up to the kitchen window and take food while she was doing her washing-up at the sink, not a bother on them to be so close to a human.

Nancy lay there feeling cosy and comfortable and thought back over the night before and the wedding. The party had gone on into the wee hours, and she had had great fun with a group of girls almost a quarter of her age who were doing vodka shots. Nancy didn't actually drink the alcohol, but she'd enjoyed the buzz nonetheless. In fact, she and alcohol had parted company many years ago, but she still loved to party.

One of the things she really enjoyed about getting older was that it was so easy to shock people. She'd found out that presumptions were a powerful thing. Once people saw her grey hair – even though it was cut into a funky choppy bob – they saw 'old woman' and treated her accordingly. She loved to stay quiet, listening as they rabbited on about the weather or teabags of whatever inane subject they thought she'd be interested in, and then pounce with a sharp comment or a well-judged swear word. It worked a treat every time. Their eyes would widen, then, depending on their personality, they'd either shun her or sit closer and want to hear more.

It had been just that way last night. She'd found herself sitting next to a group of Lily-Rose's friends, and she got chatting to them. Oh, they were fabulous. All dressed up in amazing gear and each one more stunning than the next. They were politely making conversation with her, on their best behaviour, when she held up her hand and said, 'You all look so beautiful and are so full of youth, I'm going to give you some advice and you'd do well to listen to it carefully. Old age is an absolute bitch. One minute you're twenty, the next minute you're seventy, it just creeps up on you like that.' She clicked her fingers. 'You have to party your hearts out while you can. Be outrageous. Go crazy. Follow your heart. Do whatever the feck makes you happy. Trust me.'

There was a stunned silence after her little rant, then one of the girls said, 'Jesus, fair play to you. You're right, and I'm going to write that down and remember it. And look at you, still going strong. What age are you your-self?'

'Seventy next year,' Nancy said, 'but that won't stop me. It's just an even better excuse to be wicked,' and she winked at them.

The girls shrieked with laughter.

'I wish you were my mum,' one of them said. 'Can I adopt you?'

Nancy shook her head. 'Forget it. I like my life too much to be adopted by anyone.'

'Oh, I love it,' one of the girls said. 'Since I hit thirty I've been coming under such pressure from my parents for a grandchild, and I haven't the heart to tell them I don't want to be a mother. So it's okay not to want that?'

'Of course,' Nancy said. 'It's the single biggest commit-ment you can make in life. There's no breaking it. So you have to want it from the core of you. If you don't, don't do it. You can't live your life to make other people feel good about you. They have to suck it up and feel good about who you are, the real you. Otherwise tell them to take a running jump.'

'I'm Natasha,' the girl said, holding out her hand and smiling widely. 'And you are my official new favourite person.'

They shook hands and the girls toasted Nancy.

'To wisdom!'

'Ah now,' Nancy said, 'I'm only alive long enough to be able to tell it like it is. I'm not sure that's wisdom. But you won't go wrong if you take my advice, I will say that.'

The girls took her into their circle and the chat flowed, along with the vodka, as they told her about their lives and asked her opinion and laughed at her anecdotes and stories. Nancy felt wonderful – being with young people brought out her own youthfulness and she revelled in their attention and energy. As the night darkened around them, the chat became more personal, and Nancy listened to their worries about the future.

'What do you regret most, looking back?' asked Natasha. 'Or are you a person with no regrets?'

'Ah, I've a few regrets of course,' Nancy admitted. 'My main regret, if you could call it that, is that I didn't spend more time with some of my husbands and less with others.'

'Husbands?' Natasha said. 'How many times were you married?'

Nancy held up her right hand. 'Four times. Mercifully, I married the first three over in the States or I'd probably still be shackled to the first miserable sod. I lived in America for a long time. I loved it then, but I'm happy to be home now. Only the last husband, my real love, was from here.'

'How many children have you?'

'I missed the boat with children, I'm afraid. I was too much in love with alcohol to manage to fit anyone or anything else in. A sad and silly mistake that I regret massively. You asked me my regrets,' she said turning to Natasha. 'It's booze. Never allow it to take over your lives, ladies.' The girls all looked uncomfortable, but she desperately wanted to stop them from making the same mistake.

'Did all of your divorces happen because of the drink?' asked a stunning girl with waist-length hair and legs that went on for ever.

'No, darling,' she said. 'I fell out of love with one. He was a very kind and sweet man. He was too nice, though, if you get my drift? I know that sounds crazy. At first I loved the fact that he adored me so much, but then I found him stifling. Eventually, I totally fell out of love with him.'

'I do that all the time,' said another girl. 'I'm all about the new relationship stuff, the chase, the spark, the excitement and then when I have him, I don't want him anymore!'

'Yeah,' Nancy nodded, 'falling out of love is just as much of a body blow as falling in. Oh it's a killer, and every part of me ached. I thought I had flu at first. Then I knew it was the physical gut-wrenching fact that I no longer loved Maddox.'

'Cool name,' said someone.

'I know, right? But I had to leave him. I divorced him, and I can still see the sadness in his eyes. God, I felt so mean.'

'So are you married now?'

'No,' she said with a sigh. 'I'm widowed. The last guy, Liam, died of unexplained causes twenty-two years ago. I cried for a month. Losing him was like losing a limb. I felt utterly changed and sort of useless.' A tear trickled down her cheek as she thought of Liam. The pain was still there, just beneath the surface. 'You know that phrase that it's better to have loved and lost?'

The girls all nodded.

'What a sack of horse shit.'

They all giggled, in spite of trying to hold it in, as she was clearly upset.

'Hey, it's okay to laugh,' she said, smiling at them. 'I love the sound of laughter. There's nothing better. I miss having someone to laugh with, so I see my neighbours a lot. I love it when they drop by for a chat.'

The girls would have happily talked on until morning, but Nancy performed her usual escape trick by saying she was popping to the loo and then walking on out the door and home. Pearl had already retired for the night, so she didn't have to make a big song-and-dance about saying goodbye.

She smiled to herself now, remembering all the fun, hoping the girls had heard her words and would take them on board. Seven decades gave you a good bit of perspective, and if that could help someone younger make the most of their time, that would make her very happy.

There was a snuffling sound and her bedroom door creaked open a little and Nelly padded across the floor and jumped up onto the bed.

'Morning, Nelly,' Nancy said, reaching to scratch her behind the ears. 'I'd say you're hungry, are you? I'm later than usual this morning because I was kicking up my heels last night.'

She had decided after Liam died that a dog was a necessity because the house was so quiet and lonely. After her first dog passed away, she'd found Nelly at the animal rescue centre and it was love at first sight. Nelly was a Bichon Frise. Nancy picked her up and kissed her warm, furry head. She wriggled and writhed with excitement, making Nancy giggle.

'Okay, calm down, little girl!' she said. 'I know, I know, I love you too.'

Nelly settled down on Nancy's tummy, and Nancy sighed and gave in to the luxury of lying on a bit longer. The chat last night had made her think about her husbands, little flashes of the past rising up and falling away again. Given this famous perspective she felt she had now, it wasn't surprising that none of her marriages had lasted. Maturity and hindsight showed her that she'd been a dreadful wife – impossible to live with when all she really wanted was drink.

One husband had filed for divorce, saying the final straw was her disrespect for God when she'd turned up for mass on Christmas Day looking like a homeless person. He actually wrote on the divorce papers that she had fries in her hair. On that occasion she'd gone on a bender, bought takeaway as she staggered home and fallen asleep with her face in the box of fries. Not her finest moment, she knew.

Then there was husband number three, Barney. She'd bumped into an old college friend while staying at his parents' home. Her husband had gone home early, disgusted with her, and she'd partied on into the night, not caring what he thought. They had a family lunch the next day, preceded by a special mass at her in-laws' home. She'd rolled in during the mass and proceeded to sing 'Swing Low, Sweet Chariot' with gusto, much to everyone's astonishment. After that she heckled the priest and made loud burping noises and howled with laughter.

Barney had dragged her by the arm up to their bedroom and flung her inside the door. She sat on the edge of the bed, feeling a little scared by the anger that was rolling off him in hot waves.

'How could you embarrass me like that?' Barney hissed. 'Where are your manners? You're from out of town. My parents have never met you and they've been excitedly telling the neighbours that we were arriving to share the holidays with them and you show up to their home and to a mass looking like this!'

Sitting on the bed, she'd looked down at her ensemble. There was a man's brown overcoat she'd found in the cupboard in the hallway last night. She'd figured her pyjama bottoms would be acceptable seeing as they had

Santa figures all over them. She'd pulled on a clean white blouse and a sleeveless red sweater vest.

'I look festive,' she said, attempting to defend herself.

'You're a walking obscenity,' he cried, throwing his hands up in the air.

Confused, she looked down at her pyjama bottoms, then suddenly realised the Santa figures were either flashing or doing rude things to themselves.

'Oh honey, I got them in a Kris Kringle box from Maggie at work.' She thumped her forehead with the heel of her hand. 'It was a lucky dip and she's twenty. She must have thought they were a hoot.'

'Well my folks, their neighbours and I do not think they're a *hoot.*'

They'd stayed there for three further torturous nights, during which time Nancy's in-laws barely spoke to her.

As soon as they got back to New York and walked into their apartment, Barney delivered a New Year's surprise. She was on the floor in utter shock, and it took her a few moments to realise he'd punched her.

'Never embarrass me like that again. You need to learn some manners. By the time I'm finished with you, I'll ensure you know how to behave.'

She had no cuts and the bruises were down her back where she'd hit the wall, but she was broken and damaged all the same. And it wasn't the only beating either. Barney was only getting started. Slowly, bit-by-bit, he took her personality and pushed it behind her terror. For a year and a half she was lost to herself, living in fear, constantly told she was a useless, rude, stupid whore. Then one day she just walked out. She still didn't understand where that bravery came from, but she had packed a bag with what dignity she had left and walked out of that apartment and away from Barney's hatred. She didn't understand how she did that, any more than she could understand why she'd stayed for eighteen months. The drink had turned her into something she wasn't.

Then later, after she'd kicked the drink habit and turned things around, she'd met Liam while she was working at a makeup counter in a very fancy store on New York's Fifth Avenue. He was looking for a gift for his grown-up daughter. His accent took her right back to home. They chatted and laughed together while she picked out a little hamper of goodies for his daughter. He took the glossy bag from her, then looked her in the eye and asked her out for a drink after work. She wanted to say no because she'd decided men were not for her, but an invisible force pulled her towards him. Three hours later, they were sitting in a bar, Liam sipping Guinness and she sipping a diet soda. Liam made a face at his Guinness and she laughed.

'What do you expect? You're in New York. It might be the city that never sleeps but it's not Dublin. The Guinness is shockingly awful here. You'll have to go home for that.'

'Well, this is just a holiday,' he said. 'So I'll be downing a decent pint in a few days' time.'

They regarded each other in silence.

'When are you coming back to Ireland?' he asked.

She smiled at him. 'Sadly, never.' And she'd meant it. Her job and one-room apartment were cosy and safe. She could go to work and go home, eat a proper meal in the large canteen at work and make a toasted sandwich in the evening. She had a small TV and that was enough. She knew she was existing, not living, but she simply didn't trust herself to do anything more.

Liam wasn't prepared to give up on her, however. Over the next six months he begged her repeatedly to come back to Ireland and be with him. 'Come for one month and if it doesn't work out, you walk away with no hard feelings, okay?'

In the end she reckoned she didn't have anything to lose on those terms, so she'd agreed. She sublet her apartment, left her New York life ready to move back into, and booked a flight home. Liam collected her at the airport with a dozen red roses and a smile as wide as the Shannon. He drove her straight to the new house he had just bought on Kingfisher Road and Nancy honestly thought she'd died and gone to heaven. The stream, the garden, the mountains as a backdrop, the neat and calm spaces created by the lovely neighbours – it was perfection.

Liam told her every day how delighted he was to have a woman in his life once again. His first wife had died of heart disease and although it took his children a little while to accept her, Nancy formed a polite relationship with them. She was happy to be partners and live together, but Liam proposed one memorable night with champagne under the stars in their garden, and it felt so right that she cast aside all her feelings about marriage and gave him a resounding 'yes'. It was a simple ceremony, but beautiful, and it made them both very happy.

When Liam died suddenly just three years after she'd moved over, his children kept up a forced sort of exchange with the odd phone call, then text message, and then nothing. She hadn't heard from them in years. She still missed Liam desperately, but she had made a very firm decision that she was now finished with men. She'd had her fair share and she'd come to a point where she was happy with Fraser, her first dog, and her neighbours. They rallied around her and once she got over the initial shock of Liam's death, she began to enjoy her life again. Slowly she built relationships with the other women on Kingfisher Road and before she knew it, twenty years had passed.

Nancy got up and did some light stretching, enjoying the suppleness that her all-important pilates classes bestowed on her body. She went down to the kitchen and switched on the kettle. She enjoyed a proper cup of green tea first thing, made the old-fashioned way with teapot, strainer and leaves. The aroma rose up and enveloped her and made her feel instantly more awake.

She pulled a warm cardigan over her pyjamas and took her cup outside, loving the feeling of the dewy grass on her bare feet. She wandered around the garden, sipping her tea and making mental notes of what work she needed to do in the beds. She went down by the stream, to the spot where Liam had proposed, and she gave thanks that after all her years of bad habits and bad men, she had got a taste of proper, grown-up romantic love. She missed it so badly, yet was so grateful it had been hers – even for such a short time.

She walked on down by the stream edge, listening to it burbling and gurgling. She had planted montbretia all along here some years ago, and it had proved an inspired choice. The heat of the orange was glorious, a real show-stopper. As she walked on, a flash of blue caught her eye and made her smile. Her kingfishers were busy at work, looking for food no doubt.

She made her way around to the front garden, checking on the progress of new plantings and the effects of autumn on the flowers. There was quite a bit of work to be done, she mused. She should get into her gardening gear now and get going on it. As she turned to head back to the house, she saw a van outside number ten. It was a large removal van, and six men were fetching and carrying out of the back of it. Nancy watched with interest, wondering if one of the men was the new owner. It was such a crucial moment when they met a new neighbour, and she felt nervously excited at the prospect of it.

Back inside the kitchen, she cut some bread and popped it in the toaster, then opened a tin of food for Nelly. At the same moment, the toast pinged up and her phone beeped loudly. It was a message from Betsy: Come for coffee. We have the new neighbour!

Chapter 5

DANIELLE FELT AS IF SHE WERE HAVING SOME SORT of a weird out-of-body experience. One minute she was helping Justin to move things into their new home, and the next she'd been catapulted into a neighbour's kitchen that suddenly seemed full of people all looking at her expectantly. The introductions were swift and she hadn't really taken in any of the names. She was confused as to who even lived here. Two of the women seemed to be in charge and she was trying to work out if they both lived in this house.

They were all being friendly to her, but they were a bit scary. They were very posh and kept staring at her as if they were waiting for her to entertain them. She didn't know whether she should tell them a bit about her and Justin or not. Was that considered bad manners or good manners? She wished her mam had taught her about this kind of situation. But then, she could just imagine what her mam would say about this group. 'I'd rather eat my own leg off than walk into a room full of poshies like them.'

She silently cursed Justin for dumping her right in it. One of the women, the small older lady who was dressed in a skirt and blouse and a navy blazer with a perfectly tied silk scarf, had come over with a big smile and a hamper of stuff and basically insisted she go with her. Danielle had surveyed the chaos of her life that was being dumped from the van and said 'No, thank you' about fifty times, but the woman was stubbornly insistent.

'Just pop in and say hello for five minutes, that's all. The other women are dying to meet you. It would be so lovely. You'll come, won't you?' Danielle had begun shaking her head yet again, so the woman had switched her attention to Justin.

'Can you spare her for a few minutes, do you think?'

Justin grinned and reached over to take the hamper from the woman's hands. 'Oh of course! Take her. She'd love to go and meet everyone, wouldn't you, darling?'

She'd glowered at him, but it was too late. The lady had taken her by the arm and frog-marched her into house opposite Danielle's. There were two other women there, too, sitting in the perfectly spotless kitchen. It was so clean, Danielle even tried to breathe minimally. She'd accepted a cup of tea and a small home-baked biscuit and tried to focus on the conversation. They all seemed to know one another very well and she hadn't the first clue what to do or how to be. All the talk was about some party that was clearly happening soon.

'Of course, you two will have to come along,' said the most glamorous one of the bunch. She was exactly the type of woman Danielle would normally avoid – red lippy, a tonne of mascara, fake tan and cleavage all pushed up so that it was straining out of her shirt in a way that was far too eye-catching. All glam and no shame, as her mother would have said. 'Freddie and I are celebrating twenty years of marriage, God help us all. I'm having a major blow-out in the garden. Well, in a tent in the garden.'

'A marquee, Maia,' said the one who'd dragged her here.

'Oh yeah, sorry, in a marquee,' she said in a put-on posh voice. She cackled laughing and Danielle forced a laugh. This was torture. She'd be making damn sure Justin didn't throw her to these lions ever again.

'Stop talking about me, I've arrived,' a voice called from the hallway, then the door to the kitchen pushed open and an even older lady walked in, smiling widely.

'We weren't talking about you,' said the glam one, going over to hug her. 'And if we were, it would be about how adorable you are.'

'Adorable, my ass!'

'Nancy, for goodness sake,' said the lady in the blazer and she looked shocked. 'Language, please.'

'Lighten up, Betsy,' the woman said, grinning at her. 'My ass is entirely inoffensive, I can assure you.'

They all started giggling at that, even blazer Betsy, even Danielle. She felt like this woman was different from the others. She was older, for starters, but she was funny and didn't seem to give a toss what the rest thought. Dressed in an ankle-grazing dress covered in a daisy motif that looked as if it were genuinely vintage, she had a warm and inviting smile. When she sat on a high stool beside Danielle, they were all treated to a view of her bright Kelly-green patent Mary-Jane shoes. The look was finished off with a headband of yellow artificial flowers.

'Hi, I'm Nancy,' she said, extending her hand.

Danielle shook it awkwardly. 'I'm Danielle. I just moved in to the road.'

'Did you now? I passed the removal vans and was wondering who was joining us on Kingfisher Road. Well,

I hope you'll be very happy here. We're all great friends and I'm sure you'll fit right in too. I live in number five, at the bottom of the road, and you're welcome any time.'

'Thank you,' Danielle said, sure she'd never have the guts to knock on any of their doors, and hopefully never the need to either.

'Have you been introduced to the rest?' Nancy said, looking around.

'Of course she's been introduced,' Betsy said, sounding offended again. 'What kind of a home do you think I run?'

Nancy winked at Danielle. 'What's her name?' she said, pointing to the woman who was the quietest one.

Danielle blushed. 'Em . . . I'm not . . .'

'Hah, you see,' Nancy said triumphantly. 'You over-whelmed her and she's not taken anything in. I knew it from the look of her, like a frightened cat.' She turned to Danielle and smiled. 'That woman is Pearl,' she said, and the quiet woman waved at her. 'She's in number two, next door. This is number one, Betsy's house. Utter perfection, I think you'll agree. And that looper over there is Maia, our resident hot chick. She's in number three.'

'What about the other five houses?' Danielle asked, looking towards the door and fearing another stampede of people and names to remember.

Nancy ticked off five fingers. 'Unfriendly widower who won't even look at you if you're not his grandkid; high-flying couple who spend only about one month here a year; another high-flying couple, retired but still on aero-planes most of the time; a businessman who seems to treat it as a pad to shag his mistress; and finally an opera singer who we suspect has it only for tax purposes.'

Danielle's head was reeling from this rapid-fire delivery

of strange information about her unseen neighbours. 'Oh right,' was all she could manage.

'Nobodies, basically,' Nancy said with a shrug. 'And then there's us, who look out for each other and have a bit of fun together and it suits us. You'll have to find your side of the fence, I suppose, but I hope it's here with us.'

She smiled again, and Danielle liked her even more. She was a straight talker, that much was obvious.

'So, how is everyone feeling this morning?' Nancy asked, looking around at the others. 'Because I'm pretty whacked.'

'At least you could have a lie on,' said Maia. 'I had to bring the twins to swimming early this morning. Honestly, I can't drink the way I used to and get away with it. Ugh, I just die if I go hell for leather.'

Danielle tried not to stare at Maia. She was a typical yummy-mummy, with a loud, booming voice with a slight whine added in for good measure. Her accent seemed to be a mish-mash of at least two and much as she was trying to be open-minded, Danielle wasn't drawn to her. She guessed she drove a massive jeep and let the nanny raise the kids most of the time. She seemed to be looking for a medal for turning up at the swimming pool this morning.

'Well, let me tell you,' Nancy continued as she elbowed Danielle to get her attention, 'I had a lesson on how the young ones do it these days. It's all shots and slammers. We were at a wedding in Pearl's house,' she said leaning across her to pat Pearl on the leg. 'They put on some spread.'

'Was it your son or daughter's wedding?' Danielle asked politely.

'My niece's,' said Pearl. 'Lily-Rose. She's a dote and we were delighted to host it because we have the space after all. She lives in Westwood and their house doesn't lend itself to large weddings.'

'I'm from Westwood,' said Danielle.

'That's where me and Seth came from originally,' said Pearl. 'I thought I recognised the accent. What are your parents' names? Maybe I know them.'

'My mam is Rachel O'Brien.'

Pearl shook her head. 'No, the name doesn't ring a bell. But you must introduce us if she's ever over visiting you.'

'My husband is from County Meath,' Danielle said, changing the subject. 'His family are all into horses, but I prefer this type of place. I'm not a country girl.'

'Oh I don't blame you,' said Pearl. 'Given the choice between Kingfisher Road and a mucky horse yard, I'd pick here without a contest.'

'A horsey family sounds very la-di-dah, though,' Maia said, studying her. 'What did you say Justin's surname was?'

'I didn't,' Danielle said, staring right back at her.

There was an awkward pause, then Maia started laughing. 'We're doing the nosy neighbours things, aren't we?' she said. 'But there's no use pretending we don't want to know about you, is there?'

Even though she was annoying, Danielle couldn't help admiring her honesty.

'He's Justin Johnston,' she said. 'Although we're not married, so I'm just plain old Danielle O'Brien.'

Maia's mouth fell open and she stared. 'What, as in *the* Johnstons from Meath? The filthy rich lot?'

'Yes,' said Danielle. '*Those* Johnstons.' She didn't look away, but she hated having to admit who Justin was because it made her feel like people were looking at her and wondering how the hell she had managed to land a catch like him. She was afraid someone would actually ask some day because she couldn't answer it herself. She had no idea why Justin had fallen for her like he did. She wasn't from his circles at all, and yet he was mad about her. She wasn't a Maia, all dickied up and sexy, she was completely ordinary. She was sure that's what they were all thinking as they stared at her in silence now.

'That's a wonderful family,' Betsy said, beaming at her.

'Maybe you'll end up in the family business,' Pearl said.

Not on your nelly, Danielle thought to herself. If this lot had actually met the Johnstons, they'd soon realise money couldn't buy you intelligence, or manners for that matter.

'Jesus Christ,' Maia said, her eyes still wide. 'The bloody Johnstons. You are a dark horse, Danielle, if you'll excuse the pun.' She looked delighted with her little joke.

Just then, there was a loud beeping sound and they all saw the truck reverse by the window and then pull out onto the main road.

'Looks like we're all moved in,' said Danielle, standing up. 'It's been lovely to meet you all, but I'd better get back to Justin.'

'You're moved in already?' asked Maia. 'When we moved here it took ages to empty the trucks. You must have hardly anything if they're finished. I would have thought you'd have oodles of fancy stuff with money like that.'

Danielle was trying not to take an instant dislike to this Maia one, but it was challenging.

'That's because most of the trucks were probably full of your shoes and handbags, Maia!' said Nancy.

'You're not wrong,' said Maia as they all laughed. 'Then

I had to try and put things away before Freddie saw them. The stress was something else. If you haven't already worked it out, I'm a shopaholic,' Maia said proudly. 'If you need help with shopping of any sort, I'd be delighted to help you, love. I know where everything is in Vayhill shopping centre.'

Danielle almost said something sarcastic but held her tongue. Instead she smiled and nodded, hoping she looked appreciative.

'I'm the opposite,' said Nancy. 'I don't like shopping, but I reckon I'm a pretty good listener and I can make a mean cuppa. Call on me any time.'

'Thanks, Nancy,' Danielle said. She knew there was more likelihood of her dropping into the old lady than brash and loud Maia.

'I'd be happy to help any time too,' said Betsy. 'My son is coming home from Australia soon with his wife and baby, but apart from that, I'm usually free, so don't be shy.'

'Does he have a firm date yet?' Maia asked Betsy.

The conversation was obviously about to take off again, so Danielle made her move before she got stuck there for another hour. She felt shy and out of place with these women. She could feel sweat trickling down her spine from the stress of trying to do and say the right thing, and she desperately wanted to be with Justin in their house.

'I don't mean to be rude, ladies, but I'm going to have to run. I'm anxious to get the house done and I've abandoned poor Justin.'

'You run along, love,' said Nancy. 'I think you were great to come in and sit with us lot when you don't know us from Adam *and* you're trying to move in. But I guess what we all want you to know is that we are here for you. We're a tight-knit bunch and we're here if needed.'

'That's so kind of you to say,' Danielle said. She was genuinely smiling now, but mostly because she was moving swiftly towards the door. 'Once we get our furniture sorted I'll have you over. Well, it's been great to meet you all. Take care now.'

Danielle walked quickly down the hall and let herself out of the front door. The fresh air was blissful and she breathed deep. Freedom. She knew they were probably discussing her the second she left. But at least it was out in the open *who* they were, so at least that box was ticked. She could understand that they all wanted to see who the new people were. Her own mam would be exactly the same if someone new moved in on their road at home. She'd be straight over to the front door with a lasagne or an apple tart, just so she could have a bit of a nose!

They were clearly good friends and wanted her to join in with that. She genuinely liked them all, except for Maia. Danielle decided to stay well away from her. As for joining the housewives' gang, she really wasn't ready for any of that. She was way too young to be spending too much time with that lot.

Her phone began to vibrate in her back pocket and she pulled it out. A text from Hazel. *Hey you, first day back and I miss u! it's all so mad. Feel lost without u. hope u ok. Xx*

Danielle stared at the screen and felt tears gather behind her eyes. Her dream, her big moment was happening without her. How the hell had she let this happen?

She jumped as Justin grabbed her in a hug.

'Hey,' he said, looking into her face with concern, 'what's up? You look like you just saw a ghost.'

She held up her phone and he read the words.

'Oh,' he said, nodding. He held her face in his hands and kissed her deeply. 'It's just postponed, that's all.'

'I know,' she said quietly. 'I just worked so hard for it, you know.'

'And that work wasn't wasted,' he said, putting his arm around her and walking her towards their house. 'We just need time to sort ourselves out and settle, and then you'll take up that law degree again and you'll be brilliant, I've no doubt about it.'

Danielle tried to smile at him, but she knew it was a weak effort. Hazel was immersed in books and cases and continuing her law course, and here she was, hanging out with a gang of old women who probably swapped knitting patterns and recipes. She knew she was right to stick with Justin, but at what price?

Justin passed her a Coke from their newly installed fridge and they went and sat on a couple of boxes.

'So how did the coffee go?' he asked. 'Don't hate me for pushing you in there. I know how shy you can be and I thought it might help you to break the ice. Were they okay?'

'Yeah, mostly,' she said. 'But please don't do anything like that again, yeah? I could've done without anything else zooming around in my head today. Next time I'd prefer to make my own decisions about where I go and with whom.'

'Aye-aye, Captain!' he said, saluting her.

Danielle stared around the empty front room. With a beautiful bay window that overlooked the gate and part of the front garden, it was really gorgeous. The carpets had all been laid and they were waiting for the curtains. They'd chosen a duck-egg blue shade for the carpet and it looked stunning. But as Danielle scanned the room, she couldn't help thinking that they could probably fit the entire downstairs of her mam's house in here and yet this was the smaller, cosy room! She'd never get used to having so much space.

'It seems like a massive job to take on, now we're here,' said Danielle. 'I hope I can do it.'

'*We* will do it together,' said Justin. 'Don't forget, I'm with you all the way. I'll support you in everything you do. If you can be there to do the same for me, I think we'll be very happy.' He put his arms around her and she rested her head on his shoulder. She needed to stop obsessing about not being in university. This was her life now and her studies would resume later. Next year to be exact. She'd arranged to take a year out. The time would fly and she'd be well settled here and even more ready than she had been.

'It's been a bit of a whirlwind, hasn't it?' Justin said, kissing her hair. 'I've fairly swept you off your feet. You don't regret it, do you?'

Danielle looked up into his face, and her heart melted with love. She was cracked about him, that was the bottom line, that's why she was here and nowhere else. She felt unbelievably blessed.

'No, I don't,' she said. 'This place is amazing, and I'm sure I'll get to grips with it all in time. And you're amazing.'

He smiled at her. 'You'll be great. In fact, those old biddies might prove very useful to you.'

She frowned. 'How?'

'You know, when we're throwing dinner parties and being cosmopolitan hosts, they're the kind of women who would know all about that. Be good for advice and a bit of help. You said your mum never entertains, so I know that might be a worry for you.'

Danielle felt her stomach lurch. The idea of being a host terrified her. She'd have no clue what to do, or how to cook fancy food or anything. She'd be useless. She'd grown up in a two-up, two-down terraced house with furniture from the local St Vincent de Paul. She'd never been at a dinner party in her life.

'Do you really mean we'll have to cook for people?' she said, stricken.

Justin laughed. 'You look like I just asked you to do a striptease outside on the lawn. Without music! I only mean having friends over and showing them a good time. Enjoyable stuff, like.'

'But I don't know how to,' Danielle said. 'Cook, I mean. I'm no good at that. I couldn't do a dinner party. I'd poison everyone and end up in prison.'

He laughed. 'Well then I can show you some stuff, and we can enrol you in a cookery class. You'll be grand.'

'I'm not like you,' she said, feeling almost panicky now. 'I didn't grow up like you did, the big house and everything. I can't be that kind of partner, you know. I'm just not . . .'

He stopped her with a kiss. 'You're nearly hyperventilating,' he said. 'Calm down. I'm not trying to upset you, I'm just saying we're going to enjoy this place and our life in it and sharing that with our friends. That's all. I'm not expecting anything from you or demanding anything you can't give.'

'You're just way above me in terms of . . . well, everything,' Danielle said.

Justin looked at her. 'Don't ever say that,' he said seriously. 'I love you for who you are. None of the rest of it matters. My name doesn't make me a better person, you know that. Plus where you come from doesn't govern where you'll end up. You should know that too.' He put his hand on her belly. 'We've got a whole life ahead of us, Danielle, and I can't wait to dive right into it. I want us to enjoy it, not worry about doing things for show, I hate that kind of thinking. I just want you, and this little one inside you, and I'll be happy.'

Danielle took a deep breath and nodded. 'Me too,' she said.

'I can't wait until we can tell everyone you're pregnant,' he said.

'Your mam was adamant we had to keep it private for another month,' Danielle noted.

'She's just superstitious or something,' Justin said. 'They'll come round.'

'At least she didn't cry uncontrollably and tell me I'd ruined my life,' Danielle said wryly, 'like my own mam did.' She shook her head. 'I still can't believe she took it so badly. It was so horrible. I knew she'd be disappointed about college, but I thought she'd be happy at the same time. She just kept saying the whole point of her life was to help me make a better one and not do the stupid stuff she'd done.' She glanced at Justin. 'Presumably I qualify as stupid stuff.'

'Ah now,' he said, rubbing her back. 'Your mum just got a shock, that's all. She'll be fine in time. She just needs to get used to the idea. We'll just keep reiterating that your law degree is only on hold, then she'll be okay with it all. You're only twenty, Danielle, it's only natural she's concerned about your choices.'

'I know,' Danielle said, 'it's just . . . how will we make it through all this, the baby and everything, without the support of our families? I'm not strong like you. I can't take people on and fight them and all that. I just can't.'

Justin opened his mouth to reply, but there was a loud honking from outside. He stood up and looked out of the window.

'Sofas,' he said. 'Come on, we'll have to save the deep and meaningfuls until later. We've got an Italian leather sofa to welcome!'

He hauled Danielle to her feet and she did her best to shake off the feeling that there were rocky times ahead. Deep down, she felt scared of everything – making a home in this massive place, letting Justin down, being judged by everyone, including her own mam, failing to achieve the one thing she had set her heart on – becoming a lawyer – and having a baby. That one was so huge, she had to just not think about it or she'd drown in fear. A baby at twenty – was she absolutely mental?

Chapter 6

BETSY HUMMED TO HERSELF AS SHE PUT THE finishing touches to the small guest room. She figured it would be the best one to put little Arnie in while they were here because a large strange room might seem too scary. With that in mind, all she'd put in was a cot and a chest of drawers. Freshly painted a lovely shade of cornflower blue only a couple of months previously, it complemented the pristine crisp white bedding she'd bought in the mother and baby store. In Graham's day there weren't so many lovely things to choose from. But then, everything was different back then. The doctors had discouraged breast feeding and thought nothing of it when women smoked in the labour wards. These new ways of doing things were probably for the best, she thought with a smile.

She went in to check on the room she had prepared for Graham and Tasha. She felt her nerves go taut every time she thought of Graham's wife, but she was holding on to the hope that marriage and motherhood had softened Tasha and they could get on this time. Their room was next door to Arnie's, but it was large and spacious, with a king-size bed, a chaise longue at the foot of the bed and a big wardrobe that had belonged to Noel's parents. It would be plenty big enough for both their clothes. Betsy had bought a lovely print in the local gallery – a watercolour of the beach that was about twenty minutes away. She admired it again, wishing she had put it in her own room. But then, guests deserved the very best. She wanted any visitors to her house to feel truly at home. She had scrubbed and vacuumed and dusted until the bedroom was spick and span. She looked around once more before closing the door, happy that Graham would feel welcomed and comfortable and cosy once he got here.

Betsy made her way back downstairs, to check that everything was perfect. The kitchen was spotless, and she had set the table for coffee and snacks once they arrived. She checked the clock: one o'clock. Noel would be standing in arrivals, waiting for them. She was so excited every time she thought of the baby, and she knew Noel couldn't wait to hold him, too. They were due to land at a quarter-past, so it wouldn't be long now.

Noel had been so nervous before leaving.

'Do I look okay?' he'd asked her anxiously. 'I don't want our Graham walking through the arrivals doors and being ashamed of me.'

'Why on earth would he be ashamed of you, love?' she asked, filled with concern. 'You're his father and you're a wonderful man.'

'Thanks, darling,' he said. 'But it's been a while, and I'm sure I've aged a lot.'

'Haven't we all. Time tends to do that to a person,' she said with a warm smile.

'How do you think Tasha will be?' he asked for the umpteenth time.

'Don't allow that woman to make you feel uncomfortable,' Betsy said. 'With a bit of luck, she's grown up and mellowed out. And besides, she's on our turf this time, so if she has anything between her ears, she'll behave.'

Betsy really hoped Tasha didn't cause any trouble or disharmony. She badly wanted this to go well. If it didn't, would they ever see Arnie again? The Tasha they'd met in Australia would cut them out without a second thought, she knew that much. That's why it was essential they all made an effort to get on.

It had been a horrible experience when they'd flown out to Australia for the wedding three years previously. Graham and Tasha had made them feel so unwelcome, and her family was even worse. They didn't so much as invite them for a cup of tea. They'd gone out there for three weeks, expecting to spend time with their son while they got to know their new daughter-in-law, but that simply hadn't happened.

They'd made the most of it, of course – booked tours and taken in as much of the area as possible. But they'd only seen Graham a couple of times and each time Tasha was there, ready with a put-down or a snide remark about his *bourgeois parents*. She was insufferable. Being a polite and reserved man, Noel hadn't wanted to argue with her or take her to task. Betsy, on the other hand, was used to speaking her mind and telling cheeky young ones like Tasha where to go. But for some reason, she'd decided to keep her mouth shut after the first altercation. Graham and Noel had both looked pained and she knew any further arguments would only upset them. So she'd resolved to keep quiet. It had been incredibly hard, but she'd done it.

That first taste of Tasha's unique way of behaving had occurred when she didn't want them to go for dinner at the restaurant they'd booked. 'For crying out loud, guys!

What's the point in sitting around like old fogies in a nursing home when we could be on the beach with a whole pile of great people who'll ensure we get some fun out of the night too?'

So they'd found themselves on a beach, in the dark, with a gaggle of drunken louts who were smoking joints, drinking their body weights in beer and behaving like savages. It was an ordeal Betsy never wished to repeat as long as she lived.

'I can't do this,' said Noel after half an hour. 'Graham, your mother and I are leaving. We'd really love it if you and Tasha would come with us.'

'Gray, if you leave, don't come back,' Tasha had warned. 'I'm not going to be dictated to by *them*. Your life is gonna be with me from here on in, so it's up to you, mate.' She'd stood with her hands on her hips, challenging him to do what she wanted.

Much to their horror, Graham chose Tasha, putting his arm around her as she swigged out of a beer bottle and grinning at them.

'Cheerio then, folks,' she shouted. 'Catch you later, right.'

The three-week holiday they'd been so looking forward to turned out to be a lonely time for them. They were forced to come to terms with the fact that their son had pretty much dumped them for this demanding and rude woman who clearly disliked them and didn't want them there.

The wedding was a shambles. Betsy shuddered to remember it. There was a makeshift ceremony followed by another dreadfully unorganised event at the beach. Nobody was introduced to them and anyone they attempted to make conversation with cut them short and walked away. Tasha's family didn't go and so there was no in-laws' introduction made either. They'd ended their trip with heavy hearts and a horrible sense of loss as they said goodbye to their only child for good.

Since then, they had been the ones who'd pushed to stay in touch with Graham. They Skyped him once a week and had the same brief, one-way conversations each time. Tasha never spoke to them, and for the past year or so Graham hadn't even mentioned her. They'd begun to hope that maybe a divorce was in the offing, but that obviously wasn't on the cards.

Betsy tutted at herself – such a terrible attitude! She shouldn't be wishing divorce on her Graham. No, it simply had to be the case that Tasha had grown out of her nasty ways. Babies had a habit of changing a girl to a woman. Come to think of it, they had a habit of changing a boy into a man, so perhaps she'd meet a much more grounded Graham, someone capable of standing up for himself – and for them. She'd love to see him gain confidence and forge a more equal relationship with his wife. Imagine! Graham was a father. She felt overcome with emotion every time she thought of it. Please God, this trip would bring about healing and a new beginning for them as an extended family.

The sound of Noel's car crunching onto the gravel outside made her gasp with excitement. She rushed to the front door to see Graham already out and taking the baby out of the back seat. Betsy could hear him crying and she assumed the poor little mite was fed-up of being shoe-horned into a seat.

'Hello, love,' Betsy called as she approached the car, suddenly feeling a bit nervous.

'Hey Ma,' said Graham. He beamed and rushed to hug her. She was taken aback momentarily, forgetting his Aussie accent, which was thick and so different from the way he'd spoken growing up. It was fine on natives, but she found it so odd to hear her son speaking that way.

Graham held up the car seat. 'And this is Arnie,' he said. 'This is your grandma, mate.'

'Oh hello, love,' Betsy said, as tears rolled down her cheeks. She touched the baby's soft cheek. 'I've been living to meet you, Arnie.'

Much to her surprise, the little boy was extremely big for five months old and went to her with no sign of making strange. He settled in her arms immediately, sticking his thumb into his mouth and resting his head against her chest. That gesture made her feel sky-high with happiness.

'Hello, my little sweetheart,' she said as he lay there, hiccupping as if he'd been sobbing for hours.

'Oh thank God,' said Graham. 'He's whinged the whole way across the world, haven't you, mate? The entire plane hated us by the time we changed over and I kind of thought he'd give up, but no, he kept on going like a broken record.'

'Oh dear. Lots of babies and small children hate flying and the sore ears, so we can't blame him,' said Noel.

'Lots of adults hate flying,' Graham said, 'but they don't scream the whole time! Oh and I've said it to Dad, but I go by Gray now, Ma. If you wouldn't mind going with that too?'

'There are a lot of things you're going to have to try and get used to,' Noel said as he walked past her towards the boot. 'I'll help *Gray* in with the luggage if you want to go on in with the baby.'

'Sure. Where's Tasha?' she asked.

'She's following in a taxi,' said Graham.

'Don't ask,' said Noel. 'I'd stick with that little man if I were you.'

More than happy to do as she was bid, Betsy cradled her precious grandson and carried him into the house.

'Look Arnie, this is your nana and grandad's house! You're going to have a lovely holiday here with us I hope.'

She brought him into the small TV room, where she had set up a baby paradise. Noel had tried to restrain her, but she'd bought a few things to entertain him. 'We haven't so much as a toy car here for him, Noel,' she'd argued. 'I don't want him to be here and bored out of his mind.' Eventually, Noel had gone into the attic and found a large box of Graham's favourite things, but only after she'd gone to the shops and bought a pile of stuff.

Now there were all sorts of toys and books waiting for Arnie, from a robust car garage to building blocks to a small work bench with tools, all of which they agreed he was too small for, but they figured that maybe they could be posted to him in a box when he was a bit bigger. The board books with either a furry animal or a squeak to press would be just right to read to him, Betsy mused. She could just picture the two of them, Arnie nuzzling her neck, sitting in front of the fire having a lovely story together.

They'd never believed in allowing Graham to smash things or ruin his toys, so everything he'd owned as a little fella was perfect. They'd had a great trip down memory lane as the toy aeroplane was found. It had little people and a pilot. It even had a hostess trolley with a little lady pushing it. 'Not very PC these days,' Betsy had laughed to Noel, 'but sure, what harm?'

Betsy had also bought a playmat with a baby gym over it, with dangling toys that were meant to keep him happy while he lay there. But now that she was holding him, Betsy realised that Arnie was a lot more advanced than Graham, or Gray, had made out.

'Look Arnie, there are some gifts for you to open,' she said with excitement in her voice. He looked up at her and smiled. She set him down gently on the floor, sitting behind him in case he wasn't able to sit up alone. As she rightly guessed, he was pretty sturdy on the floor and well able to stay sitting upright.

He looked around a bit and back at her and sighed. He twirled both his hands as if his wrists were wound up. The mannerism made her cry instantly. Graham used to do the exact same thing when he was a little baby. He did it for toys and his dinner!

Arnie took a present from her and smiled. He was dribbling like a little tap and one of his cheeks was red. No wonder he'd cried so much, the poor little fellow was clearly teething madly. The distraction of the present meant his mind was taken from being in pain. As soon as he opened the new toy pick-up truck with little chunky people to sit in the cab, he squealed and clapped.

'Good boy!' Betsy said, clapping too. He grinned and tried to free the toys from the packet, but when they wouldn't come out immediately he began to cry again, rubbing his eyes. The poor child was utterly exhausted and needed some painkillers. Hearing the men clambering into the hall and straight up the stairs she walked into the hall.

'Graham, have you anything to give the baby for pain? He's teething like crazy and he's worn out.'

'Ah nah, we don't go in for drugging him,' he said.

'Tasha and I feel really strongly about people giving their kids over-the-counter drugs.'

'But he's so sore and he needs some sleep. He's not going to lie down and rest when he's in this much pain.'

Graham thundered down the stairs and peered out the front door. He looked around at her nervously. 'You really think he needs something?'

'I'm not into giving babies lots of drugs myself,' Betsy said, 'but sometimes it's necessary. And I really think he's in a lot of pain.'

Graham looked out again. 'Well look, there's no sign of Tash, so maybe lob something into him quickly, yeah?'

'I've got Calpol here,' Betsy said. 'That should do the trick. His cot is all newly made up and I'd say he'll sleep if we change his nappy and make him more comfortable. I think you're making the right decision to let the poor little mite have some relief, Graham.'

'Yeah sure.' He blushed and scratched his hair, which she noted was well overdue a trip to the barber's. He had a heavy beard too, which she knew was all the rage with young men, but his was like a rat's nest and she had an immediate urge to trim it so it wasn't quite as scraggy. 'And please call me Gray. It annoys Tash so much when people don't.'

'Yes,' said Noel as he passed them to get more things from the car, 'we're not to call him the name we chose and called him all his life. That's fine, isn't it, love?'

Betsy gave Noel a warning look and he stopped being sarcastic and continued with the unpacking.

Betsy rushed to the kitchen to find the Calpol and then she gave Arnie the dose suggested on the bottle. He snatched the plastic measuring spoon, biting down on it.

Knowing he'd bawl if she took it away, she replaced it quickly with a teaspoon.

'Now, pet, that's nice and cool and it'll help with those bold teeth.'

Noticing a changing bag slung over the banister, she wondered if there'd be a supply of nappies. Mercifully there were nappies, but no wipes, no cream and no bags to put the soiled one into. Noel had scolded her for 'going overboard' and buying everything at the supermarket, but now she was glad she was so prepared. She carried Arnie up to his bedroom.

He looked around at everything with wide eyes, chewing on the spoon all the while. Betsy laid him on the change mat she'd bought and opened his onesie and removed his nappy. She gasped at the sight of his bottom. His poor skin was scalded and on fire with the worst nappy rash she'd ever seen. No wonder he was screaming during the flight! The nappy he was wearing was a cloth one, although there were a couple of disposable ones in the bag. While she had no objection to using cloth nappies, Betsy did have a problem with allowing his poor tender skin to become so horribly sore. Delighted to be free of the heavy, soaked nappy, Arnie kicked his legs.

Almost in tears, Betsy kept one hand on him in case he rolled off the mat while she rooted in the drawers.

'Yes!' she said with such gusto that Arnie giggled. She'd secretly built up quite a lovely wardrobe for Arnie and had been planning on gifting it all to them when they were leaving. The little tracksuit looked as if it would fit him perfectly. She couldn't remember if she'd bought the matching long-sleeved t-shirt and so was thrilled when she found that too.

'Who's got a clever nana, then?' she said, tickling his tummy. Biting the tags off with her teeth, she lathered his bottom with nappy rash crème and dressed him in his new dry, cosy clothes. As she stood him up and told him how handsome he was, there was a loud bang on the front door, almost as if it were being kicked. Scooping Arnie into her arms, she peered out of the window to see Tasha pulling enormous bags out of a minibus taxi. Betsy braced herself.

'Right, sweetness,' she said. 'Mummy's home. Let's see what wonderful transformation you've brought over her, shall we?'

Betsy carried Arnie downstairs, expecting Tasha to rush in and grab him. Instead, she barely looked over at either of them. She didn't even start with hello, but chose instead to yell at Graham like a fishwife.

'Eh, are you expecting me to do all this on my own, ya lazy shit? In front of your parents too!' she shouted, rolling her eyes. 'Pay your man too, yeah,' she said to Noel without greeting him. In utter shock, poor Noel walked out and paid the taxi man and joined them in the 'playroom'. All the bags and boxes were abandoned higgledy-piggledy in the hallway. Betsy stepped over them and brought the baby into the room, where Noel soon joined them too.

'Wow, look at all this stuff!' Graham was saying. 'Ah yeah, I remember this. Oh, and this,' he said as he looked at the things. 'Look Tash, Mum and Dad have kept my old stuff as well as buying a whole heap more, isn't it great?'

'I assume you've told them our plans?' She folded her arms and stared at him as if she might punch or kick him at any given moment.

'Hello Tasha,' Betsy said tightly. 'I hope you had a good flight.'

Tasha didn't look at her. 'Well?' she demanded, still staring at Graham.

'Yeah, so I hope you don't mind, Mum and Dad, but we've decided to come back home for good.'

'I beg your pardon?' said Betsy. Her head was spinning. 'For good as in, you're moving back?' She was astonished. 'Sorry, I must sound like an eejit, but I'm so shocked. I'm delighted, though,' she said, recovering and then promptly bursting into tears. 'It's the best news, isn't it, Noel love?'

'Ah that's super news, son, we're delighted we'll have you both, and especially little Arnie who seems to be best friends with his nana already!'

'Yup,' said Graham, 'if you'll have us, can we stay here for a bit? We won't be in your hair for too long, I hope. I aim to find a place for me and the wife and the little fella and we'll be all set.'

'We don't want to stay with his olds for any longer than we have to,' Tasha said, looking at them as if they were depriving her of something rather than coming to the rescue of her family.

'Well, rental accommodation really isn't easy to come by,' said Betsy. 'So don't worry about it for the moment. You're welcome to stay here for as long as you wish, isn't that right, Noel?'

'Of course,' he said. 'Let's wait until you settle in first. We have all the time in the world for figuring out the logistics. The important thing is that our Graham is home, and with little Arnie!'

'It's Gray,' Tasha spat, but they all ignored her.

Half an hour later, the house was still littered with bags and boxes and Betsy was at a loss. She liked order. Everything had its place and she was the first to admit that it was over the top, but she hated shoes inside the house. That was why there was a shoe rack to the side of the porch with slippers of all sizes ready for people to help themselves. She'd bought them at IKEA and they were made of towelling material and could be washed.

Making a mental note to explain that particular house rule and a few other things, she let it go for the moment. She knew the best policy was to start as she meant to go on, though, so the house rules would be put up sooner rather than later.

'Let's have some lunch and we can discuss plans,' she said. At least if they were in the dining room and the kitchen, she wouldn't have to look at the chaos.

'Jeez-Louise!' Tasha shouted as she walked into the room. 'Look at this! A full-on fancy dining room, with handmade-expensive dishes and all! Ah, thanks so much for going to so much effort, Mum.'

Betsy winced. She didn't expect her daughter-in-law to be formal around her. She wouldn't like it, in fact. But she wasn't keen on being called Mum by anyone but Graham – Gray.

She served the prawn cocktail with a little wedge of lemon that she'd wrapped in gauze and tied with a little bow.

'This is just dinky!' Tasha said.

Betsy wasn't sure if she was being overly sensitive or what, but that girl shouted and bellowed every word. If she didn't stop, Betsy would have a permanent headache. Arnie was in his new high-chair and seemed very pleased, if a little perplexed. The redness of his cheeks had subsided and he seemed in much better form.

'You needn't have bought that chair,' said Gray. 'We

brought his old one. But having said that, this is far nicer. We bought his at a garage sale. I think we paid four or five dollars for it, didn't we, Tash?'

'Yeah, something like that. We don't believe in spending tonnes of cash on stuff. We were living in shared accommodation for the last while. Since Arnie here was a baby really.'

'Yeah,' Gray said, shovelling tuna pasta into his mouth. They weren't the manners he'd been reared with, Betty thought, but like everything else, she let it go. 'That way we didn't need to work too much. Paying rent and lecky bills and all that stuff is a total waste of energy.'

'How did you avoid paying bills?' Noel asked, looking confused. 'Every house costs money.'

'Not ours,' Tasha said, grinning. 'We didn't own it.'

'But the landlord didn't let you stay there for free,' Noel said. 'Or do your parents own it?'

Tasha laughed. 'Nah, I don't come from the bourgeoisie, mate. I'm a real person. I don't mind roughing it a bit. It's good for the planet if we live more simply, ya know.'

Noel shook his head. 'I still don't get it,' he said. 'You can't acquire a house without acquiring bills with it.'

'We were squatting,' Tasha said with a shrug. 'That clever solution wouldn't even occur to someone like you, with your fancy stuff and your too-big house and your climate-changing emissions, but to people like us, people who care, it's obvious.'

Betsy and Noel exchanged a look.

'You mean . . .' Noel said, staring over at Arnie, 'you had a baby staying in an illegal situation, with no electricity or warmth or comforts?'

Tasha shook her head. 'See, I knew it was beyond your

tiny, narrow view of the world. Completely beyond you, mate. But yeah, we had our baby living with us the way we love to live. Me and Gray. That's our way of making the world a better place. And as soon as we can, we'll find a squat here and we'll be out of this frigging monstrosity of a house. Can't happen quick enough for me.'

As she tried not to choke on her prawn cocktail, Betsy looked at Noel, whose face had gone an oddly florid shade.

Chapter 7

MAIA PUT DOWN HER PHONE AND SIGHED. THE party was going to be stupendous, but my God there was a lot of work to get through to get it right. She'd just been on to the marquee people, explaining how it had to be blush and gold because that was the colour theme of the night. Eventually the woman had offered to have it tailormade – for an extra five grand. Maia had agreed. It had to look right, and she wasn't changing her colour scheme now she'd got the chair covers, pelmets, napkins, plates and banners all sorted in blush and gold. Anyway, Freddie wouldn't mind. He trusted her to make the money decisions in the house and she'd never let him down. He'd want it to look right as much as she did.

She hoped he'd feel the same way about her dress. It was from Harvey Nicks and it had cost an absolute fortune, but it was blush and gold, so it had to be done. She knew he'd love her in it. It had a plunging neckline and a slit up the thigh, so it was exactly the kind of dress he loved her to wear. It was all going to put a dent in the bank account, but it would be worth it.

Speak of the devil! Freddie walked into the kitchen, looking preoccupied as usual. He was staring at his phone as he walked, frowning.

'Jesus, Freddie, the meaning of life must be on that screen you study it so much,' she said, teasing him.

'What?' He looked up. 'What?'

She sighed again. 'Nothing. We have to be ready to go at six o'clock, okay. The school wants everyone in their seats by six-forty-five, so we can't be late. Can you believe it, our kids graduating? It sounds daft, doesn't it?'

Freddie was still staring at his phone. 'Yeah,' he said absently.

'I'm having an affair with the milkman,' Maia said.

'Yeah,' he said again, then he suddenly looked at her. 'What did you say?'

Maia rolled her eyes. 'It seems I have to be dramatic to get your attention these days. Is that work?' she said, nodding at the phone.

'Do I ever do anything else?' he muttered.

Maia walked around the counter and went over to him. She snaked her arms around his neck and nuzzled him. 'Come on, do you not have any nice words for your wife?' she said. 'Or maybe a few minutes to hop upstairs and make each other happy?'

The phone began to ring and Freddie nearly jumped.

'Not now, love,' he said gruffly. 'This is a private call.' He turned and walked quickly out of the room and into the study next door, shutting the door tightly behind him.

Maia stood there feeling stupid and unattractive. That seemed to be how things were between them lately. He never had time for her and wasn't interested in anything she had to say. There was something eating him up, but he refused to talk to her about whatever it was. It had to be work, but she hadn't a clue beyond that. She'd never really known the ins and outs of that side of his life, so she was in the dark.

He'd always been private about his business affairs, and that was fine with her. It was his business and he ran it well. He had a jewellery shop in Vayhill and it had seen off all competitors and pretty much had a monopoly in the area now. He'd always done well, but over the last years the money had really been rolling in, and that had made her wonder, but she didn't want to rock the boat.

'You don't ask no questions and I'll tell you no lies, yeah?' he'd said recently, when she'd tried to ask him about it.

She was worried, but at the same time she knew Freddie was no fool. She just had to trust him that he wasn't into anything he shouldn't be, like illegal stuff. She had a dread in the pit of her stomach that maybe he was, that that's what all the secret phone calls were about, but she just couldn't bring herself to ask him. He had never involved her in the business in any way, it was his domain, so she pushed down her fears, kept spending money and prayed he knew what he was doing.

She went off to get ready, knowing her new dress and makeup would help her feel better. The graduation ceremony was the biggest night of the year in the twins' private school, and with that lot, that was saying something. Freddie was shelling out twenty grand a year each for Zach and Zara, but he always said it was a solid investment. No kid ever came out of that school and didn't end up wealthy and successful, and that's what they wanted for the twins.

She was just zipping up her royal blue off-the-shoulder cocktail dress when Zara walked in.

'Wow, Mum, you look amazing,' she said, eyeing her from head to toe.

'Well you look utterly gorgeous in that gown,' Maia said, feeling teary at the sight of Zara looking like a well-groomed woman. 'We nailed it with that Alaïa number, didn't we?'

'I love it,' Zara said, looking down at herself admiringly.

The graduates wore evening wear for the ceremony, and they had spent weeks finding the perfect dress. It was a pearl grey silk gown, with beading on the bodice, and cinched in at the waist to show off Zara's perfect figure. Her hair was loose and made her look youthful and very beautiful.

'Are you ready for Sorcha?' Zara asked. 'She's just arrived.'

'I certainly am,' Maia said. 'Bring her on up.'

Sorcha was Maia's makeup artist, and she came to the house regularly to get them ready for nights out. She was quick and professional and made Maia look ten years younger every time. She knew she'd get a big tip at the end of each session, so she made it her business to be the best, and Maia made it worth her while.

At six o'clock, Maia and Zara were waiting in the kitchen, made up to perfection. They each had a matching fur wrap for their dresses, made especially by the seamstress in the village.

'Come on, boys!' Maia shouted. 'Time to roll.'

Zach wandered into the kitchen, grinning at them. 'How are the super models?' he drawled.

'You look so handsome,' Maia said, admiring his tux. 'Just perfect.'

'And do I pass muster?' Freddie asked, walking in from the study.

'As ever,' Maia said, straightening his dicky-bow. 'And I'm so glad you've torn yourself away long enough to join us.'

'Just doing business,' he said quietly. 'It's important.'

'Okay,' Maia said, smiling at him. 'But now it's time to have some fun.'

The school assembly hall was almost unrecognisable from its normal daytime look. It was set out with chairs for the audience, and the stage was bedecked in a heavy red velvet curtain. The lighting had been designed by a professional team, and the caterers were on standby, ready to move away the chairs and set out the buffet meal and disco after the ceremony. The crowd was so glamorous, that even Maia in her stunning dress felt a bit dowdy. Everywhere she looked were designer outfits and Louboutins, and as for the car park – it was wall-to-wall Land Rover, Lexus, Audi and Porsche.

'It's like bleedin' Maxwell Motors out there,' Freddie said, grinning. She hadn't seen him look so like himself in ages. He used to feel intimidated by these sorts of gatherings, but over the years she reckoned he'd come to enjoy the feeling that he'd paid his way in and actually belonged here.

It was rare to see so many parents because so many of them were high-fliers, with incredibly demanding jobs, and their children were full-time boarders. But they had turned out for this special night in their children's lives. The school had come top of the league tables for the Leaving Cert results, so there was much to celebrate. This was the final farewell, and they were sending off their students in some style.

'It's a far cry from St Assumpta's, isn't it?' Maia whispered to Freddie.

'You can say that again,' Freddie said, looking around. 'This is like a film star party, like something in Cannes.' He shook his head. 'If our kids don't make it big after this, Maia, they've only themselves to blame. We've given them some start.'

Maia smiled. 'Yeah, we have, and I'm proud of us. I'm really proud of you, though, for bankrolling it all. You're an amazing dad.'

Freddie looked as though he'd burst with pride. 'Thanks, love,' he said, kissing her cheek. 'And I've the most beautiful wife here by a country mile.'

Maia appreciated the thought, but she was feeling far from beautiful. The other women looked so classically stylish, it was effortless chic. Her loud dress and silver skyscraper heels and matching wrap suddenly didn't look so hot. She felt a bit cheap. She felt like exactly what she was, in fact – a woman from the wrong side of the tracks made good, but not quite hitting the mark. These women didn't have a Marjory, that was for damn sure.

Nobody in the world knew it bar her and Freddie, but they'd paid this woman called Marjory to come and teach them stuff. How to talk nice, how to be a host at a dinner party, what to do when you're invited to someone's house . . . pretty much the A to Z of how to be posh without people noticing and thinking you were stupid. They weren't thick at all, it was just that where they'd grown up, people didn't *entertain*. If it was someone's birthday, they went to the pub, got smashed, ate chips on the side of the road as a fight inevitably broke out and ended up in someone's gaff smoking weed and drinking cans. She'd be lying if she said she'd never liked it, though. She enjoyed a good night out with the girls. The lads would be up at the bar and the girls sat at the round tables chatting and having a great laugh. But she detested the fighting, the crude language and the depressing way they'd been shoe-horned into a tiny house with far too many mouths to feed. Freddie had taken her far away from all that – much further than she'd imagined. And now her precious twins would never know anything of that world, not ever. This was their world.

Zara came over and took her hand. 'Mum, I want you to finally meet Lottie's parents. You've known her, like, for ever and I've never got to introduce you. But they're here.'

'Oh yeah, sure,' Maia said.

'I'll get us a glass of wine,' Freddie said, heading for the bar.

Maia followed Zara over to where Lottie was standing next to a man who was handsome in the professor kind of way, and a woman who was rake thin and wearing what Maia knew was a Versace wraparound silk dress. She looked stunning.

'Veronica, Charles, this is my mother, Maia,' Zara said, giving Maia a gentle push on the back towards them.

'Delighted to meet you,' Charles said, and he actually took her hand and kissed it. Maia nearly burst out laughing before she realised he was serious. Lucky Freddie wasn't there, he would have laughed in his face for sure.

'Lovely to meet you, Charles,' she said, concentrating on not letting her accent slip. 'Lottie is one of my favourite people in the world. We love having her around.'

'You've been so kind, having her to stay so often,' Veronica said, but her smile wasn't exactly warm.

'You look so gorgeous,' Maia said. 'I love your dress.'

Veronica reached over to kiss her cheek, and Maia pretty much poked her in the eye with her nose when she swooped around for a second kiss.

'Oh sorry,' Maia said, blushing, 'I always forget the second one.'

Veronica looked amused. Bugger, thought Maia – two grand in Marjorie's pocket and she still managed to mess up the basics.

'You look . . . striking,' Veronica said. 'That colour certainly announces your presence.'

Maia knew she was being a bitch, but she bit back her anger because she wouldn't embarrass Lottie and Zara for anything. But this woman was obviously a prize cow, and she just wanted to get away from her.

'Zara tells me she's taking up a place in Queen's University next year. That's an excellent choice. I did my first MA there. How about you, Maia, where's your alma mater?'

Maia swallowed. 'Em, I didn't attend college, Veronica. But I've invested all my time and energy in my twins' future and I'm so happy it's paid off.'

'Well,' Veronica said with a laugh, 'steady on, Maia, it's only Belfast, hardly Ivy League.'

'Mum!' Lottie said, looking upset.

Maia put her hand on Lottie's arm. 'Don't worry, Lottie my love, your mum's only having a little joke. I'm sure she knows that Zara scored eight As and one B and is basically a walking brainbox.'

'The whole year did well,' Veronica said, refusing to give Zara her credit.

Maia decided it was time to fight fire with fire.

'Are you still travelling as much as ever, Veronica?'

'Oh yes,' she said, running her fingers through her sleek bob. 'My life is the complete opposite of a stay-at-home mother like yourself, Maia. As vice CEO I'm hugely busy. I'm on business class constantly. Airport private lounges are basically my second home,' she said, looking to her husband, who laughed dutifully.

That, thought Maia, is a man who isn't getting any, and hasn't been getting any for years. She smiled warmly at him and he winked at her. It gave her a little thrill of satisfaction to know she could have him if she wanted to. Put that in your pipe and smoke it, Veronica.

'So you probably weren't there when Lottie and the team won the hockey cup, were you? No? What a shame. It was a fantastic match. And the best after-party ever. We had it at our house and Lottie was a smash-hit at karaoke. She came for the night and stayed for the week. She's so much part of our family. I think of her as my second daughter. We're so close.' She smiled innocently at Veronica. Out of the corner of her eyes, she could see Zara and Lottie stifling a giggle. They knew what she was up to and obviously felt Veronica deserved it.

'Sounds lovely,' Veronica said, through gritted teeth. 'There I am paying thirty thousand a year, and Lottie keeps bunking off to stay off-campus. Marvellous. And karaoke?' She turned to Lottie. 'I hope I never hear of you doing something so silly again. It's beneath you, darling.'

'I'll just pop over and say hello to Mr Woods,' Maia said, turning on her heel and walking off.

She bumped into Freddie and he handed her a glass of white wine. She took it and gulped down half of it.

'Jesus, go easy, love,' Freddie said. 'I don't want to be carrying you out of here over my shoulder.'

Maia grimaced. 'I just met the mother from hell. How someone as gorgeous as Lottie came out of her loins, I will never understand.'

Freddie laughed. 'You'll have to introduce me. Sounds like the kind of woman I'd enjoy annoying.'

'I was going to say hello to the principal,' Maia said. 'He was over there a moment ago.'

'Here comes trouble,' Freddie said.

Zach walked over to them, hand in hand with a tall girl with red hair, long white limbs and a vintage style dress. Maia had never seen her before, and she was immediately intrigued. She looked a bit other-worldly, not remotely like the girls Zach normally went around holding hands with.

'Hi guys,' Zach said. 'This is Delia. I just wanted you to meet her.'

'Hi Mrs and Mrs Jones,' the girl said. 'I'm stoked to meet you. I've been asking Zach for ages to take me home for dinner so I could, you know, get to know you.'

'For ages?' Maia said. 'Really?'

The girl nodded enthusiastically. 'Oh yeah, sure. We've been together five months, like, so I felt it was time, but he's so shy about it.'

Freddie looked at his son. 'Shy, Zach? You? Why the hell haven't we met this beautiful girl before now?'

'Five months!' Maia couldn't believe it. She thought her and Zach were close, that he filled her in on his life.

'Don't freak out,' Zach said. 'I was just enjoying having Delia all to myself.'

Maia instantly felt paranoid. Why didn't he introduce them – were they not good enough?

'Are you a boarder, Delia?' she asked.

Delia nodded again – she was like a happy little puppy.

'Yeah, like, since first year. My parents live between Monaco, New York, London and Dublin, and they didn't want me to be raised by the staff, so yeah, I'm like part of the furniture around here.'

Maia felt like crying. That was it, Zach hadn't wanted Delia to meet his unemployed mother and not posh father. She felt sick. When had it happened that she wasn't good enough for her own children? And would it just get worse as they moved on into colleges and everything – would they not want to know them?

'I'm so upset that Zach is going to UCLA,' Delia said. 'But I'm going to Columbia, in New York, so we're hoping to keep our relationship going. I know it's a flight over to him in California, but we think we can do that a couple of times a month. I'll happily use up my allowance on going to see him,' she said, gazing at Zach adoringly.

'Why don't you come for dinner soon, maybe this weekend?' Maia said.

'I'd absolutely love to,' Delia said, looking delighted.

'Thanks, Mum,' Zach said and he gave her a peck on the cheek. It placated Maia a bit, but she could feel the worry settle in her stomach. In exactly how many ways was she going to lose her children?

'Oh, there's Mr Woods,' she said, spotting him through the crowd. 'I just want to thank him. Excuse me.'

She made her way over and tapped the principal's shoulder. He turned around and smiled at her.

'Maia, lovely to see you. And you look beautiful, if I may say so.'

'You certainly may,' she said, laughing. She'd always liked Mr Woods, he didn't have a stick up his arse like so many of the others here. 'I just wanted to say thank you, for educating my two so well, and putting up with them all these years. You've been fantastic. They'll miss you.'

'You're very kind,' he said. 'But we were the lucky ones. Zara and Zach have been wonderful students. I can't wait to see what they go on to achieve now. Zach will head off soon, won't he?'

Maia nodded. 'Yes, both of them will be gone in the New Year. All new lives. Very exciting.'

'Well don't be a stranger, Maia,' he said, taking her hand. 'You were fantastic on the fundraising committee and we'd love to have your dynamism to draw on. Can we stay in touch?'

'Of course,' Maia said, feeling flattered. They probably just wanted to extract more money from Freddie, but still, she had contributed hugely to the committee, so it was nice to have that noticed.

'Please take your seats as the ceremony is about to commence.'

The students made their way to the front of the auditorium, so they could easily go up to collect their certificates. Maia and Freddie found seats and Freddie began recording on his iPad.

Maia sat there, feeling numb and cold. She watched her children take their places among these elite and privileged young men and women, and for the first time she wondered if this school had been a good idea. The fact that people like Veronica thought it was wonderful made her feel uneasy. Yes, she wanted her children to be successful and happy, but she didn't want them to be stuck-up and obnoxious. She felt the lead weight of her grief at their leaving. It was all happening too soon. Zach was going to the US in January, and Zara would head off for a year of travelling before settling to do her degree in Belfast. The house would be empty – and with Freddie being so distant, what would she be left with? Who would she even be if she wasn't the twins' mother? That's all she'd been for eighteen years. That's all she was. She had nothing else to offer – no skills, no job, no passions, nothing. If she wasn't a mother, she was nothing at all. The idea made her feel scared and lonely and lost.

Chapter 8

'HELLO THERE, ARE YOU LOOKING FOR SOMEONE?'
Nancy called out. The young woman she was addressing
was sitting on a wall looking very glum.

'What, me? No, I'm fine.'

Nancy registered the Australian accent. 'Are you . . .
Tasha, by any chance?'

The woman glared at her. 'What of it?' she demanded,
sounding ready for a fight.

Nancy smiled. 'I'm Betsy's neighbour, Nancy. I live over
there. You're Graham's wife, aren't you? It's lovely to meet
you.'

Tasha continued to glare at her. 'And?'

Nancy looked at her in surprise. It was like talking to a
truculent teenager, but she looked too old for that lark.

'And what?' Nancy retorted. 'And you're too high and
mighty to be civil to a neighbour?'

Tasha shrugged. 'I don't care about this place, or Gray's
mum or her neighbours.'

Nancy frowned. 'But you'll take her free and generous
hospitality, is that it? Why are you standing out here anyway?'

Tasha nodded in the direction of the house. 'Baby's
crying. I've had enough.'

'I see,' Nancy said. 'Well I'm glad that baby has a grandmother as warm-hearted as Betsy.'

Tasha turned and walked up the driveway to the house without another word. Nancy stared after her, and her heart broke for Betsy and Noel. What a piece of work that young lady was! What the hell had made Graham fall for her? Poor Betsy. Nancy decided to bake her some scones when she got in. Betsy always said Nancy's were the best scones in the world, and she was sure Betsy would need some cheering up now.

She headed on over to her own house, glad she didn't have to share her space with Tasha. It seemed unending, when she looked at her friends with children, no matter what their age, that they could turn up on the doorstep looking for shelter. Better off to be on your own than prey to other people's whims, Nancy thought.

'Come on, Nelly,' she said. 'Let's get home and light the fire and make a cuppa.'

The evenings were getting dark so quickly now, and the chill in the air was unmistakably winter. Nancy loved getting in and shutting the door behind her and switching on the lamps and lighting the fire. Her house was so cosy, she didn't mind the weather at all.

She collected her post from the box at the gate on the way in. Bills and brochures, no doubt, the usual pile for the recycling bin. Inside, she put out food for Nelly, then got the fire going in the grate and moved Nelly's basket to the hearth, just as she liked it. She heated up some soup, cut some bread and brought it in to the table by the fireplace and set herself up nicely. She was reading a good novel, and she savoured the idea of an evening of losing herself in it.

While the soup cooled, she checked through the post. Nothing very interesting, but there was one letter that looked official, with a harp stamped on it. Nancy slid her finger along the gummed flap and pulled it open. When she saw the name at the top, she fell back in the chair like she'd been shot. She sat there, staring at the ceiling, trying to get her breathing back to normal, thinking, no, no, it can't be. It's not possible.

Slowly, she picked up the letter again and tried to focus her eyes to read it. It was short and to the point.

Mill Hall Adoption Agency

Dear Miss Smyth,

We have recently been approached by your son, Steve Mannion. He has been working for years to trace you. Some years ago, his adoptive parents told him he was adopted, and that they had found him via the nuns at Lemon Street Magdalene Laundry. He has been researching the available records since then, and he finally made the connection to yourself. He has enjoyed a good life with his adoptive family and bears you no ill-will. If you were willing, he would very much like to meet you. If this is something you feel you are able to do, please contact me at the number/address below and I will set up an appointment.

Best regards,
Alice Fitzsimons

Nancy dropped the letter into her lap and put her face in her hands. She was completely overwhelmed by emotion. Things she hadn't thought about in years – hadn't let herself think about – rose up now and fought for her attention. *Your son.* She had banished that whole episode to the darkest reaches of her mind, convincing herself it was over for ever. How had he found her? And after all these years. It seemed impossible.

The nuns at Lemon Street Magdalene Laundry. Nancy didn't want to think about those cold bitches again as long as she lived. Even just reading the words on the page made her shudder. The image of the tall, dark building with the heavy wooden front door and lion-head brass knocker rushed back into her mind and she gasped at the pain of the memories. There she was again, standing on the doorstep, with the wind whipping around her knees, forcing her to hold her hat firmly in place. She raised the knocker and let it drop, and when that sound echoed around the draughty building, it signalled the end of her happiness and the beginning of six months of horror.

She had been a girl of just sixteen when it happened. One of the travelling farm labourers employed by her father had taken a shine to her that year. PJ had been coming to work the farm every summer since she was seven, so she knew him well, but that year he seemed different. He made comments and jokes she couldn't quite understand, but the tone of them made her toes curl. He was always looking at her, no matter what she was doing. She started to avoid him, going the long way round so as not to bump into him, but he was a cute one and she was as green as the grass in the fields, so it didn't take him long to get her on her own.

She had been walking back along the Holly Lane, as they called it, returning after delivering eggs to a neighbour, and there he was, leaning against a gate, pipe stuck in his mouth. He was probably only about thirty, she reckoned now, but to her then he was an old man. So many years had passed, but Nancy still felt tears at the thought of it.

He had robbed her youth from her that day, pushing her into the field and down onto the ploughed earth. She didn't even really know what was happening, just that it hurt. She'd seen the animals go about their baby-making, but she hadn't fully grasped that it applied to humans as well. They were sheltered times – too sheltered, she thought to herself, that's how young girls got caught and cornered, because ignorance made them vulnerable.

She shook herself to get rid of that memory. PJ had left her there in the field, warned her not to speak of it. She thought no one would believe nice old PJ was capable of such a thing, so she said nothing. She thought no one would ever know, that she'd just have to live with it in silence. But then her tummy started to bulge and, God love her, she still didn't understand. She went to her mother and asked her why her belly was fat and hard but the rest of her was the same. Nancy could still remember the colour draining from her mother's face as she looked down at her. She'd made her strip off her clothes and stand in front of her on a chair. Pulling her down by the arm, she'd smacked Nancy across the face so roughly that she'd ended up on the floor. Blood streamed from her eye where she'd caught it against the chair edge. But that did nothing to deter her mother, who yelled and called her names and told her she was a sinful disgrace.

That was that. Within days she'd found herself dumped at a mother and baby home in the midlands, far away from where she'd been raised and all she'd ever known. The nuns had taken her in, given her a narrow hard bed to call her own in a dormitory of thirty girls, all in the same shocked state as herself. They were a sorry bunch, that's for sure, broken by what they'd been through. No girl should ever have to experience being abandoned by her family, Nancy thought, then realised that her son might feel the same way about her. It wasn't her fault, though. The laundry had its own, never-ending routine and the girls were powerless to change it. It ended the same way for all of them.

They were woken at dawn and brought into the laundry where they scrubbed sheets and blankets. When their time was near, they were moved onto ironing. The food was basic and horrible, and as a result fainting was common. Nancy remembered blacking out quite often, coming to with a nun standing over her, glaring down, ordering her back to her feet. They were treated like animals, as if they were dumb and stupid and a lower order than everyone else. It created a sense of black despair that ran through the whole place like a poison. It seeped out of the walls, affecting every one of them. As your belly grew, your sense of self shrivelled up and vanished. Nancy wiped away a tear. She hated thinking about it.

Luckily for her, she was small and not at all developed, so the priests never sent for her. But she watched the girls who were called dragging their heels, their faces dark with fear and dread. The stories they came back with would curdle your blood. Sexual abuse was rampant and it was no wonder so many of the girls ended up with severe psychiatric issues afterwards, and sometimes for life. Sure, wasn't that what had happened to Nancy herself?

When the pains started, she was taken to a bare room with one of the narrow hard beds in the middle of it and nothing much else. She was told to lie on the bed and stay there until she was done, and not to be screaming the place down. The next twenty hours were a blur of pain and terror, but when her baby slid out and the nun caught him and held him up, Nancy had been astonished at what she'd done. This perfect little creature, crying for her. She had been overwhelmed by the reality of him. Even after all the pain, she felt a rush of love for him and his tiny vulnerability. He was perfect.

She was allowed to stay with him for a whole month. That was more than most and she'd always wondered if it was because he was colicky and had cried a lot. She'd tie him onto her with old sheets while doing her work, and that would soothe him. She'd named him David.

Then one day, without warning, she was summoned to a room in the main house where the nuns all lived. She was told to be a brave girl and to hand her baby to the head nun. In return, she was given a single photo of her precious son. The nun put it on the table beside her and told her that she could have that as a reminder of what a fallen woman she was. She didn't feel like a woman, she felt like a terrified and traumatised child who had nobody on her side. There was no contact from her parents and nobody came to see her.

She had tried, God knows. She told them no. She argued, told them she loved him and would mind him always. That earned her a lashing across the backs of the legs with the cane. Then two nuns held her while the head nun prised little David from her arms. When his warm little body left hers, she felt a cold run through that had chilled her for years. All the drinking, that had been an attempt to erase that cold, even for a while. She drank to ward off the sorrow and the shame, but it never did. It took her decades to realise that, Nancy thought, with a tired smile. She reached down and rubbed Nelly's head, desperately needing to anchor herself in the present, to remind herself that that was then and this was now. It was amazing how something could be so long ago and yet feel so raw and real.

David had been given to a couple who arrived that very day. The deal was done, and Nancy had no way to challenge it or undo it. She was a fallen woman, the lowest of the low, and anything she felt or thought didn't matter in the slightest. She couldn't have felt any worse if they'd reached in and pulled her heart out with their bare hands. The pain was as much mental as physical, maybe more so. It was so awful that she went into a decline and refused to speak or eat or drink, so the nuns sent her to a hospital, where she was told in no uncertain terms that the next stop was the nut house. That put the fear of God in her, so she had pretended to be fine. Mercifully, she was released from hospital.

She couldn't go home, so she had gone to Dublin first and the nuns helped get her a job in a big house, cleaning and learning to cook. She was clever with money and saved up enough for a ticket to London, and from there she went on to America. Each day, she'd look at the single photo she carried of her baby. Years of nightmares, drinking binges and bouts of depression followed. She'd married and divorced three times, but never managed to have any more children. She'd long thought God or the nuns had cursed her womb, but then later, when the drinking stopped, she realised she was glad it hadn't happened for her. It was better this way. She liked her independence, travelling freely, putting herself first, it suited her. She wasn't cut out to be a mother, she reckoned, so being not-a-mother had become an important part of who she was.

She told no one about David, not even her friends on Kingfisher Road. He was her one true secret.

She picked up the letter again. So now what? She had spent a lifetime forgetting him, grieving him, wrecking her life because of him, and now here he was, wanting to meet her. He carried the whole of her painful past with him and she wasn't sure she had the strength to relive it. What would he want to know? Could she tell him the truth about his tragic beginnings? It did say he'd had a good life, so at least she didn't have that on her conscience. It was her who'd paid for it entirely, it seemed. PJ went on as if nothing had ever happened, and David had a normal childhood, so it was only her who was almost destroyed by it. She felt a flash of anger and jealousy to think of it, then immediately gave out to herself for thinking it at all. See, she thought to herself, I'm not a proper mother if I can be jealous of my own child for getting off lightly. I should be rejoicing.

It was all so complicated. She was nearly seventy, and this person – Steve – wanted her to be – what? Did he want a mother, or just the truth of his own origins? She shook her head, wishing the letter had never arrived. She had to answer it, which meant she had to decide, and she'd banked on getting through life without ever having to make that decision. But then, what about his decision, his need? Wouldn't it be wrong to deprive him of this reunion? Shouldn't she put him first, because really, as she knew from her friends, that's what a mother always does – puts herself last in line.

'That's why I'm no mother, Nelly,' she said, rubbing the dog's ears. 'He'll be sorely disappointed if he meets me. I'll never live up to any expectations he's carrying.'

She sighed and laid her head back in the chair again. Fifty-three years. One month together and fifty-three years later, a letter. It was too much to take in. But slowly, in the corners of her mind, she could feel curiosity growing. She could feel the memory of holding his little perfect body taking root. Who had David turned out to be? This might not be what she wanted, but could she really live out her days without finding out?

Chapter 9

SETH WAS RETURNING TO CYPRUS FOR THE LAST time. He'd spent six weeks there finishing off a training course he'd been running. He'd had a two-week break at home and now he was headed out for the month of November to tie up loose ends. After that, his retirement would begin just prior to Christmas.

As she dropped him to the airport where he would meet with the rest of his troop, Pearl could see a visible change come over Seth. His chest puffed out a little and his frame rose higher and it was clear he was getting ready to do what he loved best. To be the person he was most comfortable being.

Neither of them was exactly comfortable when he was at home. He had nobody to order around properly, which was really his favourite thing. He also loved being in uniform and being around other people in uniform. If he had his way, they would all stand in a line and have their shoes looked over, a thing he did to Drew when he was small. Drew hated it, but Pearl kept saying that Daddy was simply trying to help them. Deep down, though, she hated it too. She couldn't understand how polished shoes or standing straight had any bearing on the real world. But Seth was a bully, and she knew the safest thing was to just go along with him. His temper could flare at the drop of a hat and once that happened, they were all in danger of being on the end of a tongue-lashing, at the least.

Whenever he was home, he spent his time correcting Drew and, in a more subtle way, criticising her. During his summer furlough, he'd built a log shed in the back garden. He'd instructed her to have a large tree stump delivered from a woodland he had a connection with. He chopped it up into rounds at first, then logs. Poor Drew was ordered to don his work clothes and help out.

'His mind might be a bit muddled,' Seth had barked, 'but that doesn't mean his body can't do the work of a proper man.'

The word *proper* had hit Pearl harder than a brick to the back of the head. He'd never accepted Drew's limitations. He'd never even tried to understand his son. He wasn't interested in who Drew actually was, although that meant Seth was the one missing out, she'd always known that. When she saw Drew with Tommy, she daydreamed that he'd been Drew's father from the get-go.

The thought of Seth's imminent retirement had brought her into a state of such dread, she'd developed eczema. The rash had begun behind her knees and had spread to her arms and even her scalp. She'd gone to the doctor, who had prescribed a cream and told her to try and avoid stressful situations.

But the fact of the matter was that she was completely stressed, because she lived in terror of Seth's retirement. She'd lain awake at night for months, wondering how on earth she'd cope with having him there all the time. It would be torture. She'd never get away from the sly, barbed comments, and he'd reduce poor Drew to a gibbering mess on a daily basis. Her skin would be raw and no amount of magic cream from any doctor would be able to help.

How would she get to spend proper time with Tommy? The way it worked right now was that she'd visit him in the mews. Some days they'd go to bed for a while, if Drew was at school. Other days they simply chatted and shared a cuppa while laughing at the ups and downs of life. It was easy and relaxed and reliable, which was exactly what she needed.

That was the biggest difference between her relationship with Tommy and with Seth. She and Tommy laughed. It might be over the simplest thing, but they had such a joyful time together. She also knew that Tommy loved them both – her *and* her darling Drew. He told them often enough. When he said it to Drew, a fine big man with the gentle mind of a six-year-old, he'd almost purr. If she was there to witness it, he'd point at Tommy and tell her, his shoulders rising and falling in the glee of it all, 'Tommy loves me, Mama.'

'I know he does,' she'd say. 'Isn't that wonderful?'

Twice a year, for a week in the summer and for two weeks at Christmas, Tommy packed a bag and returned home to his family in Cork. Those days were the longest and most lonely of Pearl's life. If she was lucky, Seth wasn't around during Tommy's holidays. At Christmas, he was usually away. She often suspected he offered to work the Christmas schedule, the one no one else wanted. Drew adored Christmas and still believed in the magic of Santa Claus, which had become a bone of contention over the years.

Seth had tolerated this notion while Lily-Rose and the boys were little. Of course, Drew was only small then, too.

But when the others moved on and Drew became a deep-voiced man with a chest size bigger than his father's, Seth couldn't cope with his juvenile ways. 'He needs to be sat down and told there's no Santa Claus and that all this nonsense with stockings must stop.'

'Don't be cruel,' Pearl had pleaded. 'You'd break his heart. He doesn't understand. He never will. Don't you get it, Seth? This is the way he'll stay. His mind is frozen in time, but that doesn't mean his body is. He isn't trying to annoy you. He doesn't do anything with nasty intent.'

Seth had muttered under his breath, but he'd let the subject drop. Instead she noticed he wasn't there to witness his son's glee at the Easter Bunny leaving eggs around the garden. He avoided Christmas like the plague and was rarely there for his birthday parties. Drew still wanted a traditional party at home, with Rice Krispie buns, jelly and ice-cream and a big birthday cake with candles. Last year they'd had a magician come along and he and the others from his day care centre had been mesmerised by the tricks. Each of them got a balloon animal to take home and Drew had hugged her and Tommy saying it was his 'bestest party ever'. Seth's absence wasn't even noted by Drew, who looked to Tommy as the male figure in his life.

When the temper tantrums hit, that was when she needed Tommy's brawn. Drew had a tendency to fly off the handle for no apparent reason. She'd ended up with countless black eyes and on one occasion, when his precious and much-loved brown bunny toy had been left in a shop, she'd ended up with a broken rib. Tommy had heard her screams or God only knew what might've happened. She never told Seth about it. Tommy managed to calm Drew down and the three of them went to the local A&E where she was strapped and given painkillers.

Drew slept for twelve hours afterwards and she barely slept one. Tommy stayed over that night. The golden rule about being together in Pearl's bedroom was broken, but they only lay in each other's arms, so Pearl reasoned that she hadn't performed any acts in her marital bed with another man. On bad days, she still thought back to that night and tried to remember what it was like to be in the embrace of a person she truly loved. She was in love with Tommy, and with all her heart too. It wasn't an affair that was ruled by sex, although he was able to make her feel things that Seth probably thought were illegal.

'Why don't you leave him?' Tommy had asked her, many years ago.

'I can't,' she'd said. 'I wouldn't be able to stand the stress of the break-up. We'd have to sell the house . . . It would be awful for Drew, and Lily-Rose and the boys look to me as their stability too.'

'It's okay,' he'd said, putting his hand on her arm. 'I won't ask again.'

She'd told him to go and find a single woman, someone who could give him children and the full relationship he deserved, but Tommy had smiled and told her that he'd rather an hour a week with her than twenty-four hours a day with anyone else.

As the years rolled by, she forgot that she was keeping him from a life as a husband and father. They were a lovely unit and she knew that nobody suspected a thing. It had all worked out so well, until now.

Nothing would ever be the same again once Seth retired. There'd be very little time for her and Tommy to be alone together. Even their walks in the park when Drew brought his scooter – something Seth didn't approve of – would have to be done when Seth was otherwise engaged. There'd be very little fun allowed, that was for sure.

She'd tried to organise a little family outing to the local park yesterday, before Seth headed off this time. Drew was out the front of the house wearing a very thin rain jacket with no warmth in it.

'Please come back inside and put on your puffa jacket,' she'd begged him. 'You'll freeze in that coat. It's only for the summer. It's October and there's frost on the ground.'

'No,' he'd said. 'I like this one. It fit me and it's mine.'

Seeing as he'd insisted, she hadn't wanted to waste time arguing. She knew he'd end up freezing and miserable and she'd have to run him a warm bath as soon as they got back. Still, that wasn't the end of the world. He had knee and elbow pads and a helmet, a set Pearl had bought after one too many falls where he'd come down heavily on his poor knees and ended up with nasty cuts. But the ensemble had made Seth flare with rage.

'He'll look like an idiot at the park dressed like that. A great big fat man, fumbling along on a scooter that could buckle under his weight at any second. And as for that dreadful mac-in-a-sac jacket? It's pure comedy. And you're worse, encouraging him.' Then a hateful curl of his upper lip spurred him on. Once Seth started being nasty, he couldn't help himself. 'And as for farmer Joe who lives in our shed, laughing and skitting with Drew as if life is just a doddle. It's a bit like a game of spot the idiot. *Which one of these men is truly mentally handicapped and which is just mental?'*

Pearl was shocked by his language. 'Seth, please, can you stop?'

He glared at her. 'I'm not a fan of that country bumpkin you insist on having around the place. When I retire, we can get rid of him too.'

She froze with fear at the thought of him firing Tommy. Life would be unbearable without him.

'He's very good with Drew and you know how Drew hates change . . .' she began, before realising she was talking to herself. Pearl followed her husband out to the front gate. Drew had disappeared.

'Drew?' she called frantically, worried that he'd gone out by himself. 'Drew?'

'I'm heeeere,' he said as he ran around the side of the house. 'Look, I found some more stuff in the shed. I'm winter-ready now, right?' He had found lots of reflective clothing and put it on. In fact, he'd gone to the large trunk in the shed and had put on every belt, gilet, jacket and reflective item they owned.

'For crying out loud, you couldn't have made him look more ridiculous if you tried.' Seth chuckled and pointed at Drew, who joined in with the laughter.

'Do you like my things, Dad? Mama says I need to be seen to be safe.'

'Maybe we'll take off one of the belts or the large over-jacket, seeing as it's not dark just yet,' Pearl suggested. 'I promise you'll be safe at the park without them all on. One or two is enough, okay?'

'No.' Drew shook his head and went to scoot out of the gate. Before she could stop him, Seth ran and grabbed Drew by the back of his reflective jacket.

'Don't speak to your mother like that. Now get inside

and take this stuff off. Put that blasted scooter away and we'll go to the park like a normal family.'

'No,' Drew repeated, pointing to the gate. 'We're scooting to the park now, please.'

'If I have to tell you again, you'll know all about it,' said Seth.

Drew was on a mission and Pearl's blood ran cold as she realised there was going to be a clash of horns.

'Come on, Mama. We're going now,' Drew insisted. He turned to face Seth. 'If you can't be more cheerful, maybe you should stay home.'

Seth grabbed him and dragged him roughly by one arm back into the house. Drew stumbled awkwardly and called out her name. Pearl raced after them but wasn't quick enough to stop the punch that Seth landed on Drew's cheek.

'You will do what I say, when I say it. Do I make myself clear?'

Drew curled into a foetal position on the floor in the hallway of the house and covered his head with his hands. They all knew from previous outbursts that his father detested crying, so he tried to hide his sobs. Pearl longed to drop to the floor and cradle her poor confused boy in her arms. But experience, yet again, told her that any such actions would enrage Seth further. So she made eye contact with Drew and tried to let him know that she'd be with him as soon as Seth was gone from the scene.

'We won't be going to the park. Instead you'll stay in your room. Now take that junk off and put it away neatly. Don't let me see you dressed like some sort of neon clown again, do you hear?'

Drew had his hands over his ears.

'I said, do you hear?' Seth yelled.

'Yes I can hear,' said Drew. 'I can hear.'

'Now move and do what I said.'

Drew had a dark red mark on his face where he'd been hit.

'Move,' Seth yelled.

Unable to hold back any longer, and terrified Drew would be punched again, Pearl dropped to her knees to try and comfort him. The last time she'd come to Drew's defence like this, Seth had dragged her away from him and his roughness had left her bruised all along her arm and left side. But this time he'd grabbed one side of her hair and yanked. She heard a ripping noise as some of it came away from her head. She felt no pain, she simply wanted to get to her son. When Seth kicked her, right under her stomach as she was on all fours, the force lifted her off the floor so she crumpled in a useless sobbing heap beside Drew.

'Mama, it's okay. I'll mind you,' he said as he crawled to her.

'Get away from her,' Seth yelled. 'Stand up and take that crap off this minute.'

'No, you've hurt her and that's not nice. You're a bad man,' Drew shouted.

With that, Seth grabbed him and with all his might dragged Drew to the bottom of the stairs. 'Go up and take that stuff off and then stay in your room. I don't want to see you again tonight.'

'No,' Drew yelled as Pearl closed her eyes and begged him to do as Seth asked.

Drew stood up and wouldn't move, so Seth smacked

him with full force across the face and then again. The boy reeled and fell back against the stairs, whacking his back on the banister.

'Ow,' he said and burst into tears. He tried to reach out to Pearl, but Seth was having none of it. Grabbing his son, he dragged him up the stairs and pushed him into his bedroom. 'Take that stuff off and stay in here until I'm gone. You're the bane of my life and you will not disobey me, you moron.'

As he came back down the stairs, Pearl remained in a ball, sobbing.

'I'll leave you two to your warped little club,' Seth said. 'I'll be leaving now. I'll spend a night at a hotel so I can be calm and in the right state of mind to greet my men tomorrow. If I stay here, I'll be caught up in your weakness. I'll text you which hotel to collect me from so you can drop me to the airport, as planned.'

She waited for him to pack his bag and leave before she climbed the stairs to help her son.

'Come on, darling,' she said. 'Let's get ourselves out of our coats. I think we'll have a duvet day today. It looks as if it might rain anyway.'

'Is he going away quickly?'

'Don't be scared,' Pearl soothed. 'It'll be just fine.'

'Is he never coming back? 'Cause that's the only fine I can think of,' Drew said, sniffling. 'He's got a bad and mean heart. Not like Tommy. I wish Tommy was my daddy,' said Drew.

So do I, she thought, more than you'll ever know.

Seth phoned later that night to tell her where he was staying. He didn't apologise, far from it.

'I hope you took heed of what I was trying to say, Pearl.

That boy needs more manners. He's going to kill you one of these days. Spoiling him isn't helping matters. What I did today was for his own good and yours, Pearl. You'll understand that once you stop being so soft.'

She didn't argue nor did she agree. She wasn't prepared to even try to have a conversation with a man who thought his brutal attack on her and their special needs son was in any way, shape or form right. And to even suggest that he was doing her a *favour*? The man was an animal and she detested him for what he'd done.

The following day, Tommy took Drew on a trip to the zoo. Pearl told him quickly what Seth had done but said that she couldn't talk about it. She was still sick to her stomach, which was completely true. Drew, darling boy that he was, had forgiven Seth. In fact, he'd just buried it and appeared the following morning for breakfast with a smile on his poor bruised face.

Pearl wanted nothing more than to kick Seth out. She wished she had the guts to tell him to pack his stuff and never come back. But she also knew that wouldn't come to pass. She'd do what she always did. She'd use the time apart to heal and come to terms with the man she was married to and prepare herself for the next stint as a family. By the time he returned, she'd be able to pretend again.

As she drove back from the airport, her heart was light and heavy. Light because Seth was safely gone, but heavy because she knew all the pretending in the world couldn't get them through his retirement. Once he was there full-time, the wheels were going to come off this whole thing. She was kidding herself by even thinking it was a manageable situation. She and Drew had only one joy in life: each other and Tommy. That was the family unit that made them happy. Her life with Seth was a sham, but she hadn't the courage to change it. Her eyes blurred with tears and she had to pull over on the motorway. She bent her head to the steering wheel and cried with a breaking heart. It felt like her life was slipping through her fingers and out of her grasp.

Chapter 10

DANIELLE WAS READY TO DROP WITH TIREDNESS.
She had cleaned the house from top to bottom, even
though Justin had ordered her to leave it to the new housekeeper he'd hired. Maggie was a lovely woman, but
Danielle felt bad when she saw her cleaning their house
and doing private things, like stripping and washing their
bedsheets. It was totally normal for Justin, but not for her.
She kept wanting to tell Maggie to take the weight off and
have a cuppa while she did it. So she had worked alongside for the two hours Maggie was there that morning,
then she'd done another two hours on her own. Now she
was wrecked. This pregnancy was making her feel like an
old woman.

She had a long hot shower, put on a nice dress that hung
loose and hid her little belly and tried to prepare for what
lay ahead. This was the day Celia-Ann and Jeremy, Justin's
parents, were coming to visit. They'd only been in the
house ten days, but Celia-Ann had insisted they wanted
to be the first to see it. She had basically ordered them to
invite her to afternoon tea and Justin had, of course, given
in. He'd moan and bitch about his mother, but when it
came down to it, he'd go along with what she wanted.
'For a quiet life' he kept saying to Danielle, but she was
sick of his quiet life already.

She went into the kitchen and opened the fridge and surveyed all the stuff she'd bought, according to the list Justin had given her. Standing there, she realised she hadn't a clue how to put it all together – what even was afternoon tea? She'd thought it was a pot of tea and a Bourbon Cream, but Justin had burst out laughing at her and then written out all this stuff – paté, smoked salmon, cucumber, chocolates. It looked like a hell of a lot for an afternoon snack. She sank into a kitchen chair and started crying. She felt like a complete idiot. Justin wouldn't be back until 3.30 p.m., when his parents were due, so the success of this visit was entirely on her shoulders – and she was the one person who couldn't carry it off.

She couldn't sit here weeping like a princess in a story, anyway. That wasn't going to get her anywhere. She could Google it – yeah, that was a great idea. The university of Google would educate her about bloody afternoon teas for people with too many hyphens in their name. I mean, Celia-Ann Mulroney-Johnston, who wants to have that much going on in one name? Her mam would laugh herself stupid if she heard that.

She went over to the sink and splashed some water on her face. As she stood there, looking out of the window, she spotted a figure working in a garden at the end of the road. It was a brightly coloured and petite figure. Nancy! She would know what to do, wouldn't she? Danielle felt a rush of hope fly through her. Nancy had told her to pop over whenever, so she wouldn't mind giving a bit of advice. This was her best chance of not messing up.

Danielle grabbed her house key and let herself out of the front door and hurried down Kingfisher Road to Nancy's cute cottage.

'Hi Nancy!' she called out as she reached the wall, panting a little.

'Oh hello, Danielle,' Nancy replied, standing up straight and stretching out her back. She came over to the wall. 'Hmm,' she said, peering at Danielle.

'What?' Danielle said.

'You've been crying,' Nancy said. 'What's up?'

'You're not a great believer in keeping your thoughts to yourself, are you?' Danielle blurted out.

Nancy laughed. 'Got it in one,' she said. 'No point in pretending at my age. So come on, what has you upset? Can I help?'

The kindness was too much for Danielle. She started crying again, covering her face with her hands in embarrassment. Nancy came around the wall and put an arm around her.

'You just let it out, my love, then you can tell me and we'll sort it, whatever it is.'

When Danielle could finally speak, she told Nancy about the invite and the food and the fact that she was about to make a fool of herself in front of the very people she had to impress.

'Afternoon tea's a cinch,' Nancy said. 'I'll come over and help and once you've done it once, you'll be throwing them like a pro. We'll have you hostessing à la Martha Stewart in no time.'

Danielle had no idea what she was talking about, but Nancy was going to dig her out of the hole she was in so she didn't care. She waited while Nancy went inside and washed her hands and changed her shoes, then the two of them went back to Danielle's house.

'Right, what have you got?' Nancy said. She rifled

through the kitchen shelves. 'Ah sure, you've everything. This'll make itself.'

She showed Danielle how to make salmon and brown bread. 'No butter,' she warned, 'just a squeeze of lemon juice.' Then they made cucumber sandwiches, which seemed a mad idea to Danielle, but she rolled with it. Nancy went through the cupboards and got out lovely plates and serving dishes and arranged it all beautifully. She cut the Madeira cake and set out the chocolates on their own dish. She set out the bite-sized scones from the bakery and found ceramic ramekin dishes to use for jam, butter and cream, setting them all on a round slate platter she found in the cupboard. The centrepiece was a freshly made chocolate fudge cake – also from the local bakery – which they put on a cake stand with a glass lid. It immediately looked fancy and gorgeous and Danielle breathed a sigh of relief.

'Right, now for the table,' said Nancy. 'Where do you want to set up? In here? Or maybe a table in the sitting room so people can help themselves?'

'Em . . . yeah, whatever you think,' Danielle said.

'Come on, let's have a look at the sitting room,' Nancy said. Danielle led the way. 'Oh my, this is a really beautiful room,' Nancy said, looking around. 'I adore that duck-egg blue on the carpet. Inspired choice.'

'Do you really think so?' Danielle said anxiously. 'I was so sure, and I'm afraid Celia-Ann won't like it.'

Nancy raised an eyebrow. 'She doesn't live here. You do. If she doesn't like it, tell her to take a running jump.'

Danielle giggled. 'I can just see her face – and Justin's – if I ever came out with anything like that. They are seriously rich and fancy. I'm not in their league at all. They probably eat like this every day. I have a bowl of cereal in the morning and a cheese sandwich for lunch. I've never even had smoked salmon before. And it looks revolting, by the way.'

'It does,' Nancy said, laughing. 'But it is gorgeous. And don't you be worrying about those sorts of things. If this Celia-Ann woman is decent and kind, she won't care about using the correct fork or whether you scalded the pot. She'll be far more interested in you and her son and your happiness. Just be yourself and don't sweat the small stuff.'

'I'll try,' Danielle said, but she could feel the tension spreading through her body at the idea of the Johnstons sitting in this room and sizing up her efforts.

'If you don't mind me asking,' Nancy said, 'how did you meet Justin?'

Danielle laughed a little. 'That's probably been wrecking your head all along, has it?'

'Well I am a nosy old cow,' Nancy said, laughing too. 'You just keep saying how different they are, so I was wondering how your paths crossed.'

'I met him at a gallery in town,' Danielle said. 'My friend in college, Hazel, her dad owned it, and there was a show being launched, a show of horse portraits, and Hazel asked if I'd like to serve wine at it and earn fifty quid for the night. So I went along and we had to wear black skirts and blouses and walk around with trays of wine. It was mad, because I thought it would be fancy people being all intelligent and talking about art, but they were knocking back the wine and getting really loud.'

'That sounds about right,' Nancy said. 'They have notions, but they don't always live up to them, that's my experience.'

'Anyway, Justin was there because the artist was an old family friend, and I noticed him because he was the only person in the whole night who said thank you when he took a glass of wine.'

'Sounds as though he didn't get his good manners from that mother of his,' Nancy said.

'At the end of the night, we were cleaning up and nearly everyone was gone, but Justin was still there talking to Hazel's dad and buying a few paintings. Then he came over and asked if he could buy me a coffee on the way home. I told him I didn't drink coffee after six o'clock and he called me a Gremlin and that made me laugh. So we ended up going to a café that stays open late, and we sat there for about an hour and it was the easiest conversation I'd ever had. Then he walked me over to Trinity. I had a scholarship and was rooming there. I was in second year and loving it. So we sat on a bench in the cricket field and talked until dawn. If you'd told me before that it was possible to fall in love in one night, I'd have laughed at you. But it's true. That's what happened.'

'That's an amazing story,' Nancy said. 'Proper old-fashioned romance.'

'It was an incredible night,' Danielle said, smiling to remember. 'And I suppose everything's moved very fast since then, and here I am. But his mother isn't happy about it. That's why I'm so anxious this goes well.'

'Well then, let's make sure it does. Come on, let's get this set up nicely.'

Nancy moved tables around until she had the place looking just right. There was a round table to one side, and she set up the food there, with plates and cutlery and napkins ready to be used. Then they moved the two sofas so that they were facing each other on either side of the fireplace, and Nancy put a low table between them.

'That looks brilliant,' Danielle said, standing back to admire their work. 'I should have thought of putting the sofas like that. It looks just right.'

'It's easy to come in with an objective eye,' Nancy said. 'Now,' she said, glancing at her watch. 'It's quarter-past three, so I'm going to skedaddle and let you catch your breath before they all descend on you.'

'Won't you stay?' Danielle pleaded. 'You're so welcome.' She would actually pay good money for Nancy to stay and be her ally.

'I won't, thank you,' Nancy said. 'I better go feed Nelly and finish that work I was doing. You'll be great. I'm sure everyone will be on their best behaviour anyway, so it'll be fine.'

'Thank you so much, Nancy,' Danielle said. 'I don't know how I could ever pay you back for this. I was a wreck before you helped me.'

Nancy winked at her. 'That's what neighbours are for.'

As she let Nancy out, Danielle felt a bit bad for all the things she'd thought about the women of Kingfisher Road. Yes, they were old and a bit nosy, but she would have made a fool of herself in front of the Johnstons if she hadn't been able to call on Nancy for help. She made a mental note to be a nicer neighbour herself in future.

She heard the sound of car doors slamming outside and ran to the window. They had all arrived at the same time – Justin in the jeep he used for work, and his parents in a big Mercedes. Danielle gulped when she saw how Justin's mother was dressed. She looked like she was going to a wedding. She was wearing a dress with a pleated skirt, and it looked like silk. Her shoes matched the navy of the dress, and she was encased in a calf-length fur coat. A navy hat perched on the side of her head completed the look. Danielle looked down at her 'good dress' and felt a bit sick, but she heard the key in the lock and it was too late to change.

'It's so suburban, Justin,' Celia-Ann was saying as they came through the front door. 'No, I can't see you being happy here. I think you'll be back in Meath with us very soon. And what in the name of God is that thing in your driveway?'

Danielle frowned, wondering what she could be talking about.

'That's Danielle's car, Mum,' she heard Justin say.

'That's a heap of junk, darling, and it's completely ruining the look of your house. They don't belong together, your beautiful Beamer and that piece of trash.'

Danielle sucked in a breath. She just knew Celia-Ann was really referring to her and Justin when she'd said that. It was exactly how she saw them – mismatched, uneven, one far superior to the other.

'It's a grand little run-around,' Justin said loyally. 'And if you must know, I've just ordered Danielle a brand new Range Rover. We'll have it in a couple of weeks.'

Every time Danielle thought about the new car, she felt a bit sick. While she was grateful that she was being showered with yet another atrociously expensive gift, she was terrified in case she scraped it or, even worse, banged it off a gate or a wall, or crashed. Her own little Yaris had been passed down to her from her mam. She'd learned to drive in it, passed her test first time in it and she was basically comfortable about driving it. More to the point. she was grateful to have it at all. The jeep scared the living daylights out of her, but Justin had been absolutely certain she needed a new car. He'd argued the safety angle, for when she was driving the baby about, and how could she argue with that?

'Well a Range Rover sounds far more suitable,' Celia-Ann said as their voices came closer.

There was a pause – Justin must be taking their coats, Danielle thought. And then his mother's annoying posh voice started up again.

'This is a terribly narrow vestibule, Justin. And why did you choose those insipid grey tiles? It doesn't work at all.'

Danielle's heart sank.

Justin opened the door to the sitting room, and she could see his face relax into a smile when he saw the set-up.

'Hi darling,' he said, winking at her. 'Mum and Dad arrived just as I did.'

Danielle stepped forward, hand outstretched. 'Good to see you again, Celia-Ann,' she said.

Justin's mother looked her up and down, nostrils flaring. 'Did you forget the date?' she asked pleasantly.

Danielle was confused. 'No, I . . .'

'You seem dressed for a different event perhaps?' she said, her mouth twisted in a smile but her eyes cold. 'I thought maybe you had forgotten we were joining you for afternoon tea today.'

'No, no,' said Danielle, feeling about two inches tall. 'I have everything ready and I hope you'll enjoy it.'

Celia-Ann looked around the room and saw the food all laid out and pursed her lips. God bless you, Nancy, Danielle thought. Obviously this obnoxious woman was expecting Danielle to have got it all wrong and was annoyed to see she had pulled it off expertly.

'Please come in and sit down, Jeremy,' Danielle said, taking Justin's father's hand. He smiled warmly at her and kissed her on both cheeks

'Lovely to see you looking so well, Danielle,' he said. 'Are you feeling as well as you look?'

Danielle nodded. 'Yes, I'm very tired but otherwise . . .'

'You chose a terribly difficult colour for the carpet, Danielle,' Celia-Ann interrupted loudly. 'It'll look grubby and unkempt. That shade of blue is far too delicate for flooring. You should have asked me about it.'

'We're just trying out things to find out what we like,' Justin said quickly.

He was always smoothing things over when it came to his mother. Danielle had only met them once before, at a restaurant they had brought them to after Justin had told them he was in love with her. The place was dead fancy, and Danielle was uneasy all throughout the meal. She liked Jeremy, but he just moved in his wife's shadow and said very little. Celia-Ann was most definitely the queen of her little world, presiding over Jeremy and their four sons and expecting everyone to do her bidding. She had made Danielle feel small that night too, making comments in that pleasant tone that were cutting and cruel. She had remarked on Danielle's background, the fact that she was 'the product of a single mother', as she put it, and managed to get the word 'gold-digger' into the conversation five times, all under the pretence of talking about someone else. She had talked constantly about Justin's ex and Danielle knew she saw the ex as worthy and herself as entirely unworthy of Justin's affections. It looked like she hadn't changed her mind one bit on that score.

'How was the mare this morning?' Jeremy asked Justin

as he put scones onto his plate and accepted a cup of tea, then took a seat on the sofa.

'Temperature is still up,' Justin said, sitting down, 'but I think she's more comfortable than yesterday. I'd say the fever will have broken within another twenty-four hours. I'm not worried about her anymore. I think she'll be fine.'

'Wonderful news,' Jeremy said, biting into a scone. 'Fantastic,' he said, smiling at Danielle. 'Lovely and buttery. Did you make them yourself?'

Danielle channelled a bit of Nancy, looked him straight in the eye and said, 'Yes, I did. Fresh out of the oven an hour ago.'

Celia-Ann looked sceptical, but didn't say anything.

'The mare – what's wrong with her?' Danielle asked. She hadn't a clue about the horse world, but she wanted to learn for Justin's sake.

'An infection,' Jeremy said. 'At any other stables it probably would have finished her off, but we have the best horse-whisperer on this island on our books, thankfully,' he said, smiling at Justin. 'So she'll be back on her feet soon.'

'Have you ever been to a stables, Danielle?' Celia-Ann asked.

'No, just the one time. Justin brought me out to see it,' she answered. 'I really enjoyed it.'

'You have to be born into it,' Celia-Ann said grandly. 'Horse families are a particular breed, as we always say.' She let out a peal of laughter. Danielle smiled politely.

'Well, when Danielle's name is Johnston, she'll be adopted into it,' Justin said loyally.

His mother's eyes went wide and she looked from him to Danielle and back. 'Never marry in haste, Justin,' she said sternly, 'or you'll regret it for a lifetime. Especially, when, if you'll excuse my forthrighness, Danielle, you are thinking of marrying outside of your own circle. That's a particularly delicate situation and must be handled carefully. If you are seriously thinking of such a thing, we will of course get our solicitor to draw up a pre-nup and cover every single angle.' She looked pointedly at Danielle. 'It has to be watertight when you come from a family such as ours, Justin,' she said.

Danielle could see the little vein in Justin's temple starting to throb.

'Mum, you know full well that Danielle and I are having a baby, and that we will of course be getting married. I'd marry Danielle in the morning, but I've agreed to your suggestion of waiting until after the birth.'

'It's the right choice,' his mother said. 'Trust me.'

'More tea anyone?' Danielle said. She thought Justin might fling a plate into the fireplace if his mother kept up this kind of talk.

'Yes, I'd love some,' said Jeremy.

'No you won't,' Celia-Ann said sharply. 'We're leaving now. I have an appointment and I don't wish to be late.'

'Wouldn't you like a guided tour?' Justin asked, sounding disappointed. Danielle felt disappointed too, given all the work she'd done to make every room perfect.

'No thank you,' his mother said. 'Judging by the tiles and the carpet, I can't imagine Danielle's taste has much in common with mine.'

Danielle blushed, but said nothing. This woman wasn't worth it. Like Nancy had said, if she was a decent person, she wouldn't go out of her way to make her feel bad about herself. She might be rich, but she was a nasty piece of work all the same.

'Now, both of you, keep the night of thirtieth October free, please,' Celia-Ann said as Justin helped her into her coat. 'I'm planning a rather fun bash, a masked ball, and I want you both at it. And Danielle, I'd like to invite your mother as well. I think it's important we all meet, don't you?'

Danielle was taken aback, but Justin looked so delighted she just stammered out a thank you and assured Celia-Ann that they would both be there.

'Good. Now come along, Jeremy.'

'Yes dear,' he said as he hugged Justin awkwardly and banged him on the back. 'Good show, son, good show.'

'See you in the morning with the vet, Daddy.'

'Yes, indeed. See you then. Bye-bye, young lady. Thank you for a marvellous tea. Catch you later!' he said and tried to make a peace sign that ended up being a V-sign. Danielle and Justin just managed to hold their laugher until they shut the door behind them.

Justin wandered back to the food table to fill another plate, chatting all the while about the mare and 'the bash' and the box-set he wanted to watch that evening. Danielle was pleased that he was happy, and relieved she had played her part well enough, but she didn't share his conviction that Celia-Ann had somehow changed her mind and wanted to play happy families. She was astonished about the party invite, but unlike Justin, she found herself wondering about motives. What did Celia-Ann stand to gain from inviting Danielle and her mother?

Chapter 11

BETSY WAS ENJOYING EVERY MOMENT WITH BABY Arnie. He was the most cheerful little boy and so easy to mind. He ate anything she put in front of him and loved playing with his toys. She was glad she'd gone to the trouble of fishing Graham's old things out of the attic and buying a few more, otherwise he'd have had nothing. He'd arrived all the way from Australia without so much as a teddy. She'd made up for that now. It was such a joy to have a grandchild to spoil.

'He's so good, isn't he, Noel?'

'He's a little star. But I suppose the poor child is delighted with anything after living in a squat and eating gone-off food from a skip.'

Noel had never got over Tasha's admission of how they'd been living, and every time Betsy thought of it she shuddered. How had Graham gone from being so well brought up to that? She couldn't help feeling it was partly her fault. Clearly she hadn't raised him well enough or else he would've made better choices.

Noel was constantly telling her that the past was in the past and that things would be different from here on in. 'Arnie was only a dot when they lived in that dreadful squat,' Noel reasoned. 'With a bit of luck he won't have any memories of that time. Instead he'll know about living with his loving grandparents and his doting parents.'

The doting parents comment was a bit of a stretch, Betsy mused. Tasha wasn't any nicer than she remembered, and she didn't lift a finger around the house. There wasn't a single offer to help with the washing or cooking or cleaning. Instead she sat on the sofa reading Betsy's magazines while calling Gray and asking for a cup of tea, a glass of juice, a coffee, a few biscuits, a packet of crisps . . . She never stopped, and Graham ran after her like a little lap dog.

Betsy was in the kitchen, preparing dinner for Arnie and for the adults when Noel stormed in, his face red with anger.

'I'm going to strangle that woman if she doesn't start to pull her weight,' he growled.

Betsy absolutely agreed with him, but she knew that they needed to butt out of the situation.

'It's not our business, Noel.'

'It bloody well is if they're living in our house,' he said. 'I've told her that she's to stop sitting in the front garden smoking those roll-up cigarettes. If she must do it, she's to keep it to the back where nobody can see her. The cheeky cow has been shoving her cigarette butts into the planter at the front door. My poor cyclamen display is being burned and ruined.'

'That's not on,' Betsy admitted. 'Did she say she'd stop?'

'I got the usual glower followed by a nudge in the shoulder as she bumped past me.'

'What is that all about?' Betsy said, as anger rose inside her. 'She's dreadfully aggressive and seems to have no respect for the fact that she's living in our home – for free, I might add.'

'Maybe I'll have a word with Graham later on, in private, and suggest he prints off a CV,' said Noel. 'Much as I adore little Arnie, neither of us is really able to mind him full-time. We're not getting any younger, Betsy, and young children are a lot of work.'

Noel had been a wonderful hands-on father with Graham and Betsy knew he would gladly do it again for little Arnie, but he was right, people in their sixties weren't really cut out for full-time parenting. There was a good reason why Mother Nature didn't give babies to pensioners.

'Leave it with me, love. I'll do it now in fact,' Noel said, suddenly looking determined. 'No time like the present, and I reckon Graham will listen to me. No offence, pet, but I think it's time for a man-to-man talk.'

'None taken,' she said holding her hands up in defeat. 'Anything you can do to improve things will be most welcome.'

Before Betsy could blink, Noel had taken Graham into the parlour, which wasn't often used, although it was a beautiful room and contained her most prized ornaments. The three of them knew that a summons to the good room meant business. Betsy huddled close to the door with her hands clasped and her eyes shut and prayed Graham would listen to Noel.

There was no noise at first, but then the shouting began in earnest. Clearly, what Noel had said wasn't going down too well with Graham. Meanwhile Tasha appeared with Arnie, dumped him on the floor with an armful of toys she'd scooped up from the playroom and flicked on the TV. As Arnie played on the floor, Tasha sat watching a dreadful programme where people with missing teeth and tattooed knuckles were hurling abuse at one another. There was more beeping than talking and Betsy longed to change the channel.

'They're not the nicest of people on there, are they?' Betsy ventured. 'It might be an idea to put on a children's programme for Arnie to watch.'

'He's a baby, Ma,' she said, without so much as a glance in Betsy's direction. 'Besides I can't stand kiddies' programmes. They do my head in with all the crappy music and stupid storylines.'

'Well they aren't aimed at us, dear.'

'Exactly my point,' said Tasha. 'So that's why I watch something that *I* enjoy. God knows I spend enough time doing what he wants.' She pointed to Arnie as if he were nothing more than a nuisance. Betsy opened her mouth to speak but nothing came out.

A short time later Graham appeared, looking flushed and furious.

'How did it go?' Betsy asked with trepidation. 'We both love you, darling, but this situation has to change.' She gave a vague wave of her arm so as not to point at anyone in particular.

'Come in here for a moment please, Betsy,' Noel said.

Arnie began to cry, so Betsy picked him up and brought him with her. Graham closed the door behind her and went over to the bay window and stood there staring out with his back to them. Noel shot her a look and she knew things weren't good.

'We'll be gone as soon as I can find some place we can squat,' Graham said, his voice flat with restrained anger. 'I had a bit of a tip-off from a guy I met at the park yesterday.'

'You can't take that baby to a squat again,' said Noel.

'It's not right and it's not the way you should be raising a child.'

'It's fine. You don't know the first thing about it so keep your nose out of it, yeah?'

'Don't speak to your father that way,' Betsy said. 'We all need to calm down a bit. Arnie deserves to have a proper home where he has warmth, food and love. I don't know about squats, you're dead right there. But I have an imagination and I'm using it. Correct me if I'm wrong, but it wouldn't be similar to living here?'

'Mum, don't go down the smart-ass route,' Graham said, spinning around. 'Nowhere is as good as bloody Kingfisher Road, I get it. But sadly, I'm not having a house handed to me so I can become all high and mighty.'

'That's enough!' Noel shouted, making them all jump.

Arnie burst into tears and Graham instinctively took him and cuddled him until he stopped.

'Right, I'm now laying down the law. You won't be going to a squat,' Noel said. 'You will stay here until you are in a position to fend for yourselves. But you and Tasha must pull your weight with the housework and you will be pleasant while you do it. Do I make myself clear?'

Much to Betsy's astonishment, Graham seemed to back down. He nodded and then left the room. They filed after him to where Tasha was still watching TV.

'Eh, what's the problem, babes?'

'My folks want us out of here and they're saying they don't want Arnie near a squat.'

'Right,' she said, seeming totally uninterested. She turned back to watching her programme.

Arnie was plonked down on the floor and Graham stormed out of the front door, slamming it for added drama.

Much to Noel and Betsy's astonishment, Tasha's gaze still didn't leave the TV and she didn't look as if she might be ready to have a conversation with them either.

'Eh, Tasha . . .' Noel said. 'We're wondering if you've had any thoughts on what you might do. You can't carry on doing nothing and, as I've just said to Graham, we'll gladly help out as much as we can . . .'

'Yeah, great,' she said and turned up the volume.

Not sure of what else to do, Betsy put a howling Arnie into the buggy and said she'd take him for a walk.

'I don't mean to be awful,' Noel said. 'I'd love a walk in the fresh air, it's also getting dark so I don't like you being on your own, but I'm not leaving Tasha here on her own. I don't trust her.'

'No, neither do I, unfortunately,' Betsy agreed. 'I won't be long, love. I'll only go until Arnie falls asleep.'

As she followed the path through the park, Betsy spotted Graham sitting on a bench. He looked stressed to the hilt and very alone, and Betsy's heart went out to him. Arnie was nearly asleep, so she pushed the buggy over to the bench.

'Mind if I join you?'

Graham looked up tiredly. 'No, it's fine. Sit down, Mum.'

She sat, rolling the buggy back and forth as she tried to think of how to get through to her son. In the end, she didn't have to, because he started talking and it was clear he'd been doing a lot of thinking.

'I'm so sorry about all this, Mum,' he said suddenly, taking her by surprise. 'I know you're trying really hard and this situation is tough, and I know you love Arnie as much as I do and you're just thinking of him. It's just hard, you know, because Tash is so set in her ways. She won't hear of us living any other way. It's her way or no way.'

Betsy took a deep breath. 'She's difficult to live with, Graham, but I would live with the devil himself if it meant being able to mind you and Arnie. Your father and I feel so blessed to have Arnie in our lives, but we just can't bear the idea of a cold and dirty squat. It wouldn't make him happy. And,' she ventured, 'I'm not convinced it would make you happy.'

Graham rubbed his face with his hands. 'I think I have had enough of it, especially now that I've experienced being home again. The problem is, I want to make Tash happy, but now I'm wondering if it's possible to do right by my wife and my son. The needs of one seem to cancel the other one out. But I don't want to choose, Mum. I really want Tash to come round and see that we can have a place and give Arnie a good life without compromising our beliefs.'

'I really don't know about Tasha's beliefs,' Betsy said drily. 'She seems fine with handouts from us, and for all her talk of communal living, she doesn't actually contribute, not in our house anyway. It seems to be a philosophy of convenience, if you ask me.'

'Yeah, I'm beginning to question it myself,' Graham admitted, which Betsy admired, because it's hard to say you might be wrong about something – especially your marriage. 'I can't believe how disrespectful she is towards you and Dad. I've noticed and I'm sorry, Mum.'

'You've no need to apologise,' Betsy said gently. She was thrilled to see this new side to her son, it was definitely a sign of maturity. He'd been such a difficult teenager, but it was like he was finally learning to see things from other people's perspectives. 'We love you and we'll help you find somewhere to live, but you'll need to think about getting a job, love.'

'I know,' he said, sighing deeply. He peered over at Arnie and smiled. 'He's such a good boy. I think he's the main reason I've stayed with her.'

Betsy remained silent, because she could see Graham was working things out as he spoke about them. She was like that herself: she came to the truth by talking her way towards it. True enough, bit-by-bit Graham began to reveal his true feelings about his life with Tasha. He hated squatting, he couldn't bear being smelly and dirty and eating out of dumpsters. He hated the drugs and drink scene. Betsy thought she might yelp when he mentioned drugs. She knew so little about them, but she did know they scared her.

'What kind of drugs?' she asked. 'I know I should probably be all cool about it, but I'm not. I'm shocked. You're not a drug addict, are you, Graham?'

He laughed and then hugged her because she looked as if she might cry. He said it was mostly weed, but that Tasha was always stoned.

'She even smoked while she was pregnant. We had so many arguments over that. I wanted to leave at that point, but I felt I owed it to the baby to stay.'

'Oh love, why didn't you ask us for help sooner?'

'I couldn't see the wood for the trees,' he said. 'But now that I'm home, I know that I want what's best for my son. I want a proper home where he can grow up with his grandparents nearby and go to the school I went to . . . all those things matter to me now. But Tasha doesn't give a toss. She'd live in a shoebox on the side of a motorway in Timbuktu if the idea took her fancy.'

'Or if the shoebox was full of weed,' Betsy said, elbowing him and smiling sadly. 'We'll work it out with you, okay?'

He nodded, and she could tell he was so relieved to have her there. Betsy was delighted. In fact, she was happier than he would ever know. When her only child had chosen to go to live on the other side of the world, she'd taken it personally. She knew that was daft, but she couldn't change the way she thought. She'd cried for weeks after he'd gone. Especially when she was at home on her own. She wasn't sure she'd ever get used to him being gone. So having him sitting beside her, confiding in her, was a dream come true.

'Come on,' Betsy said, taking his hand. 'It's getting cold, we'd better get Arnie back to his cosy cot.'

'Sure,' Graham said, and they walked slowly home. He was lost in thought, and Betsy knew better than to interrupt him.

At the house, Betsy wheeled Arnie inside then left Graham to put him up to bed while she served dinner. As always, the table was set beautifully for four, with fresh flowers, proper napkins and white and red wine glasses, so everyone could choose their own tipple. Betsy was a firm believer in making her guests feel like royalty, even if, as in Tasha's case, they behaved like savages.

True to form, Tasha only came to the table after everyone else was seated, making them wait. Then she filled her white wine glass up to the brim with red wine and slurped it down greedily. She regularly consumed a full bottle on her own each night, and it pained Betsy to see it. In her mind, a mother of a young child should be very restrained when it came to alcohol, but she kept quiet about it. Tasha's table manners were awful, and Betsy suspected they were deliberately awful, just to make a point. She chewed loudly, spoke with her mouth full, and sat with one leg under her, often using her hands or just a fork. It drove Betsy absolutely mad but again, out of respect for Graham, she reined in her anger.

'Lovely tucker, Ma,' Tasha said as she shovelled casserole into her mouth.

'Mum is so good to do this for us every night,' Graham said quietly. 'You know, how about tomorrow night you and me cook for them? We could take turns.'

'You mad?' Tasha said, staring at him. 'Miss Housekeeper of the Year here loves doing it, and she'd go nuts if we were roving around her kitchen, wouldn't you, Ma? Let her at it, Gray.'

'I think it's a good idea,' Noel said. 'Thanks for suggesting it, Graham.'

Tasha pointed her fork at him. 'Nose out, grandpa. Don't go flattering him into skivvying for you lot. It's your house and we're the guests, alright? End of.'

Noel took a very deep breath and Betsy could feel the anger pumping through his body. Even Graham looked worried.

'I think we need to show respect to each other for this to work out,' Betsy said, hoping to defuse the situation.

'So what will work out?' Tasha said.

'Living together,' Betsy said. 'It will probably be a while before you find a place, so while we're . . .'

'I found one,' Tasha said.

All three of them stared at her. She looked like the cat that got the cream, smugly enjoying her moment.

'What?' Graham said. 'Where?'

'I forgot to tell you earlier,' Tasha said, grinning, 'but

yeah, I got us sorted, mate. Found a great place. It's a squat in the city centre, an old house on the north side. They told me it used to be a tenement, so it has this really fascinating history. Anyway, there's a room going in it. There are mostly men there, lovely blokes, but they said they wouldn't object to a baby joining them. They smoke and said they wouldn't be prepared to do that outside, especially not in this cold-ass country, so I could take Arnie to another room while they do that.' She batted her hand as if to say it wasn't important. 'So don't worry, Betsy, mate, we'll be out of your hair in a couple of days. So you don't have to bother with the lecture on respect, thanks.'

Her big announcement was greeted by total silence. She shovelled another forkful of casserole into her mouth and stared at them defiantly. It was Betsy who found her voice first, and she no longer gave a fig about respect or family relations or Graham's feelings or anything. She was so angry she felt like she was going to explode into flames.

'You horrible creature,' she yelled. 'You sit around watching TV all day and listen to us worrying and trying to help and all the while you knew *this*! You are out of your tiny mind if you think my grandson is going into a tenement squat with some drunk old men. It's *winter*, or haven't you registered that fact? That place won't have heating or electricity. If you take Arnie there, he could die of exposure . . . or . . . or a rat bite . . . or God knows what. You can't do that to him!' By now, her chest was heaving with sobs as the thought of Arnie in danger was more than she could bear. She was overcome and collapsed into her chair.

'Jesus,' Tasha said, recovering from the shock of Betsy's meltdown, 'no need to lose your shit over it. The place is perfectly fine. I'll mind Arnie like always, it's not a problem.'

'But you don't mind him,' Betsy said, sitting up and leaning across the table towards her daughter-in-law. 'I do! You sit around staring at the TV and do nothing for him. I cook and clean and buy his clothes and change his nappy. You're not interested in being his mother. You don't care enough . . .'

'Mum,' Graham said quietly. 'Please don't say things you'll regret.'

She knew what he meant. Tasha held the trump card here because she was Arnie's mum. Betsy knew she had to get a grip on herself and get down from the ledge she was teetering on, or she could risk losing Arnie altogether. She took a deep, shaky breath and fought to compose herself.

'Tasha, I don't want to fight with you. I hate confrontation. But please understand that I just want us to talk about this because it's a question of Arnie's well-being. Ireland gets very cold and wet in winter, and he really could become ill if he's in a building that's damp. That's the history of those buildings, in fact. People died there in their droves. So please, please, will you consider these angles and rethink your decision.'

Tasha smiled maliciously at her, knowing that she was in control here.

'That's more like it, Betsy,' she said, 'bit of the old respect you keep banging on about.'

'Tash, please,' Graham said. 'They mean well.'

'These bleeding heart bourgeoisie types always mean

well,' she spat. 'They think there's only one way to live and it's their way. You go on about living on this road as if it's the be all and end all of your life. This place is bricks and mortar. Who gives a shit if you have spotless carpets and the whole place smells of furniture polish? I happen to hate where you live. I think it's insular, limited and I'd say your neighbours are just as full of shit as you two morons.' She was enjoying herself now, and Betsy hated her for it.

'We want what's best for Arnie,' Noel said. 'If you don't like us, that's fine. You're married to Graham, not us . . .'

'Gray,' Tasha said.

'Yes,' Noel said, sounding exhausted. 'We are happy to have you all here and happy to help any way we can. We're not saying the squat sounds awful because we want to control you two or dictate how you live your life, but we do have to be honest and say it does sound unsuitable for a baby of Arnie's age.'

Tasha chewed a mouthful of food and seemed to consider it.

'Alright, here's what I'm prepared to do,' she said. 'How about we stay on here for another month, see how things go, and you can give us, say, two hundred quid a week so me and Gray can have a life. Then after a month we'll see how things are going.'

Betsy knew they were over a barrel, but what else could they do? They'd have to bargain with her for Arnie's sake.

'Thanks for thinking about it,' she said through clenched teeth. 'Noel and I really appreciate it and we'd be delighted to continue with our current arrangement.'

Tasha burst out laughing. 'Sounds like you ate a dictionary instead of this delicious casserole, Betsy.'

Graham caught Betsy's eye and gave her a little nod. She knew he was thanking her and Noel for saving Arnie, and for not stabbing his horrible wife with the bread knife. It was going to be the toughest thing she'd ever done in her life, but Betsy could do it for Arnie.

Chapter 12

MAIA FELT LIKE A BIT OF A TOOL STANDING outside the gates of Danielle's house with a candle in a little sparkly bag in one hand and a pot of jam in the other. As she peeped into the garden, she could see how much work had been done. They'd pulled up a lot of the plants and made space for the cars instead. If she were truthful, she'd love to do the same, but when she'd suggested it to Nancy years ago, she'd more or less told her that would be tacky.

She'd gotten so much support from Nancy in the beginning. She'd been so kind when she asked for advice. Now looking back on it, she must've bombarded the poor lady with an endless stream of stupid questions. But Nancy never made her feel stupid; instead she'd answered and advised her without making it seem as if she was telling her what to do. She still maintained a great relationship with her. The children almost thought of her as their grandmother and they adored her.

'Hello?' said a nervous sounding voice. 'Who is it?'

'It's Maia from number three. I just thought I'd drop by. If you're busy, I can call back at a better time for you.'

'No! Come in, please.' The monstrous gates, which were also new, opened slowly, but as if they were gliding in mid-air.

Danielle was waiting at the front door when she walked up.

'I made a load of jam in the summer. I make things when I'm hassled or bored. Anyway, I thought you'd like it. I discovered these candles recently and I'm addicted to them! I could go home and swap them for an empty cup and ask you for sugar if you'd prefer?' Maia said, making it a joke.

Danielle stood blinking, clearly not picking up on what she'd said. So Maia thrust the things at her, feeling awkward. Danielle was dressed in a faded black tracksuit that had definitely seen better days with worn-out looking slippers. Not exactly lady of the manor garb. Freddie would have seven fits if she ever looked like that when he got home from work. By comparison, Maia looked like she might be headed to a flash nightclub. Her black leather mini-skirt was designer and she'd teamed it with a plain black top and sandals. For her, it was very ordinary, but she felt OTT next to Danielle.

'Did I see that skirt in Bella's down in the village?' said Danielle.

Maia smiled. 'Yeah, I saw it in the window and couldn't resist.'

'I saw it too, and Justin tried to get me to buy it, but I couldn't justify the price.'

'Really?' Maia said. 'I never think of things like that. If I see something I like, I just buy it. Freddie will give me the money and he says it's important that I'm happy.'

'Justin would love you,' Danielle said with a laugh. 'I'm not used to having so much money to spend, and with all the furniture and the endless outgoings on the house, I just couldn't justify the price tags in that shop.'

'You'll learn,' said Maia as she tried to hide her disgust. What was wrong with this girl? She was in a position that most would kill for – living with Justin Johnston and, if she played her cards right, no doubt married to him in time. It wasn't as if one designer outfit would leave them bankrupt . . . she needed to get with the programme. Her poor husband was clearly trying to get her to look the part. She was so dowdy and miserable-looking with her stringy blonde curls and her totally makeup-free, pale skin.

'That's so kind of you to bring a gift,' Danielle said, looking at the candle and jam. 'Will you come in for a coffee? My mam's here.'

'I don't want to crash in on you and your mam,' Maia said.

Danielle leaned forward and whispered, 'You'd be doing me a favour. I'm kind of struggling in here.'

Maia couldn't help smiling. 'Mams can be hard work,' she whispered back. 'I know that from painful experience.' Then she raised her voice and said loudly, 'Oh thank you, Danielle, I'd love to come in and see the place.'

Danielle gave her a thumbs-up and pulled the door open wide. 'You're very welcome,' she said, stepping back to let her in.

'Oh dear Lord, I'm having serious house envy here,' Maia said, her jaw almost hitting the exquisite and understated grey tiles. 'I would gladly swap if you want? I could arrange for all your things to be moved within the hour.'

Danielle giggled and led Maia down to the kitchen.

'Mam, this is one of our neighbours, Maia. Maia, this is my mam, Rachel O'Brien.'

A woman looked up as Maia stepped into the room, and she clocked the look of disapproval that crossed her face.

Maia was well used to women like this. They let themselves go, got a little flabby around the waist, dressed to be invisible, didn't take care of their skin, and then they looked at Maia as if she was a traitor for looking so well. This kind of woman hated the kind of woman Maia was. It was going to be one long cup of coffee, Maia reckoned.

'Hiya Rachel,' she said brightly. 'I'm delighted to meet you.'

'Hello,' the woman said stiffly. 'Over for a gawk, are you?'

Maia burst out laughing. 'Yeah, that's it exactly. I brought the candle and jam, but that was just to get me through the door really. Am I that obvious?'

'I can see through you like glass,' the other woman retorted, but Maia could see the hint of a smile.

Given that there was no need to make a secret of the fact that she was here to have a good look, Maia looked around and took it all in. The kitchen and living room had been knocked through and the place was bright and spacious. She'd been here once with the previous owners – with a candle and jam in her hand – and then the décor had been dull and old-fashioned. Now, most of it was white, including the sofa.

'You have a white sofa, and in the kitchen,' Maia said, going over to pet the arm of it. 'This would be destroyed within the hour if it were in my house.'

'Tea? Coffee? Glass of something like juice or sparkling water?' Danielle asked.

'I'd love a coffee,' said Maia and she perched on one of the white bar stools. It had a chrome stand that brought out the sparkly silver in the marble worktops that seemed to go on for ever. The cupboards were also white, with chrome handles. The place should, by rights, look like an operating theatre, but there were splashes of deep pinks and turquoises in the picture frames, the matching kettle and toaster, the enormous American fridge and some cleverly placed flowers and pots and decorative boxes.

'Who did your décor, Danielle? It's magnificent and although it's girly, it's not *so* much that your husband would prefer to eat his dinner in the shed.'

Danielle laughed as she gave Maia her cup of coffee. The matching cup and saucer had large peony roses emblazoned on them with silver trimming at the edges. The milk jug and sugar bowl matched and the napkin she was offered to drape over Maia's lap picked up the colour. Everything was totally gorgeous to the extent that Maia felt as if she were messing the place just by being there.

'She did it all herself,' Rachel said, looking half proud and half annoyed. 'You would never be able to tell that it's far from all this she was raised.'

Danielle bit her lip and looked at her mother, and Maia could see there was a huge tension running between them. What had they been talking about before she arrived, she wondered. There was a definite atmosphere, and it wasn't one of a cosy mother–daughter chat.

'I was raised very far from it myself,' Maia said, taking a sip of the good, strong coffee.

'Is that so?' said Rachel, cocking her head to one side. 'You're such a peacock, you look like you come from somewhere exotic.'

'Mam!' Danielle said, looking horrified.

Maia held up her hand. 'Don't worry, Danielle,' she said. 'I admire a woman who speaks her mind and looks out for her kids. Well, Rachel, if you must know, I was born and reared in Westwood. I had a mother who pushed me into modelling, which I hated, but then it was through that I met my lovely man, Freddie, and it's thanks to him I live like a queen now in a place like this.'

Rachel considered this, then nodded her head. 'I come from Westwood as well,' she said. 'Which road you from?'

'The Avenue,' Maia said. 'You?'

'The Mill,' said Rachel. 'It's on the other side. Across the park. I'm still there.'

'So that's where you were raised?' Maia said to Danielle.

'Yeah. That's who I am,' Danielle said, looking sad. 'All of this is lovely, but it's really weird as well.'

Maia could feel herself warming to the girl. She was obviously being pulled between two different worlds, and Maia could relate to that. And she was so young. It was hard to trust your own instincts at that age. That was the one thing Maia loved about getting older, you got way more bolshie into the bargain. Danielle could do with a bit of edge to her.

'That's gas we're from around the same area and ended up here,' Maia said.

'Both of you on the coattails of men,' Rachel said, her eyebrow raised.

'Whatever it takes,' Maia murmured.

'This one has great notions now,' Rachel said, nodding at Danielle, 'but she can't cop on to the fact that all this bling is blinding her to what she should be doing.'

'And what's that?' Maia asked.

'I put blood, sweat and tears into her education,' Rachel said proudly, 'and it paid off. She only went and got a place in Trinity, to study law. I was made up for her. Nothing like it ever seen in my family. And what's she doing? Sitting here, on her pampered arse, buying stuff and wasting time.'

So that's what they were talking about, Maia thought. She could see both sides of this immediately, and she understood why there was so much tension in the room.

'Have you given up on it?' she asked Danielle.

'No!' Danielle said, her eyes wide. 'Of course not. I slogged for it and I've dreamed of going to college since I was little. It's just . . . things happened and I didn't expect them and . . . you know . . .'

'Are you allowed to tell her?' Rachel demanded, 'or has that mother-in-law of yours got you to sign a confidentiality agreement? In blood, knowing her.'

'I don't want Danielle to talk about anything she doesn't want to,' Maia said, feeling uncomfortable. 'We only just met and . . .'

'I'm pregnant,' Danielle whispered. 'No one's supposed to know.'

'Oh,' Maia said. 'Well . . . that's wonderful news. You and Justin must be so happy.'

'We are,' Danielle said, casting a fearful glance at her mother.

'Happy,' her mother spat. 'Happy that your life's over, is it? That you'll be elbow-deep in nappies instead of law books? I can't do this, Danielle. I'm going home.'

'Hang on,' Maia said, reaching out towards her. 'Can I just tell you one thing?'

Rachel sat back down heavily with a sigh. 'Go on then.'

'My husband, Freddie, once he started making money, my family started making comments, you know, about me having notions about myself and getting above myself, all that kind of thing. When he started making big money and bought us the house here, my family couldn't handle it at all. They did visit a few times, but it was a disaster. My mam couldn't bear to be in the house. It was way outside her comfort zone, and she couldn't handle it. I tried, but it just created this big rift between us, like the Grand Canyon suddenly opened up between there and here.' She looked Rachel dead in the eye. 'I haven't seen or spoken to my mam in seventeen years,' she said, pausing to let that sink in. 'She saw my twins about six times in their first year, and not since. Her sense that I was living a lie meant she could never, ever be happy for me, and that ended our whole relationship. Things are more fragile than you think, Rachel, believe me.'

Rachel stared at her for a few moments, then bent her head. It took a few moments for Danielle and Maia to realise she was crying quietly.

'Oh Mam,' Danielle said, rushing around to hug her. 'It's okay.'

'I know,' Rachel said, patting her hand. 'This is so hard for me, Danielle, after all your work and getting that place, I just felt so proud of you.'

'I'm going to go back,' Danielle said. 'I've just taken a year out. But I'll be finishing that degree, I promise you. Justin is one hundred per cent behind me and he's going to help me make it happen. I still want it, Mam, I just have to be patient.'

Her mother nodded, and Maia's heart broke for her. She wasn't being a cow, she was genuinely upset for her daughter and all she felt she'd lost.

'Rachel,' she said gently, 'once you marry into money, you're made up, everything's possible. Danielle won't be a struggling single mother trying to afford childcare while studying. She'll have the backing of a very wealthy family. She'll easily be able to pick up her studies and see them through.'

Rachel nodded wearily. 'Do you know what, Maia? You're right. I thought you were a dense airhead walking through that door . . .'

'Jesus, don't hold back, Rachel,' Maia said, 'tell me how you really feel.'

Rachel and Danielle both shook with laughter.

'*But*,' Rachel said, 'you've your head screwed on right, and I do hear what you're saying. I'm glad Danielle has you nearby. You'll be a good influence.'

Maia laughed. 'Well that's the first time in my whole life anyone's ever called me that!'

Danielle looked so relieved, Maia couldn't help smiling.

'Come on, you,' she said. 'Where's your hostessing? You must have some cake around here. Let's freshen up these coffees, break out the cake and have a proper chat.'

Danielle started opening cupboards and getting out plates.

'So, Danielle, what's this mother-in-law like? Your mother mentioned something about signing stuff in blood?'

Danielle sliced an apple tart and filled the three plates and handed them out.

'Don't get me started,' she said.

'Ooh, my favourite conversation opener!' Maia said. 'Tell all.'

Danielle shook her head. 'She dresses like royalty, but she has no basic manners. Too much money and it's gone to her head. She treats me like I'm after her son for his money and nothing else. I'd say she thinks I got myself knocked up on purpose to trap him. She ordered us to keep it quiet, and I keep wondering if she's hoping we'll break up before anyone knows.'

'She sounds like a right piece of work,' Maia said. 'Makes Freddie's awful mother look like a pussy-cat.'

'Don't take it from her,' Rachel said. 'You're as good as anyone. And if you change your mind about Justin, you just come straight home. I'll help with the baby while you go back to college.'

Maia could see Danielle's shoulders stiffen. It was going to take more than one honest conversation to clear the air fully between those two.

'Actually,' Danielle said, looking at the mother, 'she's insisted you and me go to some big party at their house.'

'Me?' Rachel said. 'No way, forget it, Danielle. I can't mix with that type. I wouldn't have the clothes, for starters. I don't want to be going all the way out to Meath for her to laugh and sneer at me. No thanks.'

'Just think about it,' Danielle pleaded. 'I can't get out of it because Justin wants us to go, and it would be great to have someone to talk to. Don't say no yet. Just think about it.'

'You can borrow clothes from me,' Maia said.

Rachel looked at her, then threw back her head and laughed. 'Eh, we don't quite match up, Maia, love, in case you haven't noticed. If I put on that get-up, I'd be pure mutton dressed as lamb.'

'I've a walk-in wardrobe full of stuff,' Maia said. 'There'll be something in there you like, guaranteed. Don't let the clothes thing put you off is all I'm saying. You can go through everything I have and pick whatever you want. Take the eye out of the grand Mrs Johnston.'

'Thanks so much,' Danielle said. 'I was dreading having to pick something.'

'Sure, we can go shopping in Vayhill,' Maia said. 'I'll get you decked out good and proper.'

'What about you?' Rachel said. 'You said you have twins.'

Maia nodded. 'Zach and Zara, they're eighteen. Just finished school. Zach is heading to America to start college in the New Year, and Zara is travelling and then taking up a place in Queen's next year.'

'Impressive,' Rachel said.

Maia shrugged. 'Just sounds lonely to me.'

Rachel smiled. 'It's a tough time, when they fly the nest,' she said.

'Better change the subject before I start blubbing everywhere,' Maia said, and she meant it. She was so emotional these days, she was crying at the drop of a hat.

'What about the famous Freddie then?' Rachel asked. 'What does he do to keep you in such luxury?'

Maia felt her face redden. What does Freddie do, she thought, good question. She felt like she no longer knew.

'He's in jewellery,' she said. 'Has a shop down in Vayhill. Actually,' she said, looking at the clock on the wall, 'I'd better be getting back because he'll expect dinner when he gets in.' She got up and brushed crumbs off her skirt. 'Your house is magnificent,' she said to Danielle, 'and I hope you'll be very happy here.'

Danielle smiled gratefully. 'Thanks so much for coming over. And the gift. I'm really glad you got to meet my mam.'

'Me too,' Maia said. 'It's been an interesting afternoon.'

'I better go, too, before my car turns into a pumpkin,' Rachel said. 'This is all a bit fairytale for me. I still can't get my head around it.'

'I'm still just me,' Danielle said, and it hurt Maia to hear it because she remembered saying those exact same words herself. Not that it had made any difference.

She said goodbye and headed back across the road to her own house. Freddie was rarely home before 9 p.m. these days, and he never wanted dinner at that hour. He'd just raid the presses for crisps and beer and eat junk on the sofa staring at the telly. She'd just said that to get out of there before Rachel could think up any more questions to fire at her.

All the same, it had been a very interesting afternoon. She'd had an insight into the Johnston family and it was fascinating. Who knew that the glamorous woman who graced the society pages in her glossy magazines was such a cow? And Danielle pregnant, now that she hadn't seen coming. She'd have to invite her and Justin to her party and get a good look at the two of them and how they were together. Danielle definitely didn't strike her as the man-trapping type, and God knows he'd have his pick of far more savvy and groomed women, so on the whole, she reckoned it probably was love. She just hoped Rachel could come to see that and forgive Danielle for not going along the path she'd laid out for her. Poor Danielle, she thought, everyone had an opinion on what she should be doing, and she was trying to find a way to suit them all. Maia knew from bitter experience that you could never please everyone. It just might take Danielle a while to figure that out.

Chapter 13

NANCY COULDN'T SIT DOWN, COULDN'T STAND still, couldn't even think straight. She felt like she was in a dream, the kind where moving feels like pushing through water and if you scream, nothing comes out. She hated those dreams.

She looked at the clock for the millionth time. Fifteen more minutes. She felt sick, but she tried to breathe deeply and calm herself. She focused on preparing a pot of coffee on the stove and then showering the jam and cream sponge cake she'd baked with icing sugar. The aromas from the baking filled the kitchen and made it feel warm and homely. She really hoped she had made the right decision.

After she'd received the letter from the adoption agency, she'd been able to think of nothing else for a week. She felt she should reply in a timely fashion, so she set herself a deadline to reply. One week to the day after receiving the letter, she took her courage in her hands and wrote a reply, confirming that she would meet with David, or Steve as she had to keep correcting herself. She had received a phone call the very next day from a nice woman called Angela who had set up the meeting. She was going to come to the first one, just to help break the ice.

'You might feel very emotional, Nancy,' she had said.

No shit, lady, Nancy had wanted to say, but managed to hold her tongue.

So now it was the day, and almost the time, and Nancy was a bag of nerves. She had no idea what to expect. And she almost felt a little afraid of who she would be after this meeting. She'd be a mother, someone's mother. Would she still feel like herself?

'Silly old woman,' she scolded herself. 'Just focus on him and stop being selfish.' Nelly looked at her enquiringly. 'Don't mind me, Nelly,' she said, 'just talking to myself as usual.'

The doorbell rang and Nelly barked and Nancy had to steady herself on the back of a chair.

'Alright Nelly, my love,' she said, 'it's time.'

When she opened the front door, all she could see was a large woman in a black skirt suit.

'Hello, I'm Angela,' she said, sticking out her hand.

'Hi Angela,' Nancy said, shaking her hand. 'Come on in.'

Angela stepped inside, and there he was, standing on the doorstep, smiling at her.

'Steve?' she said uncertainly.

'Yes,' he said, and he looked as shaken with emotion as she felt. 'My God, I can't believe I'm finally meeting my mother. May I hug you?'

Nancy was so taken aback, she stood there like a fish, her mouth opening and closing and no sounds coming out. She managed to nod, and this tall man engulfed her in a warm embrace. Nothing about him was familiar – not his body shape, his smell, his facial features – she'd never have picked him out as a Smyth. She realised now she had expected him to look like her father, but he wasn't a bit like him. Mercifully, he didn't look anything like PJ either. That would have been incredibly difficult.

'Thanks so much for letting me meet you,' he said.

'I . . . of course,' she stammered. 'I didn't want to let you down.'

'I brought you this,' he said, picking up a wine bag from where he'd left it on the doorstep. 'Hope you like red.'

'I love it, thank you,' Nancy said. She wasn't going to get into her teetotalism just yet.

'I think we'll all step inside now,' Angela said. 'Let's sit down and get acquainted.'

Steve looked around as Nancy led them through to the kitchen.

'This is a lovely home. Do you live with your family?' he asked tentatively.

'No, I live alone,' Nancy said. 'My husband died twenty-two years ago, so it's just me and Nelly now.'

'I love dogs,' Steve said, bending down to pat Nelly's head. 'Best companions in the world.'

They sat down at the table, and Nancy saw that her hands were shaking as she cut the cake and poured coffees.

'So, this is our first meeting,' Angela said, beaming at them. 'And hopefully there will be more, but I just want to emphasise that there's no obligation on either of you to meet up again, okay? This is just exploration, toe in the water stuff for now, okay? Are we clear?'

Nancy felt deeply irritated by Angela's schoolteacher tone, but Steve didn't seem to mind. He was looking all around, interested in everything.

'I love this kitchen. I've always wanted a table like this, that's good solid wood, last a lifetime. And it's so cosy. Must be well insulated, well built, I'd say. It's a great spot to live, so close to everything but when you're here, it's so quiet, like being in the country. Although I'd say the mortgages on these places are huge, are they?' he said, talking a mile a minute.

Nancy looked at Angela, then back at Steve. She'd imagined he'd have a million questions for her, but that wasn't one of them. Why on earth was he talking like an estate agent?

'Are you an estate agent?' Nancy asked.

He threw back his head and laughed. 'God, no. I'm a plumber. Love doing that. I'd never make an estate agent. No good with numbers. Sorry, I'm . . . I'm just really nervous and I talk utter gibberish when I'm nervous.'

Nancy laughed. 'I know exactly what you mean. My head's gone blank. It's all very strange, isn't it?'

He nodded. 'I'm making an eejit of myself here, but it's because I've waited for this moment and now that it's here, I barely know what to say.'

Nancy's heart went out to him. Here she was, worrying about her own feelings and he was in turmoil.

'It's only natural that you're feeling a bit stressed. I am too. It's the kind of thing you can't really prepare for, isn't it? But is there . . . anything you want to ask me?' she said, although she dreaded his answer.

'Em . . .' he looked over at Angela. 'Well, I don't have much information on my life pre-adoption. You were in a Magdalene Laundry, weren't you?'

'Yes, we were,' Nancy said. 'I was only sixteen when I discovered I was pregnant.' She hesitated, she didn't want him to know the circumstances of his conception. It was long ago now, and it would only hurt him unnecessarily to know the truth. 'Those were very different times, so being pregnant out of wedlock was a terrible sin.'

'I understand,' he said. 'And I'm so sorry you had to go through that. But thank you for getting me through it.'

Nancy swallowed back tears. 'I named you David. I adored you. I was allowed to keep you for a month, and I minded you and planned to bring you up myself. But then the nuns found a couple who wanted to adopt and they forced me to give you up. I did want you Da—, Steve. You weren't unwanted. But I had no way at all to prevent them taking you away from me.'

'That must have been so hard,' he said.

He looked at her so kindly and with such empathy that Nancy felt a stab of grief that she wasn't bowled over by love. Was she so utterly non-maternal that she couldn't even feel a connection to her own flesh and blood? What kind of woman was she?

'They were wrong to do that, but they were very different times, as you say. But it means the world to me to know that I was wanted. I did wonder over the years. And in case you were worried about me, my adoptive parents were good to me. I had a happy childhood and I'm doing well and they have always treated me as their own.'

'I'm really glad to know that,' Nancy said. 'I'm so sorry you had such a start in life.'

'You know,' Steve said, looking towards the window, 'I love gardens. Would you like to show me around the garden? It's easier to walk and talk.'

'You're absolutely right,' Nancy said, standing up. 'Good idea.'

She led him out to the garden, leaving Angela to enjoy the cake. She told him about the kingfishers and what she'd learned about them. He talked easily, telling her about his childhood and his job, the fact that he was single but okay with it. The whole time, Nancy was watching him, hoping she'd feel something, some pull that would let her know this was her David, some connection. But she felt nothing. It was all too long ago, she supposed.

'You know, I used to write you letters,' he said, as they stood looking at the river. 'Once I found out I was adopted.'

'Really?' Nancy said. 'That's kind of heartbreaking.'

'My parents told me I was adopted when I was fifteen. They were scared to tell me, I think, that's why they left it so late. It was hard to hear, to be honest. I hadn't a clue, so I felt like I'd been sort of tricked, you know. I pulled away from them for a while, and the only person I could confide in was you, my mother. So I'd write letters telling you all about myself and asking you to come for me. I had nowhere to send them, of course, but it made me feel better to write them.'

'That's so lovely,' Nancy said. 'And I'm so sorry I wasn't there. If there was any way, I would have made it work. But I was only sixteen then, powerless, and I was up against the Church. Talk about David and Goliath.'

He smiled. 'Exactly. And I really do get that, Nancy. I don't blame you or think that you gave me away or anything, just so you know. I believe you that you tried and the system broke you. I've read up on the Laundries, and the stuff that went on was incredible. There was no way a young girl could have changed anything.'

Nancy nodded. 'It's a dark part of our history alright,' she said. 'It scarred my life for a long time, and I made some terrible decisions, but I've made peace with myself over the years. And to hear that you had good parents, that really helps as well.'

'I was just born at the wrong time,' he said.

'Yep,' Nancy said. 'The odds were against us.'

They smiled at each other.

'Are your parents upset that we're meeting?' she asked.

He sighed. 'I think they are a bit, yes. I've been very honest with them all the way along, to try to make sure they're okay with it, but I think they do feel a bit mixed up about it. But then, they love me, and they know it's important to me to meet my real mother.'

Real mother. Nancy was beginning to feel upset that she didn't feel anything maternal towards him. He was a lovely guy, easy-going and chatty, but he was just a stranger. There was no big 'oh' moment, no falling in love, no sense of her son coming home . . . nothing. He chattered on, but Nancy was feeling overwhelmed. She reckoned this proved what she'd said all along – she was not cut out to be a mother. It just wasn't in her. And now this poor man was looking for his mother, and all he'd found was her. This was meant to be special, and she was failing him – again.

'Well this has gone really well,' Angela said when they came back into the kitchen. 'We always recommend no more than half-an-hour for the first meeting, as it can be a bit difficult to process. So I'd like to suggest that we leave now, Steve, if that's okay by you, Nancy?'

Nancy nodded. She felt like crying, so the sooner they left, the better.

'Okey-dokey, we'll say our goodbyes then. And maybe you two could indicate if you'd like to meet up again?'

'I'd like to, if that's okay by you, Nancy,' Steve said. 'Could I maybe drop by next week?'

'Sure,' Nancy heard herself say. She wasn't at all sure, but how the hell could you say 'No thank you' to the son you'd abandoned. It wasn't really an option.

'I'll send you each other's numbers then,' said Angela, 'and you can take it from here. Thank you for your hospitality, Nancy.'

When the front door closed behind them, it was all Nancy could do not to slither to the floor, curl up in a ball and wail. What the hell had just happened? She was a stone, an unfeeling stone – why hadn't she felt a sense of homecoming? She had to be there for him now. He was a wonderful man, easy company and not pushy, and he deserved a good mother, an open-armed mother who made him feel loved and special. He didn't deserve Nancy, she was useless at this. The poor man!

She ordered herself to calm down. This was silly. He was only one month old when she'd last seen him, and he was a middle-aged man now, so of course he felt like a stranger. Why wouldn't he, for crying out loud? She just had to be sensible and let time take its course. They'd get used to one another and no doubt forge a connection. It didn't matter that it hadn't happened immediately. She resolved to be the best mother she could be to Steve. It might not come naturally to her, but she had to put him first now, think of his needs and strive to fulfil them. She wanted to give him back whatever she could, especially as he had been so brave to come looking for her. She'd have to park those feelings of not being maternal towards him and work on their friendship. She wanted to do that for him.

She was just walking away from the front door, trying to steady her breathing, when the doorbell rang. They must have left something behind, she thought, looking around as she walked to the dor.

She opened the door, but it wasn't Angela and Steve, it was a man in leather motorcycle gear with a helmet under his arm.

'Hiya missus,' he said. 'Just delivering this to you.' He pushed a padded envelope into her hands, then turned and walked away without another word.

She looked down at the envelope he'd given her. It had a Vayhill and District Local Authority stamp on it.

'Oh God, what the hell now?' she said to Nelly. 'Given the way this day is going, it could be anything.'

She went back to the kitchen and sat down at the table and opened up the envelope and took out a sheaf of papers. She sat there staring at them in utter shock. The letter told her that she had two months before her home was demolished. She stared at the words *Compulsory Purchase Order*. Dear sweet Jesus, they couldn't! They were giving her four hundred grand to get out and buy a new place somewhere else. And she had to be out by Christmas. She looked around her cosy kitchen. There was no way she could give up Kingfisher Road.

Shaking, she picked up her mobile and called her solicitor.

'Read that again,' said Sean, who'd taken her call immediately, bless him. 'It says . . . *Due to the volume of traffic coming in and out of Vayhill town centre we have decided to widen the road. In order to carry out these works we will need to remove numbers five and six Kingfisher Road.* Then they give the amount I'm being offered and how they would like me to vacate the premises as soon as possible. Oh dear Lord, Sean. It's a CPO and it seems there's damn all that I can do about it. Please tell me I'm wrong about that.'

'Don't panic,' Sean said briskly. 'I'll get straight on to it. Can you pop by sometime today with the letter and I'll take a copy of it? Then I'll start proceedings immediately to stop this.'

'Can I take a picture of it and email it over?' she said.

'Yes, do that,' Sean said. 'It's quicker. I forget I'm living in the technological age sometimes.'

'Do you think I've any chance of saving my home?'

'It'll be a tough one to overturn, I can't lie to you,' said Sean. 'But if you could get your neighbours together and ask them to back you up and perhaps send letters of complaint to the Authority, that wouldn't go astray.'

'Oh yes, they'll help,' she said. 'Damn right, they will. We're a very tight community here. I can definitely count on my neighbours for support.'

As soon as she had finished the call, she smoothed out the hated letter on the table and took a photo and emailed it straight to Sean's office. Then she sat there, just staring until the words swam on the page. It all looked so official and final. *Vacate the premises . . . compulsory . . . please accept the current market value . . .*

Nancy was in a state of shock. She knew she should get up and go over to one of her friends, to Maia or Betsy or Pearl, but she couldn't move. She felt like her body was paralysed. Tears rolled down her cheeks, but she didn't make a sound. This was all too much. First Steve, now this. She had a horrible feeling that Steve turning up had somehow heralded the end of her life as she knew it. If she had to leave Kingfisher Road, she couldn't cope. Her best friends in the world were here, and she adored her life with them. She wanted to grow old and die here and have her ashes scattered in her flowerbeds. This just couldn't be happening.

Out of the corner of her eye, she spotted the gaudy wine bag. Her hands started to shake. She jumped up and rushed over and grabbed it, yanking the bottle out. She didn't even look at the label, just twisted the cap and brought the bottle close to her lips. She smelled the alcohol curling up out of it, twisting around her, so seductive. She put the bottle a little closer, touching her lips now. One small lift of her arm, and it would be done. Her troubles would float away. She could chase her fear down the neck of that bottle and drown it.

With a cry, she suddenly turned the bottle upside-down and let all the wine flow out and down the plughole. She collapsed against the counter, sobbing. She let it all out, let herself cry it out. Her breath came in gasps, shuddering through her, then slowly it began to subside. Eventually, she stood up straight, rubbed her eyes with the back of her hand.

'Right, Nancy old girl, it's time for one hell of a fight.'

Chapter 14

LILY-ROSE ARRIVED AND IT WAS AS IF THE HOUSE had been lit up. She was larger than life and always full of stories. In fact, most of her visits began with, 'wait until I tell you Auntie Pearl' and ended with 'see you again soon, oh, oh I almost forgot . . .' as she ran back in again for just one more story that had popped into her head. Pearl loved her so and was always thrilled to see her coming in the door.

'Come in, come in,' she said to Lily-Rose and her new husband, Leo. She hugged them both tightly. 'I'm so delighted to see you.'

'We just flew in this afternoon, so we thought we'd hop in and say hello to you on our way home. We won't stay long, but we're hoping we can take you out for dinner next week and bore you with honeymoon photos?'

'Any time,' Pearl said, thrilled at the idea. 'I'd love a nice meal out, that would be lovely. But do stop for ten minutes anyway. Would you like a coffee?'

'After being on that plane for twelve hours, I'd murder one,' Leo said.

Pearl ushered them into the kitchen, where Drew and Tommy were playing Snap.

'Lily-Rose!' Drew squealed. 'I love you.'

He enveloped his cousin in a bear hug, and she laughed.

'Still the best welcomes, Drew. No one will ever beat you!'

'My God, I'll have to up my game,' Leo said, going over to shake hands with Tommy.

'He adores her,' Tommy said. 'No wedding ring is going to change that.'

'It's lovely,' Leo said, smiling over as Drew held Lily-Rose's hand and led her to the sofa. 'You must get such joy out of minding him.'

Tommy smiled and nodded. 'Yep, that's for sure. I'd be lost without Drew. I learn more from him than he does from me.'

Pearl's heart soared – she loved to hear Tommy speak of his affection and love for Drew. It was the opposite end of the spectrum from how Seth looked at Drew, and it made her so happy that Drew had that constant love from a male figure in his life. It made her love Tommy, too, and she smiled a private smile for him. He winked at her.

'So how was the honeymoon?' Pearl asked, bringing a tray of coffees and biscuits over to the table.

'New Zealand is so amazing,' Lily-Rose said. 'It was so hard to tear ourselves away and come home. We had just the most incredible holiday.' She smiled adoringly at her new husband.

'Going back to work will be a real culture shock,' Leo said. 'But at least we have another few days before we have to face into that.'

'Enjoy every second of it,' Pearl said. 'It's such an important time.'

'And I brought a present for my favourite cousin,' Lily-Rose said, reaching into her bag.

Drew clapped his hands, his eyes shining. Lily-Rose drew out a brightly coloured gift bag and put it into his hands. Drew yanked it open and pulled out a soft, cuddly penguin.

'I love it,' he announced, cuddling it tight. 'I'll take it to bed. What's its name?'

'That's for you to decide, Drew,' Lily-Rose said. 'It's a blue penguin, one of the native animals. They are so adorable.'

'Em . . . its name is . . .' Drew held up the cuddly toy and peered at it, 'I know . . . Bluebob.'

Pearl laughed. 'You know what, Drew, that suits him perfectly. Hello, Bluebob!'

'Hello Mummy,' Drew said, waving the penguin at her. 'He likes you. And he likes Tommy, too. I think you and Tommy are his favourite people.'

'Ah, that's so cute,' Lily-Rose said, giving Drew a kiss on the cheek. 'I hope you and Bluebob will be very happy together.'

'Can I show him your house, Tommy?' Drew said, jumping up.

'Sure thing,' Tommy said. 'I'll take him down with me,' he said to Pearl, 'so you can have a chat and get ready for tonight.' He and Drew walked off hand in hand.

'What's tonight?' Lily-Rose said.

'Oh, just supper club,' Pearl said. 'In other words, me and my neighbours get together to eat, gossip and drink wine. We do it about once a month, and the new neighbour is coming along for the first time tonight.'

'So is the emphasis on the gourmet cooking?' Leo asked with a grin.

'I'd love to say yes,' Pearl said, laughing, 'but with my cooking skills, I tend to try to blind them with wine and then bleed them for gossip!'

'That's my kind of night out,' Lily-Rose said. 'Sounds like great fun.'

'You're both welcome to stay,' Pearl said.

'Oh no.' Lily-Rose shook her head. 'We're pooped, and there's no way you'd have good-quality gossip with us in your midst. No, we'll head on home and enjoy a night's sleep in our own bed.'

'No problem,' Pearl said. 'Seth's away on duty, so I'm free any night you want next week.'

'I'll be in touch,' Lily-Rose said. 'Although, before we go, we got a little something for you too.' She pulled out a small gift bag, wrapped beautifully with a pink satin bow. 'This is for you, from both of us.'

'Oh you shouldn't have,' Pearl said. 'Wasting time shopping for me while on your honeymoon.'

'We wanted to thank you from the bottom of our hearts for the wedding day you gave us,' Leo said. 'It was even better than we'd dared hope, and that was down to the care and attention you lavished on it. We appreciate it so much.'

Pearl felt like crying. It wasn't often anyone noticed her efforts, let alone commended them. She carefully untied the bow and slipped a square jewellery box out of the bag. She opened it, and on a bed of pink velvet lay an exquisite gold necklace. It had a thin, elegant chain, with a gold heart shape adorning it, complete with tiny pink stones.

'Oh I love it so much,' Pearl said, running her fingertip over it. 'It's beautiful. Perfectly me. Thank you,' she said, going across to kiss each of them in turn.

'Here, let me,' Leo said, and she turned so he could place the necklace over her head, then clasp it shut.

'It's beautiful,' Lily-Rose said. 'And it hangs just in the right spot.'

'I think I'm going to cry,' Pearl said, feeling embarrassed. 'I feel very spoiled.'

'You deserve a bit of spoiling,' Lily-Rose said. 'You've been doing that for us all our lives.'

After they'd left, Pearl admired her necklace in the hall mirror, then remembered she had only an hour before the ladies all descended. She went to the kitchen and set to work. She had prepared a simple chicken pie, and now she got going on the sides – a warm mustard-seed potato salad, a beetroot slaw, a tasty dish of paprika-fried chick-peas and a simple green salad. She had made brownies for dessert, and they were already on a serving platter, ready to go. She was just opening a couple of bottles of wine when Drew and Tommy came back in.

'I'm tired, Mum,' Drew said.

The three of them had gone swimming earlier, and that always worked its magic on him and made him easier to manage at bedtime.

'We're going upstairs to get into PJs and I'll read him a bedtime story,' Tommy said. 'You go on up, Drew, I'm right behind you.'

Drew wandered off and when he was out of sight, Tommy slid his hands around Pearl's waist and drew her close for a kiss. She wrapped her arms around his neck and kissed him deeply.

'I love you,' she said.

'Well I'm going to love you and leave you,' he said, teasing her. 'I don't want to be in the middle of the ladies, so I'll put Drew to bed and then I'm going to meet Cormac for a pint or two down the road. Is that okay?'

'Of course. Do you good to get out,' she said. 'And when you come home, I'll creep down to the mews to see you.'

'I look forward to it,' he said with a grin, giving her one last kiss. 'Don't let them eat all of those fabulous looking brownies.'

'I'll do my best,' she said as he left to go to see to Drew.

Pearl left the wine to breathe, checked the clock and decided it was time to light the candles, draw the curtains and switch on some low lamps. Everything was perfect. She was looking forward to a glass of wine and a good chat.

At eight o'clock exactly, the doorbell rang. Pearl smiled to herself, knowing it had to be Betsy. She was always punctual. She went to open the door.

'Betsy, come in,' she said, giving her a big hug. 'You're the first. The perfect guest, as always.'

'Well, maybe not tonight,' Betsy said, looking anxious. 'I'm sorry, but my daughter-in-law has insisted on joining us. I couldn't dissuade her.'

'Where is she?' Pearl said, peering into the darkness behind Betsy's shoulder.

'She wouldn't dream of being on time,' Betsy said drily. 'She's doing something or other and will follow over.'

'Right, well come in and we'll get fortified with a bit of wine before then,' Pearl said.

She poured out two generous glasses of red, then the doorbell rang again. On the doorstep were Maia and Nancy.

'Good evening,' Maia called. 'I'm so hungry and this place smells good.'

'Great to see you,' Pearl said. 'Come on in, Betsy's inside. Apparently we're being joined by Tasha tonight. Are you okay, Nancy?' she asked, looking closely at the older woman. 'You look pale. Are you tired?'

'I'm okay,' Nancy said and gave a watery smile. Pearl

wasn't convinced. She'd have to pursue this once they were all relaxed and fed.

'Come on in, the stove is lit,' she said. 'Red or white?'

She poured a white wine for Maia and an elderflower cordial for Nancy. When the doorbell sounded again, Maia said, 'I'll get it. You concentrate on feeding me.'

Pearl laughed. 'I'll get the plates warmed,' she said.

Maia went out and returned with Danielle and Tasha. Danielle looked a bit shell-shocked and kept looking over at Tasha as if she might do something crazy any minute.

'Welcome to both of you,' Pearl called out. 'Delighted to meet you, Tasha. And delighted you're joining us, Danielle,' she said warmly. 'May I get you a drink?'

'I'll have the same as Nancy,' Danielle said. She smiled nervously. 'I'm not really a drinker.'

'Great. I'll have hers as well then,' Tasha said loudly. 'I'll take a glass of each, mate. Can never decide between red and white, so I just go for both.' She laughed at her own joke, but no one else did. Pearl could see that Betsy was mortified, and she felt for her.

'I'll start you on a red, Tasha, okay, and then you can help yourself as we go along. Right, if you'll all sit down, we'd better feed Maia before she has a hangry tantrum.'

The food was delicious, but the atmosphere was a little strained because Tasha seemed determined to behave as badly as possible. She sat cross-legged in her chair, swigged down the wine like it was water and ate with her mouth open. Pearl had to continually avert her eyes so she wouldn't feel sick. How Betsy was living with her every day was beyond her. She was a nightmare.

'So do any of you have a job?' Tasha asked, her tone already accusing. 'Anyone go out and earn a living, no?'

'I'm retired,' Nancy said. 'I worked all my life, though.'

'We've all had jobs,' Maia said, 'but having a family changes things.'

'Women who give up and blame it on their kids are weak,' Tasha said.

'Oh, and what's your career, Tasha?' Maia said with a dangerous edge to her voice. Pearl knew that tone, it meant Maia was struggling to keep her temper.

'I don't believe in the corporate, consumerist culture,' Tasha said, gulping down more wine. 'I choose to exist outside of all that bullshit.'

'Right, and how does that make you different from us, then?' Maia asked.

'I am *so* different from you, mate,' Tasha sneered, pointing her fork at Maia. 'From all of you,' she said, jabbing her fork towards each in turn. 'You are consumer-zombies, housewives, spongers. You've never made a choice because you've gone through life blind. All this fancy stuff and comfort,' she said, looking contemptuously around Pearl's kitchen, 'it's all masking the fact that you're sexually dissatisfied and living without purpose. I feel sorry for you. Your lives are meaningless.'

There was a stunned silence, then Nancy burst out laughing, making everyone jump. Tasha looked at her in astonishment.

'You're a right little pain in the ass, aren't you?' Nancy said. 'I've never heard such codswallop in my life. You're a jumped-up little madam who probably comes from a nice middle-class family and believes you're a radical revolutionary because you don't shave your armpits.'

Pearl couldn't help noticing those hairy armpits herself. Tasha was pretty much showing them off in her vest top.

Tasha's face went red and she appeared to be having trouble breathing. She was staring at Nancy in shock.

'What the hell do you know, you daft old woman?' she snarled.

'Plenty more than you,' Nancy retorted, her voice equally icy. 'Don't you come in here and tell us you're better than us. You haven't even the intelligence to talk to people, to find out about their lives. You're just a walking set of assumptions based on nothing. Now you either sit up, behave and talk like an adult, or you leave. Pearl didn't produce this beautiful meal to have you sit there like a sulky child and ruin it. You like choices, so here's your chance to make another one – stay with respect or leave now?'

Pearl looked over at Betsy, to see what she made of her daughter-in-law being treated like this. She had never seen such a wicked smile on Betsy's face before. She was positively glowing. Fair play, Nancy, Pearl thought, you're doing everyone a favour.

Tasha jumped up so fast, her chair fell over. 'I'm leaving. You are a pack of witches and there's no way I'm sitting here listening to you talk about frickin' . . . nails or . . . dresses or something stupid like that. I'm out of here.' She grabbed the bottle of wine and stalked out, slamming the front door shut behind her so hard, the whole house seemed to shake. Then there was silence.

'Jesus Christ,' Danielle said, then she started laughing. 'If these supper clubs are always like this, I'm definitely coming again.'

That set them all off, and they sat there laughing like bold schoolchildren. Betsy had to dry her eyes with her napkin.

'Oh Nancy, that's the best thing I've seen in a long time,' Betsy said. 'I'd have paid good money to see that. I love you for doing that. She's making my life a living hell, but at least you gave her a taste of her own medicine.'

'I just wish I'd been quick enough to wrestle that bottle out of her hand,' Nancy said. 'Cheek of her to take it like that.'

'Oh Betsy,' Maia said, 'you have got to get her out of your house and quick. Are you putting up with that at every meal?'

Betsy nodded. 'Every one,' she said, no longer laughing. 'I've never met anyone like her. I've no idea why she's so angry all the time, but it's just exhausting. Noel and I are at our wits' end.'

'Can you not ask her to leave?' Danielle said.

'But then she'd go and take Arnie,' Betsy said, twisting her napkin in her hand. 'I can't bear the idea of that. She wants to take him to a squat in Dublin, some cold ancient building with a pile of men living in it. She's mad.'

'Well, look, as long as she's there, use our houses as much as you like,' Maia said. 'You don't even have to talk to me. Just set yourself up on a couch and enjoy the peace and quiet.'

'Thank you,' Betsy said, smiling at her. 'You're always so kind, Maia.'

'And mine too,' Danielle said. 'It's usually just me anyway, and it's huge. Come over anytime.'

'Lord, I need a top-up after that drama,' Maia said. 'Is there another bottle of red, Pearl?'

'I'll get it,' Pearl said, and she went and took another bottle from the wine-holder and opened it. She poured some into Maia's glass, and into her own.

'Well I'm very, very glad you made her leave, Nancy,' she said, sitting down again. 'It was ruining the whole vibe. Talk about tension!'

'I've seen her type before,' Nancy said. 'Think they're remaking the world. She'll learn. Although probably the hard way.'

'What Graham ever saw in her I'll never know,' Betsy said. 'But thank you, all of you. For running her off and for making me laugh. I really needed that. I tell you, if I didn't live on Kingfisher Road with you all, I'd be a basket case. You're my sanity.'

'Cheers to that,' Maia said, raising her glass and they all joined her in the toast.

Pearl saw Nancy bend her head and thought she was laughing about Tasha again, but then she saw her shoulders shuddering.

'Nancy?' she said.

Nancy held up her hand. 'Sorry, I'll be alright in a sec. I'm such a silly old fool.'

'Jesus, Nancy, what is it?' Maia said, looking stricken. They had always been very close. Pearl knew that Maia relied on Nancy hugely, especially for parenting advice, funnily enough, given that Nancy wasn't a mother. But she had always had a way with the twins and had helped Maia to keep them on the straight and narrow.

'Let's just chat and have fun,' Nancy said, raising her head and rubbing her eyes.

'No way!' Maia said. 'If something's upset you, out with it. We can help.'

Nancy shook her head sadly. 'I don't think you can,' she said. 'I have a bit of a desperate situation.'

'Tell us,' Maia cried. 'I'll do anything to help.'

'I got a letter from the council,' Nancy said, looking around at them. 'There's a road-widening scheme that's getting underway in a couple of months, and they need some of the land from Kingfisher Road. Two houses. Mine and number six.'

'What do you mean, need them?' Pearl asked.

Nancy's eyes filled with tears again. 'They want to acquire our houses and land by compulsory purchase order and demolish them to make way for the road. I have my solicitor on it, but it's not looking good.'

Pearl was absolutely stunned. The others were obviously deep in shock, too. They were all staring at Nancy, eyes wide.

'My God,' Betsy said, putting her hand to her chest. 'They can't . . . I mean . . . no . . .'

'What did your solicitor say?' Danielle asked. 'Surely there's some sort of appeal facility? I can research into it for you.'

'He's working on it and has contacted the council on my behalf. They've agreed to a meeting with me, but it sounds like they are holding firm. I'd say they'll just reiterate everything in the letter in person and order me to leave. A CPO is a legal instrument, so you don't really have any counterargument, you know?'

Maia looked like she was about to start crying too. 'They are *not* putting you out,' she said fiercely. 'It's your home. This is disgusting. How can they just swoop in and grab someone's property? It's not right. And I'll tell you something, I'll chain myself to your garden gates if I have to, because this is not happening.'

'I'm with you,' Pearl said. The idea of watching Nancy being forced to leave made her feel sick. 'If we stand together and get the other residents involved and reach out to any contacts we have, we can challenge this. There has to be a way to put them off and if there is, we'll find it. And if the worst does come to the worst, which it won't, you can come and live with me, Nancy. I genuinely mean that too. You will never be without a roof over your head as long as I'm living on Kingfisher Road. I'll build a second mews if I have to.'

Nancy smiled weakly around the table at her friends. 'Thank you so much,' she said. 'You're so wonderful. With you lot at my back, it makes me feel like maybe I can fight this.'

'Oh you can,' Maia said, looking scarily determined. 'They have no idea who they're messing with. We can set up a campaign.'

'What do you mean?' Nancy said.

'We can get your story out there,' Maia said. 'Radio, TV, social media. We get out there and make the council look like the vultures they are, damage their reputation, malign the whole shagging road project and get an army of voices on our side. They can't just steamroll through here then.'

'Yes, that's a brilliant idea,' Betsy said, sitting forward. 'We can plan a campaign to save the houses and keep the road further away. No one along this stretch will want a busy road being brought closer to the houses. I know that local radio presenter, Mattie what's-his-name, I've dealt with him on Residents' Association issues before. I'll call him tomorrow and see if we can book an interview.'

'I can look into the legal angle,' Danielle said. 'I know I'm not qualified yet, but I can read up on CPOs online and see if there's a loophole anywhere.'

'Excellent,' Maia said. 'I'll get the twins working on the

social media side of things. They will definitely want to help you, Nancy, they adore you. And I'll call my friend Julia, she works in PR, she'll be good for advice.'

Pearl looked around at these women, these old friends, and felt the force of the determination and their love for Nancy. The council didn't know what was about to hit them.

Chapter 15

'I'M WORRIED ABOUT HER,' MAIA SAID.

Silence.

'Freddie!'

He looked up guiltily from his phone. 'What?'

'I'm speaking to you,' Maia said, feeling stupidly close to tears. He was always staring at that bloody phone. It was like a barrier he put up between them so he didn't have to listen to her. She missed him so much at times like this, and yet the big lump was right there. Here and far away, that seemed to be her marriage now. 'I said, I'm worried about Pearl.'

'Pearl?' Freddie said, clearly tuning in for the first time. 'Why?'

'Seth has gone on his last tour of duty. By Christmas he'll be retired. I've tried to talk to her about it, but she keeps shutting down. It's as if she can't bear to think about it.'

'Jesus, who'd blame her?' Freddie said. 'I'd rather be thrown into the gorillas' den in the zoo than put alone in a house with that fella for any length of time. He's so army, he can't adjust to just being normal. Remember that time he told me he'd teach me how to polish me shoes properly! I nearly decked him.'

'Yeah,' said Maia, frowning. 'You're right. I feel so sorry

for her. And I've never been convinced that she actually loves him. He hides behind his holier than thou soldier crap, but at the end of the day I don't like the first thing about him. I've always felt there's stuff going on behind closed doors over there that the rest of us don't know about.' She sighed. 'I'll just have to stay close and let Pearl know I'm there if she wants to talk.'

'Right,' said Freddie, picking up his phone again, 'so is that what you wanted to talk to me about? I'll just head into the . . .'

'Oh no,' said Maia. 'You're not locking yourself in that study. I've two more things to talk to you about. I think you can give me ten minutes of your precious time.'

Freddie sighed and put his phone on the table. 'Two things. Right, hit me.'

Maia wanted to fling her arms around his neck and kiss him long and hard, to try to bring him back to her, but she pushed down that urge and sat down opposite him.

'The party,' she said. 'Just so you're up-to-date on things, I've sorted almost everything now. They're making us a marquee, and I've everything picked to go into it. I called that guy you recommended, and he's sending bar staff, glasses, the whole works. And the caterers are going to serve on the night as well as do all the cooking and everything. Invites have gone out now, and I've started getting replies, but I just wanted to double-check your invite list because it seemed short. So can you go through it again and add anyone else you want?'

'Yeah, sure. Just email it to me and I'll sit with it when I have time.'

'Okay. And on the food, do you think we should have

people go up to serve themselves buffet-style, or have the meals brought to the tables?'

'Definitely served up,' Freddie said. 'I want it to feel like a big party restaurant, you know. No wandering around with paper plates. I want proper Delft and cutlery and guests sitting back and enjoying it all.'

'Ooh, I love it when you're all decisive,' Maia said, grinning sexily at him. 'I think I've got it all under control then. So just get back to me on your list within twenty-four hours, okay?'

He saluted her. 'Yes, ma'am.'

'Now the other thing I wanted to mention is a bit, em, delicate.' Freddie's eyes kept darting to his phone, but Maia willed herself not to snap at him. 'Something has happened to Nancy.' That got his attention good and proper. He thought the absolute world of Nancy, especially as she was the one who had kept Maia together when the babies were small. Without Nancy, they would have all sunk into a depression.

'What's happened?' Freddie asked, focusing on her fully for the first time.

'The council have issued a compulsory purchase order for her cottage,' Maia said. 'They said she has to be out within six weeks. They're giving her money to buy a new place, but you know what it's like in Dublin now with the house prices. She'll have a hard time getting anywhere like it. Plus, she loves it here, of course, and wants to see out her days in that house. But they have the lawyers on their side and her solicitor is saying he can't see a way around it.'

'Jesus Christ,' Freddie said, his eyes bulging. 'They can't put an elderly woman out of her own home. That's crazy.'

'I know,' Maia said. 'It's to widen the bloody road. But we're going to fight them tooth and nail.'

'Too right,' Freddie said. 'Would she like to talk to our solicitor? Barry is a right terrier, and if he gets his teeth into the council, they'll know all about it.'

'I was thinking,' Maia said, looking at him steadily, 'that there might be other friends of yours who could go talk to the council.'

Freddie looked confused. 'Who?'

'You know, the kind of friends who know how to make a baseball bat count, how to get people to change their minds.'

'I don't know people like that,' Freddie said quickly. 'What are you talking about, Maia?'

'Don't you?' she said. 'All these years I've kept my mouth shut, Freddie, and asked no questions, but all the secrecy, all the money, I reckon you probably do know the right people to go put the fear of God in the relevant council people.'

Freddie looked at her like she was mad. 'Jesus, Maia, we're not living in *The Sopranos* here. I'm not Tony bleedin' Soprano by any stretch of the imagination. I make good money from a legit business. I certainly don't go around with baseball bats. Have you gone mental?'

'Look,' said Maia, 'you don't have to tell me a thing. But if it's possible, just know that I'd be quiet about that too.'

He shook his head. 'You've the wrong end of the stick, love. I'm just an ordinary businessman, working to make a good living. You need to stop watching so much Netflix.'

'I just want to help Nancy,' Maia said. 'Seeing her so upset and scared is killing me.'

'I understand completely,' Freddie said gently. 'I hate

the idea of her not being down the road from us. I'll get on to Barry today and get his advice. And I'll call into Nancy to see how she is and look at the documents myself. We'll figure out something.'

'Me and the girls are organising a campaign,' Maia said. 'We made a plan at supper club the other night. I've been on to the local radio station and TV Ireland, drumming up interest in the story. I think I've got the *Vayhill Recorder* interested, I'm negotiating them sending down a journo and photographer to cover the story. And I've got Zach and Zara doing stuff on social media. Danielle is looking into the legals and the others are pulling in any contacts they think can help.'

Freddie looked at her admiringly. 'That's my girl. Loyal to the end. I'm proud of you for thinking of all that. It's the right way to go about it. Get the public involved and weighing in with opinions, and the council will soon realise they can't just quietly take an old woman's house. You're bang-on, there, Maia. Fantastic work.'

Just then, his phone started to buzz and he nearly levitated off the seat with fright. He glanced at the screen and said, 'Eh, sorry, love, I have to take this.'

Maia sat back. 'So you leap to the ceiling when your phone rings, but they're all just ordinary, normal colleagues at the other end, yeah?'

His face tightened into a frown. 'Yeah, that's right,' he said, and there was a warning tone in his voice. 'You saying all that other stuff could land me in a right heap of trouble. Everything I do is legit. End of. So you just stick to running the house, and I'll run the business, just like we've always done, alright?' He pressed a button to take the call and walked from the room, talking quietly.

Maia looked after him, disgusted that he couldn't just be honest with her. She was his wife, she'd never sell him out. She had always played her part perfectly – look gorgeous, run a perfect home, ask no questions. Surely she'd earned the right to be a little more involved, a little more trusted? She was getting sick of all this cloak-and-dagger stuff. He was going to lose her if he kept it up. But then, the thought of being without Freddie made her heart hurt in her chest. He was the best, and she loved him, no matter what.

She decided she'd go over to Pearl, see if she could have a coffee with her and get her talking about herself. She was sure there was trouble there, and she didn't want Pearl to feel alone. She was just gathering her phone and keys into her bag when the doorbell rang.

On the doorstep stood Danielle and Rachel.

'Hello, you two,' Maia said, surprised to see them. 'Do you want to come in for a coffee?'

'We were just wondering . . .' Danielle began, looking nervous, ' . . . like, if this isn't a bad time, but we'll come back again if it is, you can just tell us a better time . . .'

'Eh, is there much more of this, Danielle?' Maia said. 'Because it'll be time to start my Christmas shopping soon at this rate.'

Danielle and her mother started laughing.

'What she's trying to say,' Rachel said, 'is may we come in and take up your offer of lending us clothes so we don't put ourselves to shame at this swanky party we have to go to.'

'Yes!' Maia said delightedly. 'You absolutely can. Try-ons and fashion shows are my favourite pastime. In you come.'

She flung the door wide and Rachel shook her head and smiled.

'Of course time wasted trying on stuff makes you happy. I should have known.'

'Ah now, Rachel, don't get all sour on me and spoil the fun,' Maia said, wagging her finger. 'I might get my revenge by putting you in a tutu. You're in my control now, don't forget.'

'Lord, help us,' Rachel said, rolling her eyes. 'The things we do for our children.'

As they made their way upstairs, Zara came out of her bedroom.

'Oh hi,' she said, smiling at Danielle. 'Are you our new neighbour?'

Danielle nodded. 'Yes, nice to meet you, Zara.'

'Danielle's boyfriend is Justin Johnston,' Maia said, giving Zara a meaningful look. 'His snobby mother has invited these two to a big bash at her place, so they're trying on stuff to look the part. I get to be Fairy Godmother!'

'Really?' Zara said, eyes sparkling just like her mother's. 'Can I help?'

'I see you've ruined another life,' Rachel said drily.

Zara looked a bit put out, but Maia laughed. 'You'll have to get used to Rachel,' she said. 'She thinks we're dreadful for loving fashion and spending a small fortune on clothes. *Very* disapproving.'

'Oh right,' Zara said, grinning. 'We'll have to see if we can change her mind.'

'That's the spirit!' Maia said. 'Right, in here everyone.' She pushed open a door that led to her private dressing-room. It was a large room, with a big window at the far end, and rails of clothes along both sides. In the centre was a long, rectangular wooden cabinet that had shoe racks on all sides – all of them full. On high shelves were hat boxes and handbags. Behind the door, the wall was studded with small hooks, on which hung every type of necklace. There was a tall, narrow chest of drawers under the window, and its drawers pulled out to reveal rings and bracelets and Maia's most expensive items of jewellery, including a collection of watches. There were soft rose-coloured fairy lights garlanded near the ceiling and a tall floor lamp in one corner with a rose-coloured tasselled shade. It was like walking into an incredibly tasteful boutique.

'Well, dear God, I've seen it all now,' Rachel said, staring around in wonder.

'My dressing-room,' Maia said, 'and I'm not going to apologise for it.'

'Where's your husband's stuff?' Rachel asked.

'He has his own dressing-room across the hall.'

'*Grand Designs* has nothing on you,' Rachel said. 'This is unbelievable. Are you getting one of these?' she asked Danielle.

'Well, now I've seen this,' Danielle said, 'I might have to. It's fabulous, Maia. I'd actually sit and read in here.'

'Well, you'd certainly never find me doing that,' Maia said, 'but I'm glad you like it.'

'I'm going to get a few things from my room that might suit you,' Zara said, sizing Danielle up. 'If you're with a Johnston, you'll need to be sort of classy sexy, you know?'

'No, I don't know,' Danielle said. 'I'm completely useless at all this. So I'll just trust you and Maia.'

For the next hour, Maia and Zara pulled out dresses and held them against Danielle and Rachel and laid out some for trying on and put others back. They picked out matching shoes and jewellery, argued about their choices, agreed about others. They cast expert eyes over the two women's bodies, hair and features. They had long discussions about the right and wrong colours and kept mentioning someone called Sorcha who would 'pull it all together'. Danielle and Rachel sat there, watching all this whirling around them.

Finally, Maia and Zara had exactly what they wanted assembled.

'Trying on time!' Maia said, clapping her hands together. 'Let's sort you first, Rachel, seeing as you're a grumpy cow about all this.'

Rachel got up heavily. 'You better not expect me to wear anything short or see-through or low-cut or anything of that sort,' she said.

'See,' Maia said, looking at Zara, 'grumpy. We've our work cut out for us here.'

'And I'm not getting changed in front of you lot,' Rachel grumbled.

'I've laid it all out in my bedroom,' Zara said. 'You can go in there and put on what's on the bed and come back to us.'

Rachel walked out of the room as if heading to the scaffold for hanging. As soon as she'd shut Zara's bedroom door, Maia burst out laughing.

'She's hating this so much, it's making me enjoy it all the more.'

'You're so bold,' Danielle said, shaking her head and grinning. 'She could well run out of here and insist on wearing her tracksuit to this party. I wish we'd never been invited,' she said, looking glum.

'Are you mad?' Zara said. 'It's going to be amazing. The

Johnston parties are legendary. I know a girl, a friend of my friend Lottie, and she's in all those circles and her Insta account goes absolutely wild whenever she's at a Johnston event. Everyone is gagging for a look. You've got to send me photos, okay?'

Danielle laughed. 'Okay, I promise. I'll have to play dutiful fiancée, though, don't forget. Justin wants me to meet so many people.'

'You're so lucky,' Zara said. 'I'd give my right arm to meet a man like that. And he's cute into the bargain. Your ring is utterly gorgeous, by the way. I noticed it the moment I saw you.'

'Thanks,' Danielle said, looking shy. 'Justin picked it. I would have gone for something smaller, but he wanted a sapphire and diamonds, for some reason. Although,' she said, holding up her hand and admiring it, 'now that I've got used to it, I really love it.'

'You're learning,' Maia said. 'You've just got to relax and let him spoil you from time to time.'

From the hallway outside came Rachel's disgruntled voice. 'I look stupid. I'm not wearing this.'

Maia rolled her eyes. 'Come in and let us be the judge of that.'

Rachel walked in, wearing a navy pleated, calf-length skirt, with a silver boat-neck top. It sparkled as she moved. She had a pair of red suede ankle-boots on with it.

'Oh!' Danielle said.

'What does that mean?' Rachel said defensively. 'I look awful, is that it?'

'No,' Danielle said, staring at her wide-eyed. 'You look amazing, Mum. I would never, ever have picked that outfit for you, but it's actually perfect. It suits your shape and makes you look younger. It's so chic and yet funky as well. I absolutely love it.'

Rachel moved over to look at herself in the mirror. Maia could tell that she was struggling with the fact that she liked it too. She stood sideways, then frontways, looking at herself from every angle.

'No, it's awful,' she said. 'I'll go try the next one.'

Danielle opened her mouth to protest, but Maia put her hand on her hand and shook her head. Once Rachel had gone back to Zara's room, Maia whispered, 'Just let her try them all. She does like that one, I can tell, but she's not ready to admit it. We'll just humour her and she'll come back to it. You'll see.'

Rachel tried on a black short dress – 'mutton as lamb' – a red halterneck – 'slutty' – and a green two-piece 'mother of the bride, no thank you!'

Finally, she came in wearing the last outfit, a beige dress from Cos that hit her in all the wrong places.

'I think this is the one,' she said.

'No it's not,' Maia said. 'It does nothing for your arse.'

Rachel turned on her, face red with anger. 'Feck off, Maia!'

Maia laughed gleefully. 'You can take the girl out of Westwood . . . ' she said. 'You better not tell them poshies at the party to feck off and ruin all my good work. Jesus, they had it easy in *My Fair Lady*. There wouldn't have been a film if they'd had you to work with, I can tell you.'

Rachel started laughing, in spite of herself. 'Look, it's beige, it's anonymous, it suits me.'

Maia shook her head. 'That makes me really sad to hear, Rachel,' she said. 'You're a woman. I know you've spent your life putting others first, but here's a chance for a bit of fun, a bit of sparkle. Why shouldn't you make the most of it?'

Rachel's head drooped. 'I don't know,' she mumbled. 'It's just not me.'

'Please,' Maia said gently, 'for yourself, put the first one back on. I know you felt good in it.'

Rachel raised her head and looked at her. 'Jesus, you should be a counsellor,' she said. 'You've a gift for persuasion.' She looked down at the beige dress again. 'Alright, give me a minute.'

Danielle couldn't believe it. 'You've actually convinced her,' she said when Rachel had left. 'I didn't think it was possible.'

'There's no competition,' Zara said. 'That first outfit is a no-brainer.'

When Rachel came back in, wearing the navy and silver ensemble, she was smiling.

'Alright, you win, Maia,' she said. 'I do love this one. And I feel like I ruin it, but if you'll lend it, I'd love to wear it.'

'Sense at last,' Maia said. 'You're welcome. And I've already texted my makeup girl, Sorcha, and she's going to come to Danielle's on the evening of the party to do you both up. Hair and makeup. And it's on me, my treat.' She held up her hands as Danielle and Rachel both started talking at once. 'Forget it. It's done. Now, we've got Danielle to sort, so let's keep moving.'

Danielle went off with Zara to her room. They were back in minutes.

'I think I have my one already,' Danielle said, looking shy again. 'Zara's a genius.'

'I had a gut feeling about this one,' Zara said proudly. 'And I was right.'

Danielle walked into the dressing-room and did a twirl. She was wearing an ankle-length dress in sunburst yellow. It was strapless, with a sweetheart shape and tight corseting, but then it softened at the waist into ruched folds that fell gently down around her legs. Zara had teamed it with red strappy heels and a daisy-chain state-ment necklace.

'Wow,' Maia said, appraising her. 'You are a genius, Zara, that's perfect. You look effortlessly chic, like you haven't tried at all but hit the nail on the head anyway.'

'That's exactly what I wanted,' Danielle said, smiling. 'I just want to look right, so no one can make any snide remarks.'

'I have a bolero jacket to go with it,' Zara said, dashing back to her bedroom. She returned with a sweet little cream bolero with silk lining and piping.

Danielle slipped it on, and it was like she stood taller and straighter. It never ceased to amaze Maia how some women could dismiss fashion as stupid, and yet it had the power to transform. You could be the shyest little thing, but the right dress and heels suddenly made you feel like a tiger. That was why she loved it so much.

'Our work here is done,' Maia said to Zara, holding up her hand for a high-five.

As Zara pulled out some dress bags to hang all their clobber in, Rachel asked about her school and plans.

'I'm going to study Classics and French at Queen's in Belfast,' Zara said, zipping the clothes in carefully and boxing up the shoes. 'But I've deferred the place for a year and I'm heading off travelling with a friend. We're hoping to see lots of Europe and then finish by hopping across to South America.'

'Oh my God,' Danielle said, 'that sounds amazing. When do you go?'

'After Mum's big party,' Zara said, smiling at Maia.

'You must have worked hard to secure your university place,' Rachel said.

Zara nodded. 'Yeah, the Leaving Cert was really tough, but I knew what I wanted to do and how many points I needed, so I just focused on it and kept at it.'

Rachel nodded, and her eyes drifted over to Danielle. 'It's good to have focus,' she said softly. 'Just keep your eyes on the prize, girl.'

'Okay,' Maia said quickly, feeling it could degenerate into an argument if Rachel kept talking. Danielle was looking uncomfortable, and it was obvious Rachel's regrets about the pregnancy hadn't dissolved in any way. 'Right, you two. I'll help you cart all this across the road.'

'Thanks so much, Zara,' Danielle said, giving her a hug.

'Pictures,' Zara said. 'Lots of them. Don't forget.'

'I won't,' Danielle said. 'You've earned them.'

They headed downstairs and towards the front door.

'You're okay, Maia,' Danielle said. 'We can manage them. You've done enough.'

'If you're sure,' Maia said. 'And by the way, it's all go on the Nancy front. I'm waiting for a call, but I think we're going to get someone from the local paper down to cover the story, which is a good start.'

'That's great,' Danielle said. 'I'm still researching options, but it's not looking good in terms of legal appeal, I'm afraid.'

'Well, we can focus on getting the story out, then,' Maia

said. 'I'm going to suggest a meeting to review progress and make more plans, so you'll come to that, won't you?'

'Absolutely,' Danielle said, nodding. 'Just tell me when, and where.'

'I'll be in touch,' Maia said.

She saw them out, then went back to the kitchen to make a Nespresso. She smiled to herself thinking about Danielle. She had seemed so reticent about getting to know them all, and now here she was, in the thick of the campaign to save Nancy's house. Kingfisher Road had a funny way of drawing people in, she thought, and she reckoned it was happening again.

Chapter 16

NANCY'S PHONE BEEPED. A TEXT FROM STEVE. *NO problem that you have to cancel. I understand. Meeting is important. What time it at?*

Nancy sighed. She appreciated his support, but she wanted to focus on the meeting with the council and not on a ping-pong game of texts. People these days seemed to think nothing of constant interruptions, but she felt like each one was an intrusion on her train of thought. She actually preferred the world thirty years ago, when she could be uncontactable, and even get lost from time to time. Things had felt more open and adventurous back then. All this constant monitoring and checking was irritating.

Eleven, she texted back.

She returned to her vanity table, using her well chosen makeup pieces to create a soft, happy-in-my-own-skin look. She didn't want to try to look younger because she felt looking her age might benefit her in the meeting. She wanted them to see that she was an older woman who should be left to live out her years in her own home.

She hadn't told the others about today's meeting. She knew Maia would kill her when she found out she'd gone to it alone, but she felt she had to face it by herself. If she brought Maia or Betsy, they would become emotional and angry, and then sparks might fly. She'd dealt with enough pen-pushers in her time to know that they didn't take well to emotional displays, or anything that smacked of emotional blackmail. Instead, she'd called Sean Claffey, her solicitor, and asked him to accompany her, which he'd been only too happy to do. Between the two of them, they could present her case calmly and rationally. Hopefully, that would have the desired effect.

Each time she thought of losing the cottage, her insides caved in. She had to hold firm and believe that this could be overturned. She wasn't much into mantras and vision boards and the like, but she had taken to repeating the words, *I will not be leaving my home*, over and over again when she woke up in the morning and before she fell asleep each night. What else could she do?

She took a last look at herself in the mirror and nodded. Ready as I'll ever be, she thought.

'Right, Nelly, you're on guard while I'm gone,' she said, as Nelly trotted along at her heels. 'Your bowl is full, I've refreshed your water and I shouldn't be too long. With a bit of luck, you and me will be staying put.'

Her phone beeped again. Goddamn it, she thought, picking it up. It was from Sean. *Outside.* Nancy rolled her eyes. Was that how gentlemen carried on these days? No wonder he was divorced. She took her coat and bag from the chair in the hallway, took a last look around, steadied herself and went outside, locking the door behind her.

'Morning, Nancy,' Sean said as she opened the door and sat inside the car. 'You look very fetching, I have to say.'

'Thank you,' Nancy said. 'I feel sick, but if the exterior looks right, that's one battle won.'

'Indeed,' Sean said, pulling out of Kingfisher Road. 'We'll

present a good case. I received a number of letters from the other residents, someone called Maia forwarded them to me.' Nancy smiled. 'They all support you vehemently, so perhaps they'll hold some sway.'

'I hope so,' Nancy said. 'I don't have much else in the armoury.'

They arrived at the council offices at ten-fifty and made their way to the reception desk. The council offices were a lot nicer than Nancy had expected. In fact, she was instantly impressed until she remembered that she was here to fight with them, and that they shouldn't be spending a pile of cash on having a place that would do Donald Trump on a flash day.

'Mrs Smyth and Mr Claffey to see Mr Derek Small, please,' Nancy said to the receptionist.

'I'll let him know you're here,' the young woman said. 'Please take a seat.'

Nancy and Sean sat down on the plush banquette that ran along one wall.

'No expense spared,' Nancy said out of the corner of her mouth.

'Makes my office look like a hovel,' Sean replied. 'I'm in the wrong business.'

'Mrs Smyth?' A man was walking towards them, hand extended. He could do with losing several stone in belly fat, tidying up his clothes, hair and dreadful straggly beard and polishing his shoes. A lifetime in retail had left Nancy with a very strong sense of how to make a good impression, and this man obviously hadn't got the memo. She smiled inwardly to think of him going through life with the word 'small' attached to him.

He led them down a warren of corridors to a cramped,

overly warm office. 'Take a seat, please. Can I get you tea or coffee? A scone, biscuit or pastry to go with it?'

'Is this the charm offensive?' Sean said drily.

The man smiled. 'Not at all. I offer the same to all my visitors.'

'Thank you, but no, Mr Small,' Nancy said. 'I'm not here to socialise. I'm here to fight for my home. Have you ever been in this position yourself?' She raised an eyebrow and paused so he could answer.

'Please call me Derek and, no, Mrs Smyth, I haven't.'

'Good for you,' she said. 'Because it's not a great feeling, let me tell you. I couldn't swallow a scone right now. I'd probably choke on it and die right here on your herringbone carpet.'

'I'm sure it's not a nice feeling,' he said carefully. 'I didn't mean to annoy you by offering a snack. We'll just get to it.'

He looked uncomfortable, and Nancy could see a slight tremor in his hands. Excellent, she thought, I've got him on the back foot.

'So I've brought you here today to give you some good news,' he said, as he licked a finger and turned over some pages that lay on the desk in front of him.

Nancy and Sean exchanged a look.

'You have?' Nancy said, leaning forward.

'Yes, I'm very happy to say that I can offer you a wonderful property in the new St Helen's Garden complex, not far from Vayhill. There are only two properties remaining there and although there's a long waiting list, we'd be prepared to give you first option on them. What do you say?' He looked at her with a hopeful expression.

'St Helen's?' Nancy said. 'Isn't that the new old folks' home?'

'Well, it's not . . .' began the man, but Sean cut across him.

'Yes, it is, Nancy,' he said.

Nancy felt a rush of anger. 'I don't want to live in an old fogey complex where nurses come and change your nappy and feed you blended carrots each day,' she said crossly. 'I'm not ready for that, and I can't ever imagine a time when I will be. I'd rather get pizza delivered every day for the rest of my life and live in squalor than go there, so you can keep your two remaining units.'

'I see,' Derek said, as his forehead began to bead with sweat. He wiped it with the cuff of his jacket, making her recoil.

'Didn't your mother ever tell you not to wipe your nose or your head with your sleeve?'

'Eh, not really,' he said as he clearly tried to think back.

'Well don't do it,' she snapped. 'It's rude and looks awful. So have you any more good news for me?'

He was looking at her in astonishment, no doubt thinking her a grumpy old cow, but Nancy didn't care. Everything about him and this whole conversation annoyed her, and she was past hiding that fact.

'Yes, yes, I do as a matter of fact,' he said, rifling noisily through the pile of pages. 'I have another property I think you might like . . .'

'Excuse me,' Sean said, 'but is this an estate agent's or the council offices? Can we not discuss the option of Nancy *not* being turfed out of her home?'

Derek put down the papers and looked at them. 'I'm afraid it's gone beyond that,' he said. 'I do realise that you're angry and it's a big thing to get a CPO, but the road-widening scheme is well advanced, the road crew are ready to roll, so we really need numbers five and six vacated asap.'

Nancy bit back another sharp comment. She couldn't bear it when people said 'asap'. It sounded so silly.

'But work *hasn't* commenced,' Sean insisted, 'so there is still a conversation to be had here. Are you the man who can make decisions, or do we need your superior sitting in on this meeting?'

Derek bristled at that. 'I'm the exact person you need to talk to,' he said, all hint of a smile vanished now. 'Now, the council regrets the inconvenience this will cause to Mrs Smyth, but a CPO is a legally binding order, backed by the courts. I am perfectly within my rights to serve this order on Mrs Smyth and Kingfisher Cottage. We need Mrs Smyth to move out within the next six weeks. We are very willing to help find her alternative accommodation where she will be comfortable and happy. The Kingfisher Road houses fetch an excellent market price, so with all due respect, Mrs Smyth will most certainly be able to find a comparable property.'

'But I don't want or need any alternative accommodation,' Nancy said, hating herself for sounding so desperate. 'I'm not budging from my home on Kingfisher Road.' She folded her arms. She was playing at being defiant, though inside, she was crumbling. She bit her lip, willing herself not to cry, not here in front of this little upstart with his legal chatter. In order to ward off her tears, she went full-on anger instead. 'I said I'm not budging,' she shouted, sounding like someone possessed. She was impressed with herself, she sounded so scary.

'My client is deeply distressed at the thought of losing her home,' Sean said in a placatory tone. 'She wishes to see out her days in Kingfisher Cottage, which is exactly what would happen if the council didn't interfere in her private business.' He opened his briefcase. 'I have a sheaf of letters here from local residents, all condemning the council's action and requesting that the road-widening scheme be amended to take it further away from Kingfisher Road, not closer. The residents are up in arms at the idea of traffic noise coming closer.'

Derek held up his hands. 'That's as may be,' he said. 'But it doesn't change the facts of the matter nor the decision taken by the council in league with the Road Authority. This widening scheme is necessary to make the Vayhill road safer for all users. I know you think we're terrible people, but honestly, we don't take these decisions lightly. The engineers have assured us that this is the very best solution, so we have to implement it. My hands are tied.'

Nancy wished she had accepted a scone, because she dearly wanted to pick it up now and biff him in the head with it. The thought of flinging a scone across the table and hitting him square between the eyes nearly made her start giggling. But then the enormity of the situation rolled over her again, and she could feel the tears threatening.

'Oh, please don't cry,' the man said, looking distinctly uncomfortable. 'We really will do right by you, get you a house just as fantastic, honestly.'

'A house that contains all my memories?' Nancy said coldly. 'I lived with my husband in that house, he proposed to me in the garden, he died in the back bedroom, I waked him in the sitting room, I planted a tree for him down by the stream.' She leaned forward. 'Now tell me, how do you propose to find a house that can give me all that?'

The man gulped, his Adam's apple bobbing up and down. He looked down at the desk, avoiding Nancy's unblinking stare.

'I'm so sorry,' he mumbled. 'But the CPO stands.'

'Right,' Sean said, gathering the letters, stuffing them into his briefcase and standing up. 'I'm going to lodge an appeal at the High Court.'

'We have an appeal mechanism here,' Derek said quickly. 'It's much quicker and . . .'

'No,' Sean said sharply. 'I will go above the council to the courts. You'll hear from us in due course.'

He offered Nancy his arm and helped her up. She felt weak in the legs, but she managed to maintain a dignified composure.

'Goodbye, Mr Small,' Sean said, then he escorted Nancy from the room. He didn't stop until they were outside, in the fresh air.

'Are you okay, Nancy?' he said, his face full of concern.

She nodded sadly. 'Just a bit overwhelmed,' she said quietly. 'That didn't exactly go well, did it?'

Sean shook his head. 'No, it didn't,' he admitted. 'But I will get straight on to the appeal. If nothing else, it should buy us a little time.'

'Alright,' Nancy said. 'If you need me to sign . . .'

'Nancy!'

She looked up in surprise at hearing her name being called. Coming towards them down the street was Steve, hurrying along. His right arm was held up in greeting.

'Steve,' Nancy said. 'What are you doing here?'

'I just wanted to be there for you when the meeting ended,' he said. 'I couldn't stop thinking about you. How did it go?'

'Excuse me,' Sean said tactfully, 'I'll leave you two to your discussion, if you don't mind. I have papers to file.'

'Of course,' Steve said. 'Nice to meet you.'

God bless Sean's tact, Nancy thought, he didn't even ask who Steve was, although he must have been wondering.

'I'll be in touch, Nancy,' he said. 'I'll update you as soon as I hear anything.'

'Thank you so much, Sean,' she said. 'And thanks for coming with me today. You were a great support.'

He headed off, and Steve suggested a coffee at the café across the road. Nancy looked from the council offices to the café.

'Would you mind if we went a bit further away?' she said. 'I'd hate to be sitting in there and have that horrible man come in. I don't want to see him again until I absolutely have to.'

'Of course, I should have thought of that,' Steve said. 'How about I drive you back to Vayhill and we can pop into The Bakehouse?'

'That would be lovely, thank you,' Nancy said.

He found a parking space on the road outside The Bakehouse and they went inside. Nancy prayed none of her friends were about, because she didn't want to have to explain Steve's existence just yet. She would soon, but just not yet.

Steve brought over two coffees and a coffee slice with two forks. The sight of the cream turned Nancy's stomach, but she took a smidgen of it, just to be polite.

'So, how did it go?' Steve asked. 'Was it a tough meeting?'

'Not well,' Nancy said, sipping her coffee. 'They won't change their minds. They just kept saying how I have to move out.'

'I'm so sorry, that's just terrible,' Steve said. 'They'd make you feel powerless, wouldn't they? You've paid your taxes and earned the right to keep your home. It's outrageous.'

Nancy nodded. 'My sentiments exactly, but try telling that to the council.'

'Is there an appeal process?' he asked.

'Yes, Sean, he's my solicitor, he's going to pursue that angle. He'll do everything he can, but CPOs are legal instruments, so I wouldn't be expecting him to be successful.'

Steve shook his head. 'I really feel for you, Nancy. I could see how much you loved your home just by how you kept it. If I can help in any way, money or helping with form filling, anything at all, just say the word.'

'Thank you,' Nancy said, feeling a bit embarrassed. 'I really don't want to impose on you, though. No one goes looking for their mother hoping they'll find her in dire straits and needing help straight off the bat.'

Steve burst out laughing. 'You have a way of saying things straight, Nancy.'

'We're all adults here, no need for me to beat around the bush.'

'True,' Steve said. 'But if I can help, just let me know.'

'I will. If you have a decent cardboard box, I'll take it off your hands if it comes to it.'

'Oh no, they won't see you go homeless,' he said. 'I presume they're offering you the market value so you can relocate?'

'Yes, that's how the CPO works. They do give you the money, but I don't want to move.'

'A place came up for sale on your road not long ago, would there be a chance of someone selling up and you could buy?'

Nancy shook her head. 'The neighbours that are there are very happy. I can't see anyone selling up in the next two months. I'd have to buy elsewhere, but then I'd lose my friends as well.'

'What about down-sizing?' Steve said. 'I hear that's all the rage now. You know, you buy a bijou place that would suit you and Nelly and cost less than your current place, then you'd be able to put the money you didn't spend to take care of yourself as you get older.'

'There's a sense to that, of course,' she said, 'but I want to stay in my home. No money can recompense me for what I'd lose if I moved out.'

'Your memories and everything?' he said.

'Yes, my husband and I were so happy there. I'd hate to leave all that behind.'

'That's understandable,' he said. 'What can we do?' he said, tapping his head. 'There must be a way around it.'

'Sean is working on it,' Nancy said. 'If there's a way, he'll find it.'

'You know, the Chinese word for crisis is made up of the characters for danger and opportunity. I heard that once and it really struck me. Maybe you need to see this as being a blessing in disguise.'

'How?' Nancy asked, puzzled.

'Like, maybe you'll move somewhere smaller and a new world will open up to you. Most people would love the idea of having extra cash as well. You could invest and possibly make more. I mean, I'm getting into an investment at the moment, run by a friend of mine. I'm looking at a ten per cent return if I play my cards right.'

'Be careful of schemes like that,' Nancy warned. 'No one gives you ten per cent without a price attached to it. Those are the kind of promises they make to sucker you in. Your money is hard-earned, Steve, so don't let anyone take it away from you.'

'Oh, I'd be very careful with it alright,' he said. 'I don't have enough to be throwing it around. But this is a guy I trust. He's had amazing success already. I'm going to give him a lump sum, and I know at the very least I'll get it back. I'm certain of that. And you know, if you do end up down-sizing, you're very welcome to come in on this scheme with me. We might both get a windfall.'

Before she could answer, Nancy became aware of someone looking in the window at her elbow. She turned her head, and Freddie was standing there on the path, looking in at them. He was frowning. She waved at him.

Freddie turned and walked to the door of the café and then came in and over to their table. 'How are you, Nancy?' he said, staring all the while at Steve.

'I'm good,' she said. 'This is Steve,' she said. She didn't want to get into specifics right now, and she'd prefer to tell Maia about Steve first. 'Steve, this is my neighbour, Freddie.'

The two men shook hands. Freddie kept looking at Steve, as if he was trying to remember something.

'Have we met before?' Freddie asked him. 'There's something familiar about you.'

'No, we haven't,' Steve said, pushing back his chair and

standing up suddenly. 'Now, if you'll excuse me, I'll just pay for this and say goodbye to Nancy.'

He walked off to the counter and Freddie turned to her.

'Would you like a lift home? I'm heading that way.'

'I won't, thanks Freddie,' she said, smiling at him. 'I'd prefer to walk and get some fresh air.'

'Alright,' Freddie said. He glanced over at the counter. 'That fella reminds me of someone, but I can't think who.'

'Well, don't let us keep you,' Nancy said. 'You're probably heading home for your lunch.'

He looked at his watch. 'Yeah, and it'll probably be served on my head because I'm late.'

Nancy laughed. 'I definitely don't want to be responsible for you wearing the soup. Go on now.'

By the time Steve returned to the table, Freddie had left.

'God, he probably thought I was dead rude,' Steve said, helping Nancy with her coat. 'I jumped up and ran because I didn't want you to have to explain who I was.'

Nancy blushed. 'I'm not ashamed to tell people,' she said, 'it's just I'm very close friends with Freddie's wife, Maia, and I'd prefer to tell her first. She might be offended if she found out through Freddie.'

'So no one knows about me?' Steve said.

'No, I've never confided that part of my life in my friends,' Nancy said. 'I was so young, and I've just never wanted to talk about it. They are difficult memories. So I will of course be telling them and introducing you, but just not yet.'

'That's not a problem,' Steve said. 'You do it when you feel ready. I'll stick to the line that I'm your ex-husband's son until you tell me otherwise.'

'You're so kind,' Nancy said, and she really meant it. He was incredibly thoughtful and patient.

'We'll take things at our own pace,' Steve said. 'There's no rush. But do think about what I said, you know, that crisis could be turned into opportunity. It really could.'

'Thanks for coming to meet me,' Nancy said, 'and for the cake and coffee.'

'No problem. I've to head off to a job now, but I'll be in touch. Do you want a lift?'

'I'll walk,' Nancy said. 'Clear my head.'

'Grand. Take care.'

Once he had driven off, Nancy dropped the smiles and her face crumpled. She'd had to pretend in front of Steve, but she was gutted by the meeting with the council. She wanted to go home, close the door and curl up on her own without any need to pretend that she was hopeful or strong. It was terrible that she would be thinking of being alone, but she honestly enjoyed her own company. Steve was lovely to chat to and so considerate, but the thought of being alone with Nelly was a solace.

It struck her again how the connection she so badly wanted to feel wasn't materialising. She wanted to look at Steve and feel a solid sense of love and belonging. So far, it hadn't happened. It made her feel so bad. She wanted to be a loving mother to this man who had sought her out, but she felt out of kilter with his expectations. He must have come looking for her in order to bond with her and feel that he'd found his roots, and she felt like she wasn't giving him that. She wanted to, but she felt she wasn't. It was driving her nuts. Here she was, being given an unexpected chance to be a mother to a lovely son, and she felt she was messing it all up. How long would he hang around if he felt she wasn't fully there for him? It worried her. She had to focus on him and forge that connection, for both their sakes.

Chapter 17

THEY DROVE ALONGSIDE THE WALL OF THE ESTATE for a few minutes, its long white curving line presenting a very effective barrier against seeing anything beyond. They reached the entrance, which was flanked by two high gate pillars, each topped with a statue of a horse rearing up. The imposing gates, which also featured horses, opened slowly, noiselessly, and Justin put the car in gear and drove up the wide and long boulevard that led to the house. There was a gate lodge on the left, just beyond the gate. It was a beautiful stone house, single-storey, with two tall chimneys. There was a barrier just in front of it, and a man dressed in uniform and holding a clipboard indicated for them to stop.

'Evening, Hanley,' Justin called out as he lowered the window. 'How are you?'

'Ah, it's yourself, Mr Justin,' the man said, smiling in at them. 'The place is hopping up there. Enjoy yourselves.' He raised the barrier and Justin's BMW slid on past and up the sweeping driveway.

Orange lanterns hung from the trees that lined the drive, lighting the way towards the house. It stood regally at the end of the driveway, massive in its Georgian proportions, with ten windows adorning its upper floor and four each on either side of the red front door. The front was festooned with Virginia creeper, glowing red in the wintry gloom thanks to the uplighters that cast a beautiful light on the whole exterior.

'It's beautiful,' Danielle said, feeling a bit overwhelmed by the grandiosity. She had thought Kingfisher Road was a mansion, but this blew everything else out of the water. It was like something from *Downton Abbey*.

The drive ended in a fanned-out car park, and it was filled with cars Danielle had only ever seen on *Top Gear*. She looked over at Justin, incapable of imagining what growing up here as a child would have been like. It was so far from her house in Westwood, it was comical. They came from two different planets. And yet, Justin was so down to earth, you'd never guess he came from all this. He didn't feel so terribly different from her. But this, this was so far out of her league, she wanted to belt back down the drive and keep on running.

Justin put his hand over hers. 'It's just a house,' he said. 'Don't think it changes anything.'

'Just a house?' Rachel said disbelievingly from the back seat. 'Jesus, Justin, you can't really say that to people who call a two-up, two-down home. I'd say you could fit my whole house in one room here.'

'It's just extra space,' he said, looking at Rachel in the rear-view mirror. 'Doesn't mean better people.'

Danielle squeezed his hand. 'We're not trying to make you uncomfortable,' she said. 'It's just a lot to take in.'

He parked the car around the back, where the family's vehicles were kept out of sight. Danielle knew Justin's parents and two brothers lived here, but there were eight cars and SUVs ranged around. More than one for every day of the week, she thought, shaking her head at the mad excess of it all.

'Right, ladies,' Justin said. 'Are you ready to go inside?'

'No,' Rachel said.

Justin laughed. 'Well I'm not sitting out here freezing my nuts off, so you're going to have to. Come on, we'll find a drink and a quiet spot where you can people-watch.'

'Perfect,' said Danielle. 'I have to take photos for Zara as well.'

They made their way around to the front door, which stood wide open, light spilling out to welcome them in. Another uniformed man stood at the top of the wide set of steps leading up to the door.

'Welcome, Mr Justin,' he called out. 'And this must be the beautiful Miss Danielle you've told me about,' he said. 'You look perfectly stunning, if I may say so, madam.'

'Thank you,' Danielle said. 'You may definitely say so. It might settle my nerves.'

He winked at her. 'You look the part, so just hold your head up high.'

'Thanks, Morton,' Justin said. 'I've been dying for you to meet her.' He grinned at Danielle. 'Morton's been here since I was two years old, so he's my oldest friend.'

'Delighted to meet you,' Danielle said.

'Right, in we go,' Justin said, and he proffered an arm to each of them. Danielle linked one side and Rachel linked the other. 'I am going to be the envy of every other man in the room,' he said.

'Not bloody likely,' Rachel muttered.

He led them down the long hallway, then through a set of double doors into . . . a ballroom. An actual ballroom. Danielle stared around in wonder. She hadn't expected a full-on ballroom, even though the house was big enough. It had a beautifully polished dark oak floor, draped curtains with tassels, a bar down one side, fully stocked with every kind of bottle and beer taps as well, and gorgeous velvet armchairs in different colours dotted all around the room. There were tall tree-like plants and incredible flower displays on the glass tables set in the gaps between the windows. There was an aroma of food cooking and perfumes on the air, and the guests were talking and laughing loudly.

'Look at the dresses!' Danielle said to Rachel. 'They're so amazing.'

The women looked like exotic peacocks, in all colours of silk and feathers. Many were wearing diamanté-studded eye masks, although none of the men were masked. Danielle was so glad she had gone to Maia and Zara for help. She didn't look anything as good as this lot, but at least she didn't stand out as terrifically badly dressed.

As they walked through the room, Danielle could feel how the chatter died down and everyone turned to look. She could feel her face burning, just knowing that they were all sizing her up. This was her first time in the Johnston house, so the first time for people to get a good look at her. They were openly staring, looking her up and down, and the women, in particular, didn't look too impressed.

'Keep your head up,' Rachel whispered, 'just like the man said.'

Justin led them over to where Mrs and Mrs Johnston were standing with some friends. Celia-Ann was wearing an embellished gown, the like of which Danielle had only ever seen in the fashion glossies she sometimes indulged in. It had to be couture, she thought. Even the colour was exquisite, a sort of turquoise that you'd never see in the shops. It looked like a shimmering jewel. Celia-Ann wore her hair in a perfectly chic chignon, but her face was set in a pained smile.

'Justin, darling,' she said, reaching out to receive a kiss on both cheeks. 'And you brought the girl and her mother.'

'Good evening, Celia-Ann,' Danielle said, but her voice sounded high and thin. It was all she could do to keep breathing normally. *The girl and her mother.* Obviously, she wasn't going to bother being nice in front of her guests. Her own mother, she noted, said nothing at all, just kept staring down Celia-Ann, a look of disapproval on her face.

'Ah, Danielle,' said Jeremy, walking towards them. 'I'm so delighted to see you. And don't you look beautiful, my dear.' He took her hands and kissed her cheek. 'Is this your mother?' he asked, smiling at Rachel.

'Yes, Jeremy, I'd like you to meet my mam, Rachel O'Brien. Mam, this is Justin's father, Jeremy.'

Rachel held out her hand and Jeremy took it and held it.

'I'm so pleased you could come,' he said warmly. 'I'm very fond of Danielle, and it's lovely to meet her family.'

Danielle could tell that Rachel was thoroughly charmed.

'That's kind of you,' she said. 'Danielle's a great girl. Any family would be lucky to have her.' She shot an unmistakable look at Celia-Ann, and Danielle held her breath, fearing an argument right there in front of everyone. But Celia-Ann was looking over their heads, at the room behind them.

'Here she is now, my favourite dressage award-winner,' Celia-Ann said, clapping her hands together. 'Gold in the finals. You are just incredible, Mallory.'

Danielle turned and saw a supermodel walking over to

them. She was tall and willowy, with hair like Kate Middleton – to die for, in other words. She was wearing a deeply sexy strapless gown that clung to her narrow hips as she walked. The necklace she was wearing looked like it cost a million euros. She was so beautiful, Danielle felt almost winded. The whole room was staring at her, and she knew it.

'Celia-Ann,' she said, brushing past Danielle and Rachel and straight into the arms of Justin's mother. 'Thank you so much. And what a party. You've surpassed yourself yet again.' They embraced, and then she turned to Justin.

'Evening, Mallory,' he said, looking oddly formal.

'Justin, my darling,' she said, reaching to kiss his cheek. 'You look devilishly handsome in that tuxedo. You'll have to save a dance for me.'

Danielle knotted her fingers tightly together, trying to stop herself from shouting, or breaking down in tears. There was something between this woman and Justin, she could just feel it. She grabbed her engagement ring and twisted it about her finger, willing herself to remember that Justin was hers, that he loved her. But the way this woman was with him, it was like she knew him intimately.

'Danielle,' Celia-Ann said, smiling dangerously, 'have you met Mallory?'

Danielle shook her head.

'Mallory and Justin were together for two years. Match made in heaven.'

'Mother,' Justin said through clenched teeth. 'No need to bring up the past. Mallory and I are just friends.'

'Of course,' Celia-Ann said, laughing. 'I'm just introducing her so Danielle will know where she fits into your life.' She turned to Danielle. 'Mallory trains here and stables her horses with us as well. She and Justin share an absolute passion for horses. That's how they fell in love.'

Danielle felt light-headed. They worked together. Every day. And he'd never mentioned her? That alone felt like a betrayal. She felt utterly foolish, standing there, not knowing the most basic things about her own fiancé's past. She felt an arm around her waist, and Rachel was suddenly beside her, pressed against her.

'This room is so lovely,' she said, to everyone and no one. 'I think we'll find a nice place to sit and admire it, excuse us.'

She walked Danielle down the room and then to a velvet two-seater sofa. They both sat down and Rachel gripped her hand tightly.

'Keep smiling and look like we're talking normally,' she hissed. 'Do not let that woman get to you. That bitch set that up. Justin loves you, Danielle. He picked you. Don't let any ex make you think otherwise.'

'Look at her,' Danielle said. 'She's like a princess. Jesus, Mam, why the hell did he bother with me at all?' She looked over, and saw Justin leaving the group and walking straight for her and Rachel. His expression was fierce.

'I'll go get us a drink,' Rachel said, standing up. 'Christ knows I need one.'

She left, and Justin plonked down in her place on the sofa. He wrapped his arm around Danielle and kissed her long and softly on the lips, then he leaned his forehead against hers.

'Don't worry about my mother or Mallory,' he said, pleadingly. 'You never mentioned exes, so I decided to follow your lead and just let it be.'

'But you see her every day,' Danielle said.

He shook his head. 'That's just Mother stirring things,' he said. 'Mallory does stable her horses here, but she only spends one day a week with them. When she's about, I make myself scarce. I don't see her every day, I promise you. Obviously my mother has decided to be mischievous tonight, so we just have to stand united and ignore her, okay?'

Danielle's head was spinning. Which was the truth? How could she ever know what Justin got up to out here?

'Danielle,' he said, twining his fingers in hers, 'I love you. I want you. This is all just show and swagger. Don't let it confuse you about what's real. We're real. This ring on your finger is real. You're the only one I want.'

She opened her mouth to answer, but Justin was suddenly clapped roughly on the back.

'There you are, Tinny. How's things?'

Justin grinned up at the young man and stood up to hug him.

'Danielle, this is my baby brother, Michael. This is Danielle.'

'Oh, the one and only!' Michael said, smiling at her. 'He never shuts up about you. But do you mind if I steal him for a few minutes? Rasher and Grimmy have just arrived, and we thought a little whiskey in the gun room, perhaps?' He raised an eyebrow suggestively at his brother.

'Em, no, I'll follow you in later,' Justin said.

Danielle stood up and held out her hand to Michael, who shook it uncertainly.

'Lovely to meet you, Michael,' she said, smiling at him. 'I hear lots about you too. Don't miss out, Justin,' she said, looking at him. 'I'm perfectly fine here. You go have a whiskey, honestly.'

'Thank you,' Michael said, giving her a theatrical bow. 'Much indebted. Come on, Tinny, make haste.' He dragged Justin off by the arm.

Danielle needed time to think, which was why she'd let him go. This was all too overwhelming. She glanced over and saw Mallory staring at her, smirking. Jesus, she thought, of all the bloody exes it's possible to have, he has to have one who looks like she just stepped off the pages of *Vogue*. Danielle sank back in the chair, willing the night to go quickly so they could just get out of there.

'Here you go,' Rachel said, arriving at her side again and handing her a glass of champagne. Rachel sat down and held up her glass. 'Cheers,' she said, and downed half of it in one go. 'God, I needed that. My nerves are shot.'

'I can't drink alcohol,' Danielle said, wishing she could just knock back the whole thing.

'Take a sip to know what quality tastes like,' Rachel instructed, 'then hold the glass like a lady and hand it to me when this one's gone.'

Danielle lifted the delicate flute glass to her lips and sipped. It was smooth, bubbly and delicious. She'd only ever had cheap Prosecco before – and this was nothing like cheap Prosecco.

'That's gorgeous,' she said.

'I know,' Rachel said, nodding. 'I'll never have the like of it again, I'm sure, so I'm going to have a few while it's going.'

'Just please don't get drunk,' Danielle said. 'We're conspicuous enough as it is.'

'We look just as good as anyone else,' Rachel said. 'And of course I'm not going to get drunk. I wouldn't let you down.'

Danielle felt a swell of love for her mother. She might not be happy about the situation, but she was here, where she always was, right at Danielle's side. Danielle reached out and took her hand in hers.

'Thanks, Mam. You're the absolute best.'

'Jesus, you'll have me crying and Maia will kill me for ruining the expensive mascara.'

Danielle laughed. 'Sorry. I just want you to know that, though. You're a brilliant mother. I hope I'm even half as good as you. And I'm sorry, Mam, about college. I know it's hard on you.'

Rachel looked at her and her face softened. 'You've nothing to be sorry about, my love. I just needed time to adjust. It's a big change,' she said, looking around. 'I just want you to be happy. And I don't want this shower of poshies making you feel bad about yourself. That would really kill me.'

'I'll try,' Danielle said.

A delicious smell reached them, and they watched as uniformed waiters carried trays of snacks around the room, offering them to the guests. Rachel flagged one of them down.

'Here, could you just leave that tray on the table there,' she said, pointing to a nearby glass table. 'Thanks so much.'

The waiter raised an eyebrow, but simply said, 'Of course, madam.'

'Now we're set up,' Rachel said, grinning at her. 'Let's eat some of Celia's money.'

While Rachel sampled the food, Danielle took some photos and sent them off to Zara. Her phone pinged with an immediate reply.

Wow! U lucky thing!!!!! Fab!

'It's all a bit boring, isn't it?' Rachel said. 'I'd actually prefer a party in a gaff in Westwood.'

Danielle smiled. 'I know what you mean.'

The next hour passed in people-watching, and it was clear the party was getting more raucous and more drunken. Danielle felt it was rude of Justin's brothers not to come over and introduce themselves, but then, it seemed like everyone was giving her a wide berth. She watched Justin come back into the room, arm in arm with another man, and she knew he was pretty well on. Obviously quite a few whiskies had been downed – what had he said, in the gun room? What a mad place.

She watched Justin's mother intercept him, laughing gaily and leading him towards the huge fireplace, where Mallory was standing with some girlfriends. Danielle felt herself go very still as she watched Celia-Ann engineer it so that Justin and Mallory were standing side by side in the middle, flanked by all her friends. There was a photographer working the room, and she waved him over, indicating that he should take a photo. Mallory put her arm around Justin's waist and leaned into him, her head against his shoulder. Justin was laughing, full of the joys, surrounded by these gorgeous women.

The waiters moved swiftly through the room, taking away the trays and any empty glasses. The same waiter came back and took away Rachel's tray.

'Why are you taking that?' Rachel asked.

'Music's about to start, madam,' he said. 'Time for the dancing.'

Once the area had been cleared, the room was plunged into darkness, and people oohed and aahed and pretend-screamed.

'Murder mystery,' someone shouted out.

'Happy Hallowe'en!' yelled another.

Red laser lights suddenly sprang on and spun around the room, like forked lightning. Danielle couldn't even see where it was coming from. Then a massive disco ball lit up in the centre of the room, and the opening bars of Michael Jackson's 'Thriller' boomed out. The crowd went wild, racing for the middle of the floor to dance.

A figure emerged from the semi-darkness and stood in front of them.

'Danielle,' said Celia-Ann, 'I'd like to have a word, if I may. Would you and your mother join me for a quick chat. Somewhere quieter,' she added.

'Sure,' Danielle said, shooting a look at Rachel, who shrugged her shoulders slightly.

They got up and Celia-Ann led them out of the ballroom and back into the hallway, then down a set of steps. She pushed open a heavy wooden door and when they stepped inside and it closed behind them, it was suddenly blessedly quiet. It was a booklined room, with a wooden ladder to access the higher shelves and a few leather armchairs scattered around a fireplace.

'Oh, I love this,' Danielle said, looking around with a smile. 'Your own library. It's fantastic.'

'Quite,' Celia-Ann said, looking unimpressed.

The door opened again, and Mallory walked into the room, closing the door behind her.

'Hello Danielle,' she said, smirking.

Danielle looked from Mallory to Celia-Ann. What the hell was this? She was very glad her mam was close by. And at least if Mallory was here, it meant she wasn't with Justin.

'We just want to have a little chat about the future,' Celia-Ann said. 'Mallory is part of that future, so I asked her to join us.'

'Okay,' Danielle said, still unable to see where this was going.

'Look, Danielle,' Celia-Ann said, clasping her hands together. 'I know you have a soft spot for my Justin, and he's such a decent boy he thinks he feels the same way, but that's only because he's got you pregnant. He doesn't actually love you, he just has a very strong sense of duty, do you see?'

'That's not true,' Rachel said fiercely. 'Have you brought us in here to lie to us? Because I, for one, don't want to hear it.'

'Now calm down,' Celia-Ann said. 'I really think you'll want to hear what I have to say. Just hear me out. I think it's plain that Justin and Mallory make a beautiful couple. They are destined to be together. Though your little . . . affair . . . has messed things up a bit. But you aren't married, so there's limited damage done.'

So that's why she didn't want a wedding, Danielle thought bitterly. I knew it.

'Justin has a stellar future in front of him, and he needs a stellar wife to help him handle it. That's just not you, Danielle,' she said, with a sickly sweet smile. 'I think you know it as well. But Mallory fits the bill perfectly. I mean, just look at them together.' She picked her phone up off the table behind her and held it out to Danielle.

Danielle didn't want to look, but she couldn't stop herself. The picture was the one taken earlier, by the photographer. The other girls had been cut out of it, so it was just a photo of Mallory and Justin. Danielle swallowed hard. They looked beautiful together.

'This is a pile of crap,' Rachel said. 'Come on, Danielle, let's go.'

'Just another minute,' Celia-Ann said, and Mallory moved to stand in front of the door. 'I know you can see it, Danielle,' she wheedled. 'And if you love Justin, you'll let him go. Let him live the life he's meant to lead. And I'll make it easy for you. This is the good bit, Rachel, so listen up. I'll give you the house on Kingfisher Road, and I'll also give you a lump sum of fifty thousand euros. It's the perfect solution. You move your mother in with you, get her out of that grotty estate, and you bring up baby together in comfort, with money in the bank. You're young, you'll meet Mister Right some day. It's a win–win situation.'

Celia-Ann stared at them, waiting for a reply. Danielle didn't trust herself to speak, because her mind was stuck on that photo, on the vision of Justin's future that looked so right. She couldn't help thinking that his mother was right – she was holding him back from a fabulous life, one where he fitted in perfectly. She didn't, not by a long shot. Her brain felt paralysed. No words would come out of her mouth, and if they did, she was terrified she would say 'Yes'.

'You are a pathetic old witch,' Rachel said, her body shaking with anger. 'How dare you! Justin is old enough to make his own choices, and he chose Danielle. You're so far up your own arse, you can't see that you have no control here. None!'

Celia-Ann's face was red. 'Stupid woman,' she said. 'It's the best offer you'll ever get in your miserable life. Take it!'

'No!' Rachel shouted. 'Now you tell Miss World here to

get away from that door because me and my daughter are leaving.' She looked Celia-Ann up and down. 'I can't believe a woman would do this to the woman carrying her own grandchild. You're a disgrace.'

Rachel grabbed Danielle's hand to lead her out, but Danielle stood her ground. She could feel tears coming, but she didn't care. If she didn't speak now, it would eat her up for ever.

'I'm a good person,' she said, looking Celia-Ann in the eye. 'I adore Justin and I will always do right by him. He can trust me and rely on me. I'll always be there for him. Because that's how I was raised. I didn't come from money, but I'll tell you what, Celia-Ann, I come from manners, and from loyalty and from decency. That's why Justin loves me, because he can't get that anywhere else.'

Celia-Ann looked like she'd been slapped. 'Get out,' she said. 'Out of my sight. You're a gold-digger, nothing more. I knew it from the first moment I set eyes on you. I'll get you out of my son's life if it's the last thing I do.'

Rachel took her hand again, and the two of them walked out, past the bitch-face Mallory and back up the steps to the hallway. Danielle was gasping for breath, totally shocked by all that had just happened. Rachel put her arm around her.

'It's alright, love. Just breathe, there's a good girl.'

'Is everything alright, madam?' It was Morton, the man Justin had introduced them to earlier.

'She's had a shock,' Rachel said. 'I need to sit her somewhere quiet. And maybe you could call us a taxi.'

'Of course. Follow me,' he said, looking at Danielle with concern.

He led them to a sitting room that was empty. Danielle

sat down, focusing on steadying her breathing. She felt broken inside. She was going to lose this battle with Celia-Ann, she could feel it. There was no way she could go up against someone that evil and win. The thought of losing Justin made her feel sick. She really did love him, she knew that from the bottom of her heart.

'Shall I fetch you a glass of water?' Morton asked. 'And shall I ask Mr Justin to come see you?'

'Yes, please,' Danielle said. 'Thank you so much.'

He headed off and Rachel stood looking down at her. 'Don't you take on anything that woman said,' she ordered. 'She's making it up for her own horrible purposes. I can see that Justin loves you. I'd tell you if I thought otherwise.'

'I don't think I can win, Mam,' Danielle said, and she gave in to the tears, putting her hands over her face.

'Oh God, what's happened?' Justin said, coming into the room and going straight over to Danielle.

'Your mother, that's what's happened,' Rachel said.

'Oh don't mind her,' Justin said. 'She's just a bit annoying, but she's fine. She likes you.'

Danielle looked up at him in disbelief, then realised he was quite drunk. He was swaying a bit where he stood.

'She just threatened me,' Danielle said. 'Threatened to break us up.'

'She won't,' Justin said. 'Don't be silly.'

'I'm not being silly,' Danielle said through clenched teeth. 'She took us into a room and told me to leave you. Told me she'd pay me to leave you. She's pure evil, Justin. I want to go home.'

'What?' he said. 'But the party is so much fun. Don't say go home. Come on, come dance with me.'

'No, I want to go home now,' Danielle said. 'I can't stay here after that.'

Justin looked at her obstinately. 'I don't want to go,' he said, looking like a little boy refusing to eat his greens.

'Fine,' Rachel said, stepping between them. 'You go on then, and we'll go home.'

Justin grinned widely at that. 'Fantastic!' he said. 'Great plan. Bye.' And he lurched out the door and back to the ballroom.

Danielle watched him go in disbelief. Who even was this person? She didn't recognise him. What about *in vino veritas* – was this his true self?

'Come on,' Rachel said. 'I asked that Morton fella to call us a taxi. Should be here any minute. Let's get out of here before they think of some other way of insulting us.'

They went out to the front door, where Morton had their coats waiting. He wrapped them around them and they stood in the cold, watching for the lights of the taxi.

'Did you enjoy your night?' he asked.

'No, not a bit,' Rachel said. 'It was awful. And that woman is awful.'

'Had a run-in with the lady of the manor, did you?' he said. He nodded. 'A difficult one at times, she is. I'm sorry to hear you didn't enjoy it.'

'I don't know how you put up with it,' Rachel said. 'All thinking they're better than everyone else, and there they are getting rat-arsed and making a holy show of themselves. Hypocrites.'

'I do so love a woman who speaks her mind,' Morton said, giving her a wink. 'Ah, here's your carriage, m'ladies.' He escorted them down the steps and shut the taxi door once they were safely inside. 'I really hope I see you both again,' he said to them through the open window. 'You're my kind of people.'

Danielle smiled weakly at him. 'Thank you,' she said. He turned and went back up the steps, to take up his post once more. 'Kingfisher Road,' Danielle said to the taxi-driver. Home, she thought, but would it be for much longer?

Chapter 18

BETSY HAD BEEN AWAKE SINCE DAWN WITH LITTLE Arnie. She had heard him gurgling in his cot, then the gurgles had turned into a whimper, which had slowly worked up to a crescendo of all out bawling. Betsy had lain there, fist clenched against her chest, willing his parents to wake up and tend to him. She knew that cry, he was hungry. How could they not respond? She waited, counting off the minutes on the bedside alarm clock. She let it count out twenty minutes, then she got up and pulled on her dressing gown.

'You're right, love,' Noel said sleepily from the bed. 'I was about to do that myself.'

Of course you were, Betsy thought. When Graham was colicky and sleeping badly, Noel had said the same thing night after night. It was always her that did the night shift, though. 'About to' isn't quite the same as getting out of the bed and doing it, she thought crossly.

She walked down the hall, not worrying about being quiet because she hoped Tasha or Graham would hear and maybe come do this themselves – even if only out of guilt. She didn't want to be accused of interfering. But nothing was stirring in the house, just baby Arnie, howling for comfort.

'How's my little boy,' Betsy said, going straight over to the cot.

Arnie kicked his legs and cooed happily at the sight of her. He reached his arms up towards her.

'Now my little divil, do you need some bottle? I think you do.' She lifted him and pressed his hot cheek against hers, breathing in his darling baby smell. He put his pudgy arms around her neck, and it made her heart melt. She felt bad for feeling cross at Noel – the truth was, she was lucky to be the one who got to do this. The rest of them were all missing out.

'Let's go down to the nice warm kitchen,' Betsy said. She could hear rain knocking against the windows, but the house was toasty and quiet, just how she liked it.

Downstairs, Betsy clicked on the lights and the kettle. She put Arnie on his playmat on the floor and set about preparing a bottle of warm milk. He was a big boy, so expecting him to sleep eight or ten hours straight wasn't realistic. He was going to get hungry and need a night feed for another few weeks yet. Graham had been just the same, needing a little bottle at about 5 a.m. until he was eight months old.

When the bottle was ready, she settled herself into the armchair in the corner, with Arnie curled up in her arms. He sucked contentedly, gazing up at her with love-struck eyes. Babies really were a little piece of heaven on earth, Betsy thought, and she gave thanks to God yet again for allowing Arnie into her life, and into her home. In the morning half-light, drowsing in the warmth of the kitchen, Betsy and Arnie both drifted off to sleep again.

'There they are!'

Betsy opened her eyes, momentarily confused, to find Graham and Noel grinning at her.

'We were wondering where you two had got to,' Noel said. 'Stay still for a minute and I'll take a photo.'

Before Betsy had time to orient herself, Noel had photographed granny and grandson curled up together.

'Thanks for doing that,' Graham said, nodding to the empty bottle on the arm of the chair.

'Well no one else was,' Betsy said. 'You two look dressed and ready for action. Are you doing something?' she asked, as she stood up stiffly and handed Arnie into Noel's arms.

'I'm going to take Graham to the golf club,' Noel said, looking pleased. 'There's a four-ball on today and some of the guys playing work in computing and IT, so it's a great chance for Graham to make some contacts.'

Betsy's heart soared with hope. Maybe Graham would make a proper go of things – and do it here in Ireland. It would be wonderful if he got well set up and they stayed for ever.

'That's a fantastic idea,' she said. 'Well you'll need a good breakfast in your bellies for that. Would you both like scrambled eggs with smoked salmon and toast?'

'Always,' Noel said, making Arnie laugh by blowing raspberries on his cheek.

'My God, we're so spoiled,' Graham said. 'This is the life, I can tell you.'

'Whaddya mean?'

They all turned, and saw Tasha standing in the doorway, glaring at Graham. She was wearing another of those unflattering string vest tops she seemed to love so much and tracksuit bottoms that had seen far better days. Betsy couldn't for the life of her understand how a young woman with a decent enough figure would want to go about like that.

'This is no life,' Tasha spat, never breaking eye contact with her husband. 'Don't you get cushy here, Gray, I'm warning

you, because this isn't us, alright? It's the opposite of everything we believe. There's no way we're going to start thinking
like *them*,' she said, putting venom into the last word.

Betsy just smiled sweetly at her. 'Scrambled eggs, Tasha?'

Tasha ignored her and looked at Arnie, nestled happily
in Noel's arms.

'And who the hell removed my baby from his cot?' she
demanded angrily.

Betsy felt a stab of guilt. 'It was me,' she said. 'I'm really
sorry if you feel I overstepped the mark, I didn't want to
interfere, but he cried in distress for twenty minutes, and
then I had to see to him because no one else woke up.'

'I did wake up,' Tasha said. 'Little blighter probably
woke the whole road, carrying on like that. You should
have left him.'

Betsy stared at her, not able to understand. 'You heard
him?' she repeated. 'But then, why didn't you go to him?'

'It's called controlled crying,' Tasha said. 'Eh, parenting
has moved on since you did it, Betsy. We know far more
about how to make a decent kid now. You're supposed to
let the baby cry, then they learn to self-soothe. You wrecked
all our work with him.' She jabbed a finger in Betsy's
direction, which was something she did with annoying
regularity. 'Don't do it again, alright?'

Betsy could feel her heart beating faster. 'Please don't
point at me like that,' she said coldly. 'You're right, I've
never heard of controlled crying, but I hate the sound of
it. If you leave a baby, they get more distressed and cry
more. That's all that's ever going to happen. And he'll have
separation anxiety. I really admire you for reading up on
parenting, but I beg you not to do that with Arnie. It's
horrible, and it goes against nature.'

'What does that mean,' Tasha said, folding her arms. 'That I'm unnatural, like a monster?'

'No, of course not,' Betsy said. 'I just mean that it's natural as a mother to respond to the cries of your baby. Those nonsense ideas are telling you to go against your own instinct.'

'So you think I'm a crap mother, is that it?' Tasha shouted.

Graham held up his hands. 'Hang on, Tash, she didn't say that at all. It's just two different ways of doing things.'

'You're such a traitor,' Tasha said, turning on him. 'Since we got here you've changed. And I don't like this version of you. I can't love Graham. I love Gray. This is doing my head in, living like this. We've got to get out of here, can't you see that?'

'I'm working on getting a job,' Graham said. 'Then we can make our own choices and pick a place we like.'

'And will it have a white picket fence?' Tasha spat. 'Do you want me barefoot, chained to the stove, cooking up apple cake, is that it? Is that your grand vision, Gray? Because let me tell you, it's not mine.'

She turned and walked off, stomping back up the stairs to their bedroom. Betsy and Noel were silent. There really wasn't anything to say. Betsy could see that the gap between Graham and Tasha was widening, and she wasn't sure it could be bridged.

'I'll go talk to her,' Graham said, and he looked so stressed and hurt, Betsy felt her own heart breaking.

Noel played with Arnie while Betsy continued with preparing breakfast. She had everything perfect when Graham came back into the room.

'It's okay,' he said, looking far from okay. 'She's calmed down, and we talked a bit. She knows I'm going out to meet some people today. We'll talk more later. But she's not feeling good,' he said, looking at Betsy, 'so would you mind . . .'

'It's no problem to mind Arnie,' Betsy said instantly. 'I want you and your dad to go out and enjoy the day, and I'll hold the fort here.' The thought of a day with an angry Tasha made her feel ill, but it was important that Graham get time out, and also tried to get a job.

By the time breakfast was eaten and cleared away and Noel and Graham had headed off, little Arnie was ready for a change of scene. Betsy knew it was perfect timing to take him out for a walk, plus it got them out of the house in case Tasha reappeared. She hadn't moved from the bedroom after her outburst, but Betsy didn't want to get another tongue-lashing from her any time soon. She bundled Arnie into a snowsuit and put him in the pram with the waterproof cover.

They headed to the park and Arnie babbled at the falling leaves, at the birds and at anyone they passed by. Betsy loved that about babies, that they showed you the world as if it was the first time you were seeing it. It did the heart good.

On the way back, Betsy saw Nancy walking ahead of her and she hurried to catch up.

'Morning Nancy,' she called. 'How are things today?'

Nancy turned, and Betsy was shocked to see how aged she looked, like she was carrying the weight of the world on her shoulders.

'Hi Betsy,' she said, smiling tiredly. 'How's baby today?'

'He's in flying form,' Betsy said. 'And how about you, do you have any word from the council?'

Nancy shook her head. 'No, nothing has changed. I had

a meeting with them, but they just reiterated the fact that I have to move.'

'I would have gone with you,' Betsy said, upset to think of Nancy going through that alone. 'You should have told me.'

'I took Sean, my solicitor,' Nancy said. 'I knew it was important he got to hear their position.'

'Oh yes,' Betsy said, nodding, 'that does make sense. I'm just glad you had someone on your side of the table.'

'Didn't do any good,' Nancy said, looking horribly sad.

'Don't give up hope,' Betsy said fiercely. 'Maia has scheduled a meeting for this evening, over in Pearl's house. There's been lots of work going on behind the scenes, so we'll talk it over then and see how to proceed.'

'You're all so kind,' Nancy said. 'But you'll have to be prepared for disappointment. Anyway, I better get back and feed Nelly. See you later.'

She walked off, looking like an old woman, her body stooped in a way that wasn't like Nancy at all. Betsy hated to see it. At their age, it didn't take much of a knock to make you feel like you were old, and once that mental switch was flicked, it had a huge effect on you physically. Betsy had seen it before, with her aunt. When she was only sixty-five she had decided she was old, and that was it, she became old. The idea quickly became her reality. They had to do everything possible not to let that happen to Nancy.

'Come on, Arnie, let's go home and warm up,' she said, shivering slightly in the cold wind.

Inside, the house was very quiet. She put away the pram and peeled the layers off Arnie, then put him sitting in the cuddly half-donut she had bought for him. He could sit up and watch her work, which he seemed to enjoy. She set about fixing lunch for him. It was only when she was feeding him, playing aeroplanes with the spoon, that she noticed it. There was a piece of paper on the kitchen table, with a pencil thrown across it. She reached over and picked it up, and her eyes went wide as she read.

Dear G
It wasn't the right sort of life for me. I hope some day you can get that. It's best this way. Arnie will get the love he deserves. Your folks will step in and sort stuff. You'll find someone better and this way we'll all be happy. Don't wait for me, I'm not coming back. It's for the best as I said,
T

'Oh my God,' Betsy said, staring at the note. 'She can't have.'

Arnie was safely belted into his high-chair, so she dashed off upstairs and flung open the door to Graham and Tasha's bedroom. One door of the wardrobe stood open, and it was empty inside. The bed hadn't been made and the curtains were still closed, but Betsy could see that Tasha's things were gone. Hearing Arnie calling out, she raced back downstairs and began feeding him again, but her mind was reeling.

She couldn't comprehend how on earth that woman could walk away from her precious baby. She was also bloody furious at her for leaving Graham, but when push came to shove, he was an adult and sadly, he needed to learn to deal with it. But leaving her baby son . . . it wasn't natural. Just like that damn controlled crying nonsense. What woman could abandon her child?

When Betsy went upstairs to put Arnie down for an afternoon nap, she suddenly noticed that the vase on the table on the landing was missing. She stood looking at the empty spot where it should have been for a few moments, then her hand flew to her mouth.

'Oh no,' she cried, then went from room to room, checking. There were other ornaments gone, including a beautiful clock that Noel's father had given them after their wedding. She went back into the bedroom where Tasha had been sleeping and nearly cried when she saw that the painting was missing. The one she had wished she'd put in her own room, it was gone.

She went into her own bedroom with a sense of dread. Sure enough, the drawers of her vanity table were open. She counted up the missing jewellery, and felt silly for being so upset, but most of it had been given to her by Noel. The sum of emergency cash she kept in there was gone, too.

'How could she?' Betsy said, rubbing the tears from her cheeks.

It was then that she spotted the second note, this one addressed to her. It was propped up behind a jar of night cream.

You got what you wanted Betsy, so I hope you're happy. I'm going back home. I need to be free. This whole marriage thing has been a total drag. I'm not cut out for it, or for motherhood. I choose life, Betsy, I recommend you give it a try. I needed a few things to fund my trip. I knew you wouldn't give it to me if I asked, so this was the only way.

Betsy put her head in her hands and cried, but it was as much from relief as anger. Tasha had ripped through their world like a tornado, but it was over. Arnie would miss her, of course, but they could work hard to make sure he was happy. And perhaps Graham would meet someone new. He was young, so surely he'd find love again and Arnie might have a lovely step-mum. Anything was possible now.

'Goodbye, Tasha,' Betsy whispered to the note.

From downstairs, she heard the sound of a key turning in the front door, and she steeled herself for what she was about to tell them. Poor Graham, his life was about to be turned upside-down. She hurried downstairs to greet them.

'We're back,' Noel called as he came into the kitchen. He registered her expression immediately. 'What's happened?' he said, looking around.

'Mum?' Graham said, looking concerned.

'I'm afraid Tasha left while I was out walking Arnie,' she said. 'And I found this note when I got back.' She walked over to the table, picked up the note for Graham and brought it over to him. She watched his face as he read it, and she could see he was struggling with a whole range of emotions.

'Right,' he said at last, clearing his throat. 'Well, she's a bit volatile, you guys know that. This is probably her just blowing off steam. I'd say she'll be back later. Even if she's angry with me, there's no way on earth she could stay away from Arnie for long.' He smiled weakly at them. 'Sorry for all the drama, but honestly, once she's had a bit of space, we'll sort it out.'

Betsy felt ill with the knowledge that this was no harmless venting on Tasha's part. The girl had made a decision, and she hadn't chosen Graham and Arnie. She knew this would hurt Graham so much, but she had absolutely no choice but to show him the second note.

'Graham, love,' she said gently. 'I think it might be a little more than blowing off steam.'

'What makes you say that?' he said, frowning.

'It's just . . .' she glanced at Noel, who was staring at her. She knew he could tell something was really wrong, but he couldn't guess what it was. She wanted to run into his arms and let him do the talking, let him break Graham's heart, but she couldn't do that. Thanks to Tasha, that job fell to her. 'It's just that, I found another note. One for me. Here.'

She took the other note from her cardigan pocket and handed it to Graham. He read it in silence, his eyes widening in shock. He looked up at Betsy, hardly able to speak.

'What . . . what did she take?'

'That's not important,' Betsy said.

'Yes, it is,' Graham said, and he was fighting back tears. 'What did she take that belonged to you?'

Betsy took a deep breath. 'Just some jewellery and ornaments and a sum of cash from my room.'

Graham stared at her, aghast. 'Are you telling me that my *wife* went into your bedroom and stole your things so she could desert her baby?'

He was so angry, Betsy felt frightened.

'Things don't matter, Graham,' she said quickly. 'All that matters is Arnie and . . .'

'She's nothing but a useless whore,' Graham shouted, eyes blazing with anger, 'and if I never see her again it's too soon. Me and Arnie are gonna be much better off without her. How could she? How bloody could she?'

'I don't think it's right to call her that,' Betsy said gently. 'I know she'll never be in the running for mother of the year, but it's not good to raise that boy to think of any woman in such a derogatory manner.'

'What's suddenly made you join the Tasha fan club?' Graham yelled. 'I thought you felt the same way about her?'

'Easy now, son,' Noel said.

'I did. I do . . . it's just, she's still the child's mother . . . and just because she has no idea of how to behave or conduct herself doesn't mean we should be as bad. Wouldn't it be better to let the anger go and that way that woman has no hold over us? We can't raise Arnie to think and believe that all women are worms. I mean, I hope he'll grow up to love and respect me.'

'Of course he will, Mum,' Graham said. His shoulders dropped and he suddenly looked worn out. 'I mean, it's taken me quite a while . . . in fact, I probably wouldn't have copped on had Tasha not behaved like this. She's shown me the type of person I'd be ashamed to raise. I want my little fella to know right from wrong, just like you and Dad always instilled in me.'

Betsy could feel tears trickling down her cheeks as she listened to Graham. She'd never actually believed she'd hear her son talk this way. He'd rejected them and acted as if he hated them for so long, she'd feared they'd lost him for ever. What Tasha had done was unthinkable, but she actually wanted to shake her hand in one way. She'd given them their son back, with interest! Little Arnie would settle with time, she and Noel would see to that. They'd be around for quite a few years and they'd go out of their way, gladly, to be a grounding influence in this little boy's life.

'It's going to be okay,' Betsy said now, looking at her

husband and her son. 'We'll get through this together and Arnie won't know anything but love. Now, I'm going to boil the kettle and then I want to hear about your day. Let's focus on something positive.'

She wasn't being dismissive, but Graham had a lot to process, and he needed to do so quickly and move on so that he could be a good father to his son. There was no point sitting around mourning Tasha; it was best foot forward now, that was best for everyone.

Chapter 19

PEARL LOVED HOSTING GET-TOGETHERS. WHENEVER Seth was away, she flung open the doors and had her neighbours around and enjoyed sharing good food and wine and having a laugh. She couldn't do it when Seth was there, as he was like a hulking presence that made everyone uncomfortable, but it was something she really enjoyed. That's why she'd leaped to offer to hold the meeting about the CPO in her house. As the women started to arrive, she pressed dainty pastries and red wine on them.

'I won't be able to focus on the agenda,' Maia said, swatting her away. 'Alcohol and battle planning do not go hand in hand.'

'Spoilsport,' Pearl said, smiling at her. 'I'll make you have some when we're done.'

'Thanks for doing this, Pearl,' Nancy said. 'You've really gone to too much bother.'

'This is the most important meeting we've ever had,' Pearl said. 'I'd do anything to ensure we knock this CPO thing on the head.'

Nancy smiled. 'Well, as I said to Betsy, we must be prepared for disappointment. The meeting with the council didn't go well, and they aren't budging an inch.'

'We'll see,' Pearl said. She looked around. 'In fact, where is Betsy? She's always early.'

'I'll text her,' Maia said. She was just typing out a message when the door to the sitting room opened and Betsy came in looking flustered.

'Oh hi everyone,' she said, sitting down and catching her breath. 'Tommy let me in, Pearl, I'm so sorry I'm late. I'm all at sixes and sevens at the moment.'

'Is everything okay?' Pearl asked.

'Everything's great,' Betsy said, smiling at them. 'You won't believe this, but Tasha upped and left today. Back to Australia. Dumped Graham and Arnie, stole my jewellery and cash, and left a note to say we won't see her again.'

Pearl stared at her in disbelief, and Maia, Nancy and Danielle were obviously shocked into silence, too.

'Sorry, Betsy,' Pearl said, 'did you say *stole* jewellery?'

Betsy nodded. 'I did. The selfish little madam helped herself to a pile of stuff. Left me a note saying she had to in order to buy her plane ticket. I feel so sorry for Arnie, but I'm glad to have seen the back of her, I can tell you. Australia's welcome to her.'

Pearl burst out laughing. 'Oh I'm sorry, Betsy, but I did not see that coming. I can't believe she stole stuff on the way out the door. Talk about cheek! You're right, better off without her. I think having a mother who resents being your mother would be worse than no mother at all, if you know what I mean.'

Betsy nodded. 'That's my thinking as well, Pearl,' she said. 'We'll pull together and make it work.'

'If my Zach ever brings home a girl like that,' Maia said, shaking her head, 'I'll brain him.'

'Anyway,' Betsy said, 'I don't want to take up any more time, so let's get talking about the protest.'

'Okay,' Maia said. 'Well, the good news is that I've got the radio station sending a reporter to talk to us and – drumroll, please – my friend in PR I told you about, she has got us Channel 1. They are sending a cameraman and reporter as well, so it will go out on the six o'clock news tomorrow night.'

'So it's all happening tomorrow?' Nancy asked.

'Yes, we are good to go for eleven o'clock tomorrow morning,' Maia said. 'Zach and Zara leafletted the wider area, so I'm hoping for a good turnout. There are local elections in a few weeks, so I've encouraged people as a chance to vent whatever frustrations they have about how things are being run around here. Lots of people are frustrated with the council, for various reason, so that works in our favour.'

'I've made a pile of banners,' Pearl said, 'thanks to help from Tommy and Drew. And we made one large, long one that we can walk behind, with Nancy centre-stage behind it of course.'

'Excellent,' Maia said. 'How about your progress, Betsy?'

'Yes,' Betsy said, 'I have all members of our Residents' Association coming along, plus I petitioned the associations of the surrounding districts, any within ten miles, and there's definitely some interest there. Like you say, Maia, there are a lot of misgivings about the council, so they see it as a chance to fight back.'

'Great stuff,' Maia said, ticking things off the list in front of her. 'And Danielle, any news for us?'

They all looked in Danielle's direction, but she was staring into space, oblivious to the conversation. Pearl had felt she'd been acting strangely ever since she'd arrived. She was sort of there and not there. Danielle suddenly realised they were all looking at her.

'What?' she said, looking startled.

'Are you alright?' Nancy said. 'You're miles away.'

'Fine,' Danielle said.

'I was just asking if you'd made any progress,' Maia said. 'With the legal end of things.'

Danielle shook her head. 'No, I'm sorry. The CPO is perfectly legal, and the council have the law on their side. It's possible to appeal, but I haven't been able to figure out any grounds on which an appeal might be successful.'

'Oh well,' Maia said, 'we'll just have to rely on people power then. Is there anything else?' She looked around, and everyone shook their heads. 'Right, then we're ready. We'll assemble in Nancy's garden at 10 a.m., so we're sorted before everyone else arrives. Are you all good to go at that time?'

The ladies all nodded.

'Kingfisher Road goes to war,' Pearl said with a smile. 'Who would have thought?'

'It's not the first time,' Betsy said. 'There was a couple many years ago fought the council because they disagreed over the boundary line. That was in your house, Danielle.'

Pearl looked over and, again, Danielle looked like a zombie, tuned out and lost in her own thoughts. I wonder what's on her mind, Pearl thought.

'And what happened?' Nancy asked.

'It went on for months, but eventually the council was forced to agree. I mean, they had the map with the title deeds, so it was silly for the council to take the position it did. In the end the land was added to the end of the garden of number ten and that was that.'

'We've got a good case, I think,' Maia said. 'And they'll hate getting bad publicity, so hopefully they'll listen to us.'

'I appreciate all your efforts so much,' Nancy said quietly, 'but please don't be upset if we don't succeed. We'll kick ass tomorrow, but it might not change anything, okay? We need to be ready to accept that.'

'I'm accepting nothing,' Maia declared. 'That's your home.'

'We'll just see how it goes,' Pearl said. 'Now, how about that glass of wine, Maia? And can I tempt you, Betsy?' She began pouring out glasses and relished the prospect of a glass herself, too. She'd share one with Tommy later as well. She was looking forward to curling up beside him in bed. It was the highlight of her day.

'So . . . how was the Johnston party?' Maia asked. 'Zara was mad about the photos you sent.'

Danielle looked like she was going to cry. 'Fine,' she said, and didn't elaborate.

'Well that's informative,' Maia said, looking put out.

'How are your plans coming along for your party, Maia?' Pearl said, eager to change the subject and take the attention off Danielle. There was definitely something wrong there and Pearl felt sorry for her.

'Fantastic,' Maia said, her eyes lighting up. 'The marquee has been made now, and I've everything sorted, I think. The RSVPs are flooding in, the world and its mother will be there. Freddie will have a seizure when he gets the bill, but it should be an anniversary to remember.'

'I can't wait,' Pearl said. 'It should be great fun.'

'And Betsy,' Maia said, 'do tell Graham he's very welcome, and he can bring Arnie too.'

'Thank you,' Betsy said, looking pleased. 'He could do with getting out more. I'll tell him that.'

Pearl tucked her feet under her on the sofa and took a

long sip of wine. This was just lovely. She loved these women.

'And do you know who I've booked as the band?' Maia went on, talking excitedly. 'Do you remember . . .'

She was interrupted by the door to the sitting room suddenly swinging back on its hinges with force. Seth stood in the doorway, glaring at them.

'What's going on, Pearl?' he asked roughly. 'It's Wednesday, it can't be a supper club night.'

Pearl felt like she'd been slapped in the face. She was staring at him, but no words came out. Why the hell was he here?

'Good evening,' he said, looking at their neighbours. 'I was hoping to get some dinner, but it looks like I'm interrupting.'

'I wasn't expecting you until Friday,' Pearl managed to stammer. In her head, she was making a quick mental map of the house, trying to picture if anything was out of place anywhere. The idea of Seth finding out about Tommy made her feel nauseous.

'Yes, well there was a change of plan and I was rerouted,' he said. 'Perhaps when you're finished here, you could rustle up something for me to eat.' He tried to smile, but it looked like a grimace.

Pearl was utterly mortified. He was behaving so badly in front of her friends, making her feel like a servant.

'We're just finishing up an important meeting,' she said. 'Won't be long.'

Seth's eyes moved to the glass in her hand and he sneered. 'Wine and gossip, by the look of it,' he said. 'You don't know the meaning of important meeting, Pearl.' He rolled his eyes. 'Is this the sort of nonsense you spout when I'm not here?'

'Okay,' said Maia, standing up. 'I think we've overstayed our welcome. Apologies for ruining your homecoming, Seth. And thank you, Pearl, that was an enjoyable evening. I'll see you in the morning.'

'Sure,' Pearl said, and her voice sounded weak and thin, like that of a child who was in trouble. He was only back two minutes and she already was no longer herself. How did he do that to her?

The others all gathered their things and stepped past Seth on their way out to the hallway.

'We'll need all hands on deck tomorrow, Seth,' Betsy said. 'Nancy's been threatened with eviction, so we're protesting outside in the morning.'

Seth looked at her with distaste. 'No offence, Betsy, but that sounds like a woman's way of tackling the problem. A waste of time. You need to find a rational solution.'

Pearl wanted the ground to open up and swallow her. She could see that Betsy was working to contain her anger.

'Neighbours support one another,' Betsy said curtly. 'If you'd like to be supportive, you're welcome to join us. If not, please don't insult our efforts.'

Pearl could see Maia grinning at this, no doubt delighted that Betsy had put the boot in, but Pearl's heart sank. Seth had spent the past few weeks being obeyed by everyone, all yes sir, no sir, and here was an insubordinate in his own sitting room. Someone was going to pay for that, and Pearl feared it would be her.

'Goodnight everyone,' she called.

She shut the front door behind them and turned to face her husband. His jaw was set in a hard line.

'I'm tired and hungry,' he said flatly. 'I expect you to be

ready to receive me on my return. That's hardly too much to ask of my wife.'

'I didn't know you were coming back,' Pearl said quietly. 'I would have had everything ready if I'd known.'

'You should always be ready,' he replied. 'Now please fetch me some hot food while I have a shower and change. I'll be ready to eat in twenty-five minutes.'

'No problem,' Pearl said.

Seth stalked off upstairs and she walked into the kitchen, her shoulders sagging, her spirit already broken. He was like a dark shadow suffocating everything in her life, obliterating all that was good. She wanted to sink onto the floor and cry, but she knew that red-rimmed eyes would get no sympathy at all, quite the opposite. She looked at the warm light glowing in the mews, where Tommy was reading to Drew. Both of them would be devastated when they found out Seth was home. She and Tommy had become closer than ever lately; it felt like their relationship was shifting into something even more intimate, even more loving. Not being able to be together would kill them both.

She felt like her heart was actually breaking apart in her chest. She felt jagged and breathless. She gripped the edge of the counter to steady herself. I don't love him, she thought, and she gasped at the truth of it. She'd never let herself go that far before, but she couldn't help it now. The last weeks had been blissful, so happy, and just by stepping into the house, Seth had destroyed it all. What was she going to do when this was her everyday reality? She stared at her reflection in the kitchen window. I'm going to go insane, she thought.

Chapter 20

MAIA LEFT PEARL'S HOUSE FEELING MURDEROUS. She could throttle Seth for his horrible manner, especially when he aimed it at Pearl. She was such a dote, so keen to help others, and he treated her like the paid help. It made Maia's blood boil. Every time she was near him, she could feel her skin prickling with irritation. She'd tried to give him the benefit of the doubt over the years, but really, he was just a nasty piece of work. If Pearl had any sense at all, she'd divorce him and kick him out of her life.

'Night everyone,' Nancy called. 'I'm off to bed.'

'Me too,' said Betsy. 'It's been some day. See you all in the morning.'

Danielle was ahead of Maia going down the driveway, still with that faraway look on her face. There was something going on there, Maia thought.

'Hey, Danielle,' she said, walking faster and falling into step beside her. She put her hand on Danielle's arm and made her turn and face her. 'Don't give me any lies now. What's up? Are you okay?'

To her astonishment, Danielle's face crumpled into tears. 'Oh Maia,' she said and practically fell into Maia's arms, sobbing.

'It's alright, love,' Maia said, rubbing her back. 'A good

cry will do you the world of good. Your hormones are probably going mental. Don't be afraid to just let it out.'

'I think I'm losing Justin,' Danielle sobbed.

'What?' Maia hadn't expected that. Trouble in paradise. 'Okay, come on with me,' she said, linking arms with Danielle and guiding her along. 'Come over to mine and we'll have a cup of tea. Come on.'

Danielle allowed herself to be led like a tired little child. Maia's heart went out to her. She was so young, and she was taking on so much. No wonder she was feeling over-whelmed.

Maia knew Freddie would still be at work, so she brought Danielle into the sitting room off the kitchen. It was small and cosy in there. She sat her down on the sofa and Danielle leaned back and rested her head.

'There now. You just chill out there for a minute and I'll make a pot of tea.'

Maia went out to the kitchen and flicked on the kettle. She found some chocolate biscuits that Freddie hadn't horsed into and arranged them on a plate. She put them on a tray with the milk jug and sugar, cups and saucers. She looked at her arrangement, then took off the cups and saucers. They were bone china and gorgeous, but she felt this chat might call for mugs. She pulled two big mugs out of the cupboard and put them down as well.

When she carried the tray through to the sitting room, she found Zara in there sitting beside Danielle.

'Oh, I didn't know you were here,' Maia said, kicking herself for not checking and making sure no one disturbed them. She didn't think Danielle would want anyone to see her crying.

'I came in looking for my phone and found Danielle,'

Zara said, looking a bit awkward. 'I was just asking if she was okay.'

'She's a bit hormonal,' Maia said. 'Why don't you hop on and I'll take care of her.'

'I don't mind Zara being here,' Danielle said. 'I'm tired of hiding stuff and pretending to be what I'm not.' She sat up and looked at Zara. 'Zara, I'm actually pregnant, my in-laws-to-be scare the life out of me and his mother warned me not to tell anyone about the pregnancy, I messed up my dream of college by getting pregnant, I adore Justin and want to marry him, but right now, I think he might be over me.' She collapsed back onto the sofa.

'Right,' said Zara, looking a bit taken aback, 'that sounds like it covers everything.'

Danielle smiled. 'Now you know me.'

Maia poured her a mug of strong tea and Danielle wrapped her hands around the mug.

'Did you and Justin have a fight?' Maia asked. 'I bet his mother's involved somehow if you did.'

'It was such an awful night,' Danielle said, shaking her head. 'From start to finish, Celia-Ann made me feel like a piece of horse crap she'd stepped in. When we arrived, she referred to us "the girl and her mother", and it pretty much went downhill from there.'

'What a cow,' Zara said. 'You both looked fabulous anyway. She couldn't diss your outfits.'

'No she couldn't,' Danielle said, 'thanks to you two. But she was determined to make me feel like I had no place there. She had this . . . This . . . girl there, Mallory. She looks like a supermodel and it turns out she's Justin's ex. He's never even mentioned her. But she was there, trying to wrap herself around him at every opportunity. I couldn't even begin to compete with her.'

'Mallory Beauchamp,' Zara said, her eyes wide.

'Yeah, Mallory, that was her name,' Danielle said. 'She was so sexy and beautiful. I mean, no dress in the world could make me look like that.'

'Don't make that mistake,' Maia said. 'You're not competing with anyone. He has to love you, and if he does, he wants you exactly because you're you. This Mallory one could look like Jessica Alba, but if she hasn't got your personality, your quirks, then he'd never be happy with her.'

Danielle sighed deeply. 'That wasn't even the worst bit,' she said, hunching over even more.

'It's not?' Maia said, wondering what could beat a super-model ex.

'His mother took me and Mam into a separate room,' Danielle said, her voice very quiet, 'and she offered me the house and fifty grand to get out of his life.'

'Jesus Christ,' Maia breathed.

'She said his future is to be with Mallory in this amazing life and if I loved him, I'd let him go live that life. I'm so confused,' Danielle said, starting to cry again.

'That bloody woman,' Maia said. 'She'd stoop to anything.'

Zara was looking at them in disbelief. 'Do people actually do things like that?' she said. 'She actually offered you money to leave the man you love?'

Danielle nodded miserably. 'How do I fight someone like that?' she said. 'I'm not like her. I hardly know which end of a horse is which, I don't know how to make afternoon tea, and I like to wear old PJs and slippers when I'm watching TV at night. I'm just, like, the opposite of her, and she hates me. How can I bring a baby into that, Maia?'

'You're not bringing a baby into that,' Maia said. 'You're bringing a baby into number ten Kingfisher Road where only Danielle and Justin live. Yer woman doesn't live over there. That's your jurisdiction, and you can tell her to stay the hell away from it. You and Justin will be happy, Danielle. You'll have to learn to handle her, but you can do that.'

'It's so hard when Justin won't stand up to her,' Danielle said.

'Yeah, why did you say you think he's over you?' Maia said. 'What did he say about her horrible conniving offer?'

'Not much,' Danielle said. 'He was half drunk and enjoying himself with his brothers and mates, so he just told me she's mischievous and to ignore her. When I said I wanted to leave, he said he didn't want to. In the end, me and Mam got a taxi and came home.'

'Men!' Maia said, shaking her head. 'Why isn't he clued in to what his own mother's like?'

'Well she is his mum,' Zara said. 'He probably feels he can't be nasty to her, you know.'

'He didn't come home,' Danielle said, her voice heavy with sadness.

'What, since then?' Maia said.

'Not that night,' Danielle said. 'He stayed out there, did his work in the stables the next day, then came home that evening. He didn't seem to think we needed to talk about it or anything. Just acted like nothing had happened. But I can't do that. I'm so upset about it. I'd like him to stand by me and tell her where to go.'

'Oh God, you poor thing,' Maia said, reaching over to

rub Danielle's arm. 'That's really tough. Rachel must have been spitting nails.'

'That's the thing,' Danielle said. 'She's now telling me to leave him. And Celia-Ann is telling me to leave him if I love him, and I feel I don't know what I think anymore.'

'Well, do you believe him that nothing happened and he loves you?' Maia said. 'If you trust him, that's your answer.'

Danielle stared down at her hands, turning the mug around and around. 'I'm just not sure about anything anymore.'

'If his mother wasn't a complete bitch, you and him wouldn't be having any problems,' Maia said. 'I can see her hand in all of this. You can't let her split you up, Danielle. If you fall out of love with him, fair enough. But don't let her lies and tricks be the cause of you losing someone you do love. Somehow you have to find a way of standing united against her.'

'Do you love him?' Zara asked.

Danielle nodded. 'I'm mad about him. I know other people see the money and all that, but I just love how decent he is, and how he makes me laugh. We just get on great, you know. When I hear his car pull up, I feel so happy, even if we're just going to sit on the couch and watch a film.'

Maia smiled. 'That certainly sounds like true love,' she said.

'But I didn't intend for all this to happen,' Danielle said. 'We were having a brilliant time together, but then I missed a period and suddenly my whole life snowballed. I had an engagement ring and a house before I knew where I was. It's been so fast, I feel like I'm only processing it all now.'

'That makes sense,' Maia said. 'The pregnancy was unexpected, so you'd be reeling anyhow, but to then have to move out and into a new house and you probably wouldn't have got engaged so fast if you weren't pregnant.'

'Exactly,' Danielle said. 'We went from messing around and having fun to accelerating into living together and playing at house. I think that's why I feel like everything is out of my control. And then his mother makes it all worse.'

'You've got to get her out of the equation,' Maia said firmly. 'Me and Freddie had to do that with our mothers. It's not easy, and you'll feel like a cow, but it really does make life easier.'

Danielle nodded. 'I know, I'm just not sure if I can do it. Or even how to do it.'

'Em . . .' Zara bit her lip. 'There's something . . . I wasn't sure whether to show you.'

'What is it?' Maia said.

'It's not good,' Zara said carefully, 'but it might give you the ammunition to prove that his mother is against you, and then it might be easier to get him to take a stand, maybe.'

Danielle was looking at her with an expression of fear, and Maia was worried about what Zara was going to do. Danielle already looked on the edge of exhaustion and anxiety, anything else might push her over. She tried to catch Zara's eye and give her a warning look, but Zara was focused on Danielle.

'I'll get it and show you,' Zara said, and she ran out of the room.

Danielle looked at Maia, and Maia shrugged. 'I've no idea what she's talking about,' she said.

Zara came back in carrying a copy of *Glam Life* magazine. She flicked through the pages, then handed it to Danielle. Maia got up and went and sat beside Danielle to see what it was. She gasped when she saw the photograph. It was Justin standing next to an absolute stunner, who was clearly besotted with him.

'That's the photo his mother made the photographer take,' Danielle said, her voice strained.

The caption underneath read: *Beautiful Mallory Beauchamp with the handsome and charming Justin Johnston. These two looked very loved-up at a recent glamorous bash at the family's Westmeath stud. Could there be good news on the horizon?*

Maia could have hit Zara over the head with the magazine. What was she thinking, showing Danielle this?

'You said yourself the mother organised that,' she said quickly. 'This is her doing, no question.'

'Oh God,' Danielle said, bending her head over the magazine.

Zara looked at her in alarm, and looked at her mother. 'I didn't mean to upset you, Danielle,' she said, looking anguished. 'It just proves to him that his mother is trying to split you up, doesn't it?'

'Can I take this?' Danielle asked. 'I need to go talk to Justin.'

'Now take it easy,' Maia said urgently. 'Don't go off saying things you'll regret. This isn't his fault, remember. Don't panic, Danielle. Stop and think for a minute.'

'I don't know what to think,' Danielle said. 'Everyone will be laughing at me.'

'They don't matter,' Maia said. 'If they treat you badly, they're not worth it. They don't matter.'

Danielle picked up her phone and took a photo of the

page, including the caption. She tapped at her phone, then looked up at them.

'I've sent it to Justin,' she said. 'I can't say anything stupid if I'm not there in front of him.'

They all stared at her phone. It buzzed and lit up.

I'm sorry you saw that. I love you Danielle. Mallory is long gone. I know that looks bad, but it's just people making up stuff. Please come home and talk to me.

'What are you going to do?' Zara asked.

Danielle took a deep breath. 'I can't really do anything other than go home, can I?' she said.

'Just stay calm and hear him out,' Maia said.

'Okay,' Danielle said, pulling herself wearily to her feet. 'Maybe he will be able to take her on after this. Maybe it's a good thing.' She looked like she didn't believe a word she was saying.

'Talk it out,' Maia said. 'Let him know how upset you are. Don't blackmail him or force him to choose, but try to show him how it feels from where you're standing.'

They walked back into the kitchen and then down the hallway to the front door.

'Do you want me to walk you across?' Maia asked.

'No, I'm fine,' Danielle said. 'Thanks for everything. Both of you. Goodnight.'

'Good luck,' Maia said softly.

She closed the front door and turned to find Zara standing there, tears in her eyes.

'Did I mess everything up, Mum?' she asked, and Maia's heart melted.

'No, you didn't, sweetheart. Come here.' She wrapped Zara up in a big hug and breathed in the sweet scent of her shampoo. The thought of losing this nearly made her cry out in pain, but she reined it in and held Zara tighter. 'Love is a difficult thing, Zara. It's all ups and downs. This is a difficult time for Danielle, but if she rides it out, it'll get better.'

'What if I've split them up?' Zara sobbed into her shoulder.

'She would have seen that picture sooner or later,' Maia said. 'No doubt it's up on social media. It's best that she knows about it and can tackle him about it.'

'Really?' Zara said, pulling back and staring at her. 'You really think that?'

'Yes,' said Maia, pushing a strand of Zara's hair behind her ear. 'You did the right thing. If they don't make it, it certainly won't be your fault. It'll all be on that Johnston woman's head.'

Chapter 21

PROTEST DAY, NANCY WAS UP BRIGHT AND EARLY, spoiling for a fight. She had got over the initial terrible shock of the CPO, and now she felt filled with a new energy. She wanted to knock the stuffing out of the council today, and that feeling gave her a boost. She'd been feeling like a defeated old woman since that horrible meeting with Derek Small, but now she'd picked herself up and was ready to get back in the running.

She opened her curtains and looked out. Maia was already out on the road, zooming around, sorting out banners from Pearl's garage, ordering Zara and Zach about and generally looking like a woman on a mission.

'That's my girl,' Nancy said, smiling to herself.

She got herself showered, dressed and breakfasted quickly, then pulled on a warm, fleece-lined puffa coat, a bright woollen hat and her furry boots and headed outside, with Nelly on the lead.

Zara was parading around in skin-tight jeans and a belly-top. How the child hadn't frozen solid was beyond her. Nancy wouldn't have removed a single layer if you'd paid her good money. It was November, for heaven's sake. How was Zara not blue-lipped and shivering? The joys of youth, Nancy thought.

'Morning!' Maia called out, waving wildly at her.

'You're well underway,' Nancy said, joining her.

'I want everything to be perfect when it starts,' Maia said. 'The twins have been drumming up interest on social media as well. They've been great. They actually got out of bed at eight o'clock. You are the only person in the world who could prise them out from under the covers at that hour, Nancy.'

'They're so good,' Nancy said, feeling almost embarrassed at all the fuss she was causing. 'I'll get them a little gift each to say thank you. And you, Maia, I'll never be able to thank you enough. With a huge party to organise, you needed this like a hole in the head.'

Maia waved her hand dismissively. 'I'd cancel that party in a heartbeat if it meant helping you. Don't worry about it.'

'Where shall I put this, Maia?' asked a very tall, slim girl with striking red hair.

'Just against the wall, Delia,' Maia said. 'Nancy, this is Delia, Zach's girlfriend. Delia, this is our old friend, Nancy. This is the girlfriend he hid for ages. I'm just coming around to forgiving him.'

'Oh hi, Nancy,' the girl said, smiling widely and coming over to shake her hand. 'Zach has told me, like, so much about you. He adores you.'

Nancy smiled. 'Ditto for me,' she said.

'He's so upset that you might have to move out,' the girl said. 'I just wanted to be here to support him – and you, of course.'

'Well I'm most grateful,' Nancy said. 'Hopefully I'll get a coffee with you and Zach later and we can chat properly.'

'That would be awesome,' Delia said, and she headed off, humming to herself.

'True love?' Nancy said, looking at Maia.

'Seems to be,' Maia said. 'I think he was ashamed to introduce her at first because her family is loaded and very well-to-do, but we're becoming friends now. She's a bit ditsy and out-there, but I'm getting quite fond of her.'

'It's great when they pick someone you like,' Nancy said.

'Good morning, ladies,' Betsy called, coming up to them, pushing Arnie in his buggy. 'Noel is going to take some cupcakes out of the oven for me in fifteen minutes, then he'll join us.'

'Hello Betsy,' said Zara as she rushed over to peek in at the baby. 'Aw no, he's asleep. Can I come and play with him some day?'

'Yes of course you can, dear,' said Betsy, looking her up and down. 'Zara, darling, I know you're beautiful, but really and truly, a belly-top on a day like today? It's freezing. Would you not go put on a coat?'

'I've already lost that battle this morning, Betsy,' Maia said, laughing.

'I'll put on a coat when I feel cold,' Zara said, pouting.

'Well, just don't be a martyr,' Betsy said. 'You don't want to jeopardise your trip by catching flu or bronchitis or some such.'

Maia couldn't help thinking it would be lovely if exactly that happened and Zara had to stay home longer, but she couldn't say that out loud.

'Thank you so much for all your work on this, Betsy,' said Nancy, 'but promise me not to keep the baby out here long. I'd hate him to catch a cold.'

'We'll stay as long as we can,' Betsy said. 'I have lots of cupcakes and coffee and tea ready to go, so send any cold and miserable people in my direction.' She watched Maia haring about and smiled. 'Gosh, she really is a force of nature, isn't she?'

Nancy smiled fondly in Maia's direction. 'She's amazing. I can't get over the support I'm getting.'

By eleven o'clock, the place was heaving with people clapping their hands together as much to get the thing going as to keep themselves warm. They collected at the end of the road, outside Nancy's house, and Maia gave a quick speech to welcome them and set out the reasons for the protest. Seven or eight photographers had turned up from local papers, and Zach had taken it on himself to stand with them, giving names, answering questions and ensuring they got the shots they wanted.

Everyone picked up their banners, which had various versions of Save Nancy's House across them, and they started a march up Kingfisher Road, towards the main road. Nancy and Nelly took pole position behind the first, long banner that said: Save My Home! Maia had managed to get her hands on a loudspeaker and she was bellowing, 'What do we want? No CPO. When do we want it? Now!' The crowd rallied round her cry and joined in. The TV cameras captured it all. The march didn't go far, they just paraded down the main road towards Vayhill, then turned and came back to Nancy's house. It was enough to get the image of protest out there.

Back at the house, the reporters crowded around Nancy, sticking microphones under her chin.

'I'd like to thank everyone who turned out today,' Nancy said. 'Many people have questions to put to the council, but they refused to send any representatives here today. We were forced into this protest because they have placed a CPO on my home – my home of more than twenty-five years – and they won't discuss it with me. I have no choice but to go public with it. I want to stay in my home until I die. That's all I'm asking.'

'Good girl, Nancy,' Maia said, hugging her. 'You're playing a blinder.'

The crowd fell into chatting, and the reporters knew it was over. Maia handed each of them a document with information about Nancy's case and about Kingfisher Road; she had even come up with questions they might have and given answers to them.

'If everyone did things as well as you lot, our job would be a doddle,' the woman from Channel 1 said to her. 'This will make a great feature on the evening news.' She asked to film Nancy walking up her garden path, then closing her front door with a wave. Nancy did it to perfection.

'Lovely!' shouted the film crew, giving her a thumbs-up. 'Thanks so much.'

The reporters and film crew departed, and most of the crowd started to disperse as well. Betsy invited the remaining people over to her house for a warming cuppa. The atmosphere was celebratory, and they were all certain there'd be a notice from the council in the post. After half-an-hour in Betsy's crowded house, Nancy said she'd go on home and thanked everyone profusely.

As she walked back towards Kingfisher cottage, Nancy heard footsteps running behind her. She turned around and saw Danielle jogging towards her.

'I'll come with you, Nancy,' she said. 'There were banners and papers left around your garden, so I'll help clear it up.'

'Oh, you don't have to,' Nancy said. 'I've taken up so much of everyone's time already. You go on back to Betsy's and I'll take care of it.'

Danielle shook her head. 'No, you're stuck with me.'

Nancy laughed. 'Okay, neighbour,' she said. 'Many hands and all that.'

As they worked, picking up rubbish and stuffing it into bin bags, Nancy asked Danielle what she felt about the protest.

'It was great,' Danielle said. 'So many people, and the support was very genuine.'

'But do you think it will work?' Nancy asked.

Danielle looked unsure. 'Maybe,' she said.

'Oh come on, don't go all shy on me,' Nancy said. 'I love a good fight, but my gut is telling me it won't change anyone's mind. I didn't want to say that in front of the others because of all their hard work. Tell me what you really think.'

'Okay,' Danielle said, straightening up and dropping the last piece of paper into the bag. 'I'd agree with your gut. I don't think the council does U-turns quite as easily as everyone is imagining. They'd be ready for a reaction and feelings running high, but it doesn't mean they'll turn on their heels and run away.' She shrugged. 'To be really honest, I don't think it will make a blind bit of difference to them. Although I really hope I'm wrong, obviously.'

'Yeah, my sentiments exactly,' Nancy said, with a wry smile. 'Come on, we're done here and we're both frozen to the bone. Come in and have a cup of tea with me. It's the least I can do.'

They went inside and down to the kitchen.

'You point and I'll make the tea,' said Danielle. Nancy was so weary she didn't put up a fight. She perched on a kitchen chair, but her guest ordered her into the sitting room, where Danielle quickly cleaned out the fire and relit it.

'Now we'll be much cosier in a few minutes,' Danielle said as she brought a tray in. There were enough cakes to open a shop, so they had their pick and sat back nursing a warm mug each.

'So . . . would you like to tell me what you're hiding?' Nancy asked as she lay back against the cushions and sighed. 'Ah this is truly wonderful.' She looked over at Danielle, who looked stricken. 'It's alright, love. You don't need to say anything if you don't want to. I just reckon there's stuff going on with you that's causing you some sleepless nights, judging by those bags under your eyes. You don't seem yourself. If you'd like to talk, I'll listen and I won't repeat it to anyone. It might be good to lift the burden.'

'Janey mac, am I that transparent?' Danielle said. 'It's just that . . .' She was interrupted by a loud banging noise in the kitchen. Well, it was loud enough to make them both jump.

'Oh bless them,' said Nancy. 'Don't worry about that. I've a pair of kingfishers in the garden. They've meandered over here from the local wildlife reserve and set up home. I usually put out food for them, but I guess I forgot with all the commotion today.'

'They aren't going to let you forget them,' said Danielle. 'That's the cutest thing. What do you give them?'

'There's parrot food there and some dried insects in the jar on the windowsill. Those are their favourite.'

'Nice,' said Danielle wrinkling her nose. 'But I guess that's what they're meant to eat. This house is obviously like a little takeaway stop for them.'

The two women got up and went into the kitchen.

'Can you see them?' Nancy whispered, pointing.

'Oh my God, they're so beautiful,' Danielle said, staring in wonder. 'They're so blue.'

'I know, aren't they gorgeous? I'd nearly be moved to believe in God when I look at them, they're so lovely.'

'Can I feed them?' Danielle asked.

'Sure. The stuff's there on the windowsill. No sudden movements. Just move slowly and they won't mind you.'

Danielle crept over and opened the window slowly and sprinkled some food on the sill outside. The two birds hopped closer, eyeing her cautiously. She closed the window noiselessly and stood back. Sure enough, they hopped in closer and closer, until they were standing right on the sill outside the window, jerking insect bits into their beaks.

'Yuck, and yet gorgeous.' Danielle laughed. She watched them for a while, then she said, 'Are they, like, endangered or anything? I've never seen kingfishers before.'

'I checked this out,' Nancy said. 'They aren't in danger just yet, but they are amber-listed, which means they are under threat. And do you know, they are the reason the road got its name.'

'Are they?' Danielle said.

'Yep. You know the nature reserve out on the outskirts of Vayhill? Well, the roads around here were named for the birds found there. This pair obviously hopped the fence and then I spoiled them, so they've stayed.'

'I didn't know that,' Danielle said, looking at them thoughtfully. She slowly took her phone from her back pocket and took some photos of the little birds pecking hungrily at their food. 'They've given me an idea,' she said.

'You have the photo for your Christmas card, do you?' Nancy asked.

'Not quite, but something like that,' Danielle said.

'I leave the small shed door open for them,' Nancy said, 'and I see them going in and out of there. I'm hoping they're making a nest in there for the winter, but I'm not sure. I daren't go and disturb them, on the off chance that they are. But they're the sweetest little creatures, aren't they?'

'They really are,' said Danielle as she took a few more photographs.

'So what's your big idea?' Nancy asked as they returned to the sitting room, where the fire was now blazing.

'I'll tell you when I've figured it out properly,' Danielle said.

'Oh this is lovely and cosy in here,' Nancy said, taking up her cup again. 'Thanks for getting that fire going. Now, where were we?'

'You were grilling me for information,' Danielle teased.

'I'm not being nosy, honest,' Nancy said, 'but you do seem troubled.'

'I am,' Danielle said simply.

Nancy listened intently as Danielle described her life before Justin, how they met, how his family reacted to her and all about the party they went to, where his mother had treated her with huge disrespect and made it clear she wanted Danielle out of her son's life. Nancy kept her expression neutral, but she couldn't believe the woman was capable of such blatant snobbery and, frankly, stupidity.

'So are you thinking twice about marrying him?' Nancy asked.

Danielle sighed. 'The thing is, Nancy, I'm pregnant.'

'What!?' Nancy was losing her touch – she hadn't

realised. 'That's wonderful news, Danielle. Congratulations. Oh you'll be such a lovely mother. You're made for it.'

'Me?' Danielle said, looking at her in surprise. 'I'm only twenty, Nancy. I've no idea what I'm doing. How am I going to raise a baby? And what if I end up raising it on my own, if me and Justin can't make a go of it?' She started crying softly. 'I can't think about anything else. I feel so trapped. I just don't know what to do.'

'Would you give up the baby?' Nancy asked. 'Or have an abortion?'

Danielle looked up in astonishment. 'No,' she said immediately.

'Well now, that's something you know for sure,' Nancy said. 'You answered that from the heart, and your heart knows you want this baby. That's a hell of a lot to know, my dear.'

'I suppose,' Danielle said, sounding unsure.

'Baby steps,' Nancy said. 'It's hard to know everything at once, so just start with what you do know. So, you want this baby.'

'Yes,' Danielle said, 'but it's not that straightforward. I also want to finish my degree and to have a good career. I have a feeling that's going to be very hard to get back on track, even if we have money. A baby is going to change everything, isn't it? Maybe even me.'

'That's true,' Nancy said.

'I mean, are you glad you didn't have any children?' Danielle asked.

Nancy took a deep breath. 'Seeing as you're divulging secrets, I guess I should let you in on mine. I do have a son.'

Danielle's eyes shot wide open. 'Do you? I didn't know. I thought you were the cool childless one.'

Nancy smiled at that. 'I am,' she said, 'but it's complicated. When I was sixteen I got pregnant. I won't go into it, but it was something I didn't want to happen. When my folks found out, they sent me to a Magdalene.'

'Oh God, I've heard awful stories about those places,' Danielle said. 'My mam's friends used to whisper about it, and I couldn't believe the stuff they said.'

'Believe it,' Nancy said grimly. 'It's all true. They basically imprisoned us and punished us for having sex, even if it was rape. It was a horrendous place. But I survived. I was stronger than I realised. They took my baby, though, when he was one month old.'

Nancy noticed that Danielle's hand instinctively went to her belly. It was a lovely gesture, and it convinced Nancy that Danielle would go on to have this baby and be a good mother.

'They just . . . took him,' Danielle said incredulously.

'Yep. I had no way to stop them, no one to tell, no one to turn to. That's what it was like back then.'

'So what did you do?' Danielle asked.

'I made a life,' Nancy said. 'I thought about him, sure, but I tried to put it behind me and move on. I lived in lots of different places, I drank too much and hurt anyone who tried to love me, but then I eventually did move on, in my heart and my head. And I love being just me,' she said, not sure if such a young woman could understand this. 'I realised, later, that I wouldn't have been a good mother. I'm not cut out for it like you are. My boy was better off with the family that adopted him.'

Danielle shook her head. 'That's mad,' she said. 'You'd

never guess all that from you. You're so feisty and funny.'

'Everyone's hiding something,' Nancy said, nodding. 'Of that much you can be sure.'

'But if I don't have this baby, I'll be free too,' Danielle said. 'I could go back to college and continue on and have that life, the one I meant to have.'

'You could,' Nancy said, 'but then, you've got to play with the cards you've been dealt. I had to do that. You're pregnant, you've got a ring on your finger, that's the situation right now.'

'But is it the situation I want?' Danielle said, looking almost scared at the thought.

'Only you can answer that question,' Nancy said. 'The thing you've got to remember is to be really honest with yourself. If you're honest about what you want, you can't go far wrong.'

The two women looked at one another.

'So what do you want?' Nancy said.

Danielle looked at her for a long time, in silence. Finally, she bowed her head and said, so quietly Nancy had to strain to catch it, 'I don't know anymore what I want.'

After Danielle had left, Nancy sat thinking by the fire for a long time. Her heart went out to the young girl. She was coping with so much at such a tender young age. Who the hell knew what they wanted at twenty? Normally, you got a bit more time to figure that out, but Danielle had been thrown into the deep end.

Nancy was glad she hadn't mentioned David – Steve – coming back into her life. She was still trying to process that one herself. She couldn't figure him out. He seemed to want to be in her life, and yet, what was he getting from it? She didn't feel they'd clicked or gelled or whatever, there wasn't really a bond there, and yet he wanted to stick around. If she was being honest with herself, she would be fine with saying goodbye to him and leaving it all in the past. Being with him made her feel tired and incomplete, and she hated that feeling. But how could she ever tell him that?

She had just changed so much over the years, she reckoned. She'd fully and totally accepted being childless, and that acceptance had changed her. One day she realised that the decision not to have a kid was just as important as the decision to have a kid, even though it took her years to see that. But really, deciding to be childless came with a bunch of other decisions, and making those choices shaped your whole life and how you viewed things. You became yourself right down to your bone marrow, it was through and through. And now, she was being asked to recast herself as a different person, and she was really struggling. She couldn't see a way to do that. She was nearly seventy, for Chrissakes, who wants to go doing big personal changes at that age? No one, that's who. And certainly not her. She sighed. The things she wanted were so simple – her home, her Nelly, her friends, her freedom, her sense of self and independence – and yet, suddenly it seemed that all those things were in doubt. Nancy shook her head. It really is a funny old life, she thought.

Chapter 22

DANIELLE SAT IN HER PERFECTLY NEAT, PERFECTLY empty kitchen. Those conversations with Maia, first, and then Nancy had left her feeling raw. She wasn't used to being so honest with people, and she felt very exposed and uncomfortable. But at the same time, those talks had brought home to her the enormity of what she was doing by leaving her old life and shacking up with Justin. She had to keep reminding herself that her feelings were valid and she was allowed to have them. She was worried, she was unsure, and Justin's pretty limp attempts to convince her all was well weren't working.

She'd tried again last night, after talking to Nancy, tried to make him see things from her point of view. But he'd had a stressed out day at the yard because the horses were suffering from some viral infection, and he'd been too tired to really engage with her. In fact, whenever the question of his mother came up now, she could see him struggling not to roll his eyes. Obviously he felt it was all done and dusted, and that she was just rehashing it over and over again. She'd felt stung by his reaction because, for her, it was far from over. They were supposed to have a whole life ahead of them together, but he wasn't willing to see the very sharp thorn in their side. He might be stressed and tired, but he still had to be her partner.

She looked around at her 'home'. Although the house was quickly filling up with pieces they'd bought together, Danielle still felt as if she was living in someone else's house. She twirled her ring around on her finger. The diamond and sapphire cluster engagement ring was more like a small mountain of ice. She'd never seen anything like it, let alone had one on her finger. She'd never been one to pore over wedding magazines or watch that *Say Yes to the Dress* show that was her mam's guilty pleasure. And yet here she was, living a life most girls would kill for, but one that made her question everything about herself.

Whenever she thought of her own mam, her heart hurt. Rachel still looked at her with those misty eyes, obviously thinking of the other life Danielle could be living right now. Her mam was ill-at-ease in the house whenever she visited, which wasn't often. She could tell Rachel was struggling with all this as well, and it was creating a chasm between them that frightened her. They hadn't always seen eye-to-eye, of course, but when her dad walked out on them ten years ago, they'd become a tight unit, their own little cheerleading team. The fact that it now felt they were living on two different planets really hurt. There was no way she wanted to be in a situation where she had to choose between Justin and Rachel, she just couldn't do that. But then, it felt like Rachel was making that choice for her by not coming round. Would she be there to help when the baby arrived? Danielle knew she'd be completely lost without her, and she couldn't see Celia-Ann changing stinky nappies and cheering her on while she breastfed. She needed her mam.

Danielle suddenly felt like she was in a cage, or one of those rooms where the walls close in until you're crushed. She wanted to get away from it, away somewhere she could think straight without all this luxury turning her head and making her question herself. She needed to figure out what she was going to do now, and she couldn't do that in this swanky pad that felt alien to her. She felt in her pocket and pulled out the keys to the Range Rover. It was a monster and she hated driving it, but it certainly turned heads. She hadn't even told Rachel about it, because she knew she'd be in for a pile of slagging about her 'fancy new life', but right now she needed one thing: to go home, her real home. She grabbed her bag and coat and slammed the front door behind her. She climbed into her car and switched on the engine, then pulled slowly out of Kingfisher Road and headed in the opposite direction.

When she reached Westwood, she could see people staring at the Rover, clocking how much it cost and who was driving it. She kept her eyes straight ahead, hoping her mam wouldn't kill her for bringing all this attention on them. She wished for the umpteenth time that Justin had let her keep the Yaris as a back-up car, but he'd been adamant that it had to go. As she navigated the roads near her old home, she realised with a shock that she hadn't been out here in about nine months. When she was living on campus, she hadn't wanted to leave it and then once she'd met Justin, she'd been totally besotted with him and spent every spare second with him. There she was, being hurt that Rachel wasn't visiting Kingfisher Road, but now she realised her mam could accuse her of the exact same thing. What had happened to them?

She pulled up at the gate, noting that it was still hanging on one hinge. There was very little space to park, but she did her best. Getting out, she checked her parking, then nodded, pleased with how well she'd managed. She pressed the lock button and the alarm made a very loud beeping noise. She jumped and then flushed, hoping half the road hadn't heard it.

Her heart hammered in her chest and she began to sweat as she walked up the small driveway. It was all so familiar, yet so far away from the life she'd just begun. The house looked like a tiny doll's house in comparison with where she lived now. The other houses were so close together, it felt stifling.

The sound of the ping-pong of the doorbell made her want to cry. She had the front door key in her hand, but she was afraid to use it. This wasn't her home anymore, and she felt she no longer had the right to just walk right in.

A figure appeared and stared at her through the mottled glass panel. The door opened slowly.

'Mam,' Danielle said, as her voice cracked. 'Can I come in?'

Rachel looked out and beyond Danielle to the sleek car standing outside her house. 'Jesus, Mary and Joseph, did you drive that thing here? Why did you bring it here? They'll have the wheels off before we've finished a cup of tea.'

Danielle smiled in spite of herself. 'It's okay. I don't have the other car anymore.'

'Is that so?' Rachel said, looking put out. 'Too high and mighty for any car I could give you, I suppose. Well, come on in and don't be standing there on the step.'

She stood to the side and Danielle walked past her, breathing in the longed for smell of home. They walked in silence to the kitchen, where Danielle automatically filled the kettle and flicked it on.

'Tea or coffee?'

'Tea would be grand,' Rachel said, watching her carefully. 'So what brings you down here?'

Danielle felt her mam had used the word 'down' purposely, and it made her feel awkward. But then she thought of what Nancy had said – if you're honest, you can't go far wrong. She took the plunge.

'I wanted to see you, Mam. I'm missing you so badly. I haven't seen you since the party. I thought you might visit more often.'

Rachel sighed. 'You're moving on, Danielle,' she said. 'I just can't cope with what you're moving into. That party was . . . I mean, Jesus Christ, Danielle, that woman tried to pay you to get out her son's life. I've seen a lot of things in my time, but I've never seen the like of that. I don't think I can follow where you're going. Those people are horrible. I'd prefer the mad ones around here, at least you know exactly where you stand with them. But that shower, no. It's just not for me, love.'

'But . . .' Danielle felt like her head was going to explode. For a bizarre moment, she felt like her mam was breaking up with her. 'But I need you, Mam,' she said. 'I'm all alone over there. I'm in a big house I don't know what to do with, driving a big yoke that terrifies me, and Justin's gone all day. I'm starting to get on really well with the neighbours, but my life feels so tiny and so . . . suffocating. I honestly don't know what I want anymore, Mam.' Danielle put her head on the table and sobbed. She felt her mother's rough hands on her shoulders.

'There, there, my little one,' Rachel said. 'I didn't know you felt like this. Do you mean, like, are you thinking of leaving Justin?'

Danielle nodded her head, tears flowing. She gulped. 'Maybe. I mean, what if Celia-Ann is right and I'm just holding him back? And what if I can't be happy in the life he's offering? If he never takes my side against his mother, I'm not sure we can be happy. My head is hurting thinking about it all, Mam. I just don't know what to do.'

'I'll tell you what you can do,' Rachel said. 'You can stop here until you figure things out. Your old room is just as you left it. You can move back in and just take a breather while you make your own decisions, alright?'

Danielle nodded miserably. 'Yeah, I think maybe I should do that,' she said sadly. 'I can't seem to see the wood for the trees at the moment.'

'And you know,' said Rachel slowly, 'you could give the baby up for adoption. Think of it, Danielle, by this time next year it would all be over and you'd be back in Trinity, studying law, making a life for yourself. Think of it.'

'I know,' Danielle said. 'I have thought of it. I hate the idea, but I know it's one option.'

Rachel smiled. 'That's the girl, don't close down any options. Just put everything out on the table and think about what's best for you. Now, you look exhausted, so I'm going to put you to bed for a few hours. Don't even bother arguing. You look like you need a good rest.'

Danielle didn't have the energy to argue, and it felt good to be mothered. She went along meekly as her mother brought her up to her room and closed the curtains.

'There's pyjamas in the top drawer there,' she said. 'I'll wake you for dinner.'

Danielle opened the drawer and took out her favourite tartan PJs. Her mother watched her from the door.

'It's good to have you home, love,' she said, then she went out, shutting the door quietly.

Danielle undressed, put on the PJs and crawled into bed. Her bed. The bed where she'd dreamed about being a lawyer and making something of herself and making her mam proud. She was looking at a fork in the road now, and she didn't know if she could even trust herself to make a decision. Old life or new life? She wished to God she could get some clarity. She drifted off to sleep, giving in to the delicious darkness that closed in around her.

'Danielle, love, wakey-wakey. You've been asleep for hours. I want you to get up and eat something.'

Danielle slowly opened her eyes and looked around, and remembered. The heaviness hit her shoulders instantly. Her immediate thought was: I don't want to be here. She violently pushed that thought aside.

When Danielle got downstairs, Rachel had cooked up a lasagne that smelled amazing.

'Thanks, Mam,' Danielle said, suddenly realising just how hungry she was.

'No problem,' Rachel said, filling two plates. 'Have you checked your phone?'

'No,' Danielle said, looking around. 'Where did I leave it?'

'Don't worry,' Rachel said. 'But I've had a text from Justin asking where you are, so you should probably drop him a line to say you're alright.'

'God, I hadn't even thought of that,' Danielle said, feeling guilty. She felt in her jacket pocket and found the phone and quickly fired off a text. *Need a few days to think. Going to stay with Mam. Sorry, Justin, but I'll come back soon. X*

They carried on with their meal, but all the while Danielle

was thinking about her phone, and the fact that he didn't bother to reply. Rachel talked away about her neighbours and who was having an affair with whom and all the gossip, but Danielle was thinking about Justin, wondering if she could have misjudged him so badly. She was thinking about all the hours spent twined around him in bed, laughing together, kissing and making love – could that have been a lie? It didn't seem possible. Remembering those times made her ache with longing and loss. She couldn't believe she was sitting here, actually thinking over the possibility of chucking it all in, giving her baby up for adoption and carrying on as if it all hadn't happened. Was she being clever, or utterly mental?

'I'll clear this away and make us a pot of tea,' Rachel said, standing up and taking the plates to the sink. 'It's so nice to have you here, love.'

'Thanks, Mam,' Danielle said. 'That's a cold night. Do you want me to light the fire inside?'

'Sure. That's a good idea.'

Danielle went into the sitting room and set about making a fire in the grate. It had always been her job, and she loved doing it. When she had a fire going, she pulled the curtains against the dark evening.

She checked her phone again. Nothing. Her heart broke a little. Maybe that was her answer right there.

Chapter 23

FREDDIE CAME HOME TO A KITCHEN FULL OF women. Maia, Zara, Lottie and Delia were waiting their turn for makeup, giggling and joking together. Maia laughed as she heard Freddie cursing under his breath.

'I'd say they can hear you all gossiping from the other side of Vayhill!' he said.

'No men allowed in here,' Zara shouted as she playfully threw a tea-towel across the kitchen at him. He caught it and threw it back at her with a grin.

'Hey honey,' said Maia as she breezed over in her long black satin dressing gown to give him a kiss. He looked down at her pert chest and smiled. 'You're early! That's good . . . Oh . . . your eye . . . What happ—'

'Nothing,' he said quickly, glossing over the fact his right eye looked as if it had met with a baseball bat.

Taking him by the elbow, Maia led Freddie to the small study adjacent to the kitchen.

'What the hell?' she asked, staring at him in disbelief.

'You're looking well,' he said as he plunged his hand into her dressing gown. 'God, I love your boobies. They were one of your better ideas. Let's go upstairs for a quickie while they're distracted.'

Maia knew from experience that it was always better to oblige him. It would put him in good form for the party that night. The guests would be here in two hours, and she needed her man in loved-up anniversary form, so she grabbed his hand and they snuck off upstairs. They ended up locking the bedroom door (her idea) and having a quick tumble in the sheets.

'Oh God, that felt good,' Freddie said as he lay back against the pillows, his gold neck chain stuck to his sweaty chest.

'So are you gonna tell me how you got that shiner?' Maia asked. She had tried to get into the sex but seeing his eye up-close was even worse. She was completely distracted, wondering what had happened to him. She felt a lump of worry in the pit of her stomach and his vague answers weren't helping to dissolve it.

'Just a misunderstanding that's been sorted now,' he said. 'Nothing worth worrying about, my princess. So, tell me what's happening.'

'You'll have to cover that eye with some makeup tonight. I'll get Sorcha to do it. Otherwise everyone is going to wonder why you look like that.'

'Fuck them. It's none of their business. I'm paying for the best party this year for them. Isn't that enough?' he flared.

'Hey!' she hissed. 'Don't start yelling at me. We need to have a story. It's not usual to go around with your face smashed in. Whether you like it or not, you need to come up with something and we both need to stick to it.'

Just then the door was nearly taken off the hinges.

'Open up?' said Zach, knocking impatiently.

'Sorry, love, we were having a private chat so I locked the door,' said Maia, quickly pulling on her dressing gown and wrapping it tightly around her. Freddie gave her a lascivious wink and pulled the sheets up higher.

Zach walked into the room and stopped dead when he saw his father. 'Oh God, what happened to you, Dad?' he said. 'That looks wicked.'

'Your father was jumped last night in London,' Maia said, thinking quickly.

'Yeah,' said Freddie. 'A gouger tried to rob my laptop. I gave him a good dig in the face, but the little fecker got me with one of those cheapo signet rings.'

'Ah, bad one,' said Zach. 'It looks savage, though! My mates will be well impressed tonight. Can we tell them you got it doing MMA?'

'No, we can't,' Freddie scoffed. 'I'm not bloody Conor McGregor and I'm not pretending I am.'

Zach went to the en-suite bathroom and 'borrowed' a load of hair products and left again.

'See,' Maia said. 'You're not going to get away with looking like that without people commenting.'

'Alright, alright,' he said. 'When you lot are finished, I'll let Sorcha do her worst.'

'Thank you,' Maia said. 'But I'm still worried, Freddie. You can't fob me off with silly lines. We have to drop it now because the night's about to kick off, but I am really freaked by it.'

She went back down to the kitchen. where she was next in line to have her makeup done. She laughed along with the girls, but her heart wasn't really in it. A black eye was serious. Had someone targeted him? Another idea suddenly occurred to her and made her feel sick – what if a jealous husband had caught him and given him a smack? Maia forced herself to breathe deeply and calm down. She had the party of the year on her hands tonight, so she was going to have to park Freddie's damn black eye for now.

A short while later, made-up and dressed, she scrutinised her look in the full-length mirror in her dressing-room. It wasn't perfect, but it would have to do. Sorcha had done a good job, as always. Her botox and fillers had been done a couple of weeks previously, so her skin looked nice and taut. She'd booked herself in for a little eye lift and the surgeon had mentioned the possibility of doing a little work on the underside of her chin. She patted it now with the back of her hand. She should've gotten it done at the same time last summer. That was a missed opportunity.

She stepped outside onto the landing just as Freddie stepped out from his dressing-room. He looked very handsome in a dark grey suit and black shirt.

'You look amazing, love,' he said as he caught her in his arms. 'Look, sorry about earlier. I was in foul humour after last night. I'm fine now. And there really is nothing to worry about. I promise you.'

'Good,' she said, feeling some small sense of relief. 'I actually feel scared when I look at that eye.'

'My little worrier,' he said, smacking her on the backside. Her dress was made from blush-and-gold silk and she knew she'd have to be careful she wasn't wobbling in it. It was very unforgiving, especially at her bum, but it was also incredibly sexy and cool. Paired with sky-high heels and her diamond necklace and bracelet, she wanted to look young and confident. 'I know they'll all arrive in a few minutes,' he said, 'but I just wanted to grab a minute alone with you.'

'Freddie,' she warned, 'I can't be rolling around the bed now I'm done up.'

'Not that,' he said, laughing. 'Here.' He handed her a

long, rectangular box. 'You've probably nearly forgotten with all that's been going on, but happy twentieth anniversary, my love. I'm still mad about you.'

'Oh!' Maia blushed. She actually had forgotten the point of the night in the midst of the unending arrangements.

Maia opened the box slowly. Nestled inside was the most beautiful watch she had ever seen. She gasped and touched it gently.

'Jesus, Freddie, it's exquisite,' she said. 'It's a Cartier. My God, did you rob a bank?'

Freddie laughed. 'Only the best for my Maia. It'll look perfect with the rest of your diamonds. Will you wear it tonight?'

'I feel like I'd need a bodyguard,' she said. 'Will you put it on for me? I'd be terrified of breaking the clasp or something.'

Freddie took it gently from the box, wrapped it around her wrist and closed it shut. 'There, absolute perfection now,' he said, kissing her.

'Thank you, Freddie,' she said, wrapping her arms around his neck. 'It's too much, but I love it.'

'Right then,' he said, taking her hand. 'Time to be the incredible married couple we are. Here we go.'

They headed downstairs hand in hand, and Maia just knew they made an incredible entrance. She felt a rush of happiness as the early guests turned to stare at them and clap their arrival. She felt like a movie star on the red carpet, and she loved it.

That feeling lasted about five minutes, until the ten friends each Zara and Zach had invited turned up. Each girl was more beautiful than the next, oozing style, confidence and youthful splendour. Oh well, Maia thought, I can't turn back the years, but I can be the most stunning old person at the ball!

Nancy was there, smiling at them in delight. 'Happy anniversary, you two,' she said, kissing them both. Freddie spotted an old pal and left them to go greet him. 'Maia!' said Nancy, holding her arms out to her. 'Oh you look utterly stunning, my darling.'

'Aw thanks, Nancy,' Maia said. 'And you look gorgeous. I love that yellow colour on you. Let's see if we can find a glass of bubbly. And don't worry, I ordered all sorts of non-alcoholic stuff as well for anyone who can't take high-class champers!'

A waiter immediately arrived over with a tray, and Maia took a flute of champagne while Nancy took a non-alcoholic cocktail, complete with umbrella. They made their way through the garden, waving to the stilt walker who was blowing balls of fire into the sky. A red carpet led to the marquee, lined by pretend paparazzi whose camera lights flashed and popped as they walked by. The drinks reception area encompassed the large fountain water feature in the garden, which was dressed with strings of twinkling lights she'd ordered and Japanese floating flowers. Maia was so pleased with how it had all turned out, from an image in her head to a head-turning reality.

'How many are coming?' Nancy asked in awe as they walked into the main marquee.

'I'm expecting about a hundred and forty,' Maia said, feeling a sudden shot of nervousness. 'That's if they actually turn up. Right now, I'm wondering why on earth I insisted on doing this. It's so nerve wracking. I hope everyone has fun.'

'They will,' Nancy assured her. 'And if they don't, that's

not your problem. You've everything laid on, so there's no reason why it shouldn't be a massive success.'

Over the next fifteen minutes, the place exploded with guests arriving – it felt like an instant crowd. Maia watched Freddie working the room like a pro, telling jokes, banging people on the back and laughing loudly. He looked like a natural, and she was so happy that he was enjoying it. It would help when the final bill landed on his desk.

Maia spotted Pearl, Seth and Drew entering the marquee, and hurried over to greet them.

'Evening all,' she called out. 'Give me a high-five, Drew,' she said, holding up her hand. He giggled and slapped her hand with his. 'I'm so glad you could come along,' she said to him. 'And who's this?' she asked, pointing to the blue toy penguin tucked under his arm.

'It's Bluebob,' Drew said, holding him up. 'He didn't want to miss all the fun.'

'Hello Bluebob,' Maia said, 'nice to meet you and welcome to the party. I hope he likes dancing,' she said to Drew.

Drew nodded emphatically. 'Just like me!' he said.

'For God's sake,' Seth said, looking livid. 'Why in God's name did you let him bring that stupid toy, Pearl? He's making a complete fool of us.'

Drew's shoulders drooped, and Maia felt like punching Seth in the face.

'He is not,' she said. 'You are all my guests, Drew as much as anyone. I love Drew and I'm really glad he's here.'

Drew smiled at her gratefully.

'Zara and Zach are dying to see you as well,' she said. 'Shall I take you over to them?'

'Oh yes,' Drew said, bouncing on his feet excitedly. 'I haven't seen Zach in ages.'

'Please make yourselves at home,' Maia said, keeping her eyes on Pearl. If she looked at Seth, she wouldn't be able to hide her anger. 'Nancy's right over there. I'll just walk Drew over to the kids. They have a table set up for themselves already.'

'You don't have to,' Seth said. 'I very much doubt they want a retard hanging out with them for the night.'

'Seth!' Pearl said, looking aghast. 'You can't call Drew that.'

Seth shrugged. 'Maia has two fine, intelligent children, Pearl. Someone like Drew will just embarrass them in front of their friends.'

Pearl looked like she was going to cry. Maia put her hand on her friend's arm and looked at Seth.

'We all love Drew just as he is. He's grown up with Zara and Zach and they are so fond of him. I really don't want to hear you running him down, Seth. This is meant to be a joyful get-together. I can't bear to hear that kind of talk.'

Seth looked at her, his mouth twisted into a sneer. 'Always so emotional, Maia,' he said. 'I'll get myself a drink and keep out of the way.' He walked off towards the bar.

'Jesus Christ,' Maia said, feeling her jaw ache as she finally unclenched it. 'Why do you stick with him, Pearl? I'm sorry to be so blunt, but you deserve a million times better than that sack of misery.'

Pearl took a deep breath, obviously trying to compose herself and her emotions. 'It's just . . . a difficult situation,' she said quietly.

'Come on,' Maia said, 'let's take Drew over to people who really appreciate him.'

'Thanks,' Pearl said, looking relieved.

They walked over to the youngsters' table, and Zara and Zach leaped up in delight, hugging Drew and getting a chair for him. Drew looked thrilled with all the attention, and happily introduced Zara to Bluebob, talking to her animatedly.

'Your kids are as generous and lovely as you are,' Pearl said, watching them. 'You've done a fantastic job raising them, Maia.'

Maia was taken aback. 'You're going to wreck my mascara, Pearl,' she said. 'That's the loveliest thing anyone's ever said to me, you know that? I've poured myself into those two for the last eighteen years and I often felt I was wasting myself just being a mother, but to hear that, well, it makes it all worth it.'

'Oh Maia,' Pearl said, hugging her. 'I thought you knew everyone saw you as mother of the century! Of course we do. Zach and Zara are a credit to you. How could you ever feel like that was a waste?'

Maia shrugged. 'Ah, you hear so much about stay-at-home mothers and how we're not out conquering the world and making a difference. I think I just took that onboard and felt like a bit of a failure.'

Pearl looked at her in surprise. 'I had no idea you felt like that,' she said. 'You always put forward such a strong, confident front. I didn't know you had worries like that.'

Maia laughed grimly. 'And then some,' she said. 'I just put best foot forward, Pearl, but I've plenty that keeps me awake at night. At the moment, it's the thought of not being their mother. When they leave, you know, I'll just be me. I've got nothing else to do.'

Pearl took her hand and squeezed it. 'Maybe you and

me should sign up for a course together. Sometimes I feel like I lost myself when Drew was born, because I gave up everything to take care of him. We could help each other to find some new interests, perhaps.'

'I'd love that,' Maia said, smiling at her. 'I really would.'

'It's a plan, then,' Pearl said. 'I see Nancy, but where are Danielle and Betsy?'

'There's been a spot of trouble with Danielle and Justin,' Maia said quietly. 'I don't know if they're coming or not.'

'Ah, they'll be fine. At that age you have barneys just to have the make-up sex,' Pearl said, and the two of them burst out laughing.

'Seems a lifetime ago now,' Maia said. 'Now I start barneys to make sure sex doesn't happen.'

'Oh God, I hear you,' Pearl said, shaking her head.

They walked over to Nancy, who was soaking up the atmosphere and looking very happy. The three of them clinked glasses.

'What are you toasting?' came a voice from behind them. 'What have I missed?'

'Oh Betsy,' Maia said, embracing her. 'You're here at last. I'm so glad you made it.'

'Arnie managed to deliver an almighty poo just as we were opening the front door to leave,' Betsy said. 'That halted our gallop. But we're all here now.'

Behind her, Noel, Graham and Arnie were making their way towards them, eyes out on stalks at all the sights of the party. Baby Arnie was reaching his hands towards everything, enthralled by all the lights.

'Welcome, welcome,' Maia called out, going to kiss Noel and Graham. 'I'm thrilled you could come. Hello Mr Arnie, how are you this evening?'

'He's in heaven,' Graham said. 'A fire-breather? You've gone all out, Maia. It looks amazing.'

'Just wait till you taste the food,' Maia said. 'Out of this world.'

'Well, me and Arnie won't stay long,' Graham said. 'He hasn't really got table manners down yet.'

'You don't worry about that,' Maia said, waving her hand. 'There's a seat for you, and I can send the caterers for a high-chair if you want.'

'Thanks,' Graham said. Arnie was pointing wildly and making noises. 'Think we better go back for another look at the fire-breather,' he said.

'This is lovely,' Noel said, looking around the little group. 'It's nice to be gathered for a good reason, isn't it?'

'Damn right,' Nancy said. 'I'm looking forward to letting my hair down with a bit of dancing later. Although I can't go too wild because I have another meeting at the council tomorrow.'

'Oh,' Maia said, looking at her hopefully. 'Did they mention the protest and the news reports?'

'No,' Nancy said, shaking her head. 'They just rang and said they'd like to discuss it again with me. It's probably just more of the same, but I'll drop in anyway.'

'I'm coming with you,' Maia said. 'I'll drive you there.'

'You will not!' Nancy said, looking horrified. 'You will have a wild party and dance until your feet bleed and you fall into bed at dawn. And that's an order!'

Maia laughed. 'I will have fun, and I will dance, but I will also be up in the morning with a pot of coffee, ready to stand by you with that bloody council. No arguments.'

'Oh Maia,' Nancy said. 'You're incorrigible.'

There was a beeping sound, and Maia asked Betsy to

hold her glass while she rooted her phone out of her clutch. She looked at them, and her face fell.

'What is it?' Betsy said. 'Please God, not more bad news.'

Maia bit her lip. 'Oh this doesn't look good, girls. Danielle isn't coming.'

'Ah no,' Nancy said, 'why not?'

'She says she's staying with her mam for a couple of days.' Maia looked up at them. 'What do you make of that?'

'She's feeling really conflicted,' Nancy said.

'About what?' Betsy said.

'Her life with Justin,' Maia said. 'She's feeling like a fish out of water, and his obedience to his horrible mother isn't helping.'

'Oh that's a terrible shame,' Betsy said. 'I've grown so fond of her.'

'She was looking forward to tonight,' Pearl said. 'Missing it is a big deal. They must be really at loggerheads.'

'Do you think she'll leave him, Nancy?' Maia asked.

'There's a very good chance, I think,' Nancy said sadly. 'When she talked to me about it, she seemed to be leaning towards calling it a day.'

'That's really sad news,' Betsy said.

The maitre d' tapped a glass and announced that everyone should take their seats for dinner. The guests all milled about, choosing tables and friends to sit beside. The waiters fanned out about the room, filling wine glasses and taking orders. It was a lovely relaxed atmosphere, and Maia was very glad that Freddie had insisted on table service. It would have been chaotic to have everyone filing up to buffet tables, but this way, it allowed the guests to unwind, chat and laugh. It was perfect.

Maia had a fantastic night. She caught up with old friends, wowed Freddie's business associates and laughed until she cried with Pearl, Betsy and Nancy. Seth found some other army bore to talk to, so Pearl was spared his company for most of the night. The difference in her when Seth was nearby was shocking. She'd be chatting and laughing, and then he'd join them and Maia would watch as her friend physically became smaller, her shoulders drawing tight, head bent. It was horrible. She and Pearl had been more honest with each other that night than ever before, so she resolved to build on that and try to talk to her about her marriage. It was definitely an unhealthy relationship, and Pearl didn't deserve that.

The caterers cleared the food and tables swiftly once the meal was finished, and the DJ crew quickly set up, creating a crazily lit-up dancefloor. The first tune the DJ dropped was Kylie's 'Can't get you out of my head' – one of Maia's all-time favourites – and it got everyone on their feet and moving. If Maia had any worries about people enjoying themselves, they all dissolved now. The party was absolutely rocking. At one point, Maia was on the dancefloor with the Kingfisher Road women, all of them bopping and laughing to 'Happy', and she knew this was one of those moments she'd remember for the rest of her life. They all had problems, life wasn't straightforward, but in that moment, she looked around and knew they had each other. It was the most wonderful feeling.

It was five o'clock and the first robin had started to sing when Maia stepped out of her dress and into her black silk pyjamas. She set her phone for 10.30 a.m., so she'd be ready in time to get Nancy to her midday meeting at the council offices. She knew Freddie had come inside, but she hadn't seen him yet. She walked into the bedroom and found him sitting up in bed – eating pizza from a box.

'Ah Freddie! Why are you eating that in bed? My good sheets!'

'I just paid two hundred euros for pizza for that lot, so I'll enjoy a few pieces of it. If I want to eat it standing on my head, bollock naked in the middle of the garden, then I will.'

'I'd prefer to see you do that because then my sheets wouldn't have cheese and sauce all over them.'

There was a pause before he cracked up laughing. She grinned and joined him. They'd always been able to make each other laugh. That was the beauty of their relationship.

'That,' Freddie said, licking sauce from his fingers, 'was the most amazing night ever. And you are the most amazing wife ever. That party took everyone's eye out. They'll be talking about it for years.'

'Well the bill will take your eye out,' Maia said, 'but I'm really glad you enjoyed it. It was a hell of a lot of work, but it was worth it.'

'I'm a lucky man,' Freddie said contentedly, putting the pizza box on the floor and settling himself for sleep. 'Too wrecked to shag you, though.'

Maia laughed. 'Don't worry about that. I'm exhausted myself.'

She watched as his eyes got heavy and started to close. Twenty years. It was a long time and a blink of the eye at the same time. She looked at the black and yellow bruising around his eye and bit her lip. Would he throw away twenty years for a fling? Or for money? What if he was dealing drugs, or something really dangerous like that? How far would he go for this lifestyle he'd grown to love so much? Her heart was heavy with all the questions he wouldn't answer, but at the same time, looking at him lying by her side, where he'd lain for twenty years, he was also her Freddie. The man who had always looked after her and their children. He was her rock, she knew that. She also knew she'd stand by him, no matter what. Once it wasn't another woman; that would break her in two. Once it wasn't that, he had her heart and her loyalty, no matter what.

Chapter 24

PEARL WOULD HAVE STAYED AT THE PARTY UNTIL morning, but Drew was starting to droop with tiredness and Seth was giving her dagger looks that meant he wanted to leave – and wanted her to leave as well. She would have loved if Seth had taken Drew home and let her enjoy herself, but then the idea of leaving Drew alone with him made her blood run cold. She kissed Maia goodnight, dragged herself off the dancefloor, found her things and obediently left at Seth's side.

'Well that was a long and unpleasant affair,' Seth remarked as they made their way back up the garden.

'I really enjoyed it,' Pearl said.

'You made a show of yourself,' Seth said. 'Dancing like that at your age. You're too old for that, Pearl. I was embarrassed to call you my wife.'

Pearl swallowed down her rage. 'It was just neighbours having some fun,' she said. She held Drew's hand tightly. She was afraid of him saying something and drawing Seth's wrath on himself, but he seemed too tired to talk, which was a good thing.

They walked through Maia's beautiful home and out through the front door, then made their way down the driveway and up their own driveway next door. It was a beautiful night, cold and clear with lots of stars twinkling above them. Pearl would have given anything to be walking hand-in-hand with Tommy, heading off to bed together. She remembered Maia's face when Seth had insulted Drew, and how she asked why the hell Pearl was still with him. She asked herself that question every day. She wasn't even sure she knew the answer. It was like some part of her felt she didn't deserve happiness with Tommy. Or maybe she was afraid that if she and Tommy could be proper, fulltime lovers, that his love would evaporate. There was some dark nub of fear deep inside her, but she wasn't sure what it was. She just knew that the idea of telling Seth she wanted him to leave made her sweat with fear. She couldn't do it.

Seth unlocked their front door and they all trooped inside. Pearl thought she'd boil the kettle for a cup of green tea, and maybe Seth would go up ahead of her and fall asleep. She made her way to the kitchen and Drew followed sleepily.

'I'm thirsty. Can I have a glass of water?' Drew asked.

'Sure thing, my darling,' Pearl said. 'You're so tired, sweetie. I'll give you this, then put you to bed.'

'Stop babying him,' Seth said, and she was taken aback by the fury in his voice. He seemed to have gone from irritated to all out anger in the time it took to walk down the hallway. 'I'm sick and tired of watching you treat him like some precious child. I think he's play-acting half the time, just to get attention. I can't stand to watch the freak show that is my family. It's disgusting.'

Pearl was hardly breathing. She was wondering if Seth had drunk more than usual. He was normally abstemious and controlled about alcohol, but his eyes were blazing with anger and it was obvious he was spoiling for a fight.

Her mind was reeling as she tried to think of a subject or a comment to calm him down.

'I'll try harder,' she said, hating her quavering, defeated voice. She hated who she became when she was with him, but she had to protect herself and Drew.

'You're an idiot, Pearl,' he said viciously. 'It's no wonder you produced an idiot. I watched you tonight, gossiping and laughing, throwing yourself around in that mutton dressed as lamb way you older women have, and do you want to know what I was thinking? I was thinking I managed to marry an idiot. I don't know how you blinded me to your real self, but you did. And that's how I've ended up with a retard for a son. You polluted my seed, your idiocy polluted it, and we ended up with this,' he gestured at Drew as if he was some gruesome abomination. 'I'm paying dearly for ever meeting you,' he went on. 'I rue the day I laid eyes on you.'

Pearl was clutching the counter behind her, making herself as small and unthreatening as possible. She hadn't heard him this angry before, this was a new level for him. She was shocked by his hatred. Because that's what it was, he hated her. He had never said all this stuff before about Drew being her fault, but he must have been brooding over it for years. She felt sick to her stomach.

There was a noise from the table, where Drew was sitting, drinking his glass of water. He bent his head and started to cry noisily, his whole body shaking with the sobs. He was clutching Bluebob tightly, burying his face in the cuddly toy. Pearl went rigid with fear. Stop, Drew, she screamed in her mind. But it was too late.

Seth reached him in three strides. He picked up the glass and flung it across the room, where it smashed into pieces against the wall. He grabbed Bluebob and began ripping the toy apart at the seams, stuffing fluttering around him like confetti. Pearl was frozen for a few seconds, then she shouted, 'Drew!' and ran over to them. She ran straight into Seth's fist. His punch caught her on the cheek and her whole head jerked backwards, then she slammed to the floor.

'Look what you made me do!' Seth roared. 'You stupid, stupid woman.'

Drew made a break for it, and Pearl could see that he was thinking of running straight outside and down to the mews, to Tommy. That was his safe haven. But Seth caught him by the shirt and dragged him back. He drew back his arm and punched Drew full in the stomach. Drew made a sound like an airbag going off and doubled over, his arms wrapped around his middle. Seth boxed his ears, making him scream in pain. Pearl couldn't bear it. Her face was aching with pain, but she forced herself up off the ground and stood in front of her son.

'Please stop,' she cried. 'Don't hurt him. It's okay, Seth. I'll try harder. I promise.'

'You two are the biggest disappointment of my life,' Seth said coldly. Pearl looked in his eyes and she knew this wasn't alcohol, this was him choosing to hurt them. He was stone cold sober. This was pure hatred, pure anger, simple as that. This was just Seth, the man he was. For the first time, Pearl realised that there was no excuse.

Seth grabbed her hair and swung her to the side, where she staggered and fell heavily again to the floor. Then he picked up Drew and threw him the other way. Drew landed where the glass had shattered and Pearl heard him cry out in pain.

'Blood, blood, blood,' he shouted in terror. The sight of

blood caused him to have panic attacks, which is exactly what was happening now. His breathing came out in strangled gasps, his eyes bulged and he couldn't stop shaking, his whole body shuddering in fear.

Seth looked over at Drew, then back at Pearl. He fixed his tie and tucked in his shirt.

'This is your fault, Pearl,' he said. 'Your behaviour tonight was entirely unacceptable. You need to clean yourself up, tell that wretched child to stop making that noise and tidy up this mess. We can talk properly in the morning. I do appreciate your acknowledgement that you need to try harder, but we can work out exactly what you need to do tomorrow.'

He walked out of the kitchen, down the hall and up the stairs, as if nothing had happened. Pearl stared after him in disbelief. She began to wonder if she had imagined it all, if she was going crazy, but then she looked over at her beautiful, vulnerable son and she knew this was her nightmare reality. She crawled over to Drew, sobbing his name, reaching to comfort him. His shirt sleeve was soaked in blood. She gently undid the cuff button and rolled it back. One of the glass shards had cut him badly when he landed, and it was bleeding profusely. Pearl stared at the wound, and didn't think she could manage it. Then she decided to do something she had never done before. She found her phone and shakily dialled 999.

'I need an ambulance, please. There's been a domestic accident. Number two Kingfisher Road. Quickly, please hurry.'

She cradled Drew in her arms, rocking him back and forth. 'I'm sorry, I'm so sorry,' she said over and over again. He said nothing, just sobbed like his heart was breaking.

Thirty minutes later, she heard a siren approaching. Fearing Seth's reaction to this public intrusion, she got Drew to his feet and they made their way outside and stood waiting in the driveway. The light in her bedroom went on, and she looked up. Seth was standing at the window, glaring down at them. Pearl moved Drew further down the driveway, both of them shaking in fear. The ambulance turned into Kingfisher Road, blue lights throwing jagged shapes at the houses. Pearl's bedroom light flicked off.

The paramedics didn't ask too many questions, but they were sizing up the situation, she knew that. She quietly explained Drew's condition and they were incredibly kind and gentle with him, talking to him calmly, making sure he understood what they were doing. They wrapped blankets around them both. As Pearl was being helped into the back of the ambulance, the side-door to her garden opened and Tommy appeared, in his pyjamas, hair all tousled, the picture of a man who'd just woken up. He took in the scene and immediately ran to them, his face full of concern.

'What did he do?' he said, reaching for Drew.

'He lost it,' Pearl whispered. 'Jesus, Tommy, it was terrible. I just didn't know what to do.' She began crying quietly.

'You did the right thing,' Tommy said. He turned to the paramedic. 'Can you wait five minutes and I'll throw on clothes and come with you?' he said.

'Are you her husband?' the man asked.

'No, I'm the childminder.'

'Afraid not,' the paramedic said, shaking his head.

'Okay,' Tommy said, nodding. He turned to Pearl. 'Don't

worry. I'll get dressed and follow you in the car. I'll be right behind you, okay? I'll be there.'

Pearl looked at him through her tears. 'I know you will,' she said.

Tommy raced back to the mews and Pearl stared out, unable to believe that she was leaving her own house in an ambulance because of her husband. All around her, lights had come on in the windows of the houses on the road, and now front doors started to open as people came out to see who the ambulance was for. The shame bit deep inside her. All these years, hiding the truth, and now they'd all know. She felt ragged with emotion.

'Go on, have a good look,' she roared.

'Calm down, miss,' the paramedic said, shutting first one door, then the other. 'It's alright now. No one's judging you.'

Pearl curled up beside Drew, holding the blankets tight around them. They would all find out, and what if they did judge her? What if they all thought she was a stupid idiot, like Seth did? She had put her own son in harm's way, and she'd done it for years, surely that was unforgivable? She hated herself, and she felt sure everyone else would too.

Chapter 25

NANCY WAS STILL FEELING SHOCKED BY THE events of the previous night. She had been woken by the blue light flashing across her eyelids and when she'd looked out, she could see the ambulance was outside Pearl's. It was turning to leave Kingfisher Road by the time she'd looked out, so she didn't know what had happened, but she was hugely worried.

She was just flicking on her kettle to make some coffee when her phone beeped. A message from Maia: *I've breakfast for you. Come on over.* Nancy shook her head. Maia was like the Duracell bunny; Nancy didn't know where she got her energy from. She knew from experience there was no point arguing with Maia when she'd decided on something, so she flicked off the kettle, gathered her bag and her coat and made her way down the road to number three.

The front door was flung open as Nancy walked up the driveway.

'I was waiting for you,' Maia said. 'There was an ambulance last night. Something happened at Pearl's.'

'I know,' Nancy said, stepping inside. 'I was woken by the lights. Have you heard who was hurt?'

Maia shook her head. 'I had an eye mask on and ear plugs in because of Freddie's snoring, so I didn't even

wake up, and sure Freddie would sleep through a demo-
lition team, but as soon as I got up Zara told me about it.
Her room's at the front so she saw it all. She said Drew
and Pearl went in the back of the ambulance, but she
couldn't tell which of them was hurt. Then she saw Tommy
run out, then he disappeared again, then he came back out
and hopped into his car and screamed off in the direction
of the hospital.'

'Oh my God,' Nancy said, feeling ill at the thought of
anything nasty happening to Drew or Pearl. 'Have you
tried to contact her?'

'I've sent four texts and rung twice,' Maia said, 'but she's
not answering her phone. I don't have Tommy's number
or I would have called him.'

'What about Seth?' Nancy asked.

'Wasn't he so obnoxious last night?' Maia said. 'I could
have throttled him. He actually referred to Drew as a
retard.'

Nancy's face registered shock. 'What? No way.'

Maia nodded. 'He said awful things about him.'

'Jesus, I would have blown a gasket if I'd heard that,'
Nancy said. 'How could he?'

'I don't like him at all,' Maia said. 'I wouldn't be
surprised if he's involved in this somehow.'

Nancy thought back to the ex-husband who used to beat
her. She shuddered at the thought of any of her friends
going through anything like that. 'Maybe we should go
over there,' she said.

'Do you think?' Maia said. 'I don't fancy the thought of
talking to Seth.'

'If Pearl needs help of any kind, we have to be there for
her.'

'You're right,' Maia said, looking determined. 'Let's go.'

They walked next door and rang the doorbell. Silence. Maia rang it again, long and hard. After a minute, they heard footsteps marching towards the door and it swung open.

Seth crossed his arms and looked at them. 'Maia, Nancy, can I help you?'

'We're worried about Pearl,' Nancy said. 'We saw the ambulance last night. Is there anything we can do to help?'

'No,' Seth said.

Nancy was so taken aback by his abrupt answer, her mind went blank.

'Where is she?' Maia cut in.

'There was a minor accident after your party last night and she took Drew to the hospital to be seen to. Nothing serious. They'll be home shortly.'

'She's not answering her phone,' Maia said.

'That's hardly my concern,' Seth replied. 'Now, I've satisfied your curiosity and I've got a lot to do today, so I'll have to let you go, ladies.'

'Please tell her to let us know when she's back,' Nancy said quickly, before the door closed. 'Tell her we're here for her.'

She didn't get any answer to that. The door closed firmly and they were left looking at each other.

'That man,' Maia said. 'He makes my blood boil.'

'We'll keep an eye out for her,' Nancy said. 'I hope Drew is okay.'

'He was in fantastic form last night,' Maia said, as they walked back to her house. 'He had a ball.'

'He's such a great lad,' Nancy said, smiling. 'Hopefully it is just something minor, like Seth said.'

'I'll ask Zara to keep a lookout while we're gone,' Maia said, 'so we know the moment Pearl gets back. Come on, better get some food and then we'll have to get going.'

They went back to the kitchen and Nancy marvelled at the spread Maia had laid out. There was a big pot of porridge, berries, granola, various types of bread and a platter of pastries.

'You missed your calling,' Nancy said. 'You should be running a hotel.'

Maia laughed. 'I feel like I am today. There are I don't know how many of the kids' friends asleep in bedrooms and couches around the place. But thank God I have the cleaners booked for today, so they can do the heavy lifting.'

'Good thinking,' Nancy said. She picked up a croissant and bit into it. 'Hmm, gorgeous,' she mumbled. 'And this coffee is divine. You always make the best.'

They chatted about the previous night, reliving all the funny moments.

'But what about Freddie,' Nancy said, not sure if she should ask. 'I noticed the shiner. How did that happen?'

Maia sighed. 'I don't know. He won't talk about it.'

Nancy studied her friend. 'You're really worried about him, aren't you?'

Maia nodded. 'Yeah. For a while now. He's a different man this last while, and I don't know how to get through to him. There's something going on, I know that much, but I've no idea what it is.'

Nancy felt so sorry for her friend. Her smile crumpled and she looked utterly stressed. 'Oh Maia, it'll be okay. Freddie's mad about you. I don't think he'd do anything to compromise your happiness.'

'Let's hope,' Maia said, looking unconvinced. 'It's horrible being in the dark, makes me think all sorts. He used to tell me everything. We were a little team, there for each other. Somehow that seems to have got lost along the way.'

Nancy reached out and covered Maia's hand with hers. 'He's still there, Maia, my darling. You'll just have to make an effort to reach him, let him see how upset you are about the way things are between you. I'm sure he'll want to meet you halfway.'

'Or break up with me and take up with some young one with pert boobs,' Maia shot back.

'You don't think . . .' Nancy said.

Maia shrugged. 'I think all sorts, Nancy, and an affair is right up there near the top of my list.'

She looked at the clock on the wall and jumped up. 'Enough gasbagging. Time to get moving,' she said. 'Just let me find my car keys.'

The drive to the council offices took only fifteen minutes, and Maia found a handy parking space right outside. Before they got out of the car, Nancy put her hand on Maia's arm.

'Maia, you know I love you dearly, especially your fierce loyalty, but I need you to stay calm in here today. It can be aggravating when they bang on about their rights and ignore mine, and I don't want you erupting in anger, okay, because it won't help my case. And it may be a lost case, of course, and we'll have to accept that.'

'I'll try,' Maia said. 'I'll do my best not to staple this guy's tie to the desk.'

'Well, I appreciate your self-control,' Nancy said, giggling. 'That's a beautiful image you've conjured up there.'

'If you see me reaching for the stapler,' Maia said, 'disarm me.'

'Deal,' Nancy said.

They went through the same motions as Sean and Nancy had before – giving her name to the receptionist, being made to wait for ten minutes, and finally Derek Small appeared, file in hand.

'Good to see you again, Nancy,' he said. 'I have a new office, so it's not as far into the warren, you'll be glad to hear.'

'I'm sure I'll still feel like I've fallen down a rabbit-hole,' Nancy said drily.

He led them to a more spacious, brighter office just down the hall. Nancy made the introductions, and then sat down to hear what retirement home they wanted to stick her in this time.

Derek shuffled the papers in the file, but before he could speak, Maia jumped in.

'You're totally wrong,' she fired at him. 'This is immoral. There's no way we're letting you evict Nancy without a fight. We'll do everything possible.'

Nancy gave Maia a look, to remind her of her promise outside.

'Sorry,' Maia said, 'but I'm just so upset and angry.'

'If you'll just let me speak,' Derek said. 'I called you here today, Nancy, because there has been a significant development in your case.'

Nancy felt her heart beating faster. 'What do you mean?'

'An objection has been lodged by the Conservation Society, which carries great weight in these matters. Their stance is being backed by local councillors.' He fixed the papers in a straight line again, then looked up at Nancy. She could see it was killing him to say what it was he had to say. 'We are withdrawing the CPO on numbers five and six Kingfisher Road, effective immediately.'

There was total silence for a few seconds as Nancy tried to process his words. Maia seemed to be as surprised as her. Then with a whoop, Maia jumped up and punched the air.

'Yes!' she shouted. 'Common bloody sense at last. Oh Nancy,' she cried, throwing her arms around Nancy's neck, 'it's over. You're staying. Your house is safe.'

Nancy didn't know if she was laughing or crying. The weight of the last few weeks shifted off her and she felt like she could breathe properly again. It was a delicious feeling.

'I don't believe it,' she said, looking at Derek. 'But you were so adamant. What did this society say that changed your mind?'

'Unfortunately,' Derek said, looking miffed, 'it transpires there is a nesting pair of kingfishers in your garden. When the Conservation Society was informed of this, it issued a cease and desist on the grounds that the birds are amber-listed in Ireland and therefore endangered, to an extent. We have to honour that request.'

'My kingfishers,' Nancy said, laughing. 'I was saved by my kingfishers? That's crazy. Boy, am I glad I fed them now!'

'Did our protest make any difference at all?' Maia asked, and Nancy had to suppress a smile.

'Em, no, it didn't,' Derek said. 'The CPO would have gone ahead in spite of local objections, but this is a different kind of objection.'

Maia shrugged. 'Well I'm glad we highlighted the practice anyway. And I'm over the moon that you have to climb down off your high-horse and admit defeat. This has absolutely made my day.'

'There's no need to crow about it,' Derek said irritably.

'Can we kingfisher about it, then?' Maia said, then cracked up laughing. Nancy couldn't help but join in. Poor Derek had to just sit there until they'd got their breath back.

'Okay, just a few things to get signed in order to finish this up,' he said, sorting through the papers. 'If you can sign here and here and . . .'

'Wait a second,' Nancy said. 'I won't sign anything without my lawyer's consent. Please send those to the office of Sean Claffey. Once I have his say-so, I'll get them straight back to you.'

Derek sighed deeply. 'Fine, Mrs Smyth,' he said. 'I'll get those couriered over to him now. But please try to get them back to us on Monday, okay?'

'No problem,' said Nancy happily. 'Is that it? Am I done with you people?'

'Yes, that's it,' Derek said wearily. 'We rescind the CPO and you are free to remain in your house.'

'Thank you for having the courtesy of telling me in person,' Nancy said. She got up to leave, then turned back. 'Just one thing. Perhaps you're not allowed to tell me, but do you know who alerted the Conservation Society to the presence of the kingfishers?'

He hesitated, then shrugged. 'I suppose there's no harm in telling you. Presumably it's someone you know. The name on the letter was Danielle O'Brien.'

'My word,' Nancy said, shaking her head. 'What a girl.'

She and Maia left, giggling like schoolgirls, arms linked.

'I feel like throwing another party tonight,' Maia said. 'I can't believe that just happened. And I can't believe Danielle spotted that loophole. Whenever she gets that law degree, she can count me as one of her clients. That was bleedin' genius.'

'I owe her big time,' Nancy said.

They got back in the car and headed back to Kingfisher Road, stunned at Nancy's good fortune. They were just getting out of the car in Maia's driveway when Betsy came running towards them.

'I saw your car,' she said, gasping for breath. 'How did the meeting go?'

'Follow me and you'll find out,' Nancy said, marching across the road to number ten.

Maia and Betsy followed in her wake, with Betsy begging for information every step of the way. Nancy rang the doorbell and after a few seconds, the door opened.

'Morning,' Justin said. He looked tired, and his face was all stubbly and pale. Nancy had never seen him look so rough.

'Hi Justin, is Danielle here?'

He shook his head. 'No, she's not at the moment.'

'Has she come back from her mother's?' Maia asked.

Justin looked surprised for a second, then gathered himself. 'No, she's staying there. I don't know when she'll be back.'

'Have you called her?' Maia demanded.

'I don't have to explain my life to you,' Justin said coldly. 'Can I help you with something?'

'No, it's fine,' Nancy said. 'I just wanted to thank Danielle for helping me. I was served with a CPO and they've dropped it because of her.'

'She mentioned that,' Justin said. 'So it actually worked?'

Nancy smiled. 'Damn right it worked. Your Danielle is a genius, and one of the most kind-hearted people I've ever met. I owe her so much.'

'Wow,' Justin said. 'I didn't think that bird idea would work.'

'Well, it did,' Nancy said. 'I'll keep an eye out for her and come over when she comes home.'

Justin looked uncomfortable. 'I've no idea when that will be,' he said quietly.

'It'll happen if you want it to happen,' Nancy said.

'What does that mean?' he asked.

'If you know you want something, you have to fight for it,' Nancy said. 'Just like Danielle fought for me. You've got to take the risk, just like she did. She didn't know if it would work, but she sent that letter anyway. She committed to the idea, do you know what I'm saying?'

'I'll be late for work,' Justin said. 'I better go. Excuse me.'

Nancy, Betsy and Maia walked slowly back down the driveway and back across the road.

'I miss Danielle being here already,' Betsy said. 'She'd be a huge loss to the road.'

'It's not looking good,' Maia said. 'Poor Danielle.'

'But what about Pearl?' Betsy said suddenly. 'Has anyone seen her since last night?'

'No,' Maia said. 'Myself and Nancy went around there, to ask Seth about it.'

'That was brave of you,' Betsy said. 'I wouldn't relish that idea myself.'

'Well, he wasn't exactly delighted to see us,' Nancy said, 'but he said it was a minor incident and they'd be home from the hospital soon.'

'Let's hope that's the case,' Betsy said. 'I was so worried when I saw that ambulance, but I didn't want to run down and get in the way. But then when Pearl shouted, it just didn't sound like her at all.'

'What did she shout?' Maia said. 'Zara didn't mention that.'

'She shouted, "Go on, have a good look",' Betsy said. 'She sounded distraught.'

'I hope she's back soon,' Maia said, looking worried. 'I can't bear this not knowing.'

'Keep me informed,' Betsy said. 'I better go in now. It's Arnie's lunchtime.' She headed off up her driveway, and Maia and Nancy walked on.

'There's a car parked outside your place,' Maia said.

Nancy looked down the road. It was Steve's car. He was sitting in it, obviously waiting for her, and when he spotted her, his face broke into a smile.

Nancy felt now was as good a time as any. 'Actually, Maia, that's someone I'd like you to meet. Come on.'

They walked on down and Steve stepped out of the car to greet them.

'Hi Nancy. I just came to see how the meeting went and if you're doing okay.'

'It went much better than I expected,' Nancy said, her eyes twinkling. 'You won't believe it, but the council has dropped the CPO. It's over.'

'What?' He looked at her in astonishment. 'No way! That's fantastic news. It's completely dropped? No CPO, no offers of money and accommodation?'

'Exactly,' Nancy said. 'It's all gone off the table. I'm free to stay and there's no threat of eviction.'

Steve picked her up and swung her round.

'Oh my goodness,' she said, throwing back her head and laughing. 'You crazy boy, you'll break your back.'

'I just can't believe it,' he said. 'I thought I'd be a shoulder to cry on, and here we are, all sorted. I couldn't be happier for you.'

Maia looked curiously from him to Nancy and back again.

'Maia,' Nancy said, 'this is Steve. My son.'

Steve looked at her in surprise, then smiled. 'Yes, I am,' he said.

Nancy thought Maia was actually going to fall down in the street. Her mouth opened and shut, but nothing came out. Her eyes nearly popped out of her head.

'Son?'

Nancy nodded. 'It's a long story, Maia, and one I never wanted to share, but I had a baby when I was sixteen and ended up in a Magdalene. The baby was taken from me, I put the whole sorry episode behind me, but about a month ago I got a letter asking me to meet Steve. I agreed, and now we're building a relationship.'

'Jesus Christ,' Maia said, turning to sit on the wall. 'I've known you seventeen years and you never told me this?'

'We all have our secrets,' Nancy said.

'Well, I'm very pleased to meet you, Mr Very Big Secret,' Maia said, holding out her hand to Steve.

He laughed. 'Thrilled to bits,' he said. 'This is all very new for me and Nancy, but we're finding our way.'

'That's lovely,' Maia said.

'Such fantastic news,' Steve said, shaking his head. 'And you know, Nancy, it still doesn't rule out the opportunities we talked about.'

'What do you mean?' Nancy said.

'Well, you've stared down the barrel of changing your life now,' Steve said, 'and you might still want to make some changes. I mean, the house is very big. Might not be a bad idea to get a valuation, just to see where it stands, you know. And that investment opportunity is still live. I got mine sorted yesterday, and was thinking I should mention it to you again.'

'You're very kind,' Nancy said, 'but I think I'll stay put and keep a tight hold on the finances.'

'No problem,' he said. 'I've got to dash now, I've got a job on, but I'll be in touch and we can celebrate in style.'

'Thanks, Steve,' Nancy said. 'I'll see you soon.'

When he drove off, Maia rounded on her. 'A son? Seriously?'

'I know it's a bit crazy,' Nancy said, 'but it was a horrible time for me back then, how I got pregnant and everything, and I never wanted to talk about it.'

'Oh my poor Nancy,' Maia said, squeezing her arm.

'It's early days, I'm just trying to be the mother he wants.'

'And is he the son you want?' Maia asked.

'I need to focus on being there for him,' Nancy said. 'I want to make a strong connection with him.'

'Okay,' Maia said, 'but that cuts both ways. What was that stuff about valuations and investments?'

'It's just a good investment he's bought into and was hoping I might do the same.'

'Is that not an odd opener when you're reconciled with your mother?' Maia asked.

'No,' Nancy said, feeling irritated. 'He's absolutely lovely and very eager to help me. He just mentioned it as something I might be interested in. That's all.'

'Right,' Maia said.

'I'm going in for a nap, I think, Maia. I'm wrecked after all that. But thank you for being there today. It was very fitting that you got that news with me. You're the one I'd have missed the most.'

'You old flatterer,' Maia said, laughing. 'And you know I adore you.'

'Well you're not getting rid of me now, that's for sure,' Nancy said. 'I'm going out of this place in a pine box and not a moment before.'

Chapter 26

PEARL FELT EXHAUSTED DOWN TO HER BONES. THE past forty-eight hours had been stressful and hectic, and she longed to crawl into her own bed and shut her eyes and disappear for hours in sleep. It was a craving for rest and escape and it burned through her whole body. But she had to push that feeling aside because she was Drew's mother first and foremost, and her boy still needed her by his side.

The doctors had kept Drew in that night they'd arrived, and then again the following night. They had dealt with his physical injuries quickly and were happy that he was in good health other than the cut on his arm, but during the treatment Drew had cried inconsolably and repeated, 'I hate Daddy' over and over. It wouldn't have taken a genius to figure out that the two things were connected, and soon a nice nurse began to gently ask Pearl about the situation at home. In the past, Pearl would have lied, or glossed over the truth, because the fear of the repercussions of being honest would have been too much for her. But she was past that fear now. Seth had turned their home into a savage place, had terrorised them and hurt Drew. This was the same man who had just retired and was going to be around them all the time. No. For the first time in her life with Seth, Pearl allowed herself to think that tiny little word: no.

She was done with the life Seth had imposed on her. She couldn't live it anymore and wouldn't make Drew live it for one second longer. He didn't deserve that, innocent Drew, who couldn't understand why his father hated him. Pearl had taken Tommy's hand in hers, taken a deep breath and through tears, she'd told the truth. She told the lovely nurse all about her life with Seth, and how Seth detested Drew's disability, and how he blamed her for it. She told her that Seth had beaten them both, and that's why they were in the hospital. The nurse listened intently, not interrupting, but her eyes were filled with pity.

'Okay, Pearl,' she'd said at last. 'I know that was really hard for you to say, but you're so brave to have said it. You're going to have to be even braver now because you have to make the changes necessary to get you and Drew out of harm's way, do you understand me?'

Pearl nodded, feeling the horrible weight of her responsibility, and her failure. She was responsible for Drew, and she had let him get hurt. The nurse was being nice about it, but she was probably appalled that any mother could mess up so badly. But Pearl knew exactly what she was saying: she had to deal with Seth once and for all. It didn't matter how scared she was, it was now or never.

A while later, two very nice gardaí had arrived to talk to her. Pearl was utterly mortified, but the nurse explained that they had to inform the police of suspected domestic violence cases. Pearl did understand, but she had really hoped she could deal with this on her own, in her own way. That wasn't an option, though. The woman, Garda O'Neill, had been very kind, listening to her story and making notes. Her colleague, Garda Regan, told Pearl he had dealt with many such cases and that he admired her for taking a stand. Pearl wanted the ground to swallow her up. Admired her? That was a joke. Her life was a shambles and it was her fault.

'Now, Pearl, I need to advise you that we are going to call to your home and talk to your husband about this matter,' Garda O'Neill said. 'You need to be aware of that because it could anger him and create a volatile situation. We also need to know, will you sign a statement and press charges of assault against him?'

Pearl glanced at Tommy, then down at her wedding ring. 'No, I don't want to go down that route,' she said. 'I'd like him gone from our lives, but I don't want to get all official and drag us all through the courts.'

'Well now, it wouldn't be you inconveniencing people, Pearl. It would be justice,' Garda Regan said gently. 'He has hurt you and your son, so making him answer for that is perfectly acceptable.'

'I suppose,' Pearl said, feeling tired and confused. 'But his family are very nice people, and his dad is elderly and still alive, and it would break their hearts if this ended up in the courts and Seth in jail. I couldn't do that to them.'

'I understand,' Garda Regan said. 'But if you change your mind, contact us immediately, okay? We aren't going to arrest him without a statement from yourself, Pearl, but we are going to call around and give him a very strong caution. And I recommend that you discuss a protection order or barring order with your solicitor or with the Citizens Advice Bureau. I can give you a contact number. You have rights, Pearl, and even if you don't want to take this to court, I think you should use the law to put protection in place for you and Drew.'

Pearl didn't even want to think about how Seth would

react when they pulled up at the house, or what the repercussions might be.

Later, after the police had left and Drew had fallen asleep, Pearl sat with Tommy, the two of them whispering, heads bent together, talking about Pearl's options and Seth's likely reaction. And then her phone lit up and vibrated and it was his name: SETH.

Pearl looked at Tommy and he nodded at her. 'It's alright, I'm here,' he said. 'You do have to deal with this, like the nurse said. Let's see what he has to say for himself.' With shaking hands, Pearl took up the phone and opened his email:

Pearl,

I'm going to stay at a hotel until this is sorted to my satisfaction. I received a visit from the local police this evening, which was deeply shocking. I explained the situation and countered your false beliefs. They seemed to think our marriage couldn't survive this incident, but I believe them to be wrong.

I can no longer live in this household in its current make-up. This has been crystallised for me by my retirement plans, which do not and will not include your son. My proposal is simple – you will organise residential care for Drew, whereby he will live in a facility that can cater for his condition. He will live there permanently, and you may visit him once a week. You will fire Tommy as he will no longer be needed. When these things have been completed, contact me and at that point I will return to our home and our marriage. I will not return until these items have been resolved fully.

You have created an unacceptable and untenable home

life for me, Pearl, and I hold you entirely responsible for that gross failure. But you are my wife, so we can renew our marriage once these issues have been eradicated. You created the problem, and I'm giving you the chance to solve it, to the advantage of you and me and our future life together. I trust you will understand that this is a gesture of compassion and tolerance on my part and respond in kind.

    Seth

Pearl stared at his words until they blurred into a big clump of grey nothingness. He was certifiably insane if he thought she was going to farm Drew out to anyone. Then the anger began to course through her, replacing the horror and giving her the clarity that she sorely needed.

'I'm divorcing him,' she said, looking at Tommy. 'I'm going to get him out of the house and out of our lives. I'll call the police in if I have to, but this is over. It stops here and now.'

'I think you're right,' Tommy said quietly. 'I'm not saying that because of anything to do with us, it's just that what he did to Drew that night . . .' he rubbed his face tiredly. 'It's vicious, you know. Drew is so traumatised by it. I swear to God, if I have to look at that man again, I'll knock his teeth out. He's a bully, the very worst kind of bully. Total lowlife.' He shook his head.

'I know,' Pearl said. 'I've let this happen, Tommy. I've been frightened of him for so long, and it made me weak and stupid. This is my fault.'

Tommy's jaw tightened. 'If you say that, you're playing right into his way of seeing you,' he said through gritted teeth. 'You've got to move on, Pearl, and see this for what it is, otherwise you'll never be free of it, even when he's moved out.'

'It's hard,' Pearl said, bending her head as the tears started to fall. 'Everything I feel, the anger, the shame, the guilt, it's all directed at myself more than at him.'

'So what are you going to do?' Tommy said. 'You need a plan of action so you don't bottle it again. Why don't you write out a list of things you need to do to get rid of him?'

Pearl was a bit stung by his tone of voice, and by the acknowledgement that she'd wimped out before, but what Tommy was saying did make sense and she tried to focus on that. If she could see a direct path to being free of Seth, that would make it easier to achieve. She took an address book out of her bag, found a blank page and dug out a pen from the bottom of the bag. Then she wrote out a list that she hoped would save her life: *1. Send Seth email to say he is to remain out of house or else I will contact the police, 2. Get solicitor to send a letter to Seth outlining allegations against him, and tell him these allegations and supporting evidence are lodged in the solicitor's safe, and warn him that if he tries to contact us again, the file will be sent to the police, 3. Counselling for Drew, 4. Research divorce proceedings and initiate them asap, 5. Research barring order and take steps to put it in place, 6. Change locks on house.*

She turned to Tommy. 'Can you think of anything else?'

He shook his head. 'That's a great start,' he said. 'Why don't you send an email to your solicitor now and go do it in the morning. I'll stay by Drew's side while you're gone.'

Pearl was too tired to argue, plus she wanted to feel like she was doing something concrete for Drew. So even though it was 4 a.m., she sent off an email asking her solicitor to see her later that day, urgently. She went online and looked up the number for the locksmiths in the Vayhill Shopping Centre and left a message on their phone saying she needed an urgent job that day, and leaving her contact number. Then she laid her head back against the wall and tried to stop the images of Seth's fists from taking over her mind. The horror kept being replayed on a loop, and each time the shame she felt increased. Why, oh why had she allowed this to become her life?

At half-seven, Pearl kissed the sleeping Drew lightly, hugged Tommy and left the hospital. She called a taxi and then made the driver stop down the main road, so no one would see her pull into Kingfisher Road. She couldn't cope with talking to anyone just yet. She snuck into her own house, head down, hurrying. When she put her key in the door, her heart began thumping madly. What if he had tricked her and was still here? She opened the front door slowly and quietly, ears strained to hear any sound. His car wasn't in the driveway, so he probably was as good as his word and was holed up in a hotel somewhere. Pearl crept from room to room, and only breathed properly again when she was sure the house was empty. She ran back downstairs and put the chain-lock across the front door.

She had a quick shower, changed her clothes, then gathered her things and some things for Drew and ran out of Kingfisher Road. It was only half-eight and the place was quiet. Once she reached the pub on the main road, she took out her phone and rang her solicitor's office. The receptionist was already on duty and after Pearl explained briefly what she needed, she was told to come in immediately. She rang for a taxi and was sitting at her solicitor's desk by nine-fifteen, relaying the events of the other night, and of the last sixteen years, since Drew's birth. Annmarie Keegan was her solicitor, and she was visibly shocked by Pearl's story, although she maintained a professional composure throughout. Once all the formalities had been carried out, Annmarie sat back and looked at her.

'I'm so sorry to hear that, Pearl,' she said. 'I had no idea. You hid it very well.'

'I was stupid,' Pearl said.

Annmarie frowned. 'No, you weren't,' she said. 'You were living under duress and you were terrified. It's no easy matter to own up to an abusive relationship.'

Pearl waved her hand, not wanting to chit-chat about the mess she'd made of her life.

'Is that everything, then?' she said. 'You have all you need from me?'

'Yes,' Annmarie said, 'but please be careful, Pearl. If there's any hint of him coming near you, ring me immediately and I'll get straight onto the local garda station. He's a dangerous man, and you must think of him like that. I'm going to lodge an application with the court office for a barring order as well, so I'll keep you updated on that.'

Pearl nodded, the exhaustion flooding through her once again. 'Thank you,' she said, getting up stiffly. 'I appreciate your help.'

'I'm here to help,' Annmarie said, standing up and shaking her hand.

Outside in reception, Pearl rang the locksmiths again and got talking to a man called Paul, who arranged to meet her at the house that afternoon. She took out her little notebook and ticked some of the items off her list. It gave her a huge sense of satisfaction to see those little ticks, showing she'd actually done something sensible at last.

When the taxi dropped her outside the hospital, she felt a huge urge to see Drew and hold him. She ran through the corridors, making her way towards her boy. When she reached his ward, he was sitting up in his bed, eating toast, with Tommy sitting on the bed chatting to him. Her heart swelled with love for these two incredible people.

'Drew, my darling,' she said, wrapping her arms around him. 'Are you okay?'

'Okay, yeah,' Drew said, but his eyes were still troubled. 'Good toast.'

Pearl smiled. 'I was just arranging things at home,' she said, 'and the doctor said we can leave soon, after they've given you a final check-up.'

Drew reared back from her, his eyes wide. 'No, no, no,' he cried. 'Not going home. I hate Daddy.'

Pearl stroked his arm. 'Daddy is gone,' she said soothingly. 'He's gone. We're not going to see him again, Drew, okay? Mummy told him to leave because he was mean to us. He won't be living in our house anymore.'

Drew watched her suspiciously. 'Really?' he said, his lip pouting. He looked past her. 'Is it true, Tommy? Tell me.'

Tommy nodded. 'Yes, Drew, that's correct. Seth was very bad, so now he's not allowed to come near you again.'

Drew didn't seem totally convinced, but he calmed down and returned to chewing his toast. Pearl's heart broke to see him so scared and edgy. Seth was an absolute monster if he could harm such a sweet boy as Drew. Any shred of love she'd ever had for Seth had withered and died now. He'd killed it.

It was lunchtime before the doctor on duty signed them

out, complete with a referral for family counselling. Pearl couldn't believe how understanding they'd been. She had been afraid they wouldn't believe her, but they had listened to her side of the story and evidently been convinced by her version of events. They were happy that she posed no threat to her son, which was why they were letting her handle the situation her own way. But she knew that if she turned up again with Drew hurt in any way, that would completely change and they'd be looking at social services or God knows what. It was probably a blessing that all the services were so hard-pressed for resources because it meant they were glad to have one less name added to their list of problems.

They made their way to Tommy's car, which had a ticket on it for being parked in two spots at once. Tommy looked sheepish.

'I just flung it in the first place I saw,' he said. 'Obviously my parking skills suffer when I'm stressed.'

Pearl smiled. 'Yes, that is the parking of a distracted man,' she said, helping Drew into the back seat.

Drew was quiet all the way home, and when Tommy turned onto Kingfisher Road, he began moaning quietly and rocking back and forth. Pearl looked at Tommy in alarm, but he stayed perfectly calm and kept going towards the house.

'Drew, you're safe with me,' he said quietly. 'I won't let anyone hurt you.'

Pearl felt a stab of pain, because she had let someone hurt Drew. If Tommy had been there that night, he would have done a much better job of protecting Drew from Seth. She tried to shush the voice in her head telling her she was useless and focus on helping Drew to get over this obstacle of walking in the door of his own house.

'Daddy's car isn't here because Daddy is gone,' Pearl said, keeping her voice quiet like Tommy's. 'He's not here.' She got out of the car and opened the door for Drew to step out. Tommy came around and took Drew's hand and held it tightly. Holding on to Tommy for dear life, Drew took tiny steps up the driveway to the front door.

Pearl unlocked the door and pushed it wide open. 'Would you like me to go first, Drew, and check all the rooms?' she asked.

He nodded, and she set off, going from room to room, opening the doors wide and calling out, 'No one here. No one here.' When she returned to the front door, Drew had his head on Tommy's shoulder.

'It's all safe, my darling,' Pearl said.

Slowly, Drew and Tommy stepped into the hallway. Pearl could see Drew's chest move faster as his breathing quickened. Tommy didn't rush him, he just let him move at his own pace, slowly going further into the house.

It took half an hour for Drew and Tommy to cover the whole house, but finally they came back to the kitchen and Pearl could see Drew's shoulders drop down as he finally believed that his father was gone. She just prayed that Seth didn't turn up on a whim and undo all their good work.

'I'd like to go to Tommy's house,' Drew said.

'No problem,' Pearl said. 'Why don't you do that and I'll make you some pasta and meatballs while you're gone. Does that sound good?'

Drew smiled for the first time in two days. 'I like pasta,' he said. 'Thanks, Mum.'

Drew and Tommy headed off down the garden path, and Pearl looked around the kitchen. She had cleaned up the glass this morning, but it still felt tainted by what had happened. She decided that she'd give away the kitchen table and chairs and get a new set. In fact, she'd change around the furniture and get the painters back to do some new colours. She needed to look around and see a different place, her place, hers and Drew's.

Chapter 27

'DID YOU HEAR FROM HIM AT ALL YET?' RACHEL asked.

Danielle shook her head miserably. 'No. I don't know if he's angry or hurt or already moved on.'

'You just focus on you,' her mother said. 'This frees you up to consider what's best for you, don't forget that.'

Danielle was slowly going out of her mind in Westwood. Justin hadn't replied to her text, and now she didn't know if she could go back to the house. Did he want to see her? Or did his silence mean, stay away? Her head hurt, her heart hurt, everything hurt. She felt lonely as hell, even though Rachel was barely leaving her side.

'Will I light the fire again?' she asked.

'Please,' Rachel said. '*Strictly* will be on soon, so we'll get ourselves all set up.'

Danielle knew her mam was really enjoying their fireside evenings by the telly, but Danielle was tired of it now. She had run away from her own house because it didn't feel like home, but here didn't feel like home either. She had moved on from Westwood, this wasn't where she belonged anymore. Was there anywhere that would make her feel happy in her skin? That possibility seemed to be disappearing fast.

As she bent to put a match to the firewood she had

built into a triangle, the room was suddenly filled with a bright white light that stretched across the wall, then abruptly went out. She was half blinded by it, blinking into the suddenly returned dim light. Then she heard the doorbell.

Rachel went out to answer it, and she could hear low voices. One of them was definitely a man. They sounded like they were arguing. Curiosity got the better of her and she went to peep through the door into the hallway. Standing on the doorstep was Justin, looking wildly desperate.

'Please, please, Rachel, just let me in for five minutes so I can talk to both of you.'

'Give her space, Justin,' Rachel replied, trying to close the door over. 'Just give her some time out and she'll be ready to talk.'

Justin looked so distraught, Danielle's heart went out to him.

'Mam,' she said. They both looked up at her. 'It's okay. We can talk to him for five minutes.'

Rachel sighed wearily. 'Fine,' she said, holding the door open. 'I'll go upstairs and leave you to it.'

'No,' Justin said, 'please, I'd like you to be there. I think the three of us need to talk.'

Rachel looked like she'd rather stick pins in her eyes, which nearly made Danielle smile, but her mother followed Justin down the passage and back through to the sitting room, where she sat on a sofa beside Danielle, and Justin sat in the armchair. The fire crackled cheerily, but the tension in the room was icy cold.

'Why did you leave?' Justin asked.

Danielle tried to think of the least hurtful thing to say.

'I just needed to be away from that whole life,' she said, 'to remember who I am and what I want.'

'And have you figured that out?' he asked, looking petrified to hear her answer.

Danielle shrugged helplessly. 'It's not easy,' she said. 'I'm feeling confused about things.'

'Okay,' he said, nodding. 'I was afraid you were going to say you want to break up with me.'

'I have thought about it,' Danielle said honestly, 'but it would kill me to do that.'

Justin looked at them and ran his fingers through his hair nervously. 'I think I owe you both an apology,' he said. 'I know you mentioned something about my mum propositioning you, but I didn't really take it in. I was well oiled the night of the party, and then afterwards, I thought you were exaggerating, so I didn't really listen. But then Morton mentioned today that you were genuinely upset leaving the party, and it made me wonder. I think . . . I think I've been an idiot, Danielle.' He paused for breath, watching them for a reaction. 'I want you to tell me what happened, and I'll listen.'

Rachel and Danielle exchanged a look.

'Okay,' Danielle said. She gave him a blow-by-blow account of the party from their point of view, including Celia-Ann's crass offer. He listened intently, never interrupting her. She finished with the photo of him and Mallory emblazoned over the pages of *Glam Life*, and how that had made her feel.

'So just to recap,' Rachel said, when Danielle finished talking, 'your mother told my daughter she wasn't good enough to love you, and then she treated her like some kind of prostitute by offering her cash to bugger off. Is that clear enough for you now?'

Justin nodded slowly. His face was set tight in anger. Danielle could see he was clenching his jaw tightly.

'I hear you loud and clear, Rachel,' he said. 'I think I didn't really believe Danielle before. I thought she got the wrong end of the stick. But given the way Mum has been banging on about Mallory lately, and given that she organised that photo to be taken and probably saw to it that it made its way to the magazine, I'm beginning to see things in a different light. You'll have to forgive me,' he said, staring down at his hands. 'It's hard for me to accept this because it means accepting that Mum is willing to sacrifice my happiness for her own gain. I'm really struggling with that.'

There was an awkward silence, then Rachel said quietly, 'She's your mother, that's totally understandable.'

He shook his head. 'The crazy thing is, Mallory doesn't like me at all. Certainly doesn't love me, though she puts up a good show. All she wants is the house and stables and to be lady of the manor when Mum kicks the bucket. That's her sole aim. I'm just the means to the end. She'd be willing to marry me to get her hands on the estate, even though she'd absolutely hate being married to me.'

'Really?' Danielle said. The idea of not falling for Justin was alien to her.

'Jesus wept,' Rachel said. 'You lot are like something from *Dynasty*.'

Justin smiled tiredly. 'You've no idea,' he said. 'I guarantee you that all the people round here are far happier than anyone I know. Money is great for the choices it gives you, but it causes so many headaches. You know, the arguments about my parents' will have been going on as long as I can remember. It used to scare me as a child, when they'd go on about after they'd died. But then I got used to it because it was a constant topic. My brothers were always vying for position and leverage, wondering what they'd get. It's something that's been bothering me for a long time. I don't want any part of it.'

'Well there'll be no need for any arguments about my will,' Rachel said with a burst of laughter. 'There's this house you're sitting in and feck-all else. And I still don't even own this outright. You'll be raking over the remains with the council.'

'Don't talk about that,' Danielle said, grabbing her mother's hand. 'I can't bear to think of it.'

'Now you see,' Justin said, gesturing at Danielle, 'that's a normal, loving reaction. You don't see that in my house. Everyone is playing the long game, wondering what the old dears will leave them. It's horrible.'

'What about Celia-Ann?' Rachel said. 'Doesn't she mind that yer one Mallory is eyeing up her bed before it's cold?'

Justin shook his head. 'She sees her as a worthy successor, so she's keen to put her in place. It's pure nonsense.' He looked at Danielle with a fierce intensity. 'I need you to believe me that there is absolutely nothing between me and Mallory. We did go out for a time, but then I realised her game. There's no way on earth I'd want to be with her. I fell head over heels for you that night in the gallery, and that hasn't changed. I was so happy when you told me you were pregnant, even though I was worried about your reaction to it, but to me, us being together and making a life together feels right. I just . . . I don't know if it's what you want.'

Danielle felt her throat constricting. This was it. This was the moment she had to decide. The next word out of her mouth would define her future.

Justin held up his hands. 'Before you say anything, let me just say something else. I haven't been a good partner to you lately. I didn't pay attention and by doing that, I let you down. My mother is a shrewd adversary, and I can only imagine that you dread the idea of her in your life.'

Danielle nodded silently. It felt so wonderful to have him understand, to get it.

'I know,' he said. 'Well, look, I've had an idea brewing for some time now, because I was feeling so annoyed about the will and all that, and now with this happening, I think it might be time to act.' He leaned forward, closer towards them. 'I'd really love to set up my own stable yard,' he said, his eyes twinkling with the light from the fire. 'It will take a lot of hard work, and we might be financially challenged while I get it up and running, but if I could manage it, then it would take me out from under my family's shadow. I wouldn't be in their place every day, and they wouldn't have any hold over me.'

'You can do it,' Danielle said immediately. 'It's a brilliant idea and you're well able. Your dad told me you're a horse-whisperer, and the best one he'd ever seen in sixty years around horses. People would flock to you.'

'It's a gamble, though,' he said. 'We'd probably have to cut back the budget and there might be some lean times while I find my feet.'

Danielle grinned. 'I kick the ass of lean times,' she said, making them laugh. 'I eat tiny budgets for breakfast. You are talking my language now, Justin. Nothing about that would scare me.'

'Well then,' Justin said. He stood up and stepped over to the sofa and went down on one knee.

'Ah here,' Rachel said.

'Danielle O'Brien, will you agree to marry me again, even if I'm a bit harder up, even if I've been an idiot, even if it won't always be plain sailing? I love you so much. Will you be my wife?'

Danielle searched in her heart and finally found that elusive thing: what she wanted. It had been Justin all along, but the whole circumstances of being with him had made her want to run away. But now, with the new future he was describing, it sounded blissful to her. With a clarity that nearly knocked her sideways, she knew exactly what she wanted.

'Yes, I will – again,' she said. She kissed him. 'I said yes before, but I didn't really know what I was getting into. This time, I have my eyes open. I want to be your wife, Justin. I want to set up a life together. I want to have this baby. And I also want to limit your mother's hold over us, and I want to have a career and I want to be happy in my own skin, just as me.'

'I can give you all that,' he said, grabbing her in a bear hug.

'Lord above, you two and the drama,' Rachel said, wiping tears from her eyes. 'I was all ready for a night in and a bit of *Strictly* and *Gogglebox*.'

'Oh Mam,' Danielle said, turning to her. 'I'll stay here tonight and we'll do that.'

'You will not,' Rachel said. 'You've made up your mind for good now,' she said. 'I can see it. And I was furious before, but what Justin's describing now sounds like a better match for you, which makes me a bit happier.'

'Just a bit?' Justin said, teasing her. 'I'm going to work hard to win your approval, Rachel.'

'It's not given away easily,' Rachel said with a sniff.

'Well we might start with this,' Justin said. 'I was thinking about you and Danielle as well, and how you haven't seen so much of each other. I'm going to be working flat out to make this new venture happen, and that worries me because Danielle will need lots of support when the baby arrives. So I was thinking about inviting you to be a much more permanent part of our family.'

'Babysitting, is it?' Rachel said tetchily.

Justin laughed. 'No. Although I'm sure we'll be hitting you for that too. But no, what I'm proposing is that we build you a little place of your own, Rachel, in the garden, and you can come and go as you please. You can keep on this house, or rent it, or sell it, whatever you feel is best for you. But I want Danielle to feel happy, and that means making sure she has you on tap when she needs you.'

Rachel was looking at him in shock. Danielle had never, ever seen her mother so lost for words. She could see that Rachel was fighting to hold back tears.

'That's really very kind of you, Justin,' she said, her voice breaking a little. 'It's . . . it's amazing you thought of that. Thank you.' She looked from her daughter to Justin. 'I don't want to sound ungrateful for one minute, but I'd have to say, hand on heart, that I'd prefer to stay here and come visit very often. I'm used to my own space, and young married couples need to get used to theirs, so while I'm very touched that you came up with that idea, I'd be much happier living my life and letting you live yours. Although I'll be in your faces a lot of the time when my grandchild arrives, just to warn you.'

Justin smiled. 'That's no problem at all, Rachel. I admire an honest woman.'

'Oh then you're going to absolutely love me,' Rachel said, making them both laugh.

Oh God, I'm so relieved,' Justin said, turning to Danielle. 'I was so scared when I got your text. The thought of losing you . . .'

'You two lovebirds need to get out now,' Rachel said, shooing them with her hands. 'Go on, go home and be all soppy about each other there. I can't watch my programmes with you cluttering up the room.'

'Are you sure?' Danielle said, feeling bad at leaving her.

'If you think you're leaving two massive cars outside my house, you can think again. I'll have every beggar from here to town coming knocking. They'll think I've won the Lotto. So get those cars out of here, come on.' She ushered them out of the room and towards the front door. 'Go on, goodnight,' she said.

'Night, Mam. I love you,' Danielle said.

Rachel closed the front door and Justin immediately wrapped his arms around Danielle and kissed her long and slow.

'I don't even want to be parted from you for the journey home,' he said, 'but I'm too scared of Rachel to leave your car here.'

Danielle laughed. 'You'd be right, too. I'll follow you home.'

As she climbed into the Range Rover she thought, home. Yes, it finally felt like it was.

Chapter 28

'I'M HUNGRY,' DREW SAID, SNIFFING THE AIR. 'IS MY lunch ready?'

'Perfect timing,' Pearl said, putting his plate down on the breakfast bar. 'You can sit up here for a change, on the high stool. I know you like that.'

Drew sat down heavily on the stool and gave his full attention to his meal. He was so big now, he pretty much inhaled food. His appetite was huge, even though he never seemed to gain weight. He was becoming a man, Pearl thought as she watched him. The future was so scary, but she was going to do right by him from now on.

'Are you okay?' Tommy said, giving her a quick and light kiss on the temple.

She nodded. 'Not great, but okay.'

The doorbell rang, and Pearl froze. Tommy stroked her cheek.

'It's okay. The locks are all changed, so if it's him, he can't get in, okay? I'll go check.'

Pearl strained to hear what was happening. She heard the front door being pulled open, then a voice that definitely wasn't Seth's. It was a woman. Then she heard Tommy said, 'No, wait, hang on, I don't think . . .' Who the hell was it? The kitchen door was pushed open.

'You're home,' Maia said delightedly, walking straight

into the kitchen. 'Oh Pearl, we've been worried sick about you. Are you alright?' Maia went straight over and enveloped Pearl in a bear hug. Pearl was caught off-guard, she wasn't ready to see them yet. But they all trooped in behind Maia, one after another, including the twins.

'We wanted to see Drew,' Zara said. 'I hope that's okay.'

Pearl nodded. 'He's over there.'

'Drew!' Zara said. 'We missed you. Are you doing okay? Oh, you have a bandage on your arm. Did the ambulance men put that on for you?'

Drew nodded solemnly. 'Daddy hurt me,' he said. 'But the doctors made it better.'

'Seth said there was a little accident,' Nancy said. 'I'm so glad it was just minor and you're both okay. We tried to get in touch but couldn't get through on your phone. We came over to Seth, but he didn't tell us much.'

'No, I'm sure he didn't,' Pearl said. She was feeling claustrophobic with all these people in her kitchen, and the feeling that they must have been talking about her and her family behind her back. She was probably the juiciest bit of gossip doing the rounds.

Danielle came in last, looking shy.

'Oh my God, Danielle,' Pearl said. 'You're home.'

Danielle smiled. 'That makes two of us. Yes, I'm home. For good this time.'

'Really,' Pearl said. 'I'm so pleased to hear that.'

'It was a rocky few days,' Danielle said, 'but we've ironed it out now. It's all good.'

Pearl envied the young woman her clarity, but then she pushed that aside and just felt happy for her.

'I'm really so happy to hear that, Danielle,' she said again.

'We all are,' Nancy said. 'We realised how much we missed her when she was gone. She's one of us now, God love her.'

Danielle laughed. 'That doesn't sound too bad.'

'I'm so glad you're all okay,' Betsy said, coming over to embrace Pearl. 'I was so upset when I saw the ambulance. I couldn't bear the idea of anything happening to darling Drew. Or to you, Pearl. You must be glad to be home.'

'Yes, we are,' Pearl said. 'Now you're all very good for coming, but . . .'

'What happened?' Maia said, and Pearl could feel the weight of her stare. Maia could sniff out a lie or a half-truth in a second. Pearl felt like she was caught in a spotlight, with everyone watching, waiting for what she would say.

'I think maybe Pearl might need some space,' Danielle said quietly. 'We've kind of landed in on top of her. We can come back later, Pearl, yeah?'

Before Pearl could say, Yes, please leave right now, Drew suddenly said, 'Daddy can't come back. He's never coming back. He won't hit me again.'

There was silence that seemed to stretch on for ever. Pearl could feel her face burning red. There was a roaring sound in her ears and she felt sick. Her friends stood around dumbly, no one knowing what to say. Drew was looking at Zach and Zara, waiting for their reaction. It was Zach who managed to speak first.

'Hey, dude, if your dad did hurt you, then I'm really glad he's gone away. No one should ever hurt you, Drew. If they do, you come and tell me and I'll hurt them right back, okay? I don't want anyone hurting my friends.'

Drew grinned. 'Thanks, Zach. If Daddy ever comes back, I'll run to Tommy or to you.'

Pearl stared at the floor, unable to meet anyone's eye. She was waiting for their shock, their judgement, their looks of contempt because they regarded her as a terrible mother. They were her friends, but they were also such strong, together women. None of them would have allowed this situation to grow to the point where their child ended up in hospital, she was sure of that.

'Oh Pearl,' Betsy cried, 'is that true? Did Seth deliberately hurt Drew?'

'I knew it,' Maia said. 'I got such a bad feeling off him. I said to Nancy that I wouldn't be surprised if the ambulance had something to do with him. And what about that bruise on your cheek, Pearl, did he do that too?'

Pearl couldn't bear the feeling of being sized up and judged. 'Look,' she said, her voice harsher than she intended, 'I know you're over to see the dysfunctional family in action, but I just can't cope with that at the moment. So yes, Seth beat Drew and he beat me and it's been going on for years and you don't have to tell me that I'm a crap mother and a stupid person because I know that already. I don't want to hear what you all think of me, okay, because I'm hanging on by a thread here.' She squeezed her eyes shut, half hoping when she opened them, everyone would have just disappeared into thin air.

'The first time my husband hit me,' Nancy said, 'I packed a bag and got ready to leave him. That bag stayed under my bed, packed and ready to go, for four long years before I actually picked it up and walked out the door.'

Pearl looked at Nancy in absolute shock. Never in all her life would she have thought of Nancy being broken down by a man. She couldn't even speak, she just kept staring at Nancy in horror.

'He killed something in me,' Nancy said, her voice so matter-of-fact it made it all sound worse. 'I couldn't leave because there wasn't enough left of me, or maybe I thought I deserved what he dished out because of my drinking. It's hard to put it into words, but leaving seemed like a mountain so high, there was no way I could ever climb it. It was just an impossibility. There was no way out. It took years for me to realise all I had to do was open the door and walk through.'

A sound escaped from Pearl that was part cry, part gasp. The world had just turned upside-down for her. She wasn't the only one, that's all she could think. Someone she admired had made the same mistake. It was incredible to think that she had been friends with Nancy for so many years and never found this out before.

'Oh Nancy,' she said, 'I'm so sorry. The idea of someone hitting you . . .'

'And that's how we feel about you,' Nancy said, walking over to hug her. 'I can see the look on your face, Pearl. You think we're all standing around judging you and thinking terrible things about you, but we're not. We're your friends. We're all gutted that this happened to you.'

'We're judging ourselves harshly,' Betsy added, wiping a tear from her eye. 'Here we are living right beside you and we never knew. We never guessed. We didn't help. What kind of friends are we?'

'I thought you'd hate me,' Pearl said hoarsely. 'I couldn't bear it, to see you all looking at me like that.'

'You mad thing,' Maia said, also starting to cry. 'We love you to bits, Pearl. We'd never think badly of you. There is only one person to blame for this and that's bloody Seth. If I ever see him again, so help me I'm going to lob something hard and sharp at his big, thick head.'

'Are you okay?' Danielle asked, her face full of concern. 'Did he hurt you badly? Were you treated in the hospital as well?'

Pearl shook her head. 'No, it was mainly Drew. Seth punched me, but he flung Drew across the room and he landed on a glass Seth had shattered against the wall, so he was bleeding. That's why I called the ambulance. All the other times, I just patched up Drew and me as best I could. It wasn't all the time, you know,' she said, feeling lighter with every truthful word she uttered. 'He was away so much, so it wasn't really regular or anything. He'd just lose it sometimes. This time it was because he thought I made a show of him by dancing at the party. But when he was in that mood, he'd always find something.'

'Daddy is a bad man,' Drew said, his chin wobbling as tears began to fall. 'I love Tommy. He's good.'

'Oh Lord, we're all sobbing,' Betsy said, rubbing her eyes. 'You two are so brave. And Pearl, to get Drew out and stand up to Seth, that took real courage.'

'But it took me so long,' Pearl said, the shame gripping her again.

'Me too,' Nancy said. 'Me too, Pearl. It's hard to get away. But saying it out loud, naming it, that's a really important step. By doing that, you've already broken free.'

'Is that why you had a guy here from the locksmiths yesterday?' Zach asked. 'I saw the van. Is that so that Seth can't get back in?'

Pearl nodded, feeling embarrassed that the twins were a party to all this. They must be shocked out of their young minds.

'Good,' Zach said. 'And I'll keep my eyes peeled, Pearl, for any sign of him. There's no way he's getting back in here again. Do you want me to stay for a while, so you've got extra help in the house at night?'

'Oh God, Zach, that is so good of you,' Pearl said. 'I'm so touched that you would think to do that. You're a credit to your mum and dad, you really are. You're so kind.'

Zach shrugged, then rolled his eyes as Maia reached up to kiss him. 'I'm so proud of you,' she whispered.

'I've some friends who have parents with alcohol problems,' he said, looking uncomfortable with all the attention. 'They've told me how horrible it is to wait for the key in the door at night, you know. I'm so sorry this happened to you, and to you, Drew. It's not right. But I will stay over any time, Pearl. It's no problem.'

'I'm very glad to know I can call on you, Zach, but thankfully I have someone in my corner, and he'd lay down his life to protect me and Drew.' She looked over at Tommy and smiled.

'Oh!' Maia said, looking from one to the other of them. 'Oh my God, you two! I had no idea. I can't believe I didn't cop that. My God, you're dark horses.'

'That's wonderful,' Betsy said warmly. 'I'm glad you've had someone kind to balance out the horrible. Pearl deserves a lovely man like you, Tommy.'

Tommy looked distinctly uncomfortable, but Pearl was floating high on the relief of her friends not blaming her and on the feeling of finally telling the truth. It was intoxicating. It made her want to spill the beans about everything. It was such a sweet feeling to acknowledge her feelings for Tommy and his for her. It made them feel like a proper couple, which was what she wanted so badly. She wanted to never think about Seth again, and to be with Tommy openly and always.

'Ah, that's so cute,' Maia said, 'the two of you blushing like teenagers.'

'I love Tommy,' Drew stated again. 'Only Tommy and Mum.'

'And we love you, Drew,' Pearl said. 'For ever and ever.'

'You'll need time to work through this, though,' Nancy said carefully. 'Don't rush any decisions would be my advice. Let the dust settle, think about what you want and put your happiness and Drew's happiness first. It's not a case of getting out of that situation and everything clicking into place. It takes time to process what happened and how it affected you.'

'Nancy's right,' Danielle said, and they all looked at her in surprise. She nervously twisted her scarf in her hand. 'My dad was a drinker,' she said. 'I've been through what you and Drew have been through. You'll need to be really kind to yourselves and not put yourself under pressure to be suddenly better and over it, you know? It takes a long time to come to terms with it.'

Nancy shook her head. 'Well there you go,' she said. 'You thought you were alone, Pearl, and actually three-fifths of us have skeletons in that particular cupboard.'

'That's mad,' Maia said. 'I'd never have guessed it about any of you. You're all such brilliant strong women.'

'My heart is breaking,' Betsy said. 'My beautiful friends harbouring such secrets. It's terrible. I'm so sorry you all experienced something so horrible. I just want to wrap you all up and hug you until it's gone away.'

'Betsy, you big softie,' Nancy said affectionately. 'Sure, none of us gets through life without something going wrong. We're all carrying scars of one kind or another.'

Pearl looked around the room and felt the love of these

wonderful people and thanked her lucky stars that she had them in her life, always nearby. She suddenly remembered something.

'Nancy, what happened with the council? Did you have the meeting?'

Nancy grinned. 'I sure did, and those silly buggers have backed down, Pearl. I'm not moving anywhere. Danielle here figured out a legal loophole and saved my ass.'

Pearl looked at Danielle in astonishment. 'You did that?' she said. 'Now that is impressive. And you called me a dark horse!'

'Kingfisher Road women,' Nancy declared. 'We may carry scars, we may have secrets, but by God we're a bunch of kick-ass women!'

'Hear, hear,' Maia shouted. 'And Pearl, you're the most kick-ass of the lot. My hat goes off to you.'

Pearl giggled. 'You're the most amazing women,' she said. 'Oh God, I'm going to start crying again. You're just so good, and to tell me these things and be there for me, it's just . . . it's incredible. I'm so glad I know you all. And it's going to be so good to live here on my own terms, no Seth, no rules. It'll be wine by the barrel-load whenever we feel like it.'

She felt overwhelmed by emotion, and by the stress and exhaustion of the past two days. But she was still standing. Seth had tried to knock them into submission, but now she was here and he wasn't. She knew Nancy and Danielle were right to say it would take time, but with the love in the room and the support of these wise and wonderful women, she felt ready to grab the future, her future, with both hands. She'd have Tommy by her side, a happy Drew, and a life that was free of fear. It felt good.

As she shepherded her friends out of the house, she heard her phone beeping from her bag in the kitchen. She went back inside and took it out with a sense of dread. Sure enough, there was his name. It was his reply. Pearl took a deep breath and pressed Open.

You are even more stupid than I thought, Pearl. I have just had a courier hand a sheaf of documents into reception, and I see that you have involved a solicitor and are threatening me with the police. This is utterly ridiculous given that this is a minor domestic matter. However, it does show me exactly what kind of person you are, and what you are is untrustworthy and hysterical. I have no desire to be married to a person like you. I'm far better off without the burden of you and your child on my back. I shall make my own plans for myself, and I won't see either of you ever again. Don't bother pleading with me when you realise the error of your ways, because it's over. Goodbye, Pearl.

Goodbye, Pearl thought, smiling through her tears. It was the sweetest word she'd ever heard in her life.

Chapter 29

DANIELLE HAD GONE SHOPPING IN VAYHILL AND picked up some new things – all with extra stretch around the waist. Zara had gone with her and helped her pick some gorgeous dresses. When she had Zara with her, it was so easy to breeze through the boutiques and pick exactly the right thing. Left to her own devices, she would probably have given up after an hour and come home empty-handed. But she was really thrilled with her purchases. They made her feel like a new woman, which matched the new contentment she felt about Justin and their life together.

She chose one of the outfits now – a red wrap dress with a pattern of little green-masted sailboats. It was cute and funky and a great shape on her. She matched it with a mustard yellow Aran cardigan that she never would have thought to buy, sheer tights and the new brown ankle boots Zara had told her were an autumn–winter necessity.

'I won't leave this shop until you've bought them,' Zara said, sitting down on a sofa and crossing her arms.

'You look just like your mother when you do that,' Danielle had teased, but she had done what she was told all the same.

She was very glad she had, because the outfit was note perfect, and she felt fantastic in it. She smiled at her reflection in the mirror while she plaited her hair, then headed downstairs to Justin.

'Oh you look fantastic,' he said when she walked into the kitchen. 'I love that look on you.'

'Thank you,' Danielle said, blushing. 'Zara helped me to pick it out. I love it too.'

'Are you ready to go then?' he asked. 'They're expecting us at one, so we need to hit the road.'

'Just let me grab my bag and coat and I'm ready,' Danielle said.

They were going to meet Hugh Somerville, a landowner who had suggested going into partnership with Justin. The two of them got on very well and over a whiskey one evening, Justin had mentioned that he might like to change things up a little in his working life. Hugh was a shrewd operator, and within a week he'd emailed Justin with a proposal – a 50/50 split for a business operated out of Hugh's stables, bringing in as many clients as would follow Justin. On paper, it was a match made in heaven, and it would make it easier for Justin to get up and running quickly. But Justin was adamant that he and Danielle share every decision from now on, so he wanted her to see the place, meet Hugh and his wife, and then they could discuss it and decide themselves what they wanted to do.

'Did you read through Hugh's proposal?' Justin asked as he cruised his sleek BMW down the motorway, headed for County Kildare.

'Yes, I've read it closely,' Danielle said. 'I was looking for any gaps that could create problems for you later, but it seems very fair and transparent. I felt he could have held out for a 60/40 split, even pushed his end to 65 given that he's supplying the base of operations, so the fact that he's offering to share equally in the profits is a real mark of respect and trust, which is a good thing.'

Justin grinned at her. 'It's so handy having a lawyer on my side,' he said.

'A wannabe lawyer,' Danielle said.

'No way; you're better than any I've met before,' Justin said. 'What you did for Nancy was incredible. I'd never in a million years have thought two little birds could be significant. I've bagged myself one smart woman.'

Danielle laughed. 'Flattery will get you everywhere.'

They pulled up at Burtonstown Lodge and drove through the large wooden gates. No horses on pillars here, Danielle thought, that's a good start. The driveway was flanked by rolling green fields stretching out as far as the eye could see. It was a really beautiful location. The house itself was an old farmhouse, with stone walls and sash windows. Danielle fell in love with it on sight.

'Oh they're so lucky,' she said. 'This is gorgeous.'

'Would you actually live somewhere like this?' Justin asked, looking surprised. 'I had you down as a lifelong city girl.'

'I think I could be happy in a place like this,' Danielle said. 'It's so quiet and green, you can think straight out here, you know what I mean?'

'You're preaching to the choir,' Justin said. 'This is my kind of place. And you know, Hugh did mention that if we ever wanted to move here, he would help us sort the planning permission. So just tuck that in the back of your mind, if you see it as a bonus of the proposal.'

Danielle knew she wanted to stay in Kingfisher Road for some time, but in the future, yes, she would be willing to consider a move like that. It would be a wonderful place to raise children, that's for sure.

Two dogs came bounding out to the car as Justin opened the door and stepped out. They were followed by a tall, slender man with a wide smile.

'There you are,' he called out. 'Delighted to see you both. Danielle,' he said, striding over to her, hand extended, 'I'm so pleased to finally meet you. Justin has me bored to tears listening to how wonderful you are.'

Danielle burst out laughing. 'I doubt that very much,' she said, 'but thanks for pretending.'

'A canny wife can be a blessing or a curse,' Hugh said, shaking her hand and pretending to look concerned for Justin.

'This one's definitely a blessing,' Justin said, coming around to shake his hand.

'How much of the land around us do you own?' Danielle asked, gazing around at the lush fields.

'I inherited a hundred acres,' Hugh said. 'I've leased some of it to local farmers, and then we kept twenty acres, which is just about manageable for us. We aren't in a position to hire many staff yet; hopefully in the future we'll turn a bigger profit and get more helping hands, but for now, Charlotte and I work our backsides off to keep our heads above water.'

Danielle was surprised by his honesty, but admired it. He wasn't pretending to be something he wasn't, which instantly put her at ease. This wasn't a display of wealth like Celia-Ann's house, where it was intended to make you feel small and unworthy. She had expected Hugh and his wife to be all hoity-toity, but instead she found him charming. Another good point in their favour.

Hugh walked them around to the stables, showing them the current operation and talking of his hopes for the future if a partner like Justin came on board. Danielle asked a ton of questions, but she didn't feel he looked down on her for her lack of knowledge. He was animated in answering her and seemed to enjoy her curiosity and interest.

'Now, I'm completely hogging you,' he said at last. 'Charlotte's been slaving over a hot stove and is itching to feed us. Come on inside.'

They went through the back door, which led straight into a spacious farmhouse kitchen with a red-tiled floor, a butcher's block table and an open fireplace.

'This is so beautiful,' Danielle said, looking around. 'I've really fallen for this place.'

'You are very kind, and you have great taste,' said a woman, coming into the kitchen with a small child on her hip. 'I'm Charlotte. Lovely to meet you, Danielle.' She hugged Danielle, then did the same to Justin. 'I've lunch ready to go, so make yourselves at home, sit down and we can chat. I'll just put this ragamuffin down for a nap so we can talk in peace.'

'What's your name?' Danielle said to the blond-haired boy. He grinned at her, but said nothing.

'This is Daniel,' Charlotte said, 'my little dote. He was helping Daddy in the yard, so he's worn out now. Normally he'd bombard you with information. Just give me a sec and I'll pop him into bed.'

While she was gone, Hugh invited them to sit and poured glasses of sparkling water. There was a loaf of homemade bread on a board in the centre of the table, with a pot of butter. There were boiled duck eggs in a bowl, some baby potatoes boiled in their jackets and a salad of lettuce and scallions. It was all so simple and looked so delicious. Danielle was making mental notes about everything – the mismatched crockery that looked so cool, the wooden serving boards and the homemade food.

When Charlotte rejoined them, they sat together and passed around the food. The atmosphere was warm and relaxed, and Danielle felt utterly at home in this lovely place with these lovely people. There was absolutely none of the silly one-upmanship that governed Justin's home, just the charm of two people devoted to one another and to their home and business, without all the fuss.

'I'm going to sound like a broken record,' Danielle said to Charlotte, 'but I really do love this place. I don't have a good sense of style or anything, but being here, I feel like this is how I want to live. The whole look of the place, it just feels so homely. I mean, even this table and the chairs – you wouldn't see them in Ikea, but I love them all the more for that.'

Charlotte laughed as she peeled an egg. 'You're very kind,' she said. 'To be honest, there's days I'd give anything to swan up to Ikea and buy a job lot and have it all sorted, but money's tight, Hugh's working towards his success, which will come, but in the meantime I have to be resourceful. This table and chairs were bought at an auction for one hundred and seventy for the lot, and I upcycled them.'

'What's upcycled?' Danielle asked.

'It's when you take an old piece of furniture and straighten out its dents, hide the scrapes with varnish and then paint it up. You make it look halfway decent again.'

'Oh,' Danielle said, looking at the table with renewed interest. 'I thought it was just old and expensive and out of my league in every way.'

'You are the best guest I've ever had,' Charlotte said,

grinning at her. 'No, it's just me with some paint and polish, and Bob's your uncle. It's easy really.'

'Well as someone who's never even heard of it,' Danielle said, 'it doesn't sound easy to me.'

'Would you be interested in learning?' Charlotte asked.

'Yes,' Danielle said without thinking.

'There's a woman who teaches a class in the village, and she's fantastic. That's how I learned,' Charlotte said. 'She's there on Monday and Wednesday mornings, and the class lasts two hours. It's well worth doing if you're interested. And you could pop in here and see me before or after. I've only got toddlers and horses to talk to, so you'd be a welcome distraction.'

'That sounds amazing,' Danielle said. 'Can you give me her details?'

'Sure, I'll text them on to you.'

They exchanged numbers, and Charlotte forwarded the contact.

'Do you just have the one child?' Danielle asked.

'No, we have three,' Charlotte said. 'The other two are at school. They're in junior infants and first class. Emily and Samuel.'

'Oh that sounds wonderful,' Danielle said. 'Actually,' she said, leaning forward, 'I'm pregnant with our first.' She felt a thrill at so blatantly ignoring Celia-Ann's express instructions. To hell with it, she thought, I'm happy and want to share it.

'Congratulations,' Charlotte said. 'That's wonderful. Oh, you'll be so happy, just you wait and see. You'll be utterly wrecked, of course, but you'll be deliriously happy too. And if this plan goes ahead,' she said, 'you'll be welcome here any time. The more, the merrier.'

Danielle felt her heart expand with joy. She already knew she'd be telling Justin that this was the perfect move to make. Everything about this place, this couple felt so right. It was all the cards falling into place, and she couldn't believe their luck. This was just meant to be.

There was a knock at the back door and a voice called out, 'Hello, anyone home?' The door was pushed open, and Mallory stepped into the kitchen. Her smile froze on her face when she saw them all sitting there. 'Oh, I'm so sorry, I didn't know I was interrupting.' Her eyes darted to Danielle, and she blushed.

Danielle was in complete shock. She had hoped never to see Mallory ever again, and now here she was. Was she following Justin? Had he told her they'd be here? Was this some other sick ploy to split them up?

'Em, Mallory,' Hugh said, looking a bit shocked. 'How can I help you?' He stood up and walked towards her.

'Didn't Johnny mention I was coming?' she said. 'I rang earlier to say I'd take a look at the mare. He said she's for sale.'

'Oh yes, of course,' Hugh said. 'No, I'm afraid he didn't mention it. But let's go outside and find him and you can take a look at her.'

Danielle looked over at Justin, and he looked back at her.

'I knew nothing about this,' he said quickly. 'It's a complete coincidence as far as I know.'

Charlotte was looking at them with curiosity. 'What's wrong?' she asked.

'Well, Mallory is Justin's ex and his mother feels I should bugger off and make way for her, so it's a little bit awkward,' Danielle said, not caring what anyone thought. It was just the truth.

'Right,' Charlotte said, nodding. 'Bloody exes, hey? Always turning up exactly when you don't need them to.'

Justin smiled, and Danielle couldn't help laughing. Charlotte's manner was so easy-going, it turned something horribly awkward into a joke. She smiled at Justin to let him know she believed him, that it was just a horrible coincidence.

Hugh returned and apologised profusely for the intrusion. 'I've left her with Johnny. She wants to buy a horse, so I can't run her out of the place,' he said apologetically. 'I hope you don't mind. Perhaps we can distract ourselves from that by discussing my proposal,' he suggested. 'I'd really like to talk it through and get an idea of how you're thinking, and what you thought of the plan I put together.'

Danielle forced herself to focus on the discussion, and they went through the various options and the finances and the legalities. She had researched a lot of it before coming here, so she was able to make an intelligent contribution, which made her feel good about herself. She wanted to be Justin's right-hand woman, just like Charlotte was obviously Hugh's confidante and advisor.

They were just polishing off an excellent dessert of apple pie and cream when there was the sound of a car driving fast up the driveway and screeching into the yard. Hugh looked up, startled.

'Who the bloody hell is driving like that?' he asked angrily. 'They'll give the horses a heart attack.'

There came the sound of car doors slamming, then an all too familiar voice shouted out, 'Justin, are you in there?'

Justin went pale. 'Oh Christ,' he said. 'It's Mum. What's she doing here?'

In a split second, Danielle knew what had happened.

Mallory had spotted the tête-à tête, probably put two and two together and rung Mummy dearest to warn her that Justin and his horrible slut were about to fly the coop. She'd put money on it. Mallory was trying to hang on to her ticket to wealth and privilege any way she could, so she'd called in the big guns. Danielle took a deep breath and steeled herself for the onslaught that was bound to follow.

Justin stood up and pushed back his chair and headed for the back door. Danielle, Hugh and Charlotte followed him. Outside, Celia-Ann and Mallory were talking intently, while Jeremy stood at the car looking mortified. As they walked towards them, Jeremy looked at Justin and mouthed the word 'sorry'. He clearly had been harangued into participating in this little show-down. Incredibly, Danielle felt very calm. None of the sense of panic that normally rose up when she saw Celia-Ann was there, she just felt calm and utterly sure of herself. It was such a new and strange feeling, she marvelled at it. Do your worst, Celia-Ann, she thought, I'm ready for you this time.

'Justin,' Celia-Ann barked when she saw him, 'what is the meaning of this? Mallory rang me, very upset, because she thinks you might be planning on going into business with this man,' she said, gesturing at Hugh in a manner that suggested she thought him unworthy of polishing her shoes, let alone being in the company of her son. 'I told her that was ridiculous. Isn't that ridiculous, Justin?'

'What I'm doing here is my business,' Justin said. 'You have no right to roll in demanding to know why I'm here. I'm not on the payroll, Mum. I don't have to answer to you.'

Celia-Ann looked like she'd been slapped in the face with a dead fish, and Danielle had to stifle a giggle. Celia-Ann's eyes bulged and she stared at Justin in shock.

'How dare you speak to me like that,' she said. 'I am merely taking care of your interests, Justin. I am well aware that that girl who trails around after you is a bad influence, and I'm just making sure you and your future are safe.'

'By that girl do you mean me, Celia-Ann?' Danielle said. 'Justin's fiancée and the mother of his child?'

'I warned you not to mention that,' Celia-Ann hissed. 'You've no right. You're not married to my son, and that's what matters. He's free to make his own choices.'

'Yes, I am,' Justin said. 'And I'm choosing Danielle, and I'm choosing to go my own way in terms of business, to get out from under your controlling grip. I'm handing in my notice, Mum, effective immediately.'

Jeremy put his head in his hands, while Celia-Ann stared at her son in horror.

'No,' she screeched. 'Don't talk such nonsense, darling. That stupid girl has turned your head. This is simply not tenable. Don't throw away your future, darling. Listen to me, your place is at Johnston House, it's your rightful place. Don't confuse love and lust. Be sensible about this. She's just a fling. She can't actually be your wife, Justin. It doesn't make any sense. Surely you can see that?'

Danielle could see Mallory's wicked delight at all this and also Charlotte's and Hugh's utter dismay, but she felt strangely detached from everything Celia-Ann was saying. It was just noise. She suddenly realised that this woman and her narrow, snobby views didn't matter at all – they only mattered if Danielle allowed them to. She couldn't control what Celia-Ann said, but she could control whether it affected her or not. It was a revelation, and Danielle nearly laughed out loud to realise it.

'You will not speak to or about Danielle like that,' Justin said furiously. 'Nor will you pick who I love or who I marry or where I live. You have interfered all my life and I'm sick and tired of it. You don't have my best interests at heart, only your own twisted view of how things ought to be. Well I'm not buying into that anymore.'

Celia-Ann looked horrified. Danielle was quite sure no member of the family had ever spoken to her like that before. Her sons mollified her, taking Justin's old stance of 'anything for a quiet life'. This was a whole new ball-game, and she evidently had no idea how to play it.

'Jeremy,' she said now, 'say something. Tell him.'

Jeremy sighed and looked directly at his wife, and then he very bravely said, 'He's old enough to make up his own mind, dear. You can't force an adult to do something he doesn't want to do. He does love Danielle, and you can't force him not to either.'

Celia-Ann looked around wildly, obviously looking for someone to back her up. Her eye lit on Mallory, who moved forward and opened her mouth to say something, but a look from Danielle shut her up quick smart. She stepped back again and hung her head. Realising she was on her own in this losing battle, Celia-Ann lashed out – at Danielle, naturally enough.

'You,' she said, pointing a shaking finger at her, 'this is your doing. My son was perfectly good and loving until you came along. You little gold-digger. You got pregnant on purpose to trap him. I can see through you. I know exactly who you are and what you're made of. I'm going to wait and watch and the day will come when Justin realises the truth about you and I'll be there to comfort him and bring him back into our family, where he belongs.'

Celia-Ann was panting after this outburst, her whole body shuddering with emotion. There was a heavy, painfully embarrassed silence as everyone stood staring at her, not knowing what to do. Danielle regarded her with cool contempt for a few moments, then she walked towards her slowly.

'That was an extremely undignified rant, Celia-Ann,' she said. 'Most unbecoming. Let's set a few things straight. I am not and never have been a gold-digger. You don't know me at all because all you see is a poor person who's not worth getting to know. You grade people by their possessions and their bank accounts and on that basis you decide if you'll be nice or nasty to them. That's why you've no true friends, why your son is getting away from you and why your other sons will probably follow suit.' She reached Celia-Ann, who was staring at her wide-eyed, seemingly rooted to the spot. Everyone was watching her intently as she stood in front of her future mother-in-law and looked her straight in the eye.

'I fell in love with Justin one night in Dublin when he asked to walk me home and we talked until dawn. After that, I wanted to be with him all the time. I was never happier than when I was with him. I'd never met anyone like him before, and I couldn't believe that he liked me back. We met in cafés or at Trinity, so I didn't know where he lived or what he drove or anything like that. I don't love him because of things. I'd live with him in a hovel and not care. I love him because he sings Prince songs in the shower, even the high bits. And because he laughs hysterically at *Father Ted*. And because his secret treat is crisp sandwiches on white sliced pan, which I think is horrible, but he adores. And because after a whiskey, he gets giggly and affectionate and makes me laugh. And because he is an incredibly loyal person, always looking out for his friends. And because when I told him I was pregnant and I was scared and thought I should have an abortion or give it up for adoption, he told me he wanted our baby and that he wanted me and he proposed to me. I love him, Celia-Ann. And I'm going to stay around as long as Justin wants me. So do you know what you're going to have to do? Build a bridge and get over it.'

Celia-Ann stared at her coldly, then turned on her heel, got into the car and sat looking straight ahead. Jeremy sighed heavily again and made his way around to the driver's door. As he passed by Danielle, he smiled at her.

'Well said,' he said quietly. 'I admire your gumption, young lady. I'll be over to visit even if I have to come alone.'

Danielle smiled at him. 'You are welcome at absolutely any time, Jeremy. Any time at all, okay?'

He nodded at her, then climbed into the car beside his wife, who was as still as a statue in her seat. He put the car in gear, waved sadly to Justin and off they went. Mallory had the good sense to do the same. She nodded at Hugh, said she'd be in touch, then jumped into her Mercedes and drove off. The four left behind stood there in silence for a few moments, then Justin walked over to Danielle and enveloped her in a huge hug, holding her tightly. They didn't say anything, just held each other in that warm embrace and a million unsaid things floated between them.

'Dear God,' Charlotte said, suddenly bursting out laughing. 'I need a drink after that. I have never in all my life seen such a display! Hugh, pop open a bottle of wine, quick, and let's toast Danielle's incredible speech. Talk about putting a woman in her place. Danielle, that was magnificent.'

Justin let her go, but slid his arm around her waist and Danielle leaned her head into his shoulder. She smiled at Charlotte.

'I couldn't have done that even two weeks ago,' she said. 'But she has pushed me to the limit. I'm not a crap person because I haven't got money and don't know about horses. Once I accepted that, all her nonsense was just that, nonsense. I couldn't care less what she thinks; now I have Justin at my side, that's all that matters.'

'You two,' Charlotte said, her eyes filling with tears. 'Love's young dream personified. You're mad about each other, and it's gorgeous. Come on, let's go back inside and raise that glass. I feel like I've witnessed some big watershed in your lives.'

'You have,' Justin said quietly in Danielle's ear. 'We've really struck out on our own now,' he said. 'Are you okay?'

'I'm fantastic,' Danielle said, kissing him lightly. 'Now, I want you to go inside, enjoy a glass of wine and close this deal. I'll drive us home.'

He looked at her in delight. 'Really? You like it? You agree?'

'Yes, yes and yes,' Danielle said. 'This place is for us, I can feel it in my bones. I want you to do this, and I want to help you. I think we've found our future.'

Chapter 30

MAIA KEPT LOOKING AT ZARA AND ZACH, worried about all they'd witnessed at Pearl's house the day before, but they didn't seem traumatised. She felt traumatised herself, but the kids seemed to be taking it in their stride. She had actually felt nauseous when Pearl confessed that Seth had beaten them up, and that feeling hadn't fully left her. Maia just couldn't believe that it had been going on right next door, and she'd been blind to it. She hadn't thought it possible that Kingfisher Road could hide such a horrible secret, but there you go, she thought, life was just so unpredictable.

'There you are, Zara,' she said as her beautiful daughter walked into the kitchen. 'Are you okay?'

'You keep asking me that, Mum,' Zara said. 'I'm absolutely fine.'

Zach came in and grinned at them. 'Is Mum still checking for signs of PTSD?' he joked.

Maia pouted. 'I don't know how you can be so funny about stuff like this,' she said. 'I was so upset by it, so I'm sure it had an effect on you two as well.'

Zara sighed. 'Oh Mum, of course it was really horrible. I had a good big cry when I got back here afterwards, but crying won't help them. I just want to make sure that I see Drew plenty while I'm still here. The best thing we can do is spend time with them and make them feel supported.'

'I don't know how an airhead like me created two such solid and sensible people,' Maia said shaking her head.

'Airhead,' Zach scoffed. 'You're one of the smartest people I know, Mum. You're on the ball.'

'Well you two are just amazing,' Maia said. 'And I'm not even just saying that as your mother. You're wonderful people by anyone's standards.' She opened her bag, got her purse and took out two hundred euros. 'And for that reason, I'm treating you to a day out. Go see that film you were saying you wanted to see. Get yourselves a nice supper. You also need to spend time with each other before you both head off.'

'Wow, thanks, Mum,' Zara said, reaching for the cash. 'Come on, bro, let's go spend this and have some fun.'

'And get taxis there and back,' Maia said. 'It's so dark, and I think it's going to rain again.'

They went off to get ready and Maia continued with her dinner preparations. She hadn't prepared such an elaborate meal in ages, but she wanted to make sure everything was just right. She did want the twins to spend time together, but she had another reason for sending them off: she had decided to tackle Freddie properly about the way things were between them, and not to let him off the hook until he had been honest with her. She was half afraid of what she might hear from him, but she had decided she couldn't keep going like this. Looking at Pearl yesterday, standing up for herself and her own happiness, it had made Maia realise that she too was guilty of cruising along on auto-pilot. Her life was happening to her, rather than her taking control of it, and that had to stop.

By the time Freddie arrived home, the plates were warming in the oven, the food was ready, the candles were lit and the wine was breathing. Maia didn't want to distract him with low-cut tops or short dresses, so she was wearing a deep green cashmere jumper with slim-fitting red pants and a cute pair of slingback kitten heels in a gorgeous mustard colour. Just as she'd planned, everything was just right.

'Jesus, this place smells good,' Freddie said, coming in and putting his briefcase on the sofa and taking off his jacket. He looked tired out, which meant he could be short-tempered, but Maia felt she had to grab the bull by the horns now, regardless.

'I've made a very special meal for us,' she said. 'Sit yourself down and I'll dish up. We haven't had quality time together in ages, so I wanted to prioritise us for a change.'

'Have you been reading some article in those magazines about how to get more money out of your husband or something?'

Maia laughed. 'I have not, you big cynic. This is about you and me and nothing else.'

'We'll see,' Freddie said. 'I'll have some of that wine, though. It's been a really long day.'

Maia let him enjoy the starter and main course and they chatted about this and that. She filled him in on the whole situation with Pearl, and he was astounded.

'That big fella hit skinny little Pearl and Drew?' He shook his head. 'That's pure bad, that is. God, I wish I could get my hands on him.'

'I think everyone feels that way,' Maia said. 'And do you know, Zach immediately offered to go over and sleep there, so Pearl wasn't on her own at night.'

Freddie stared at her in surprise. 'He did? God, that's incredible, isn't it? Talk about a good head on his shoulders. I'm proud of that.'

Maia smiled. 'We've done a good job, you and me. We're a good team.'

'Yeah,' Freddie said. 'We're alright.'

'Although,' Maia said, playing with the stem of her glass, 'lately I don't really feel that way.'

He looked at her and some sort of fear flickered across his face. 'What do you mean?' he said gruffly.

'Just that we seem to be a bit far apart these days,' Maia said. 'I don't feel you're really here. You seem very distracted a lot of the time. I'm lonely most of the time.' She looked him straight in the eye. 'Freddie,' she said, 'I want the truth and I want it now. Are you having an affair?'

Her heart nearly stopped beating while she waited for his answer. If he said, yes, what would she do? She had no idea.

'An affair?' he said, looking at her like she was mad. 'Of course I'm not having a bloody affair. I'm with you.'

'But you're not,' Maia said, trying to bite back the tears that were threatening. 'You're not with me anymore, Freddie. I don't feel it. Something has changed.'

'I'm not having an affair,' he said stubbornly. 'And I'm offended you'd think that of me. I'm not like that, Maia, never have been. I'm crazy about you.'

'Then what is it?' she pleaded. 'Don't tell me nothing. I can see the difference in you and something has caused it. If you're not shagging someone new, then what is it?'

Freddie sighed deeply. 'There's nothing to concern you,' he said. 'I'm just ironing out some problems, but I'll do it myself, okay?'

'Why?' Maia demanded. 'Why do you think I can't help? Do you think staying at home with the kids has made me stupid or something? You used to ask my opinion all the time, so why not now?'

'It's just . . .' he rubbed his eyes, '. . . it's just business stuff, Maia.' He looked at her and she held his gaze, and she could see that he was deeply troubled. The cheerful mask he always wore slipped away and she saw the extent of his fear and stress.

'Jesus, Freddie, what is it?' she said. 'Come on, a problem shared is a problem halved. Tell me.'

He looked like a defeated man. His shoulders slumped and he sighed deeply again. 'Alright,' he said quietly. 'Look, it's a business problem. I had some lads come around the shop and tell me I had to pay protection money. Real louts they were, and they let me know in no uncertain terms that I'd be messed up if I didn't give them what they wanted.'

'The black eye?' Maia said.

'Yeah,' he said. 'They were just making their point loud and clear that time.'

'Did you give them the money?' she asked.

'No,' he said, shaking his head. 'That kind, if you give them a tenner, they'll come back the next day for a grand. There was no way I was handing over my hard-earned money to them. But the thing is . . .' he looked almost embarrassed. 'The thing is, I didn't go to the cops, like I should have. I went to this other crowd, some of the old gang from Westwood, and asked them to give me protection from the first lot. That went grand for a while, but then they started demanding more and more as well. And now I'm caught between the two of them.' He looked at her. 'I'm sorry, babe, I've been really stupid about this. And now I can't see a way out of it.'

Maia felt shocked by what he'd told her, and a part of her was screaming that yes, he had been stupid not to see that it was always going to spiral out of his control. Getting involved with two gangs was never going to be the solution to being threatened by one gang. But he didn't need her anger or judgement right now, he needed her support and help.

'Right,' she said, thinking it through. 'So both sides are targeting you and the shop and its earnings?'

'Yeah,' he said. 'I can't get them off my back. They know there's good money there, and they want it.'

'Okay,' Maia said, flicking through the options in her head. 'Just let me think for a moment.'

Freddie sipped his wine and watched her as she paced around the kitchen. Her mind was whirring with the problems and the possible solutions, but eventually she sat back down and looked at her husband.

'I think I've got it,' she said.

He leaned forward eagerly. 'Well I'm all ears because I'm out of ideas.'

'Here's what we'll do,' Maia said, spreading her hands on the table. 'First, we'll put the house in my sole name, to protect our most important asset. Then we'll shut down the business—'

'Jesus, Maia, are you mad?' Freddie said, looking disgusted. 'That's not the way to handle this. We'll end up broke.'

'Just listen to me, Freddie,' she said sharply. 'Hear me out. It'll work. We shut down the business to take the heat off it, okay, and we'll put all the stuff into a secure storage facility in my name, and I'll use my maiden name. Then you go with Zach to California and spend a few months there, helping him to settle down and lying low yourself. I'll stay here and hold the fort. I'll put it about that you've run off with another woman and I'm devastated, never want to see you again. But I'll talk to the gardaí in Vayhill and tell them the truth and see if they can help us out. After six months, we'll see how things look and either reopen or sell the shop and use the money to open a new shop somewhere else. That way, the targets – you and the shop – are both gone, and hopefully the gangs will find a new target.' She sat back, out of breath from all that talking.

Freddie was listening to her in silence. 'Okay, that's not bad,' he said, 'but how do we get through six months with me not working? We've a lot of bills to pay, Maia, and they won't go away.'

'No,' she said, 'but I've got an account I've been saving into, so we can use that.' She snapped her fingers. 'And,' she said excitedly, 'I'm sitting on a pile of money in that dressing-room upstairs. I can sell designer gear on eBay or wherever and make some cash that way. If I do that, it also looks like I'm fending for myself, which is a good thing if anyone is checking up on us.'

Freddie rubbed his chin. 'It could work,' he said slowly. 'But I hate the idea of leaving you for so long. And I'd be worried sick that you'd become a target.'

'I don't think so,' Maia said, although she felt more worried than she sounded. 'Once everyone believes you've done the dirty on me too, then they know I'm not worth it. These guys want quick, easy money,' she said. 'So my guess is if this revenue stream dries up, they'll find another one that they can milk easily, you know?'

'Yeah, I suppose that's true,' he said.

'Let's get started,' Maia said. 'I'll get on to Sean Claffey's office and get them moving on transferring the house to my name. Let me open the laptop and I'll research secure storage and let's do that this week. And Freddie, I know this is hard, but I'm going to book you a flight for this week as well. Zach will follow you over, but you need to be gone.'

Maia went to the study and got her laptop, then set it up on the kitchen table. A few clicks, and she had a ticket booked for Freddie, departing in four days. She checked out some storage facilities, and quickly found the one that looked most suited to their needs. It wasn't too far away either. She looked at her watch.

'It's ten o'clock now,' she said. 'I'm going to make us a coffee and let's go to the shop then and take everything out and into my car. I'll drive it all to this place tomorrow. I've sent them an email already. I'll bring some dresses to throw over the boxes and it'll look like my dry cleaning. So that's you booked, and if we can empty the shop tonight before anyone realises what's happening, then we just keep the shutters down. Actually,' she said, thinking again, 'it might be better to leave the cheaper stuff out on display, so it looks like business as usual. That'd be better.'

'Yeah,' Freddie said, 'definitely. We don't want to sound any alarm bells for anyone.'

'Right, then we'll empty the safes and take all documents, get it all out of there. I've emailed Sean as well, so we'll get that transfer done as quickly as possible. Now, what else?'

Freddie came round the table and pulled her up into his

arms. 'You're like a whirlwind,' he said, kissing her cheek. 'I can't believe what you're doing here, and what you're willing to sacrifice. You're incredible, Maia.'

Maia melted into his arms and kissed him. For the first time in months, she felt like her husband, the man she loved, was right there with her.

'Anything for you,' she said. 'We'll sort this, Freddie. We just have to stay a step ahead and then go to ground for a while. We can do it.'

'You're some woman,' Freddie said. 'Here I was, hiding everything from you, and you're the one with the balls to actually solve it. I'm a bleedin' idiot.'

Maia grinned at him. 'Like I said, we're a team. You have to let me play my part. We're stronger together, Freddie. And I'm just so glad you've finally let me in. It's been absolutely wrecking my head knowing something was going on and you not telling me anything.'

'It just seemed too big a thing to get away from,' Freddie said. 'And I was terrified of it coming to land on you or the kids. I never thought I'd be dying to see my kids leave, but I've been counting down the days until they're gone from here and out of harm's way.'

Maia could suddenly see his behaviour over the past while clicking into place, now that she understood what was lying beneath it all. He might have been a bit foolish, but his heart was in the right place and he'd wanted to do right by his family at all times. That's what was important. The rest of it could be sorted. She'd grown up around thugs like the ones that were terrorising Freddie, and she knew how their minds worked. They wanted things to come easy and if they didn't, they went off to find the next easy thing. Freddie was a target right now, but if they took that out of the equation, time would take care of it. She felt sure her plan would work.

'Can I make it up to my beautiful wife by taking her upstairs?' Freddie said, nuzzling her neck.

'You certainly can,' Maia said. 'But once the kids are home, we're heading over to the shop, okay?'

Freddie saluted her. 'Yes, commander.'

She took his hand and led him from the room. She just wanted to be alone with her husband, to be in his arms, to feel his love again. Once they were honest and there for each other, everything else would fall into place.

Chapter 31

'I'VE INVITED DREW TO COME AND PLAY WITH Arnie today,' Betsy said to Noel as she poured him a coffee. 'He loves Arnie, and babies have a good effect on everyone, don't they?'

'They do,' Noel said, smiling. 'And if Arnie can help Drew to feel good, then tell him to come over every day. That poor child needs some support to help him over what happened.'

Betsy nodded. 'I'd do anything for them,' she said. 'It's just so sad that Pearl lived with that man for so long.'

'Well he was horribly controlling,' Noel said. 'I thought it was just the army temperament, but obviously he has a screw loose somewhere. Let's hope he stays away now.'

Betsy grimaced. 'Well he'll be getting the blunt end of four saucepans if he shows his face around here again,' she said, 'because I know Danielle, Maia and Nancy would join me in giving him a good thumping.'

Noel chuckled. 'Vigilante Betsy,' he said. 'I love it.'

Graham came into the kitchen with Arnie in his arms.

'Morning,' he said, strapping Arnie into his high-chair. 'I think this little man is very hungry today, aren't you, mate?' Arnie grinned and gurgled at him. 'And your dad needs strength for his big day today. First day in the new job.'

'You two sit down and I'll feed you up until you're full to the brim,' Betsy said, bustling around the kitchen. 'Do you feel nervous about today, Graham?'

Graham shrugged. 'Not really. It's always a bit hard going into a new place, but the work sounds interesting and Michael, Dad's golfing buddy, seems like a real gentleman, so I reckon it'll be fine. I just can't wait to have an actual salary again, so I can take care of Arnie properly. And of course I owe you two more than I can ever repay.'

'You never owe your parents,' Noel said, buttering his toast. 'Everything you get from us is out of love, with no interest.'

Graham smiled. 'I hope I can be that magnanimous to this little dude when he's bleeding me dry.'

'You will,' Noel said. 'It's just part of being a father.'

The doorbell rang and Betsy looked up in surprise. 'Drew must be early,' she said. 'Oh well, he can have something to eat as well.' She went down the hallway and opened the front door. In front of her stood a man with tangled hair to his shoulders, an unkempt beard and clothes that were giving off a distinct pong of body odour. He looked like a tramp. Betsy instinctively shut the door over, leaving a small gap to talk to him.

'What do you want?' she said.

'Sorry to bother you, ma'am,' he said pleasantly, 'but Tasha sent me.'

Betsy nearly fell to the floor in fright. Had Tasha sent this person to rob them blind as well? To murder them in their beds?

'I want nothing to do with Tasha,' she said, sounding braver than she felt. 'She has no place in this house.'

The man held up his hands. 'No please, missus, I don't mean to upset you or anything. It's just that Tasha left a bag behind here and it has some stuff in it she needs. It's got her passport in there. Couldn't believe she'd forget that, but anyway, she wants to leave Dublin and go back to Australia, so she needs it.'

'I thought she'd gone already,' Betsy said.

'She came to stay in our place,' he said, 'but she's tired of the weather now, so she wants to go home.'

'Did she tell you to come here asking for money?' Betsy asked.

'I'm to ask her husband for that,' he said, smiling at her. 'If he says no, that's grand. I'm just the messenger.'

Betsy looked up and down and although he looked a fright, he seemed gentle enough. She didn't think he was going to turn killer on them.

'Alright,' she said, 'please stand in while I find the bag. Graham might know where it is.'

He stepped into the hallway, looking around with great interest.

'This is a beautiful house,' he said. 'My mam always wanted to live on this road. It was her dream.'

'It was mine too,' Betsy said. 'I was lucky enough to have it come true. Where does your mother live?'

'In Kenilworth Square,' he said.

'Oh,' said Betsy, impressed. 'Well those houses are absolutely gorgeous. And so big. Did you grow up there?'

He nodded. 'Yeah, that's my area. I only drop in and out now, just to see her, you know.'

They walked on through to the kitchen, where Noel and Graham looked at the man with shocked expressions.

'Em, this is a friend of Tasha's,' Betsy said. 'Sorry, what's your name?'

'Alan,' he said. 'Nice to meet you all.'

'What do you mean, a friend?' Graham said, frowning. 'Why the hell are you here?'

Alan smiled and ducked his head. 'I'm really sorry to intrude, but she asked me to pick up a bag she left behind. I wasn't keen to do it, but it has her passport so she's really stuck without it.'

'Are you her boyfriend?' Graham asked coldly.

Alan shook his head. 'No, nothing like that. She's been living in our squat in the city. She's nice enough, and she kept saying she needed to go home, but no one was willing to come out here, so I said I'd do it. Are you . . . Gray?' he asked.

Graham nodded. 'Yeah, the abandoned husband, that's me. And that's the abandoned child over there.'

The man looked at Arnie and his face broke into a huge grin. 'Ah, he's a gorgeous fellow. Hello there, little man.'

Arnie smiled at him and banged his spoon on the tray. Betsy remembered her manners.

'Would you like a coffee?' she asked.

'Thank you so much,' the young man said as Noel poured him a coffee. 'This is really kind of you.' He sipped his coffee. 'Delicious. Thanks. It's mad, because Tasha told me you were absolute horrors. She made it out like you were the worst in-laws in the world, but you're really lovely people.'

Betsy smiled. 'Tasha wouldn't have a high opinion of us,' she said. 'But then, I wouldn't have a very high opinion of her, so I suppose that's fair enough.'

'About the bag,' Graham said, 'did she give any clues as to its whereabouts?'

'Yeah, she said there's a drawer at the bottom of the wardrobe and it might be in the bottom of that, she thinks.'

'Alright,' Graham said, standing up. 'I'll go check for it.' He headed off and Betsy smiled at Alan, feeling awkward.

Thankfully, Graham came back into the room a few minutes later, carrying a battered red camera bag. 'I think this is it,' he said, handing it to Alan.

'That's very decent of you when she's left you in the lurch,' Alan said.

'I didn't fit in with her lifestyle,' Graham said. 'Nor did Arnie.'

Alan looked over at Arnie. 'That's a real shame,' he said sincerely. 'She obviously has a lovely set-up here with good people, but for whatever reason she just can't see it.' He stood up and brought his mug over to the counter. 'I'll head off then. Thanks for the coffee.'

Betsy walked him out the door and then watched him walk down the driveway, then off down Kingfisher Road.

She returned to the kitchen, where Graham was finishing his coffee.

'Well that should be the last we hear of Tasha,' he said, and she couldn't tell what he was thinking when he said it.

'You never know,' Noel said. 'Life has a funny way of proving us wrong.'

Graham shrugged. 'I have to focus on Arnie now, he's what matters.'

'Speaking of which,' Noel said, glancing at Betsy, 'there's something we wanted to put to you. Your mother and I would like to offer you the money to build on to the side of the house.'

Graham listened as they explained that they had planning permission to build a townhouse-type dwelling beside the main house. They'd intended doing it as a retirement project. They'd originally thought they'd let it out or use it as an Airbnb. Either way, they planned on starting building in February next year.

'We'd like to offer the townhouse to you and Arnie,' Noel said. 'We were only letting it as something to do.'

'Yes, it's the project and the decorating and all that that we want to get stuck into,' said Betsy. 'But if we thought we could offer you two a home, it would be even better.'

'Is there enough space to do it?' Graham asked.

'There's enough to do two townhouses, in fact,' said Noel. 'The trees and shrubs take up a lot of space. Once they're cleared, the garden will be much larger. So we'd like you to take one and we'd let out the other. You'd have a separate entrance and everything. And then we'd always be on hand to help with Arnie.'

Graham looked from Betsy to Noel and back again. To Betsy's astonishment, he teared up.

'I don't know what to say,' he said at last. 'I don't want to take your retirement fund and your possible income. It wouldn't be right.'

'Yes, it would,' Betsy said firmly. 'We didn't say anything when Tasha was here because we wanted to let the two of you make your own decisions. But now that she's shown her true colours, we have no doubt that this is what we want for you. What do you think? There's no pressure. We wouldn't be offended if you don't want to live next door to us.'

'Offended? Are you crazy?' said Graham. 'I'm so delighted. I can't believe it's happening. I've been looking at the price of rental accommodation and I can't possibly afford anything within twenty kilometres of here.'

'So are you saying yes?' Noel asked.

'You bet I am,' said Graham as he stood up and hugged them both. 'Thank you so much. This is just the perfect solution, for me and for Arnie. I can't thank you enough.'

'Well that's settled then,' Betsy said, feeling a bit teary-eyed herself. She couldn't believe her luck that her son and grandson would be right next door. She could mother the pair of them to her heart's content, plus it left Graham some freedom to maybe pick up the pieces of his life and meet someone new. 'When you get home from work later we can show you the plans. I'm sure you'll have your own ideas and input as well. You'll need to think in terms of Arnie's needs as he gets older, in case you stay there for a number of years.'

Graham shook his head. 'If only Tasha could see me now,' he said. 'She'd be so disappointed in me, joining the establishment.'

'There's lots of ways to live a life,' Noel said. 'But when you have a young child, you do have to make sacrifices. It's the hard part of being a parent.'

'It is,' Graham said, nodding, 'but I still wouldn't change it. It'll mean a safe and stable home for Arnie, and having you two there to run to whenever he likes will be awesome.'

'It's for as long as you like,' Noel said. 'We're thrilled to have you home, son.'

Betsy looked at the clock. 'Right, enough of all this chatter, you can't be late on your first day. You get yourself out the door.'

Graham pulled on a warm jacket and woolly hat.

'I'll give you a lift,' Noel said. 'I need to visit the hardware shop and there's a good one not far from your place.'

'Thanks, Dad,' Graham said. 'Wish me luck, Mum.'

'You'll be fantastic,' Betsy said, kissing his cheek. 'I hope it's a nice place and you like the people. That'll make all the difference.'

Betsy and Arnie were just waving at them as they pulled out of the driveway when she saw Tommy and Drew walking towards the house.

'Ah, here's your favourite playmate, Arnie,' she said.

It had been Tommy's idea to let Drew play with Arnie, and he'd been spot-on about it. Arnie brought out the generous side of Drew and he acted like a big brother to the baby. Tommy had brought him twice before, just for fifteen minutes each time to see how they'd get on. But it was clear Drew loved visiting, and he was always very careful with Arnie, although Tommy never left them unsupervised.

'Good morning Drew,' Betsy called out. 'Come on in out of the cold. It's good to see you. Arnie couldn't wait to have his friend over again.'

'Hi Arnie!' Drew shouted. 'Do you want to play cars?'

'Morning Tommy,' Betsy said as he stepped into the house behind Drew. 'Thanks so much for bringing him again. Arnie loves it as much as Drew does.'

'It's great,' Tommy said, smiling. 'It's very good for Drew to feel like the bigger, in control person. I think he really loves that feeling.'

They went into the kitchen and Drew took out his box of cars. Betsy laid down the playmat so Arnie could sit safely, then she put a car into his hand.

'Coffee, Tommy?' she asked.

'Lovely, thank you,' Tommy said, watching the boys like a hawk. There was no need to worry, though. Drew zoomed the cars around and Arnie watched in wide-eyed fascination.

Tommy and Betsy sat at the table to drink their coffees.

'How's he doing?' Betsy asked, nodding at Drew. 'Do you think he's gotten over what happened?'

'I wouldn't say he's over it,' Tommy said, 'because it will probably always be with him, but I think he's happier in himself alright. He's learning to trust that the house is a safe space now, but it'll take time.'

Betsy shook her head. 'I still can't believe it was going on, Tommy, and I never guessed it. Did you know?'

'I felt there were things Pearl wasn't telling me, but it's very awkward when you're living with people the way I do. You're trying to be the perfect guest all the time, even though it's meant to be your home. I thought the marriage wasn't happy, but I didn't realise that Seth actually hit Pearl.'

'That man doesn't deserve either of them,' Betsy said. 'I hope he never comes near here again.'

'He won't,' Tommy said. 'He sent Pearl a message saying he didn't want to lay eyes on them again, and that was music to her ears. And he knows she'll tell the police if he does try to make contact.'

'She must be so relieved,' Betsy said. 'I hope the three of you will be really happy together now, a happy little family unit.'

Tommy took a gulp of coffee and said nothing. He looked over at the two boys.

'I'd say Drew is so happy that it's just the three of you now,' she said. 'That'll really help him to get over the past.'

'I'm there for Drew as his minder,' Tommy said. 'I'm still just an employee. I wouldn't be calling us a family now or anything like that.' He got up and went over to play cars with the boys, running the cars along the tiled floor and letting them skid away. Arnie loved it and clapped his hands.

'Again, Tommy, again,' Drew shouted.

It was wonderful to see Drew laughing and relaxed again, but Betsy was a bit taken aback by Tommy's reaction. He really hadn't liked her talking about him as part of Drew's family, and she kicked herself for being so persistent. Of course, it was none of her business what set-up Pearl and Tommy had, and she'd clearly made him uncomfortable by talking about it so openly. But Pearl had given the impression that they were a couple, so she'd presumed he'd move in now and they'd be together as a family. Did I get the wrong end of the stick, Betsy worried, or did Pearl?

Chapter 32

'DID YOU TEXT THEM?' JUSTIN ASKED EAGERLY.

'Yes,' said Danielle. 'But only just now, so you'll have to be patient and give them a chance to reply.'

'And what did you tell them?' he asked.

'I said I had a big favour to ask and could they be ready at one o'clock to attend an important meeting with me. I said the same to my mam when I rang her. She sounded seriously suspicious, but she finally gave up interrogating me and asked where it was happening. She's going to meet us on the street outside, although she doesn't know which building on the street we're going into.'

Justin grinned at her. 'I'm so happy we're doing this, Danielle,' he said, coming over to kiss her. 'I've wanted this almost from the moment I met you. It feels right to just take things into our own hands and make our own decisions.'

'I love you,' Danielle said. As she reached to kiss him, her phone buzzed. 'That's Maia,' she said, looking at the screen. 'She says she's free.'

'Great,' Justin said. 'Tell her to meet us on Southwell Street, just like your mam.'

Danielle texted that message back to Maia, and as she did so, Nancy's reply arrived confirming that she was free as well. *Anything for you D*, she texted. *I owe you big time!*

'We have Nancy on board as well,' Danielle said happily.

'And what about Pearl and Betsy?' Justin asked.

'I felt Pearl might not be up to it at the moment,' Danielle said. 'You know, with everything she's just been through and putting Seth out of the house and everything. So I hope she doesn't mind that I didn't ask her. And I met Betsy earlier when I went for a walk and she told me she has Arnie all day and was making a special dinner to celebrate Graham's first week at work. So I told her what we were doing and she was thrilled, but she just can't be there unfortunately.'

'Okay, no problem,' Justin said. 'Hugh and Charlotte said they'll pop in as well, so I think that's all the people we want, isn't it?'

Danielle nodded. 'That is absolutely fine by me. I suppose I better go get ready, then. And you should do the same.'

'Before we do that,' Justin said, 'I want you to stay there for a moment while I fetch something, okay?'

'Okay,' Danielle said, wondering what he was up to.

He left the room and came back after a minute, with his hands behind his back.

'I'm so delighted that you've agreed to marry me,' he said, walking towards her, 'and I wanted to mark our wedding day. I know we'll have our rings, but I also wanted to give you something that will always remind you of this day and how it belongs to us.' He brought his hands from behind his back and placed a long, rectangular jewellery box in her hands.

'Oh Justin, you shouldn't have,' Danielle said, immediately feeling awful that she had no gift for him.

'This is my last present to you as my girlfriend,' he said.

He kissed her deeply. 'I want to remember this moment when you agreed to become my wife.'

Danielle opened the box and gasped. Inside lay a rose gold and diamond bracelet, with a single charm on it – a little rose-gold horse.

'Oh my God, I love it, Justin. It's too beautiful for me!'

Justin took it out of the box. 'Nothing is too beautiful for you,' he said as he laced it around her wrist and fastened the clasp shut.

Danielle held out her arm and admired how it caught the light. 'It's exquisite. Thank you so much, almost-husband.'

Justin laughed. 'You're very welcome, almost-wife. I don't know if it matches what you're wearing today, but I was hoping it might.'

'I'm wearing it no matter what,' Danielle said. 'It's the most beautiful thing I've ever owned.' She hugged Justin tight. 'I can't believe this is really happening. I've got butterflies.'

'Well, much as I'd like to carry you upstairs and have my wicked way with you,' he said, nuzzling her hair, 'time is ticking on, and we should really go get ready.'

'Hold that wicked way thought,' Danielle whispered in his ear. 'We'll get back to that later.'

'Deal,' he said, giving her a final kiss.

She headed upstairs, excited to put on her new dress. She'd wanted a special outfit for this special day, so she'd gone down to the boutique in Vayhill, which was expensive, but where the clothes were gorgeous. The lady had helped her to pick out a dress that she called 'clotted cream' in colour. It was a tea length bridal gown, with a lace bodice with cap sleeves and a v-neck, and then a full skirt in the softest satin. The shape of it meant her growing bump was very comfortable, but she still felt like a million dollars in it. The boutique owner had been so helpful, insisting that it be tailored to fit Danielle's changing body shape exactly. She'd also found the perfect shoes to go with it – a pair of mid-heel t-bar shoes, also in cream satin but embellished with Swarovski crystals. They weren't totally bling, but they were sparkly and gorgeous and, most importantly, comfortable. They had also picked out a warm fur shrug in the gentlest shade of grey.

Danielle had forbidden Justin from going into the bedroom where her outfit was hung up, waiting for today to arrive. She went in there now, closing the door firmly behind her. There wasn't going to be an aisle walk or a big reveal, but she still didn't want him to see her until the last moment. She had considered asking Maia for Sorcha's number, to get her hair and makeup done professionally, but then she'd decided she would keep her look very simple instead.

She got into her dress, tights and shoes and admired herself in the full-length mirror. Then she wound her blonde hair into a low bun at the nape of her neck, using crystal-studded clips at the front. She had a sprig of white freesia from the florist, which she fixed on top of the bun. It was fiddly and took a while, but she finally got it right. She looked in the mirror and smiled at herself. She had honestly never looked so good. The shape of the dress was perfect, and with her hair styled up, it looked fantastic.

Then she moved on to makeup, which wasn't something she knew much about, but she had learned from watching Sorcha and Zara. She applied some soft peach foundation, which gave her skin a dewy look. She didn't usually wear blusher, but she'd been practising with it and really liked how it gave her a healthy glow. She wasn't good with eyeliner, so she gave her lashes a good lick of mascara instead. Then she applied the red lipstick the boutique owner had recommended. It was Hollywood red, the sort of colour Danielle normally ran a mile from. She'd put it on a few times in the bathroom and scrubbed it off quickly each time, feeling that it was too much. But now, with the makeup, hair and outfit in place, it suddenly looked perfectly right. She pouted at herself, then giggled. The bracelet sparkled on her arm and she suddenly felt like a bride. The feeling was a little overwhelming.

Finally, she pulled on the shrug and checked the small cream satin clutch bag she'd packed for herself. It was tight on space, but she'd managed to fit in her lipstick, her phone and a tiny phial of perfume that she'd siphoned from her big bottle. She was ready.

She could hear Justin moving about downstairs, so she straightened out her back, raised her head and walked downstairs in the most regal fashion she could manage. Justin heard her and came out to stand at the foot of the stairs. He watched her with such love, she felt her breath catch in her throat.

'You look incredibly beautiful,' he said, reaching out to take her hand as she stepped off the last stair. 'My God, Danielle, you're absolutely perfect.'

'Thank you,' she said, smiling shyly. 'You look stunningly handsome, of course.'

He held out his arm, crooked at the elbow. 'Shall we?' he asked.

'Yes, please,' she said, laughing with the crazy surrealness of it all.

Justin led her outside and to his BMW, which he'd had washed and buffed in readiness. Once he had seated Danielle safely in the passenger seat, he went back to lock up the house and put on the alarm. She admired his lean body in the charcoal-grey suit he was wearing as he walked away from the car. He did look incredibly handsome, she hadn't been lying. Her heart soared at the idea of him being hers, always.

It had rained that morning, but the clouds had raced on to somewhere else and the sky was a bright blue. It was really cold, but Danielle didn't mind about that. She pulled the shrug closer around her shoulders and savoured every moment of the journey, her hand resting on Justin's on the armrest between them. He had arranged with the register office that they could park around the back, so he drove on past the building and down to the side gate. As they did so, Danielle could see the others milling about on the path, obviously asking each other what they were doing there. She smiled to think of their reaction when they saw them.

As he helped her out of the car Justin said, 'Do you think your mam is going to kill me?'

Danielle laughed. 'Oh now you get nervous,' she teased. 'Remember, we agreed no one else's thoughts matter today. It's just about you and me and what we want, right?'

'Right,' he said, 'but if she does go on the attack, please put yourself bodily between us and defend me.'

'I'm not sure a pregnant woman is much of a defender,' she said.

He placed his hand on her belly and smiled. 'All this and the baby too. It's hard to take in. It just makes me so happy.' He took her hand. 'Are you ready for your grand entrance?'

'More than ready,' she said with a grin. 'Wait until you see their faces.'

They walked hand-in-hand across the car park and back out through the gate, then down the street towards their unsuspecting guests. It was Maia who spotted them first, and her hand flew to her mouth, eyes wide in shock as she pointed at them. Nancy, Hugh, Charlotte and Rachel all turned to look, their faces a picture of surprise and delight. To Danielle's astonishment, Rachel started crying.

'Are you okay, Mam?' she said when she reached her, afraid Rachel might start talking about college and lost opportunities again.

Rachel nodded her head and took the hanky Nancy offered her. 'I just hadn't expected it,' she said, sniffing. 'And you look so beautiful.'

'Oh Mam,' Danielle said. 'I'm so glad you're here. Sorry for all the subterfuge, but we just wanted a small gathering and no big fuss.'

'That's all very well,' Maia huffed, 'but you could have told me to dress up.'

Danielle stared at her in disbelief. 'You look amazing,' she said, taking in Maia's red wrap dress, sky-high heels and perfectly coiffed hair.

'I look okay,' Maia said, 'but I would have looked wedding tremendous if I'd known.'

'Wedding tremendous,' Nancy said, laughing, 'I love that. But don't worry, it doesn't matter what any of the rest of us looks like, it's only these two lovebirds that matter today.'

'Congratulations,' Charlotte said, hugging Danielle. 'I noticed the register office when Hugh was looking for a spot to park, and it did make me wonder. I'm so delighted you've allowed us to be here for this.'

'Honoured,' Hugh added, shaking Justin's hand. 'What a brilliant way to do it.'

'We decided to forget everyone else and suit ourselves,' Justin said. 'My parents will probably disown me, but I wanted this day so badly, and we'd only put it off because of Mum's objections. But after that day at your place,' he grinned at Hugh, 'we talked it over and decided it was time to take charge of our own destiny.'

'You're absolutely right,' Nancy said. 'Life's short and love is wonderful, so you should go for it every time.'

Danielle took Rachel's hand. 'Well if everyone's ready, I very much want to get in there and marry this man.'

'Proper order!' Hugh said.

They all trooped into the wide reception area of the register office, and Justin went up to announce their presence. Their celebrant was already waiting, so they were ushered straight into a wood-panelled room with a large table at one end. There were about forty chairs set out, so as there were only seven of them, it felt very empty, but they all sat together up the top and there was a lovely atmosphere of warmth and occasion.

Danielle removed the shrug and laid it on a chair with her bag. Maia then held up proceedings by insisting on taking about a hundred photos of them all from every angle. The celebrant waited patiently, smiling at them and their tiny wedding 'crowd'.

At last, Danielle was standing opposite Justin, looking him in the eye, ready to commit to him for life. She had worried that this moment might bring up old doubts, or make her think about college, but now that it was happening, she was completely present and completely sure. She wanted to follow her chosen career path, but she wanted to do it with Justin at her side. She wanted to raise his children and help him forge his new business and keep making each other laugh and keep making love to him. He was her love, it was as simple as that.

They recited their vows, all through which Rachel sniffed back her tears. When the celebrant asked them to place the rings on each other's fingers, there was more than just Rachel crying. But they were all good tears. Danielle slipped Justin's gold band onto his finger and smiled at him. Then he took her hand gently and pushed her band down to join her engagement ring. He kissed her hand and winked at her, making her giggle.

Then the celebrant asked for two witnesses to sign the register alongside them.

'Is it okay if we have five witnesses?' Justin asked. 'We'd like to have everyone present sign it, if that's okay.'

'Yes, no problem,' the celebrant said. 'That's a lovely idea. If you'll all join me up here, just sign the register across this line, please.'

They each signed their name, and it was done. Danielle was a married woman.

'Three cheers for the newly-weds!' Hugh shouted, and they all joined him in a rousing hip-hip hooray.

The celebrant posed with them for more endless photos. Maia was self-appointed wedding photographer and she didn't want to miss a moment.

'I know I'm annoying,' she announced as she put them into yet another pose, 'but you'll thank me later, you'll see.'

Rachel had finally stopped crying, and now was smiling

widely. She came up to them and laid her hand on Justin's arm.

'There's no point lying,' she said, 'I thought this was a bad idea and the baby was a nightmare scenario and that you'd swan off and leave my girl a single mother with nothing to show for all her hard work to get into university. But I want to stand here and look you in the eye and say sorry for that. I can see it now, how mad you are about each other, and it's gorgeous. I'll be there for the two of you.' She smiled at them. 'For the three of you,' she corrected herself. 'And I'm just so happy that Danielle has found a good man. Her own dad was no role model at all, but she hasn't made my mistake, and I'm proud of her for that. I wish you both a very long and very happy marriage.'

'Oh Mam,' Danielle said, tearing up. 'This mascara isn't going to last.'

Justin enveloped Rachel in a huge hug. 'Thank you,' he said sincerely. 'That means everything to me. I'd say I'll be cast out of my own family after this, so having a mother-in-law will be even more lovely.'

'Jesus, me, a mother-in-law!' Rachel said with a laugh. 'Does that mean I get to boss you about and annoy the crap out of you?'

'If that's what you want,' Justin said, laughing too.

'This could be fun,' Rachel said.

'Is this one threatening to ruin your happiness?' Maia said, joining them. 'Don't mind a thing she says, Justin, she's a grumpy ol' cow at the best of times.'

'Cheek of you!' Rachel said, swatting Maia's arm. 'I suppose you picked the dress and everything, did you?'

Maia shook her head. 'I didn't even know what I was coming to,' she said. 'I was as much in the dark as everyone else. But I'm so delighted I was here for this. I think that's the most romantic wedding I've ever been at. Mad to think my own was twenty years ago. The time just flies by.'

'That it does,' Rachel said, nodding sagely. 'Before these two know where they are, their little one will be flying the nest and breaking their hearts.'

Maia rolled her eyes. 'See, I told you, she'd make a clown cry, this one.' She put her arm around Rachel and pressed her cheek against hers. 'I know exactly what you mean,' she whispered, 'and my heart is broken too. We mothers have a heavy cross to bear.'

Justin clapped his hands to get everyone's attention. 'I know we've stolen you all away without much warning, but we're really hoping you'll be able to join us now at Pino's Restaurant, which is just down the street. We've a table booked for eight, so you're all welcome, you included,' he said, turning to the celebrant. 'We'd like to raise a glass of bubbly to toast our happiness.'

'Bubbly?' Maia said. 'I'm there.'

'Wouldn't miss it for the world,' Nancy said, smiling in delight.

'Well then,' Justin said, 'if you'd all like to follow me and my beautiful wife, we'll lead the way.' He took Danielle's hand and they walked back to the reception area, followed by their tiny gathering of guests. They went outside and walked further on down the road, with cars honking their horns at them and passersby calling well wishes. Danielle felt like she was in a movie, and she was the star. It felt delicious.

At the restaurant, the staff clapped their entrance and swooped in with trays of champagne. The maitre d' greeted them warmly and congratulated them, then led the wedding party to a private dining room, where the table was set beautifully, complete with a stunning floral arrangement. As their guests took their seats and chatted, Justin pulled Danielle aside and out of the room, back into the main restaurant. He took a tiny box from his pocket.

'And now,' he said, handing the box to her, 'this is my first present to you as my wife.'

Danielle nearly started crying at his thoughtfulness. She opened the box and on a velvet cushion lay another rose-gold charm depicting a mortar-board. Danielle took it out and Justin took it from her and attached it to the bracelet.

'Now,' he said, kissing her hand, 'you're wearing the future we hope to share.'

The tears came then, and Justin kissed them away.

'My darling Danielle,' he murmured. 'I'm going to do my best to be an excellent husband, and to make you happy. We'll achieve all we want, all that's important to us. I promise.'

Danielle looked at him. 'I believe you,' she said, and she knew it was the first time she had really, truly felt that. She let go of all the doubts and the nagging sense of failure, and she embraced this new feeling of love, proper, solid love, the kind that would hold her up, no matter what. She had made a choice, and now she was going to live that choice fully. She couldn't stop smiling. It felt amazing. It felt like she'd been on a long, gruelling journey, and she had finally made her way home.

'My beautiful husband,' she said, reaching up to stroke Justin's cheek. 'I'm ready for our future now, are you?'

'I always was,' he said, 'but I'm so glad to hear that you've joined me.'

He took her hand and they walked back into the dining

room, where their little party broke into applause and raised their glasses towards them. It might not have been the kind of wedding day either of them had ever pictured, but it was perfect. Danielle wouldn't have changed a thing. This was their day, done their way, and she was happier than she'd ever thought possible. When she thought about their life together, she no longer worried incessantly about how they'd manage or whether it would work out, now she just smiled and thought, Bring it on!

Chapter 33

MAIA WAS STILL ON A HIGH THE DAY AFTER THE wedding. It had been so simple and so romantic – and so unexpected, of course. She had reckoned it was something important when Danielle texted out of the blue, that's why she had dressed up to an extent, but she hadn't thought it was an actual wedding. When she'd seen Danielle walking down the street, all satin shimmer and confident red lippy, she had nearly fainted dead away. The change in Danielle was incredible. It seemed like Justin's love for her had just made her blossom. Maia was so happy for her.

She hadn't told anyone yet about Freddie's troubles or their plan. It all had to be handled with great care. Freddie would fly out the next day, and she was dreading it, but trying not to let him see that. It would only make it harder on him to go if he knew she was dying inside at the thought of it. She had to keep it together and stay strong, and this would hopefully all be over soon. They had emptied out the shop of all the high-end stuff, which she had deposited safely in the storage facility. So their plan was moving along nicely. She was keeping herself busy, washing his clothes and getting the toiletries and other bits he needed. He was upstairs packing, and she could tell that his heart was breaking too. But if this saved their asses, it was worth it.

Maia folded another batch of Freddie's clothes and steeled herself for going upstairs to face him. She picked up the neatly folded pile and headed out to the stairs. The front door was standing open, with the porch door locked. Freddie always did that when she was home, but she hated the front door being wide open like that. It always made her shiver, even though the house was toasty warm. As she passed by, she noticed a car parked outside Nancy's house. She stepped into the porch to get a better look. It was one of those half-van, half-car yokes, and along the side was written: Berwick Estate Agents and Valuers. Maia stared at it, her brain working overtime. Why the hell would Nancy have them around when she wasn't going anywhere? There was no way she wanted to sell the house, so what business could she have with them? There was another car parked at the bottom of the road between Nancy's house and number six. The car was really familiar – where had she seen it before?

Maia went on up the stairs, still thinking about the familiar car. She had definitely seen it before. She went into her bedroom, where Freddie's case was standing open.

'Thanks, love,' he said, taking the pile from her. 'Are you okay?'

She nodded. 'Yeah, just something bothering me. There's a car outside Nancy's and . . .' she snapped her fingers, ' . . . it's yer man's car, her son.'

Freddie stared at her in shock. 'Nancy has a son? I never knew that.'

Maia went over and looked out the window. Both cars were still there.

'It's a secret really,' she said, 'but she had a baby when she was only sixteen, and she was sent to a Magdalene.'

'Jesus,' Freddie said. 'Poor Nancy. I'm amazed she survived.'

'She's a tough one,' Maia said. 'She got out, but they took her baby son. But then just recently he contacted her and wanted to meet up. She's been seeing him quite regularly. But that's definitely his car, and there's a real estate car there as well.' Her face darkened. 'The time I met him, he was saying she should get the house valued and invest in some scheme he knew about.'

Freddie looked up. 'Sell up and invest? I don't like the sound of that. Is that what's happening over there, do you think?'

Maia was still watching the house, and now two men walked out and into the front garden, turning around to look up at the house. They were deep in discussion, waving their arms as they talked and taking a good look around.

'There he is now,' Maia said. 'Look.'

Freddie came to the window beside her and looked out. 'Is it yer man with the suit?'

'No, that must be the estate agent. The other fella, he's her son.'

Freddie stared at the man and then shouted, 'Him? He says he's her son?'

Maia nodded. 'What is it?' she asked.

'I saw him with her before,' Freddie said, frowning. 'In a café. I couldn't place him, but I knew I'd seen him around. But I know who he is now. I've seen him hanging around with some of the lads who've been giving me trouble. He's bad luck, that fella. I wouldn't trust him as far as I could throw him.' He looked at Maia. 'I'll feckin' eat my jumper if he's actually Nancy's son. He's a chancer of the highest order.'

'Are you sure?' Maia asked. She felt scared now. Who was this man, and what the hell were his intentions towards Nancy?

Freddie strode across the room and out of the door and down the stairs. Maia ran after him, shouting, 'What are you going to do?'

'I'm going to make sure Nancy is alright,' he called back. 'No one is going to get at her on my watch.'

Maia ran after him all the way to Nancy's house. He strode along like an angry bull, shoulders hunched, ready for battle. When he reached Nancy's, he flung open the gate and the two men in the garden turned around, momentarily startled.

'What's going on here?' Freddie fairly roared. 'What's your business with Nancy?' He squared up to them, and the estate agent went pale.

'Jesus, mister,' he said, shrinking back, 'I'm just doing an assessment to give the lady a valuation, that's all.'

Nancy came out then and saw them all standing in her garden, with Freddie evidently in a rage.

'What's wrong, Freddie?' she called. 'It's okay, I know these men.'

'How well?' Freddie said, still staring hard at Steve. 'And why is there an estate agent here?'

Nancy walked down the path towards them. 'This is my son, Steve. Sorry for not introducing you that last time, Freddie. He's just getting a valuation done, although I've told him a million times I'm not selling it.'

'Why didn't you listen to her?' Freddie said, and Maia could see that Steve was nervous in the face of his rage.

'Back off, man,' he snarled. 'This is nothing to do with you.'

The Gift of Friends

'Oh yes it is,' Freddie shot back. 'Nancy is an old and dear friend and I won't let anyone, and I mean anyone, upset her and try to go against her. Do you get me?'

'I've got her best interests at heart,' Steve said. 'I'm her flesh and blood. And this has nothing to do with you, so get off this property.'

'Steve!' Nancy said, sounding shocked. 'These are my neighbours, my friends, don't talk to them like that. What's got into you?'

Freddie walked right up to Steve and put his face up close to his.

'I know you,' he said. 'I recognise your ugly mug. I think you've got connections to Mad Boy McKenna, if I'm not mistaken?'

Steve looked from Nancy to Freddie and back again. Maia could see that he was actually terrified of Freddie. Although to be fair, Freddie was so angry he did look terrifying. His face was red and his veins were bulging in his neck and he was nearly sparking with suppressed rage.

'I've got your number,' Freddie said, 'and if I see you around here again, I'll . . .'

Steve didn't wait to hear what awful thing would befall him if he came around again, he suddenly made a run for it, pushing Maia over as he sped past her, then leaping into his car and screeching off up the road in a cloud of smoke.

Freddie rushed over to help Maia to her feet.

The estate agent held up his hands. 'I've no idea what's going on here,' he said, 'but honestly, I was just asked to come give an assessment. I don't know that guy.'

'This lady isn't selling,' Freddie said, 'not now, not ever, so that fella just wasted your time.'

'No problem,' the man said, backing away. 'Nice to meet you, Nancy,' he said, then he too turned and hurried off.

'What the hell is going on?' Nancy said, looking astounded.

'Nancy, my love,' Freddie said, going over to her, 'Maia told me about Steve, but I know him and he's a con man. He hangs out with some dodgy people and no doubt he's into all sorts of scams. I'd bet my life he isn't connected to you at all.'

'Not . . . not my son?' Nancy looked dazed. 'I don't understand.'

'Come on, let's go get this sorted. How did he find out about you?'

Nancy still looked utterly confused. 'He contacted Mill Hall Adoption Agency and found me that way.'

Freddie put his arm around her. 'Right then, let's go pay them a visit.'

'Now?' Nancy said.

'Right now,' Freddie said. 'If I'm right, we need to let them know he's out there trying to con people out of their homes.'

'Just let me get my coat and see to Nelly,' Nancy said.

She went inside and Maia went over to her husband and kissed him. Watching him in action, being so decisive and so protective of Nancy, had made her feel a huge surge of love.

'You are amazing,' she said to him.

'Anyone would have done the same,' he said, looking surprised. 'You're a tiger about your friends. I was just saving yer man from having to deal with you.'

Maia laughed. 'Yeah, right. You're superman to me, and nothing you say can change that.'

Nancy came back outside and locked the front door behind her. Then the three of them went across and got into Freddie's car, and he drove the thirty minutes to the adoption agency. Once there, they went in and told the receptionist they needed to discuss an urgent matter.

'The lady we need to talk to is called Angela,' Nancy said, 'but I'm afraid I don't know her surname.'

'That's no problem,' the receptionist said. 'That'll be Angela Griffith. I'll find out where she is.'

They had to wait another fifteen minutes before the receptionist called them over.

'She can see you for five minutes,' she said. 'If you just go into the boardroom over there, she'll be down shortly.'

They went into the boardroom and sat around the large oval table. Finally, the door opened and Angela came in, wearing the same skirt suit Nancy remembered her in the last time they'd met.

'Miss Smyth,' Angela said, extending her hand. 'Lovely to see you again. I presume this is about your son. Is there a problem?'

'I think so,' Nancy said, looking at Freddie.

'The man you're saying is her son . . .' Freddie said, 'are you absolutely sure that's the truth?'

Angela looked uncomfortable. 'Why do you ask?'

'Well, for starters, he seems determined to get Nancy to sell her house and give him the money to invest in some scheme, which doesn't seem very caring to me. And on top of that, I've seen him around and as far as I'm concerned, he's very dodgy. I'm finding it hard to believe that he is Nancy's son. Is it possible that he's not?'

Angela shifted in her chair. 'This is most unusual, Mr . . .'

'Freddie,' he said.

'Right, Freddie then, this is most unusual. We don't discuss clients with outsiders because these matters are very delicate. If there's any suggestion of impropriety, we will of course investigate. But I think it best that you leave it to us now.'

Freddie stared at her. 'That's it? This is something that changes Nancy's life entirely, but we're to bugger off and you'll look into it. Are you kidding me?'

Angela stared at him, but she looked embarrassed. 'I'm not willing to enter into a discussion about this case,' she said.

Freddie sat back in his chair, still staring at her. 'There's something you're not telling us, love,' he said. 'You know something, and you're feeding us these lines to stop us from pursuing this.' He stood up. 'Seeing as that's the case, I'm taking Nancy straight to Vayhill garda station and I'm going to report my worries about this individual.'

'No, don't do that,' Angela said quickly.

'Why not?' Freddie demanded.

'As I said, these things are very delicate and . . .'

'Forget delicate,' Freddie said. 'My friend here has let this man into her life, thinking he's her son, and I've a feeling you know something about that. Now either talk to us straight up, or we are going to the police. Your choice.'

Angela took a deep breath. 'Okay, look, sit down, please,' she said.

Maia could see that Nancy was on the edge of her seat, leaning forward to hear what Angela would say.

'We are in the early stages of a confidential investigation,' Angela said, 'but we have a concern that this man, Steve Mannion, is not who he says he is.'

'What gave you that concern?' Nancy asked.

Angela bit her lip. 'We think he has contacted two other adoption agencies and claimed the same thing about two other women.'

Nancy sat back heavily, looking totally shocked.

'I'm so very sorry,' Angela said quickly. 'We do our very best to ensure people are authentic, but these cases do happen from time to time. The record-keeping back in those times was very poor, and sometimes deliberately false we've found, so it leaves us open to this type of fraud. I can't say for sure if yours is a case of fraud, Nancy, but we are already investigating our concerns.'

'Goddamnit,' Nancy said, shaking her head.

'I can give you information about him,' Freddie said. 'You can take it to the police. I think it'll help you sort this out much quicker.'

'Is that so?' Angela said, looking interested. 'That would be a fantastic help, thank you. What can you tell me?'

Freddie began to tell her all he knew, as Angela wrote it all down as quickly as she could. Maia moved over and sat beside Nancy, taking her friend's hand in hers.

'Are you doing okay?' she asked quietly.

'I don't know,' Nancy said. 'My brain can't catch up with all this. I've no idea what I feel.'

'He's some lowlife to target women like this,' Maia said. 'I mean, what is wrong with people? How can he sleep at night, knowing he's messing up someone's life so badly? I hope they get him and put him away, throw away the key.'

'I'm not his mother,' Nancy said. 'I'm not a mother.'

'You are,' Maia said. 'You did have a baby, but you might never find him. I'm so sorry, Nancy.'

Angela clicked her pen closed. 'Thank you so much for

this,' she said. 'I'm sorry I wasn't helpful to begin with, but when something like this happens, we kind of go into shutdown because we don't know who to believe. But I'm going to talk to the gardaí today and set out all you've told me.'

'Good on you,' Freddie said. 'The sooner they catch him, the better.'

'Nancy, I have to offer you my deepest apologies,' Angela said, looking nervously at Nancy. 'We really do try our best, but it looks like this man might have got one over on us. I can't apologise enough. I'm so sorry.'

Nancy shook her head. 'It's okay, Angela. It's not your fault. I just want to get the truth now. If he isn't my son, I want to put this behind me and move on.'

'We will keep you updated on progress,' Angela said, 'but I really think he's not, Nancy. His description has been corroborated by the other two agencies. We have to be very careful not to jump to conclusions, but I'd be ninety-five per cent sure he's not who he says he is. And if Freddie is right, then it's definite. I'm sorry.'

'Okay,' Nancy said, taking a deep breath. 'It's a lot to take in. I need time to process it all.'

'I know,' Angela said. 'But if you'll excuse me, I really want to call the station and talk this through with them. I'll be in touch when I know more.' She left the room, and the others all looked at each other.

'I don't think I can take any more drama,' Nancy said tiredly. 'What a rollercoaster these past few months have been. My head aches just to think about it all.'

'You poor thing,' Maia said. 'I really don't know what to say, Nancy. It's just so horrible.'

'I'll be alright,' Nancy said. 'I could certainly do with a

quiet life for a while, though. Between CPOs and con men, my life feels like a freak show.'

'How about I take you both out to lunch?' Freddie said. 'We can try to get our heads around it over a steak and chips.'

'Good idea,' Maia said.

The three of them left the agency and stepped out into the cold December wind.

'Thank you, Freddie,' Nancy said. 'I don't know what would have happened if you hadn't intervened.'

Maia looked at her husband, and the pain of him leaving was intense. He was a rock, and he'd go to bat for any of them. Living without him was going to be horrible. She and Nancy would have to mind each other. She honestly didn't know what she was going to do with herself when she wasn't the twins' mother and she wasn't Freddie's wife. It felt like everything was being stripped away from her, and she didn't know what she'd be left with in the end.

Chapter 34

NANCY FELT LIKE SHE'D BEEN LIVING IN SOME strange sort of dream, and she badly needed a good dose of reality with her friends. She'd put out a call to them, inviting them over for wine and tapas, and everyone had accepted. She reckoned that, like her, they needed a chance to sit down, breathe and work through all that had happened in the past two months. They were staring down the barrel of Christmas, but the past year had to be put to bed first.

She loved doing tapas because there was no right way or wrong way, it was just a pile of tasty bites on the table and everyone helping themselves. She enjoyed the informality of it. She spent the day preparing a good variety of different dishes, then, with an hour to spare, went upstairs to shower and change. Ever since the revelation in the adoption agency, her mind had been ticking on overtime, trying to make sense of it. Whether she was in the shower, washing the dishes or watering the flowerbeds, she was thinking about her life and all the decisions that had led to this point. It was exhausting, but at the same time it felt therapeutic. Sometimes you needed a short, sharp shock, she thought, to jolt you out of the lazy old ways of thinking and give you new eyes. Well, she'd certainly had a short, sharp shock!

She was uncorking a couple of good bottles of wine when the doorbell rang and Nelly started up barking. With Nelly at her heels, Nancy flung open the front door – and all four women were standing together outside.

'Surprise!' Maia shouted. 'You're getting us as a job lot tonight.'

'Come in, come in out of the cold,' Nancy said, ushering them inside and closing the door behind them. 'You can throw the coats into the parlour,' she said. 'We're sitting in the kitchen.'

'It looks so warm and cosy,' Danielle said, admiring the candlelit kitchen. 'And it smells divine. I'm glad I'm absolutely starving.'

'That's my kind of guest,' Nancy said, laughing. 'Don't stand on ceremony, you lot. Get your asses into a chair and fill your plates.'

There was warm chatter and laughter as they sampled the dishes, poured wine and talked over each other. Nancy just adored nights like this, and she could feel its good effects like a balm on her soul.

'I think we have to acknowledge all that's happened in the last while,' she said, and her friends fell silent. 'It's been a crazy few months, hasn't it? I think it all started when Danielle moved in,' she said, winking at Danielle. 'You brought the crazy with you.'

Danielle laughed. 'I don't know about that, but it has been one thing after another, hasn't it?'

Nancy nodded. 'I don't know who knows what, but I've been trying to process all that's been going on in my life. I never spoke about it until recently, but I gave birth to a baby boy when I was sixteen, and my family sent me to a Magdalene Laundry.'

'Oh my God,' Pearl said. 'I didn't know that.'

'It wasn't something I advertised,' Nancy said drily. 'Plus, I was glad that my life was child-free, so I just let it go. But then a guy turned up claiming to be my son. He was absolutely lovely, but I didn't feel a connection to him. I thought I would in time. But then the wonderful Freddie spotted him in my garden, when he was working to try to sell my house, I might add, and Freddie recognised him as a con man.'

Pearl was open-mouthed, as was Betsy.

'Good Lord, Nancy,' Betsy said. 'I had no idea all this was going on. Have I been so besotted by Arnie that I've become a bad friend? I didn't know Pearl's situation, and now it turns out I didn't know yours either.'

Nancy shook her head. 'Don't be silly, Betsy. I'm telling you all now because you're such wonderful friends. I just need to get it off my chest, and you're the only people I want to share it with.'

'So what happened?' Pearl said.

'Freddie marched me straight to the adoption agency and confronted them about it. Turns out this guy, Steve, had contacted two other women as well. He was just looking to part us from our money. Freddie handed over what he knew about Steve, and today I got a call from the agency telling me he has been arrested. So I guess that nightmare is over now.'

'That's great news,' Maia said. 'But I hope you're okay.'

'Getting there,' Nancy said, smiling.

'It's really not fair,' Betsy said. 'You had the whole CPO stress, and then this was landed on you as well.'

'It's what they always say about buses, isn't it?' Maia said. 'You wait for ages and they all come at once.'

Nancy laughed. 'I just hope they've all gone back to the depot now and there's no more trundling down the road at me.'

'I feel bad because things are going so well for us,' Betsy said. 'I would have happily taken on one of your problems, Nancy.'

'Well, you did have the truly horrible Tasha to deal with,' Nancy said. 'Is that all resolved now?'

'I think so,' Betsy said. 'We had a young man who looked like a tramp knock at the door one morning, asking for a bag she'd left behind with her passport in it, would you believe.'

'One of the squatters?' Nancy asked. 'What did you do?'

'Brought him in and gave him a coffee,' Betsy said.

'Oh you're so good,' Maia squealed. 'I'd have hosed him down on the lawn and sent him on his way.'

'No you wouldn't,' Betsy said. 'He was actually a lovely chap. Anyway, he took the bag and told us Tasha was flying home, so that's the last of her, for a while anyway. And Graham has landed a job he likes, plus we've suggested building a townhouse next to our house for him and Arnie, and he's agreed. So I'm apologising in advance about builders clogging up the place come next February.'

'That's a brilliant idea,' Maia said. 'Builders will be a pain, but it'll be worth it. It's definitely the best outcome for Graham and Arnie.'

Nancy refilled everyone's glasses, topping up the elderflower cordial she and Danielle were drinking.

'You're really blooming now, sweetie,' Nancy said, smiling at Danielle's rounded bump.

'I'm so lucky because I feel great,' Danielle said. 'It's been an easy pregnancy so far.'

'You might get a nice placid child then,' Pearl said. 'I can't wait for a new baby on the road. It's going to be lovely.'

'And how about you and Drew?' Danielle asked. 'I don't want to pry, but I keep wondering how you're getting on.'

Pearl stared at her wine glass sadly. 'Actually, I've had a really bad week.'

'Did Seth come back?' Maia said, fear in her voice.

Pearl shook her head. 'No, he has disowned us, which suits me fine. I'm going to initiate divorce proceedings as soon as I can, which will probably take three years to complete, but I'll wait. No, me and Drew are good and we're putting the past behind us, that's all fine. It's just . . .' She looked tearfully at her friends, and Nancy felt she could guess what was coming next. 'It's just that Tommy has left.'

'No!' Betsy said. 'For good?'

'He doesn't know,' Pearl said. 'We had a big talk the other night and he said the new situation was difficult for him. He'd always wanted more freedom to be with me, but now that he has it, he just feels very unsure. He asked for time to think about it, and he's gone back to Cork until he feels ready to talk to me again.' She rubbed her eyes. 'God, I miss him so much. I finally got what I wanted, and it looks like he doesn't want me.' She started to cry softly.

'That's not true,' Nancy said gently. 'He can just see that with Seth out of the way, you and him are free to choose each other properly, in a committed way, and that has changed everything. But I do think he's mad about you, Pearl.'

'I just don't know anymore,' Pearl said. 'I thought so too, but if he's able to leave, what does that mean?'

'Just give him time,' Nancy said. 'He needs to think it through at his own pace and reach his own conclusions in his own good time, that's all.'

Pearl nodded. 'I tell you what, though, if he doesn't want me, I'm done. No more men. It's Tommy or nothing.'

'It's not a bad choice,' Nancy said. 'I really enjoy living alone.'

'The only thing is,' Pearl said, 'I feel a bit useless now. Drew is at school all morning, and I've the housework done by 9 a.m., especially now it doesn't have to be military perfect, and then I'm sort of looking around for things to do. Tommy moving out has been so hard, but you know, it's kind of giving me a new perspective. I feel like I want a purpose in life, for myself, you know? But I've no idea what.'

'I feel exactly the same way,' Maia said, putting down her wine glass and turning to Pearl. 'I know just what you mean. I've been dreading the twins leaving because I know they'll take my whole reason for getting out of bed with them. I feel like I have this energy, but I've nowhere to put it. I don't even have Freddie anymore.'

'What?' Nancy said, looking shocked. 'What do you mean? Oh Jesus, Maia, you two haven't split up, have you?'

Maia bit her lip. 'Well, that's what you're going to hear has happened, but there's more to it than that.'

'I don't think my heart can take many more revelations,' Betsy said, clutching her chest. 'What's going on, Maia?'

'I'm only telling you lot because I trust you completely,' Maia said, dropping her voice. 'Freddie hit some business trouble. A protection racket targeted him and he asked some old contacts from Westwood to step in and watch his back, but it all went pear-shaped and everyone was coming at him for money. I thought he was having an affair, to be honest, but then he finally came clean and told me. So we came up with a plan, that he would go to America for six months, help Zach to settle in, and that I'd stay here and put it about that he'd deserted me for another woman. I've talked to the police and they're aware of the situation now. He'll stay away for six months, and then we'll see what the lie of the land looks like and hopefully he can come home and start again somewhere else.'

'That's incredible,' Danielle said. 'I can't believe he's actually had to go. Ah Maia, that's horrible for you. You'll be left on your own in the new year, then. Please do knock over to me whenever you want. Don't be lonely.'

'Easier said than done,' Maia said, taking another big swig of wine. 'I'm facing a big empty house and I don't mind admitting that I'm scared. Same as Pearl, I just feel like I've no purpose to my days, no one to help or look after. I'd say I'll be cooking casseroles and cakes for you all to beat the band.'

'Well that would be a welcome side-effect,' Nancy said, with a smile. 'But seriously, though, would you not think of looking for a part-time job, or volunteering somewhere maybe? You're fantastic, Maia, you could turn your hand to anything.'

'I don't exactly have any marketable skills,' Maia said. 'Plus I'd have to explain being a stay-at-home mum for eighteen years, I'm not sure many employers would see that as a plus point.'

'We said we'd do something together, didn't we?' Pearl said. 'Maybe do a class. Or even set something up ourselves?'

Maia looked at her. 'Well, I did have one idea, but I wanted you all to tell me honestly if I'm being stupid.'

'Shoot,' Nancy said.

'I was reading an article in *Cosmo* about these women who help women from disadvantaged areas to get jobs. There was this one, and she set up a clothes hire scheme. Women from places like Westwood, where I grew up, could go and get a suit for an interview, say, and it's free of charge. It helps them get a foot on the ladder if they want to better themselves. When I read it, it just sort of clicked with me and I thought I'd love to do that. I got out of Westwood, but there must be lots of girls there who'd love to change their lives but can't. What do you think?' she said, looking at them doubtfully.

'I love that idea,' Danielle said immediately. 'I can already think of one girl I know who'd be thrilled to hear of that. I think you should do it.'

'How would we go about setting it up?' Pearl said. 'I'm definitely on for it, Maia.'

'Well, I haven't thought it through,' said Maia, 'but I suppose we'd need a space to store the clothes, where the women could come and try them on. And we'd have to build up a stock of clothes as well. We could maybe talk to Joanne, down in the boutique in Vayhill. She might be willing to put up a sign asking women round here to donate clothes.'

'I think she would,' Danielle said. 'She's really lovely, and she was telling me that she's involved with some charities already, so she believes in ethical business.'

'So, do you think I could do it?' Maia said.

'Absolutely,' Danielle and Nancy said at the same time.

'I've got some clothes to start you off,' Betsy said. 'And you can use the Residents' Association as well. I can put a note in the newsletter asking for donations.'

'So what about a space, then?' Maia said.

'What about the mews at the back of my place?' Pearl said. 'Would it be big enough?'

'You might need that for Drew in future, though,' Maia said.

'I wonder,' Pearl said, 'if you'd consider adding to the idea?'

'Go on,' Maia said.

'I would love to help women get into jobs or careers,' Pearl said, 'but if there was some way to help women who've suffered domestic abuse, that would be really important to me. I'm lucky that I have the house and money, but other women are really stuck. If we had a space like the mews, we could offer a drop-in space for women to have a coffee in peace and talk. I know we're not counsellors, but sometimes just talking through a problem in a safe space can lead to change.'

The women looked at each other in silence. It was a big ambition, but Pearl's desire to help came from her heart and it would be wonderful to see her achieve it.

'You know,' said Danielle slowly, 'you could think in terms of a digital drop-in space.'

'And in English that would be?' Nancy said.

Danielle smiled. 'I mean, there's so much you can do with social media and with online vlogs and everything, you could help lots of women that way, connect straight to them. Then it wouldn't depend on them getting physically to Pearl's garden, which might be difficult for women living in situations where their husbands control them. But if you could offer help and advice online, it's always open to them, twenty-four/seven.'

Maia snapped her fingers. 'Danielle, yet again you're

the resident genius. It's perfect. If we do it your way, we just need a couple of computers and a work room. We could have the clothes there as well, but then we could write advice columns, and we can write them from experience. I mean, look at what you have here. Between the lot of us, we've a lifetime's worth of experiences, good and bad. We could just be real women talking to real women.'

'Yes,' Pearl said. 'Just helping anyone who needs help, if we can give it. I'm on for that. If I'd had somewhere I could have talked about things with people who didn't know me, that would have really helped. This is a brilliant idea, Maia. I really want to do it.'

'Can I help as well?' Betsy asked. 'I know I have Arnie a lot, but with that kind of set-up, I could bring him along, couldn't I? I've been blessed in my life, and I'd relish the opportunity to give back something now.'

'Brilliant,' Maia said. 'The more, the merrier.'

'How about this?' Nancy said. 'I have more rooms in this house than I can live in. I just go from sitting room to kitchen to bedroom and back again. So why not use this place as our work space? We can set up whatever computers are needed in the back room, keep all the clothes in one of the spare bedrooms and then you can all drop in and out as you have time available. I don't know if it'll work, but it sounds worth a try.'

They looked at each and grinned.

'That sounds very much like a plan,' Maia said. She rubbed her hands together. 'I'm so excited. Let's get a pen and paper and start making plans right now.'

Nancy fetched a notebook and biro, and Maia began writing down the ideas they shouted out. There was so much good energy in the room, Nancy was carried away on it. She had no idea if their notions would prove useful or feasible, but it felt so good to focus on something else entirely than her own life, and she reckoned the others felt the same way, especially Maia and Pearl.

By midnight, they had exhausted all their ideas, and themselves. Nancy waved them all goodbye, then went into the kitchen to tidy away the plates and put on the dishwasher. When it was all tidy, she turned off the light, but then turned back and went and stood at the sink, staring out into the dark garden. The tree outlines were black against the navy sky, and there were so many stars twinkling, just like the night her darling husband had proposed to her. Outside on the sill, there was a little plate with the kingfishers' breakfast ready for them. She smiled again to think of a bird saving her life. It was so random. Of course, without Danielle, it never would have happened. Life could create some very strange patterns, she thought.

She was so happy that she could stay in her home, and that Steve had been outed before he could trick her any further. It was hard to think of him as calculating and horrible, because he'd been such wonderful company when he was with her. But she'd really never felt anything for him, none of the connection she'd thought would be there when you'd carried someone in your womb for nine months. Looking back, her gut instinct had been telling her the truth all along, but she'd been feeling too guilty to listen to it. She had wanted to be a 'good mother' so badly, she had ignored her own feelings. She was old enough to know better.

She still had that sense that she wasn't meant to be a mother. Steve had forced it on her, it hadn't been her choice. Nancy felt that being child-free was her natural state, and she really did enjoy it. But that thought didn't upset her or make her feel bad anymore. She felt at peace with her life and how she'd lived it. She adored her independence and her freedom, and that was the truth of who she was. She just wasn't mother material, but that was absolutely fine by her.

The end of the year was drawing close, and Nancy wanted the new year to be about growth and happiness and letting go of the past. She wanted to live out her life her own way, doing her own thing. She picked up the box of matches from the window sill and struck one, the flame throwing shadows on the walls around her. She lit one of the candles she'd blown out earlier and set the candle by the window. She gazed out at the darkness beyond the flame and spoke out into the night.

'David, I loved you when you were born. And my heart broke when they took you away. But I hope you've lived a good life, that you've found happiness. I won't ever look for you, because I'm content in my own life. I hope you found a mother who cherished you. I wish all good things for you. But I'm letting you go so I can move on happily, free from the past.'

With that, Nancy blew out the candle and the kitchen was plunged into darkness again. She felt absolved of her past and a huge sense of relief and acceptance spread through her body. This was her life, and she intended to live it her way until her last breath.

Four months later . . .

THE APRIL SUNSHINE FELT GLORIOUSLY WARM ON Danielle's face. It was the first day it had been spring-like enough to go out without a coat. She was wearing a drop-waisted floral print dress, with a light cashmere cardigan and ankle boots. It felt like summer was on the way at last and she felt a surge of joy to feel it. She adjusted the straps of the baby carrier as Isabel wriggled against her chest. She bent her head and kissed her daughter's hair, breathing in her gorgeous baby warmth.

'Let's go see Auntie Nancy,' Danielle said, stroking Isabel's plump little leg. 'Isn't that right, baby? We'll see your favourite people, then later we'll cook a nice dinner for Daddy, won't we?'

Danielle pushed open Nancy's garden gate and went up the path, admiring the jewel colours of the flowerbeds. Nancy really was a gifted gardener. She had planted a rainbow of colours, with tall, soft grasses cascading down over the whole display. It was beautiful. Danielle went on around to the side gate, and then to the back door, which was always unlocked. On the door was their sign: Kingfisher Centre for Second Chances, with its distinctive blue king-fisher logo. It was really cool, they were lucky to have Graham's design skills at their disposal.

Danielle pushed open the door and went through to the

back room, which was a hive of activity as usual. Phones rang, the printer was spewing out some document, people were making tea, trying on clothes and shouting for opinions, and laughter – always the laughter.

'It's only us,' Danielle called, patting Arnie on the head as she went by him. He grinned up at her, showing off his latest tooth. 'Good boy, Arnie,' Danielle said. 'Look at all those cars lined up so neatly, aren't you so clever.'

'Thank God you're here!' Maia shouted. She was in her business woman attire – hair in a bun, glasses swinging on a chain around her neck, tight pencil skirt and a silk blouse.

'Something wrong?' Danielle said.

'Your mother's annoying the hell out of me,' Maia said, looking exasperated. 'I keep telling her that she has to rewrite that piece on barring orders, but will she listen? Oh no she won't. I need you to talk sense into her.'

'O-kay,' Danielle said, looking around for Rachel. She was sitting at a desk by the window, focused on her laptop screen, tapping away at the keyboard.

'Don't mind Maia,' Rachel said, which was like a mantra with her. Danielle knew the two of them adored each other, but they loved arguing and sniping at each other too much to ever stop. 'She's half mad,' Rachel said dismissively. 'I've done a great job of my blog post and that's that.'

Maia threw up her hands in despair. 'See what I have to put up with?' she said. 'You deal with her. I have to prepare for a Skype chat with Laura, she has her interview today and she's bricking it. I need to calm her down.'

'Oh that's today,' Danielle said. 'I really hope she gets it. What about Gemma; has anyone contacted her today?'

'I don't think so,' Maia said. 'Can you do that?'

'Of course,' Danielle said. 'I'll do it now.'

Betsy came in with a tray of coffees. 'Anyone need a pick-me-up?' she called. 'I know I do. Oh, Isabel is here. Hello, darling. Can I have a hold?'

'She's all yours,' Danielle said, unclipping the carrier and releasing Isabel into Betsy's outstretched arms.

'She's getting more beautiful by the day,' Betsy said. 'Aren't you, my bonny girl?' She kissed Isabel's cheek and Danielle smiled. Isabel was so petted and fussed over, but she loved it.

Nancy came into the room and beamed when she saw Danielle. 'Busy day ahead,' she said. 'I'm glad you're here. I've got Dolores and Marianne upstairs trying on stuff, and they need good advice. Plus Maia has a few Skype calls to make, and we want to get Rachel's post up online.' She consulted the list in the notebook in her hand. 'I managed to get hold of the author of that book on parenting that Maia was raving about, and she's agreed to do an online interview with Q and A, so we'll need to prepare our questions for that.'

'That's brilliant,' Danielle said. 'And is she happy to come and do it in our studio?'

They called it 'the studio', but it was really Nancy's study, which had now been pressed into service as an interview and vlogging space. Maia had done a complete redecoration to provide a 'classy backdrop', as she said, and now it was decked out in fabulous swathes of pink velvet with a glass chandelier. Poor Nancy wasn't mad about it, but Maia was unstoppable when she was on a mission.

'Yes, she will,' Nancy replied. 'I described our set-up here and she said she was really interested to come see it, so I didn't have to use my famous powers of persuasion at all.'

'That will garner a lot of interest, I think,' Danielle said. 'Did you email me the to do list for the event?'

'Yes, check your inbox. It's all there, with your name against your bits,' Nancy said. 'I still find it hard to believe that we're going from a small website to a big event for women in the Vayhill Lodge Hotel. It's kind of mind-boggling, it's all happened so fast.'

'A good idea always snowballs,' Danielle said. 'It was just the right idea at the right time.'

Nancy went to collect a coffee from the tray, while Danielle settled at a free laptop and started preparing her own to do list for the day. Things were constantly busy, so if she didn't keep on top of things daily, it all got out of hand quickly. It was hectic, but she absolutely loved it. The Centre was reaching out to so many women now and going from strength to strength. She was so proud to be part of it.

Pearl came in and flopped into a chair. 'I'm exhausted already,' she said. 'It's taken two hours, two full hours, to get Dolores an outfit she'll agree to wear for her interview tomorrow. If she has any more job interviews, one of you can take care of her. She's a terror, tries on twenty different things and then puts on the first one.'

'Sounds like me,' Rachel said, winking at Maia. 'You just have to be sure with these things.'

'Are those coffees for anyone to take?' Pearl asked, reaching out for one.

'Yes, you've earned it,' Betsy said. 'Enjoy it. Has Dolores left or does she need anything else?'

Pearl shook her head. 'No, I saw her and Marianne out

the front door, with all their gear. They promised to bring it all back day after tomorrow and tell us how they got on. I really hope this is the one. Her ex isn't giving her any money for the kids, and it'll take a while to chase him through the courts.'

'We should really think about opening a crêche,' Betsy said thoughtfully. 'One that's priced very affordably, that would make life a lot easier for so many women.'

'Great idea,' Maia said, 'but expensive. We can put it on the ideas board and think about it.' She went over to the huge whiteboard that covered one wall and added 'crêche' to the list of things they wanted to achieve. The list kept getting longer and longer, but they were also starting to see some very satisfying ticks next to some of their ambitions.

'Did you get to talk to Freddie today?' Pearl asked.

Maia nodded. 'Yeah, I got him before I came over here. He's pining for me and home something terrible, and I miss him so much, but we agreed he'd stay away for another month. He said Zach is absolutely flying, which is great. He adores UCLA and the whole lifestyle out there. Plus Delia is on the scene, visiting him most weekends, so love is still blossoming. I like Delia. She's good for him. Anyway,' she said, sighing, 'there's a lot of work going on to break up the gangs here, and the police have made some arrests, so I'd say another few weeks and maybe I can book his ticket home.'

She looked so happy at the idea that Danielle's heart broke for her. It must be so hard for her to rattle around that big house on her own, but she never showed it, never complained, just turned up every day and worked her socks off. She was an inspiration.

'And Zara and Zach are getting on okay?' Pearl asked.

'Yeah, great,' Maia said. 'Freddie's keeping a close eye on Zach, which is a good side-effect of all this upheaval, and Zara texts me every day and seems to be having an absolute ball. She's actually asked me to join her for a weekend in Lisbon next month, so hopefully we can do that. I'd give anything to hug her bony little frame again.'

'When she's back for college, you'll be able to see her much more,' Betsy said. 'It's funny, when they fly the nest, you think they're gone for ever, but it might not be the case. We never in our wildest dreams would have thought we'd have Graham back living with us, or beside us. You can never predict what'll happen in life.'

'That's so true,' Nancy chimed in. 'You think you've got grand plans and you're carrying them out, but really you're at the mercy of chance and random encounters most of the time. I look back on my life and I'm amazed by the path that took me to here. I couldn't have planned it, in fact.'

'Is there a blog post in that, do you think?' Maia asked seriously.

The others burst out laughing.

'Do you ever stop working, Maia?' Nancy asked. 'You're a one-woman dynamo.'

The doorbell rang, and Nelly set up with her usual warning bark.

'Maybe Dolores forgot something,' Betsy said, and she hoisted Isabel up on her hip and went out to answer the door. She was gone some minutes, and they could tell that an urgently whispered conversation was taking place in the hallway.

'That's odd,' Nancy said. 'I wonder who she's talking to.'

Footsteps came down the hall towards the back room, then a man stepped in, his face almost hidden by a huge bunch of red roses.

'Oh my God,' Maia said.

'Well I'll be,' Nancy said, grinning widely. 'I knew it.'

Tommy stepped forward uncertainly, the flowers awkward in his arms. He looked around for Pearl, and his face broke into a smile when he saw her. Pearl was rooted to her chair, staring at him with her eyes wide. Danielle wanted to whoop and holler. He was back! He had left four long months before, and only last week Pearl had told them she was drawing a line under the relationship because he had to be gone for good. He kept texting to say he just needed more time, but Pearl had decided his heart wasn't in it. And now here he was, flowers and all.

'I'm so sorry,' he said, taking a step towards Pearl.

Maia stepped across quickly and took the flowers from his arms. He barely noticed her. His eyes never left Pearl's face. Unburdened now, his arms hung by his sides as he looked at Pearl uncertainly, obviously trying to gauge what kind of welcome he might get.

'I'm sorry,' he repeated. 'I needed time, Pearl, after all that happened. And then my dad fell ill and I wanted to stay and help out on the farm, but it was also an excuse to stay away because I felt so confused. But I can't stay away because . . . I love you. I know it's a lot to ask, Pearl, but if you still have any feelings for me, I want to win you back.'

Pearl stared at him, still without speaking. Danielle held her breath. Would she take him back? Had he stayed away too long?

Tommy cleared his throat and ploughed on. 'I was wondering if you'd agree to come to dinner with me this

Friday night?' he said. 'I'd like to take you out, so we have time to talk properly and . . .'

Before he could say another word, Pearl jumped up from the chair and strode straight across to him. Danielle winced, waiting for the sound of a slap across his face, but instead Pearl walked straight up to him, flung her arms around his neck and kissed him passionately. He was utterly astounded for a moment, then he grabbed her around the waist, pulling her tight to him and kissed her back with equal passion. There were a few beats of silence, then Danielle, Maia, Nancy and Betsy burst into cheers and clapping.

'Way to go, Pearl!' yelled Maia.

Pearl continued to kiss Tommy, oblivious to them all. Betsy reached down and put her hand over Isabel's eyes.

'This bit is x-rated,' she said, looking alarmed, and the others all rocked with laughter. 'Well it is,' she said defensively.

Finally, Pearl pulled back, her arms still wrapped around Tommy's neck.

'I love you,' she said. 'I tried not to, in order to get over you, but I love you, Tommy. It's as simple as that.'

Tommy was struggling to hold back tears, as was Danielle. It was a beautiful moment, and one that Pearl thoroughly deserved. She couldn't be happier for her.

'If you don't mind, ladies,' Pearl said, grinning at them, 'I'm going to take this man home right this minute.'

'Well thank God for that,' Betsy said, blessing herself. 'I didn't know where to look.'

Pearl laughed and blushed. 'Sorry, Betsy,' she said. 'But I'm just so happy.' She grabbed Tommy's hand and led him out of the house.

'Can you believe that?' Maia said, shaking her head. 'I didn't know Pearl had it in her.' She was about to say something else when the phone rang. She made a face. 'No rest for the wicked.'

Nancy motioned to Danielle to follow her and she slipped out to the kitchen. Danielle went after her.

'I've something special to show you,' Nancy said. 'Come into the garden.'

They went through the back door and out into Nancy's flower-filled garden, with its beautiful scents wafting on the air towards them. Nancy brought her down towards the stream that passed through the bottom of the garden.

'Lie down here,' she said, lying down herself on the grassy bank.

'Really?' Danielle said doubtfully. 'This dress is new.'

'Well dear God, when did you become a prissy little thing?' Nancy said impatiently. 'You and your new dress get down here beside me and stay quiet.'

Danielle didn't dare disobey. She lay down on her tummy beside Nancy and waited, for what she didn't know. Then she saw it – the flash of blue that announced the kingfishers' arrival. They dodged and darted along the bank, their bright feathers flashing. Danielle could see that one of them had a juicy worm in its beak. It went to a hole in the bank, and she watched with delight as a little beak peeked out of the hole, and the worm was thrust into its waiting mouth. She heard the strange *burr, burr* sound it was making, which wasn't anything like she expected.

'Oh my God,' she said, smiling at Nancy. 'A baby chick. That's amazing.'

'Brand new life,' Nancy said. 'It kind of makes sense, doesn't it?'

The Gift of Friends

They got up quietly and ambled back towards the house, back towards the Kingfisher Centre for Second Chances, back towards their friends, back towards the future that was wide open and waiting for them to fill it.

Acknowledgements

THIS BOOK WAS ONLY HATCHING. IT HADN'T THE time to crack through the shell and poke its beak out into the big bad world! I'm being forced, due to a lack of time, to leave it in the capable hands of Ciara Doorley at Hachette Ireland and Sherise Hobbs at Headline. I do hope it's a story that my readers will enjoy. As with all my books, the characters were the people who kept me company.

This time, however, they had a slightly different job. This time they were my final characters. My fond farewell to the world of writing. A world I adored belonging to. A world that saved me from going utterly do-lally over the years. As my body went through the motions of cancer treatment, I'd sit with my laptop and immerse myself in the world surrounding my characters. I loved each one. Well, some of them were annoying or a bit nasty, but I loved that too. That's the beauty of writing fiction. Nobody knows what's going to happen next.

I've whiled away so many hours thinking about the characters you have just met. I've built up a description in my head of what they look like and what type of clothes they should wear, their hair colour and how old they should be. I hope you've enjoyed getting to know them and going on the journey with each of them.

Love and light,

Emma x

Emma Hannigan valued her readers beyond words. When Emma received the news from her doctors about her final diagnosis, she wanted to share her thoughts with her readers. She posted this blog two weeks before she passed away.

16/2/2018

All Good Things Must Come to an End . . .

The time that I knew was borrowed must be given back soon, so it seems.

The conversation I never wanted to have has been said.

My medical team have thrown everything but the kitchen sink at this fight but all avenues have now been exhausted.

To say that I am heartbroken doesn't begin to cover it.

But I feel I'd like to say something; after all, that's what I've done over the years – say stuff, write stuff and tell you what's going down. So I feel it wouldn't be fair to leave you out in the cold right now.

I've gained such strength from all of you. We've shared tips and hints and stories over the years. For all of it – thank you.

Thank you for taking my hand when I needed it most and for posting all sorts from doggy snaps to moggy pics and the rest.

We've made a great team.

I have a new book out. I'm immensely proud of it and it's titled *Letters to my Daughters*.

Usually I'd spend the next few weeks chatting about it

and inevitably daring to wonder if you like it. Because this is the time when all authors want to hide in the back of the wardrobe in case nobody likes their new baby! I won't need to hide unfortunately, but I sincerely hope you enjoy it.

These characters were as real to me as all the others. They grew on me and some annoyed me at times, but as always, they were mine. Enjoy them, curl up with some chocolate or some comfort food and a cup or a glass of whatever tickles your fancy.

Faced with very little time can I tell you what screams out at me? Love.

Nothing else has much meaning anymore. Just the love I feel for the people I hold dear. My two babies (okay, they both tower over me, but I'm still allowed to call them my babies), my husband, my parents, my family, my friends and readers. Yes, you guys are up there on the short list. You've been an integral part of my existence and have championed me and held me in your virtual arms.

The love in my heart is all that matters now. I am broken-hearted at having to say goodbye so if it's alright we'll say farewell instead . . .

Mind each other. Be kind to each other and hold those you love close by.

Life is so very precious. We never know the day or hour that it will be whipped away. So fill your days with as much happiness as you can muster.

Stay away from drains. We all know them; they're the people who pull the good out of everything. The ones who suck the beauty from things and change colour to black and white. Leave them to fester – I think they're secretly enjoying being grim.

Instead, gravitate towards the light and laughter. Like a moth to a flame, remembering not to get your pretty wings burned. You'll like it better there, I promise.

Farewell and thank you, I am taking a bow. Until we meet again may all that is good and decent be yours.

Love and light,

Emma x

In Emma's Words...

Life is short. It's so very precious and it's not a dress rehearsal.

♥

Being girlie can be mistaken for being stupid.

♥

The only reason I used to swim was so I could eat chocolate and still fit into my jeans.

♥

I will be there in your hearts and you will be in mine.

♥

When it all comes down to the wire all that matters is love.

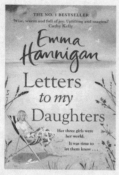

Throughout their lives, the three Brady sisters
have always been closer to their nanny May than to their
own mother Martha, a busy midwife. May always
thought of them as her daughters so when she dies
suddenly, the sisters are left devastated – especially when
they learn that letters intended for them from May with
final words of advice and love have gone missing.

But what words of advice could the sisters need?

Beatrice, owner of exclusive wedding boutiques,
is busy and fulfilled. Rose has a beautiful daughter,
a luxurious home and a thriving interiors company.
And Jeannie, married to a wealthy plastic surgeon
in L.A., wants for nothing.

Except that each of the sisters carries a secret . . .

As they gather for the reading of May's will,
they must face some life-changing decisions. Will they
ever learn the words of advice May had for them and
discover who took the letters?

Restoring a romantic, crumbling villa brings Shelly back to the small Spanish village she and her husband Gerry fell in love with before they married – fulfilling a wedding-day promise he made to her that they would return. But as plans to transform the villa into a stunning wedding venue take shape, Shelly discovers that her grown-up children might need the new move more than she does.

Jake has begun to question the things he values most: his career as a pilot, his relationship with his girlfriend Fee. Could Spain offer him the change he's desperately seeking?

And when Leila arrives in Spain with a newborn baby in tow, she soon finds herself getting caught up in the fledgling business. But then she hears some startling news she wasn't expecting . . .

As Casa Maria takes its first booking, will it turn out to be more than a romantic promise made all those years ago? Perhaps a second chance at new beginnings?

When Róisín returned home from France to the seaside village of Ballyshore heartbroken, she threw herself into fulfilling her lifelong dream of running her own artisan café. Five years on, her love life is still on ice but Nourriture, her café and delicatessen, is thriving.

But then, on her thirtieth birthday, Róisín receives two pieces of unexpected news which shake her to her core: a letter from her birth mother, a woman she's never met, and some devastating news about her business.

Meanwhile, the one person Róisín has always turned to, her adoptive mum Keeley, is hiding her own secret.

The two women must face truths about the past. Will they discover that the gift of love between a mother and a daughter is the most precious gift of all?